Rogue's Home

ROGUE'S HOME

A Knight and Rogue NOVEL

HILARI BELL

An Imprint of HarperCollins*Publishers*

Eos is an imprint of HarperCollins Publishers.

Rogue's Home
Copyright © 2008 by Hilari Bell

Library of Congress Cataloging-in-Publication Data
Bell, Hilari.
  Rogue's home / Hilari Bell. — 1st ed.
    p.   cm. — (Knight and Rogue)
  Summary: In alternate chapters, eighteen-year-old Sir Michael Sevenson,
an anachronistic knight errant, and seventeen-year-old Fisk, his street-wise
squire, tell of their journey to Ruesport, Fisk's hometown, to investigate
blackmail and a series of suspicious fires.
  ISBN 978-0-06-082506-5 (trade bdg.)
  ISBN 978-0-06-082507-2 (lib. bdg.)
  [1. Knights and knighthood—Fiction. 2. Fantasy.] I. Title.
PZ7.B38894Rog 2008   2007041728
[Fic]—dc22   CIP
                                                                 AC

Typography by Joel Tippie
1 2 3 4 5 6 7 8 9 10
❖
First Edition

To Uncle Chuck and Aunt Dorothy—
my favorite fans in the north

ROGUE'S HOME

CHAPTER 1
Michael

Most of the time, having a squire is a wonderful thing for a knight errant, but there are times when 'tis a cursed nuisance. Especially a squire such as Fisk, who notices far too much.

"That's the fourth time you've looked over your shoulder in the last hour," he complained. "If we're going to be ambushed, I wish you'd let me know. It'd be nice to be prepared—for a change."

The cobbled street was rough. Despite the Green Moon's light, I stumbled into a rain-filled pothole and swore. Chant, the destrier I was leading, pranced nimbly around it, his hooves clattering on the stone. Fisk, who was leading Tipple, swerved and missed it too. My surge of irritation was unworthy of a true knight, but I confess I felt it. And I shouldn't have. Due to a trifling bit of aid offered a carter whose wagon had become mired on the road, Fisk was, for once, as wet and muddy as I.

"In the first place," I told him, "you couldn't be more prepared to fight off an ambush—you've been twitching like a hunted hare for the last two weeks. And second, the warning Gift isn't that reliable. I once felt like this for almost a month, and I later learned that 'twas because one of my aunts was thinking of marrying me off to her best friend's third daughter. It could be anything, Fisk. It could be nothing at all."

The Gift for sensing the presence of magic, a Gift whose inheritance allowed the noble families to rise to power by *knowing* which trees were safe to cut, which animals safe to slaughter, is always reliable. Magic is either there or it isn't, and the Gods avenge themselves on those who destroy magica plants or animals without first paying the price. But there are also a host of lesser talents, which we also call "Gifts," and they function most erratically—if they function at all.

The tale of Aunt Gwen's scheme made Fisk laugh, as 'twas meant to, but he sobered quickly.

"I haven't been twitchy for weeks—just since you started looking over your shoulder, day before yesterday. Because the last time you did that, old Hackle planted that magica hide on Tipple and almost got us killed. And I didn't mean prepared to fight, I meant prepared to run. You're carrying the money just now, remember?'"

I couldn't help but smile at that, for my purse had developed a peculiar habit of ending up in Fisk's hands, whether I'd lent it to him or not. I didn't mind, for Fisk is better with money than I—though 'twas sometimes disconcerting to reach down and find it missing.

I fought the urge to look behind us yet again. Assisting the unfortunate carter had brought us into Toffleton three hours after sunset, though in mid-Oaken the sun set early enough that light and noise still streamed into the streets when a tavern opened its doors. Aside from that, and the high-sailing moon, the streets were dark, for respectable folk had their shutters closed against the damp chill.

Though I know 'tis beneath a knight errant (not to mention two lads in their late teens) to care about such petty concerns, I was tired. I only hoped we could convince a decent inn to open its doors to us—though if it got much colder, I'd settle for a not-so-decent inn and accept a few fleas as a fair exchange for warmth.

Since we were looking for an inn of the variety Fisk refers to as "cheap but clean," the neighborhood was a respectable one, so when the voice behind us called out, "Master Fisk!" there was no reason for Fisk to jump half out of his skin and draw his dagger as he turned. Though I must admit I turned quite rapidly myself, and my hand came to rest on the hilt of my sword, which protruded from the pack on Chant's rump.

"Master Fisk?" The man puffing up behind us didn't seem to warrant such precautions. As he drew near, the moonlight revealed him to be stout, sturdy, and middle-aged, with a peddler's pack on his back and a larger pack on the donkey trotting behind him.

My hand fell away from my sword, and Fisk sheathed his dagger and folded his arms as the man caught up with us.

"Who wants to know?" Fisk asked cautiously.

"I want to know. Are you the Master Fisk who once lived in Ruesport? I've been carrying this letter for almost three months—thought I'd never be rid of it!"

A number of conflicting expressions flashed over Fisk's face, and I wondered what enemies he'd acquired in his years as a con man to make him so wary to claim his identity. At least, that's how I interpreted the pause that passed before he finally said, "That's me. Who's it from?"

"You'll have to read it to find that out, won't you?" The peddler dropped his pack to the damp cobbles and burrowed into a small sack of sealed missives. "Here we are. Three gold roundels."

"What!" Fisk yelped. "For a letter? A letter three months old?"

"That was the agreed-on price—one to carry, three on delivery, no matter how long it took. I've carried it, and I've tracked you down—which wasn't easy, you know. I found someone who'd seen you three days ago, and . . ."

The rest of his complaint was lost in the surge of relief that overtook me. He'd been following us for three days! It was this harmless little man I'd sensed— for the creeping tension at the back of my neck was gone. I'd have paid him for that knowledge alone, but, as I've said, Fisk is better with money than I.

"I'm not going to pay three gold roundels for a letter that old," Fisk said firmly. "Besides, no one knows where I am—how could they send a letter after me?"

"That's probably why they sent twenty of 'em. See?" He held the letter up to the moonlight. His fingers covered the sender's name, but the date, *26 Stephen, third Featherday of Cornon,* and the notation, *9th of 20,* were clearly revealed.

Someone cared enough about something to pay twenty gold roundels sending letters off in all directions, in the scant hope that one of them would find

Fisk. And I saw from his expression that he recognized the writing.

The peddler saw it too. "Yes indeed, ninth of twenty." He rocked on his heels. "I'm lucky to have reached you first, Master Fisk of Ruesport. Traveled quite a way, this has. And for only three roundels you can have it. Or you can try to bargain with the next letter carrier who catches up to you—if another of them does. You're not an easy man to locate."

We had meant to be hard to locate. Knowing that Lady Ceciel might send men to keep us from reporting what she'd done, we'd been trying to cover our movements. In fact . . .

"How *did* you trace us?" I asked curiously.

"Very cleverly, if I say so myself." The little man beamed. "The two of you are pretty ordinary."

Indeed, we'd done nothing to call attention to ourselves. Fisk's middling, stocky build and curly brown hair make him so average as to be invisible. And though my lighter hair is growing back to its accustomed, noble length, I'm hardly more noticeable.

"I finally got smart and started asking after her." The peddler gestured to Tipple, who had snuggled against Chant's warm, gray bulk. Even in the moonlight, her ridiculously spotted coat was notable. "A little jester's mare, traveling with a destrier—now *that's* memorable.

Every groom at every inn you stayed at recognized the description."

So much for being inconspicuous. I decided that information alone was worth the price and paid him three gold roundels, ignoring Fisk's reflexive yelp— after all, I had the purse. Besides, the peddler threw in directions to the nearest inn; Toffleton was part of his regular route and he knew it well. I thanked him and we parted with good cheer.

When I turned to Fisk, I found him staring at the letter, still unopened, with very little expression on his face. Fisk can be quite unrevealing when he chooses, but still . . .

"Are you going to read it now?" The moonlight was bright enough to read by, but peering over his shoulder as I was, I couldn't quite make out the sender's name.

"None of your business, Mike."

"Mayhap not." I know Fisk only calls me Mike to annoy me, but that doesn't keep it from working. "Well, if you're not going to read it, may we move on? The horses are cold."

Fisk must have been cold, too, and he's usually the first to complain of such things, but for once he merely turned to follow me. He opened the letter and tried to read it as he walked.

"I'm glad to know it was only that peddler I sensed following us," I said. "For my warning Gift is quiet now. I told you it didn't always work properly."

"Um," said Fisk. He was concentrating so hard on his mysterious letter that he tripped into a pothole and recovered himself without even noticing it, as far as I could tell.

"'Tis entirely your affair, but you might as well wait till you get to the inn and can read it properly. If it waited three months, 'twill wait ten more minutes."

"Um." I don't think he heard me, so 'tis hardly surprising he failed to notice the two burly men who slipped out of the shadows between a shed and a harness maker's shop.

"Fisk?"

"Um."

They carried clubs, and one had a dagger in his belt. My heartbeat quickened. Two men, also armed, blocked the road behind us.

"Fisk!"

"Um?"

I thrust an elbow into his ribs, and he stumbled and swore. "Why did you . . . Curse it!"

Our attackers ran toward us.

I started to turn for my sword, but there was a better weapon to hand. I flung the reins over Chant's head and swung into the saddle. Since he'd seen the men rushing toward us, I hardly needed to make the hissing click that told my tourney-trained mount we were going to fight.

As I settled into the stirrups, I caught a flashing glimpse of Fisk, dagger drawn, edging back behind Tipple. Was he going to face the men behind us? For all his talk of running, Fisk had proved full well that he wouldn't abandon me to danger, but what . . . My puzzlement was resolved when Tipple squealed and bolted down the street. The two thugs leapt aside for her, and Fisk started to shout, "Help! Help! Murder! Robbery! Somebody help!"

As he went on in this vein, the thugs turned to each other in dismay, and I touched my heels to Chant's flanks. He thundered down the street toward them, neighing a war cry louder than Fisk's shouts.

They'd leapt aside for riderless Tipple, but seeing me on Chant's back they stepped forward, preparing to strike me off or grab the reins. Most horses won't run over a man—my good destrier bowled them over like skaddle pins. One crashed into a wall and sank to his knees, but the other retained his feet somehow and lifted his club. I spun Chant in a circle, raked my heels along his sides, and clung to the saddle, shouting in fear and exhilaration as Chant's kick hurtled me upward. The ballad makers liken riding a war horse in battle to riding the wind, but in truth it's more like trying to ride an avalanche of rolling boulders.

I heard a choked grunt and knew Chant's hooves had connected, but I'd no time to see what he'd done. The man who'd fallen into the wall rose, with a dagger almost as long as a short sword gleaming in his hand. His eyes were fixed not on me, but on Chant. A horse's long throat is vulnerable to edged weapons, but his haunches are less so. I signaled Chant to spin again, and he tried most gallantly, but as he moved I felt him lurch. I swore—his weak hind leg had given out. What should have been a graceful spin became a stumble that almost took him down. The thug stepped forward, moonlight shimmering on his blade.

Not to my horse you don't. There was no time to fumble for my sword. With a war cry of my own, I leapt from the saddle. The thug went down with me atop him, the dagger clattering from his hand. I pinned one of his wrists to the street and caught the other as he reached for my eyes. His face was dark with stubble, and his mouth stretched in a grin that revealed crooked, stained teeth. He was looking over my shoulder.

'Twas warning enough. I gripped him, rolled, heaving

with all my strength, and managed to put him between myself and another thug's lifted club. But now he was on top.

There was a moment's desperate pause as he fought to free his wrists. The second man, who'd been about to strike me down, cursed and started to move around us to where his club might reach my head.

I heard the groans of the man Chant had kicked, the thud of scuffling footsteps, and the ongoing cries for help that told me Fisk was fighting with the last of the thugs, leaving only the two on me.

Unfortunately, that was one too many.

As the standing thug circled, I punched the man atop me in the nose as hard as I could. A muffled crunch and gush of blood rewarded my effort, and he yelped and clutched his face.

Writhing from under him, I shoved him into his comrade's path and leapt back . . . into a pair of arms that closed around my arms and torso like the jaws of a trap. The man Chant had kicked wasn't injured as badly as I'd hoped.

The man with the broken nose clambered to his feet. Fisk's cries for help took on a frantic note, and I deduced he'd been pricked.

I braced my feet, thrust with my thighs, and rammed the man holding me into the nearest wall. He grunted, but his grip didn't loosen.

The thug I'd punched stepped forward, blood streaming down his chin. His fist swung, predictably, toward my face. I yanked my head aside, and the blow grazed the face of the thug who held me.

"Hey! Watch what you're doing!"

Twisting frantically, I tried to stamp on his toes, but he felt my weight shift and moved his feet in time. For a moment we performed a strange, shuffling dance.

Then the thug with the club stepped forward and swung it low, cracking it against my shin. The pain was so great that my fear became a distant thing, reduced to irrelevance.

A blow to my stomach took me down. I was on my hands and knees, dizzy, nauseous. My shin throbbed.

Rough hands hauled me to my feet. My injured leg gave way, and I collapsed against one of the thugs. 'Twas all that saved me from the descending club.

"Hold him still, Furred God curse you!"

I tried to struggle, but there were two of them, one on each arm. As the club rose with dreamlike slowness, I knew I'd not avoid it again.

A hand the size of a shovel closed around the club wielder's wrist.

"None of that, now." The voice was surprisingly

mild. But if you're the size of a small ox, you don't need to raise your voice.

A veritable crowd milled behind the man who'd stopped the club—a blacksmith, as we later learned—armed with pokers, axes, and canes. One stout dame held a sturdy-looking spindle. It was, after all, a respectable neighborhood.

Having no idea of the rights and wrongs of the affair, the good citizens who'd come to our rescue chose to hold all of us until the sheriff could be sent for. The sight of a saddled horse bolting down the street had roused several to investigate, and Fisk's shouting had drawn them to the proper place. They apologized for holding us, but I had no fault to find. Fisk was unhurt except for a few shallow cuts, though he made a great fuss about his letter, which he'd dropped when the fight began—indeed, he refused to let anyone rest until it was found.

When I walked Chant slowly back and forth, my own knee still wobbling with pain, 'twas clear that his weak tendons had been strained—his leg was already beginning to swell. The blacksmith promised to care for him for a small fee, and for Tipple as well if he could catch her. I advised him to look in the nearest place beer might be found, and was giving him instructions as to the poultice that worked best for Chant's leg, when a squad of deputies arrived to take us all into custody. I had no qualms, for I had no crimes on my conscience, and thus no fear of dealing with the law. Looking back, I can hardly believe I was such a fool.

The sheriff of Toffleton was a middling man—middle height, middle age, middle girth—whose hair stuck out at odd angles as if he had been pulling on it. At least his office was warm.

Toffleton's Council Hall was a newish wood-paneled building. Lamps in brackets along the walls had smoked from recent lighting when we first arrived. They had plenty of time to burn clear, though, for one of the thugs had the gall to ask to speak to the sheriff before Fisk or I thought of it. After the deputies checked all our wrists for the tattoo that marks a man as permanently unredeemed, the thugs were taken into the sheriff's office, while Fisk and I perched on a bench at the end of a longish hall. Finally they shuffled out, wearing satisfied expressions that filled me with fore-boding, despite my satisfaction at the purple nose one of them sported.

The sheriff listened courteously to our tale and then

made the most ridiculous statement I'd ever heard.

"I have to let them go. I'm sorry, Master Sevenson, but they say you and Master Fisk are temporarily . . . unredeemed." His voice sank on the word, as if 'twas something impolite. "And if you are Sir Michael Sevenson of Seven Oaks, as you claim, I know that to be true. I correspond with several of Lord Gerald's sheriffs, you see." He shrugged. "So I have to release them. In fact, I couldn't hold them even if they'd killed you."

"But they're hired thugs!" I protested. "They're probably wanted for crimes in a dozen fiefdoms!"

"You're probably right, but they committed no crime in Lord Leopold's fief—I checked my writs carefully. I can't hold them just on their appearance." He sounded quite sorry for it, but his eyes ran over me as he spoke, taking in my rough, now muddy, clothes and the small scar on my chin.

I could see that he thought I looked no better than they did, and I straightened up indignantly. Fisk closed his eyes, like a man refusing to watch an accident he couldn't prevent.

"I may be unredeemed while Lady Ceciel is free, but I am no brigand. I'm a knight errant, and I think my honor as bright now as it was two months ago, despite the law's opinion."

"You're *what?*"

"A knight errant," I said steadily. "In search of adventure and good deeds."

His lips twitched in the manner I've learned to ignore. When you claim a profession over two centuries out of date, you get used to being laughed at.

"I see." His manner gentled abruptly, as one who speaks to a lunatic. I've encountered that reaction, too, and find it more annoying than outright laughter. "But Master . . . *Sir* Michael, you might be the most honorable man in the realm and the law still couldn't assist you while you're unredeemed. You know that."

I did know it, but his attitude stung. And I'm Sir Michael because I'm a baron's son. The only reason anyone is knighted in these modern times is for lending the government large sums of money.

"How about me?" Fisk inquired. Despite the mud on his britches and doublet he managed to look almost primly respectable. He'd once told me 'twas his greatest asset as a con man. "They attacked me, too."

The sheriff thawed a bit. "Well, Master Fisk, according to what those men say, you're unredeemed also—"

"But I'm not." Fisk leaned forward earnestly. "*My*

debt was to Sir Michael here, and he pronounced me redeemed almost two weeks ago."

The sheriff looked startled. "Was this registered?"

"We're returning to register it now," I told him, trying to keep the annoyance out of my voice. "But it doesn't have to be registered to be legal. It requires only my pronouncement."

The sheriff ran nervous hands through his hair. "Aye, but did you pronounce him redeemed two weeks ago because he truly repaid his debt, or are you just doing it now, out of expediency?"

I lifted my head proudly. "I don't lie. Well, I did once, but 'twas not for any personal gain, I assure you." That hadn't come out quite as I'd intended.

Exasperation flashed over Fisk's face, then he leaned forward again, smiling with confidential charm. "He really doesn't lie. It's part of his . . . knightly vows. It makes . . . assisting him quite interesting. I'm his squire, you see."

Keeper, his honeyed tone implied, and I bit my tongue on an indignant protest. Fisk was up to something.

"I see," said the sheriff thoughtfully. "You've been, ah . . ."

"Helping him redeem himself." Fisk nodded. "And

if those men keep trying to kill us, we're going to have a cursed hard time of it. You're the law, Sir, and they're clearly villains. There must be something you can do."

"Hmm." The sheriff chewed his lip, and I rehearsed all the things I intended to say to Fisk later. How dare he make me out to be a lunatic! But I kept silent now, for I could see he'd gotten the sheriff on our side, and I'd no desire to be ambushed in every town between here and Willowere.

"Very well. I can't charge them for the assault, but I'll hold them for a week for disturbing the town's peace. The Gods know there's witnesses to that."

"Only a week?" Ordinarily 'twould be long enough, but remembering the way Chant had limped, my heart sank.

"Best I can do, Sir Michael." He rose, and the interview ended in a flood of warm gratitude from Fisk, who then had the cursed gall to take my arm and lead me from the room, as if he was in truth my keeper.

"I suppose you think that was clever," I snarled as soon as we were out of the sheriff's hearing.

"It gained us a week. What else did you expect? I told you what happened when I went to the sheriff in Uddersfield, remember? Besides"—we were passing the bench where the thugs had been detained, and Fisk's voice rose to a normal level—"it's all your fault, anyway. You should have let me kill them."

The change in his face was even more astonishing than his words—from prim respectability to snarling viciousness in the blink of an eye.

"What?"

"Let's just sneak up and gut them, I said, but no, you had to give them a fighting chance. I tell you, Mike, next time I'm going to go for the kill, and be hanged to your nonsense about it being 'more fun if they know it's coming!'"

He kept this up till we left the building, long after we passed out of earshot of the alarmed thugs. The full Green Moon was setting, and the small, tan Creature Moon, only a crescent, had started to rise. There was plenty of light to make out the smug expression on his face.

"I suppose you think that was clever?" I asked wearily.

"At least they'll think twice before attacking us again," said Fisk complacently. "Noble Sir."

"Noble Sir" is the other thing Fisk calls me when he wishes to annoy.

"Mayhap. Or mayhap they'll try twice as hard to kill

us before we kill them. Did you think about that, my clever squire?"

"Ah . . ." The smug look vanished from Fisk's face. I had a feeling 'twould be a long time before he passed me off as a lunatic again.

CHAPTER 2

Fisk

Despite Chanticleer's lameness, and the first snowfall, which dropped three icy inches on the roads, we reached Willowere in just two weeks, which was a great pity. At that point I'd have welcomed murderous brigands, or anything else that might have delayed us long enough for me to talk some sense into Michael. Not that time would have done much good. I might, eventually, have convinced him that his trust in the law was misplaced, but the other problem was his bone-deep stubbornness, and I don't think a lifetime of argument could cure that.

The town guard was waiting for us at the outskirts of Willowere. Having experienced the speed with which country gossip travels, I wasn't surprised they knew of our arrival—they probably knew that when we'd stopped for the noon meal, I'd mended a frayed seam on Michael's good shirt.

Seated in Chant's high saddle, Michael looked—well, not like a noble's son, but at least presentable. I'd have tried to look as respectable as I could, if I had been the one who was facing the law. (Though the one time I'd faced the law, I'd taken great pains to look respectable, and it hadn't helped a bit.) But I knew Michael was less nervous about facing the judicars than facing his father—more fool he. His father could hurt his feelings. The judicars could destroy his life.

The blue-cloaked guard escorted us, our horses' hooves echoing off the stones. Gray clouds scuttled across the sky, and the wet thatch and patches of dirty snow made the town look very different from when we'd been here in the mellow brightness of autumn. The cold, fresh wind crept under my cloak, and it was altogether a grim and miserable day—but I wasn't in the least surprised to see a crowd in the market square, surrounding the low platform where three black-robed judicars awaited us. A legal spectacle draws a crowd, as the scent of blood draws wolves, though perhaps that comparison is insulting. To the wolves.

Michael's father stood with the judicars, his expression as cold as the weather, but it was the man beside him who caught my eye. His clothes would have attracted anyone's attention, for the shirt beneath his black velvet doublet was dyed crimson, including the lace of his collar and cuffs, and matching feathers curled over his hat brim. If the ruby in the clasp of his short cape was real, it was worth half the town. But his face made his clothes irrelevant; neither handsome nor ugly, he bore the stamp of power more distinctly than Baron Seven Oaks, and foreboding filled me even before I turned to Michael and whispered, "Who's that?"

Michael, for once, looked almost as depressed as I thought he should. "That's Lord Dorian, Father's liege. He must have come to see justice done."

Justice my arse.

With Lady Ceciel's conviction, Lord Dorian had stood to gain access to his own deep-water harbor, which would have saved him a twenty-two-percent harbor fee.

Michael believed Lord Dorian was an honorable man, who wouldn't convict an innocent woman for financial gain, but I have no faith in anyone's honor. If I'd had any hope of Michael's getting off, it died right then—I've never seen the legal deck more obviously stacked. *What's the difference between a lord and a bandit? The lords dress better.*

I suppose it was to Michael's credit that he dismounted and climbed the five steps to the tribunal with solemn composure. Me, I'd have bolted under the platform and into the alley behind it. The guards probably would have caught me, but it was a better chance than trying to reason with that lot. Of course, I'd never have been fool enough to come back in the first place.

"Michael Sevenson, thou wast sent to redeem thyself by returning the murderess, Ceciel Mallory, to justice. Hast thou done so?" It was Michael's father who spoke, and the sound of the high speech, used to signify that a legal pronouncement was binding, sent a chill through me. The last time I'd heard it was when this same iron bastard laid out the terms of his son's redemption in such a way that even if he won, he lost.

Michael, twisting like an eel in a snare, had rearranged matters so that even if he lost, he won. Or so he said. I'd spent the last month trying to convince him to throw over the whole mess and run for it. Even being declared unredeemed would be better than being *marked* as unredeemed. But I hadn't been able to convince Michael of that.

"No, I haven't." He spoke serenely, and a murmur of astonishment rose from the crowd. "For she wasn't guilty of her husband's murder, or the murder of any other, though she has done things that I think should be reported to the High Liege, and her liege, that a watch may be kept on her."

Baron Seven Oaks's face showed nothing, but I saw him swallow before he spoke and knew he wasn't as unaffected as he appeared. "Then I have no choice but to—"

"Wait." One of the judicars stepped forward, which I thought quite brave given the way Lord Dorian scowled at him.

"You say that Lady Ceciel didn't murder her husband? But our investigation showed that he died of poison. If she didn't kill him, who did?"

"No one. Or rather, he killed himself. He was dosing himself with a magica potion in an attempt to cure his infertility—'twas that that killed him."

The shock that rippled through the crowd at this was greater than when Michael confessed his failure. That, they'd expected—this was news.

The judicar frowned. "Can you prove this?"

"Not here and now, for the potion was destroyed."

By me, on the mad night of Michael's rescue, when I wrecked Ceciel's alchemical laboratory. If Michael had told me that he'd recognized that potion, I wouldn't have dumped it. Not for the first time, I wondered how Michael had spotted that one bottle among all the others. He'd told Ceciel that the potions she'd forced down his throat, attempting to give an intelligent person the ability to work magic, had failed, and she'd believed him. So had I at the time, for everyone knows that only the simple ones are sufficiently close to the two Gods to wield magic. Many people are born with the Gift to sense magic, but only if they're close enough to touch it. After that wild rescue, I'd seen Michael stop to stare at a bush, or bird, or a young lamb for no reason I could see—something I wouldn't have thought twice about, except for the fear in his expression. He'd found the magica bark and herbs he used to poultice Chant's leg with remarkable ease, and he hadn't explained that, either.

Now Michael continued, "It could be proved by an investigation near his home, for all the local herbalists knew of his trouble, and the methods by which he sought to treat it."

The judicar signaled his notary, who scribbled busily as the judicar went on, "You have no proof of this?"

"No, but I'm certain of it. I would speak with you about Lady Ceciel later, if you'll permit me."

It was Michael's acknowledgment that he was about to be condemned. My heart would have sunk if it hadn't hit bottom already.

Michael's father turned to Lord Dorian, murmuring, and the lord's scowl deepened.

"To weigh her guilt or innocence wasn't your task,

Sir Michael," the judicar said. "You were to bring her back to Willowere, that we might make that decision. But given what you've discovered, and taking your youth into account, perhaps you might be granted another chance to bring her in?"

He turned to Baron Seven Oaks. Lord Dorian glared at them both, but the baron wasn't one to bend to any man's will—he thought about it.

My heart leapt. He was Michael's father. No matter how much they quarreled, he surely wouldn't condemn his own son, a youth of just eighteen, to pass the rest of his life unredeemed. Surely—

Then Michael spoke up. "'Twould do no good. I have no intention of kidnapping an innocent woman. If you want her here"—his eyes went to Lord Dorian—"then you must petition the High Liege to command her liege lord to bring you her case. I won't do it."

It was practically a statement that he thought Ceciel's trial would be rigged, and it affronted every man on the platform as only the truth can. I cursed Michael's innate honesty from the bottom of my heart.

The judicar stepped away, red staining his cheekbones. Lord Dorian didn't blush, but the look on his face sent a chill down my spine that had nothing to do with the cold wind.

Baron Seven Oaks showed no sign of guilt, but his

face hardened again at his son's defiance. "Then I have no choice but to pronounce—"

"Wait," said Michael suddenly. "I want to state, publicly and to be registered, that Master Fisk has redeemed his debt to me and is now free of all obligation." He nodded to the scribbling notary. "If you'd inform the judicars in Deepbend, I'd appreciate it."

And I'd thought I couldn't feel worse.

The men on the platform looked disconcerted at this unexpected wobble in the mill wheel of justice. The baron folded his arms and waited several moments, defying further interruption, before he went on, "Then I have no choice but to pronounce thee an unredeemed man—cast off from thy kin, honorless in the eyes of thy fellows, rightless in the eyes of the law. If any hand be turned against thee, thou mayst claim no redress, from kin, from thy fellow men, or from the law. These are my words, this is my will, let it be thus."

"Let it be thus," the crowd murmured. I said nothing. Michael's face was very pale now, but his expression was amazingly calm, all things considered.

The baron's face looked as if it had been carved in granite. "I now return thee to the hands of the law, that on the morrow thou mayst be marked with the broken circles of thy broken debt, that all men may know thee for what thou art."

I'd dreaded it for so long, the reality was almost an anticlimax. The guards led Michael off to the moderate discomfort of the town jail for the full night that tradition granted an unredeemed man—giving him a last chance to find some way to pay his debt. For the broken circles that would be tattooed on his wrists tomorrow morning would be applied with a magica ink that never faded and couldn't even be scraped or burned away, though I'd seen the scars of men who'd tried.

The men on the platform climbed down, the judicar still flushed and Lord Dorian grimly austere. Baron Seven Oaks looked perfectly composed, though rather white around the mouth.

The guard who held Chanticleer's reins looked around, baffled. No one had told him what to do with the condemned man's horse. I made my way through the chattering crowd and claimed him. After that there was nothing for me to do but find an inn, and then . . . then nothing, I supposed, though getting drunk seemed like a good idea.

I drank one brandy and gave it up. I didn't want to be drunk. I went to the jail to try to see Michael and was told he was talking with the judicars. No doubt telling them about Lady Ceciel's innocence, despite the fact that she'd tried to kill him.

It was his choice, I told myself firmly. I hoped that would be enough.

I went back to the inn, had dinner, and sat alone in a darkish corner of the busy taproom, nursing an ale. Thoughts of getting drunk, which still didn't appeal to me, alternated with wild schemes for breaking Michael out of jail—all of which involved first stealing a key. They'd probably let me in to see him now, but my pickpocketing days were years past and I'd never been good at it. Getting drunk would be more sensible. Even if I could lift the keys, or pick the lock, and find some way to elude the guards, there was a better than even chance—

"Master Fisk?"

I looked up, startled, at the woman who addressed me. She wore a servant's gown, with a clean white cap and collar, and had a plain, sensible face, but my nerves tightened. The last servant who'd approached Michael and me was an old man called Hackle, who was looking for a couple of suckers to break his mistress out of jail—though he hadn't put it that plainly, of course. If this woman asked me to rescue anyone, she was going to get a tankard of ale dumped down her dress.

"Master Fisk?" She sounded dubious, and I realized I'd been staring like an idiot.

"That's me," I admitted.

"Come with me." Her voice dropped mysteriously. "A lady wants to see you."

"What lady?"

She shook her head and walked away, obviously expecting me to follow. She'd read too many ballads—a habit Michael shares but I don't. She reached the door, realized I wasn't behind her, and came back. She looked quite surprised that I hadn't followed the script.

"What lady?" I repeated patiently.

She leaned forward as if imparting some vital secret. "Lady Kathryn Sevenson, Sir Michael's sister. She must speak with you. Urgently!"

I thought this over. Lady Kathryn and I had met, briefly, a few months ago. She seemed a sensible girl—though the sense of any fourteen-year-old is questionable. She'd asked me to look after her crazy brother, though she hadn't phrased it quite that plainly either. She'd also been careful of my pride when she'd lent me her brother Benton's second-best doublet. Her father had no doubt forbidden her to contact me . . . which was as good a reason as any to go visit her.

The maid led me through the winter dusk to Willowere's other inn and pointed to a second-story window that glowed gold in the gathering darkness.

"That's her room," she whispered. "There's a ladder in the stable yard."

And, no doubt, half a dozen grooms and stableboys to watch me putting it up—not to mention the guests who might look out a window or come outside to use the privy.

"How did you get out? Main door, or back entrance?"

She looked surprised again. "I used the back entrance. It's closest to the servants' stair."

"Excellent. Go in the same way, and signal when the hallway is empty, will you?"

I waited only a few minutes before she returned to the back door and waved me in.

To judge by the sounds from the kitchen, they were washing up. I neither crept nor ran down the hallway and up the stairs to the second floor, but walked as if I belonged there. If anyone asked my business, I could make something up. I might even tell them the truth— there was no reason I shouldn't speak to Lady Kathryn, though her father might not agree. I didn't give a tinker's curse for what the baron wanted.

Lady Kathryn, of course, didn't feel that way. The door whisked open at my knock, and she grabbed my doublet and pulled me into the room so fast I stumbled. The parlor was a pleasant room, with firelight flickering over the well-padded sofa and chairs and several branches of candles illuminating an embroidery frame that must belong to the baroness. Lady Kathryn appeared to have been hemming handkerchiefs, and I pitied whoever had to use them.

"Sorry," she said breathlessly, pushing up the gold-rimmed spectacles that had slipped down her nose. "But if someone tells Father you're here, we won't have time to talk. What under two moons does Michael think he's *doing*?"

Her straight, mousy hair was drifting free from its pins. In the manner of adolescents in the stringy stage, she seemed to have grown taller in the few months since I'd last seen her. But she hadn't changed in any other way, and her candor demanded an honest answer.

"He thinks he's doing the honorable thing," I replied. "But it isn't only that—this is his way of getting out of the second half of your father's conditions." For the terms of Michael's redemption had been not only that he must bring Lady Ceciel back, but that once he'd done so he must abandon knight errantry and take up the sensible career the baron had chosen for him. There were times when I felt some sympathy for the baron's point of view, but this wasn't one of them.

"Being Rupert's steward? He'd rather be *unredeemed*?

That's insane! Rupert's an idiot, but he's not *that* bad. Of course, Michael's an idiot, too. Master Fisk, what are we going to do?"

"Not a thing, unless you can get your father to change his mind. And what under two moons does he think he's doing? Once this is done, it can't be undone. Ever."

"Actually, it can." She turned and paced restlessly, up and down the carpet. "I looked it up when I realized what might happen. The High Liege can declare a debt redeemed. They've even got some way to remove the tattoos. But the book I read said it had been done only four times since the first High Liege put an end to the great wars, and not at all in the last century, so 'twould be a lot better if we could stop if from happening in the first place."

"Tell your father that." I sat down and made myself comfortable. This was going to take a while.

"I tried! Even Mother tried! She talked about the disgrace to the family, and Rosamund cried at him. But he still thinks he can force Michael to do what he wants. He was furious when he heard you were coming back without that Ceciel woman. He thinks if Michael is unredeemed, no one will hire him except Rupert, so he'll have no choice but to come home and do what he's told or starve!" As she spun to pace back

toward me, her skirts caught the bundle of handkerchiefs and knocked them to the floor. "Then Rupert
spoke up, which was quite brave because he *never*
argues with Father. He said if Michael didn't want to
be a steward, then he didn't want to hire him. But
Father said that being unredeemed wouldn't matter if
Michael were home where everyone knows him, and
that he'd be better off even unredeemed than wandering the countryside getting into lunatic scrapes, and
that once he grew up and settled into the job, he'd be
all right." She was breathless by the time she finished,
and her eyes searched my face intently. Looking for
hope, I suppose.

I rose and picked up the handkerchiefs. "The baron
doesn't know his son very well, does he?"

Kathryn blinked hard, but didn't cry. "He's stubborn. And he really believes what he's doing is right."

"Which one of them?"

That made her smile, though it looked strained.
"Mother and Father are dining with Lord Dorian—
smoothing him down, Mother says. *He's* furious, too,
but that's because of some stupid tax thing. Master
Fisk, could you talk to Michael? Father's going to see
him later—try to talk him out of it one last time. He
told Mother if Michael would just bring that Ceciel
woman back, he'd pronounce him redeemed no matter

how angry it made Lord Dorian. If you could persuade Michael . . ." But her voice held no conviction. I shook my head and put the handkerchiefs back on the table. Kathryn grimaced. "I'm supposed to be hemming. Mother says it's the best way to learn smooth stitches. She's going to check my progress when she gets back." She prodded the bundle. "Curse the wretched stuff. Master Fisk, what are we going to do?"

"Hemming." I took a needle and thread from the sewing kit and started on a near-finished handker- chief, taking care to reproduce Kathryn's awkward stitches as best I could. "No reason for you to get in trouble too."

"I mean about Michael."

"If neither Michael nor your father will change his mind, there's nothing you can do. I know how much you care." I made my voice as gentle as I could, which was hard, for my seething frustration matched hers. "But you're only fourteen—"

"Fifteen." She lifted her chin defiantly.

"No difference," I said. "There's nothing you can do."

I finished the handkerchief she'd started and picked up another. Sewing has always soothed me, probably because I learned it from my mother, who was a sooth- ing sort of woman. Then I thought, despite myself, of my own father. No matter how much he had harmed his family unintentionally, he would never deliberately have hurt anyone, least of all his own children.

You must come home at once. For the thousandth time, I wished I'd never received that letter. Or that I'd gotten it years from now, when it couldn't possibly matter. Or two and a half months ago, before I'd met my idiot employer.

"You're of age." The challenge in Lady Kathryn's voice drew me back to the present. "And you're a crim—" She went scarlet from collar to hairline. Then she drew a deep breath and her voice firmed. "A criminal. You could get him out of jail, couldn't you?"

In fact, I wouldn't turn eighteen for several weeks. But I was a criminal. I finished one side and stitched around a corner.

"I might," I said finally. "Though that's a lot chancier than you seem to think. The problem is, even if I do break him out, there's a better than even chance he wouldn't go."

Kathryn's mouth twisted in rueful agreement, and she sat abruptly.

"I've spent the last three weeks trying to get him to see sense," I went on with rising passion. "But the idiot wouldn't listen. He believes in the law." It still sounded insane to me. I stitched around another corner. "And he's as stubborn as they come. So you see, there's nothing either of us can do."

But that didn't stop us from discussing it for almost an hour, sharing our anger and dismay. We might have talked longer if Kathryn hadn't looked down at my work and started to giggle. Caught up in the conversation, I'd been making my usual neat, tiny stitches—we had to pick the seams out of three handkerchiefs and redo them before I left.

The next morning, ironically, dawned clear and calm—a beautiful day for a tattooing. There wasn't much to pack, for we traveled light. I led Tipple and Chanticleer into a shadowy alley on the side of the market square. I didn't think anyone was likely to recognize me, or Michael's horses, but caution is one of my few virtues. Unlike my employer.

Eight deputies surrounded Michael when they led him into the square. He wore only his boots, britches, and the shirt I'd mended—not enough, for it was chilly despite the bright sun. On the surface he looked as composed as he had yesterday, but his eyes showed the shadows of a sleepless night.

Neither he nor his father had yielded. I hadn't expected it, but it still made me angry. At both of them.

A sullen murmur rose from the crowd, and Michael looked around, eyes widening in astonishment. He'd never been hated before. *Get used to it, Noble Sir.* I'd spent the last three weeks trying to warn him, but had he listened?

I found precious little satisfaction in being right.

A mushy snowball splattered against one of the platform's supports as they led Michael up the steps. There was only one judicar today. A plump, nervous-looking man who hadn't dared to speak up yesterday in Lord Dorian's presence. I was pleased when, free of his liege lord, he stepped forward and glared at the crowd until the rustle of movement settled.

The only other person on the platform was a neat, older man who looked like a notary. I wondered whom they'd roped into the job—he might be the town's executioner, for all I knew. On the small table beside him sat a needle, a paintbrush, and a bottle of ink.

The guards hovered close as the moment approached, bravely prepared to see justice done, no matter what it took. They looked rather disconcerted when Michael sat down, rolled up his sleeves, and laid his arm on the table without fuss.

He chose this, I told myself fiercely. He could have gone home and become his brother's steward. We'd even had Ceciel in our hands. (Though hauling an unwilling woman cross-country for three weeks might have been a bit dicey.) But he'd chosen to let her go. I couldn't have stopped him if I'd tried. I had tried! It was his choice.

The older man was probably some sort of healer, for he washed the inside of Michael's arm carefully before he dipped the brush in the ink and made two small strokes. The platform was so high that no one could see the mark, but we all knew what it looked like—two broken circles, interlocked, like half-open links of a chain. The symbol was so old, no one truly knew its origin, though scholars speculated that they represented the two moons, and that once the Gods had had some part in this. Though it was hard to see how the Gods of animals and plants could be involved in a matter of man's justice.

Whatever their origin, the circles now stood only for a broken debt. A ripple of nasty satisfaction swelled as the ink was laid down, but this time Michael ignored the crowd, staring at his wrist with fixed fascination. He seemed not even to notice as the older man took up the needle, though I saw the muscles in his shoulders tense as it pricked.

It looked strangely painless for such a dire punishment. The needle rose and fell rapidly, driving ink into the skin, and the old man worked for several minutes before he took up a clean towel to wipe away a trace of blood. After ten minutes it became obvious this was going to take a while, and that as spectacles went this was neither bloody nor dramatic. The crowd began to break up, as people who had better things to do left to do them. I was sorry to see them go—the ones who stayed were the ones who'd come with intent.

The old tattooist gave Michael's wrist a final rub with the towel, inspecting his work before he released it. Michael pressed it against his stomach as if it stung, but he yielded his other arm without protest. The old man was washing it when the next snowball flew.

It passed over Michael's head, and the guards, who'd abandoned their official postures and were standing about quite casually, ducked aside. But this time, instead of glaring the crowd into submission, the judicar moved himself to the far end of the platform, out of range. The next snowball splattered messily against Michael's shoulder. It was half melted, as much mud as snow, and he flinched when it hit.

The guards looked expectantly at the judicar. He looked aside. Lord Dorian owned this one, all right.

The snow/mud balls came frequently after that, interspersed with rotten fruit—apples mostly. I promised myself that if it came to stones, I'd go fetch the judicar who'd spoken up yesterday; but it never did.

Michael endured in grim silence, his face set.

The guards followed their superior's example and backed out of range, but the tattooist had no such option. Though he winced at the splatters, he took care to keep Michael's arm clean. Finally one man with particularly bad aim caught the tattooist squarely, and he stalked over to the judicar, expostulating. I was too far off to hear what he said.

The judicar shrugged and spoke to the guards, and six of them scattered into the crowd, forcing people to drop their hoards of fruit or snow.

With the disruption stopped, the tattooist finished quickly. Michael stood and nodded courteously to the man, though at that point I'm not sure Michael knew what he was doing. The guards marched him off the platform and escorted him out of the square. A full score of rowdies followed, yelling taunts and obscenities. I hoped the guards would stick around for a while.

I swung into the saddle and was about to go after them when someone clutched my boot. I yelped and jumped, but it was only Lady Kathryn. She wore a servant's drab gown and a determined expression. Her face was whiter than Michael's, which was saying quite a lot.

"This is all I could get." The purse she pushed into my hand jingled, but it was too light to hold much gold. "Write to me, Fisk. Promise. Whenever you're in one place long enough to get a letter, I'll write back."

The odds that Michael would be able to stay in one place long enough to carry on a correspondence were small, and I couldn't help her, but what I said was, "Hasn't your father forbidden you to write to Michael?"

The ghost of a smile touched her lips. "Of course he has. That's why I'm writing to you. And if you choose to share my letters with someone, I can hardly prevent it, can I?"

I grinned despite the seriousness of the situation, and her smile grew wider, though there was more anger in it than joy.

"If Father's so fond of the letter of the law, it seems only fair to give him a taste of his own medicine. Promise me, Fisk."

I couldn't promise, and Michael had passed out of sight. "I'll do what I can." Kicking Tipple into motion, I followed my lunatic employer.

I urged Tipple to a canter, and we passed through the gang of rowdies before they had a chance to do anything. The guardsmen eyed me uneasily as we trotted up, but I simply fell in behind them, and soon they ignored me. Michael stared ahead, ignoring every-thing, walking straight through the slushy puddles unless one of the guards pulled him around them.

The guardsmen stayed with Michael until the row-dies gave up and returned to town, and I was grateful. We could have outrun the mob on horseback, but getting Michael into the saddle might have posed a problem. I wondered whose orders the guards were obeying. His father's? Lord Dorian certainly wouldn't do Michael any favors.

I brought Tipple up to Michael as the guardsmen turned back. He kept walking, like a puppet under the control of some relentless master, for a dozen more yards. I was about to speak to him, though I don't know what I'd have said, but it proved unnecessary. A bridge rose in the road before us, crossing a small river, and Michael's steps quickened. He turned off the road and marched through the thick, dead grass, hardly breaking stride to pull off his boots. He stumbled down the bank and waded into the river, which rose to mid thigh, and then knelt and ducked his head beneath the water.

I'd only a moment to become alarmed, for he sur-faced shortly, scrubbing his hair. His recently mended shirt drifted down the stream as he washed his arms and chest, followed by his stockings and britches. I contemplated the probable temperature of the water and decided it was no part of a squire's duties to retrieve them.

I did get out a dark wool blanket and threw it over Chanticleer's saddle in the hope that his big body and the sun would warm it. I also scraped the mud off Michael's boots. I was glad he hadn't worn them into the water—he hadn't another pair.

The cold drove Michael out quickly, and even so his skin was mottled red and blue. The black circles on his wrist stood out boldly. As I took his hand to pull him up the bank, he looked at them curiously.

"W-w-w-well, at l-l-least th-th-that's over." His teeth were chattering so hard, he barely got the words out, but his voice sounded natural. I grabbed the blanket and tossed it to him, trying to conceal my surging relief.

"You'll just have to learn to keep your shirt on, Noble Sir. But you have to do that, anyway." Which he did, for the scars of a flogging, no matter how nobly acquired, were almost as incriminating as the tattoos. Between them, Michael would never convince anyone he wasn't the most vicious criminal unhanged.

He was trying to dry himself without unwrapping the blanket, a task of some difficulty, but at that he frowned and said, "No longer noble—nor sir, neither.

But I still won't conceal my shame. 'Twould be a lie."

I gazed at him in exasperation. No sane man would make such a ridiculous resolution, and if he did, it would probably last about three days. But if Michael got stubborn about it, he might last . . . three months at the outside. And I wouldn't be there to help when his resolve was broken.

Come home at once.

It was a good thing Willowere was on my way. I had stayed as long as I could—longer than I should have. I turned to the pack and began pulling out his clothes. Warm clothes.

I served a late mid-meal beside the river, and Michael ate, though not with much appetite. We didn't get far in the few hours of daylight that were left, but we came across a prosperous farm just as the sun set.

Without consulting Michael, I rode forward to negotiate with the farmer for a place to sleep. The man had no spare rooms, but he was willing to let us sleep in the barn for a price low enough that for once I didn't haggle. A stew pot bubbled over the fire—mutton, by the scent—and I bought two bowls of that as well, for warm food is best if you're facing a cold night.

While the farmwife dished it up, I paid her husband and counted the remaining money into two equal parts; one part I returned to Michael's purse, and one went into the purse Lady Kathryn had handed me. It wasn't robbery, I told myself. Most of Lady Kathryn's generosity turned out to be in silver, copper, and brass. The gold was the remains of my earnings, selling wrinkle cream to break Michael out of Lady Ceciel's castle. If I'd earned it, I wasn't stealing it, right?

It was still hard to meet Michael's eyes when I went back out to the farmyard. Fortunately, I'm a very good liar.

I told Michael about my meetings with Lady Kathryn and what she'd said about letters, and he laughed for the first time that day. Somewhat to my surprise, he didn't forbid me to defy his father's will.

"You think she'd obey me any more than she obeys Father?" he asked when I commented. "I thought you had sisters. I don't suppose . . ."

"What?"

Michael's gaze slid away. "I don't suppose she said anything about Rosamund, did she?"

"Ah . . ." Rosamund was his father's ward. I'd seen her only once, but I remembered her. She was actually beautiful enough to explain, if not excuse, Michael's love-struck idiocy in her presence. I thought fast. "Yes, Lady Kathryn did mention her. She said she cried for you."

It was almost true, and Michael let the subject drop.

We finished our stew and made our beds in the hayloft. The night was clear as crystal, and the smoke from the farmhouse fires drifted into the barn, competing with the homely scents of cow, horse, sheep, and chickens. The pigpens, happily, were outside and downwind.

There was no sound but the small rustling of the slumbering stock, and the even softer rustle of Michael shivering.

After a long ride and a warm meal, I wasn't cold. And I knew Michael had recovered from his icy bath, for on the road he'd opened his cloak to admit the brisk air. It was the other events of the day he couldn't overcome.

The slightest wind would have drowned the sound. I listened for perhaps half an hour before I stood and pulled my bedroll through the hay to join his, murmuring something about the cursed cold nights. He said nothing as I lay with my back against his, but after a time the shivering stopped and his breathing took up the rhythm of light sleep. Anyone who's done a bit of burglary knows how to judge a man's sleep by the depth of his breathing.

I waited till he passed into the heavy sleep of exhaustion before rolling quietly from my bed. On a pallet of hay I wasn't that quiet, but Michael and I had been camping together for several months—his sleeping mind found me familiar.

I had no fear of waking him as I dressed and rolled up my blankets. I did lead Tipple out of the barn and down the road before I saddled and bridled her, for the thin jingling of the buckles might have roused him. Tipple looked curiously for Chanticleer, but she knew me and didn't prance or neigh.

He'd freed me from my debt when I'd rescued him from Lady Ceciel—I owed him nothing. And he'd told me then that I could have Tipple, so this wasn't theft, either. The stars glittered, for it was late enough that the Creature Moon rode the sky alone, and it was waning. Besides, I needed Tipple to get home.

Three months that letter had been on the road. Anything could have happened by now. *A dreadful disaster has befallen us. Come home at once.* I wondered again why a woman who was as sensible as Anna face-to-face couldn't write a coherent letter. I even wished that Judith had written it. My second sister had the disposition of an alley cat with a toothache, but she'd have described the exact nature of the disaster in the first paragraph, and I'd have had some idea if there was anything I could do after three months, or if it really was sufficiently dire to make me leave Michael right now.

I could have left him a note, made up all sorts of soothing drivel. But I didn't want my last words to him, even written words, to be a lie. I'd been with this lunatic too long—he was starting to corrupt me.

I could have told him the truth, too, but he'd have insisted on going with me. I'd tried to tell myself I didn't want to drag him into more trouble—and that letter meant serious trouble—but good as I am at lying to others, I generally don't lie to myself. At this point, Michael's problems couldn't get much worse. I hadn't told him because I didn't want to bring an unredeemed man home to my sisters. It was hard enough going myself, but Anna had asked for me. With or without her judicar husband's permission.

Come home. She'd filled a whole page with frantic nonsense, but those two words were all that was necessary. Especially with the three words that followed. *We need you.*

CHAPTER 3

Michael

It took over a month to catch up with my lightfingered friend, and by the time I did, I was ready to strangle him for the inconvenience of the journey, never mind the rest of it.

When I first awakened, alone in the hayloft, I paid no heed to Fisk's absence. Frankly, I thought he'd gone out to piss. Even when I saw that Tipple was missing, I thought he'd gone to fetch us breakfast—which is a sign of how disordered my mind truly was, for the only source of breakfast was right across the yard. It was only when I lifted my purse and felt its light weight that I realized what had happened. Even then I thought I must be mistaken. I had to sit down and count the wretched stuff before I could convince myself that Fisk would rob me. But once I'd counted it, there could be no doubt—he'd left me plenty of silver and copper, but a full half of our gold was gone.

My first reaction was a fury so intense, 'twas a good thing Fisk and Tipple had a fair head start. Had I caught him then, I know not what I might have done. But why shouldn't he rob me? I was as invisible to the law as I was dead to my family. No longer noble, nor sir.

I was no one at all.

I started to shiver again, in spite of the lingering warmth of my blankets. Any debt Fisk had owed me was long paid. And he'd never truly been my squire, any more than I had truly been a knight—an idea I now recognized for the mad fantasy my father had called it. A part of me had always known that, but some other part had thought that if I believed it hard enough . . .

Fisk had been right to call me crazy, and he was right to flee from me now. No sane man would tie his fortunes to mine, and Fisk was profoundly sane.

I saddled Chant in a daze of depression and rode for half the morning, pushing him a bit too hard for his still-mending leg, as I alternately cursed Fisk for his faithlessness and myself for expecting anything else. But eventually my bitterness began to wane, and a different realization crept over me: Fisk would not have done this.

If he'd wished to leave me, he'd had better chances. I had declared him free to go, debt paid, when he'd rescued me from Lady Ceciel. Even the painful conviction that he'd gone because I was unredeemed I eventually dismissed. Fisk had known that was coming for weeks. He could have left me before it occurred, openly, with Tipple and the half our funds I judged him to have taken.

So why had he gone now?

By this time I'd let Chant's pace fall to a weary walk. I was so wrapped up in my own misfortunes that a shameful amount of time passed before I remembered the letter Fisk had received in Toffleton, but once I did, it all came clear. The letter must have been a summons, and a compelling one. I remembered Fisk reading by moonlight, so intent I had to jab him in the ribs to warn him of impending attack. He'd refused to tell me of the contents so steadfastly that eventually I'd given up nagging him about it, and then forgotten it. But now . . .

The reason he'd refused to tell me, that he'd left so stealthily, must be because it summoned him into some sort of trouble or danger in which he didn't wish to involve me. Fisk was always trying to protect me from everything, from legal prosecution to chills, and cursed annoying I found it. Especially now!

I urged Chant back to a faster pace, thinking of the nearest towns in which I might locate Fisk's trail. I spent several more hours rehearsing what I intended to say to my well-meaning but wrongheaded companion when I caught up with him before it occurred to me to wonder whether I *should* catch up with him. If he was headed into danger, my presence might do Fisk more harm than good.

But I made no move to slow Chant's pace or turn him in another direction. Fisk had helped me out of too many scrapes for me to let him face trouble alone. If he wasn't trying to protect me, if he truly didn't want the company of an unredeemed man, he could tell me that and I would go with no harm done beyond some hurt to my feelings—and I was becoming accustomed to that.

At the time I had no doubt I'd catch him quickly, for Fisk is city bred, and traveling on horseback in winter takes some hardihood. But I reckoned without several factors. The first was Chant's slowly healing leg, which obliged me to set a moderate pace. The second was that Fisk knew where he was going, while I had to stop and inquire for him in each town I passed—a task that would have taken even longer if I hadn't remembered the letter carrier's trick and asked after Tipple rather than Fisk. Even so, I overshot him when he turned north to cross Blue Marrow Pass into the Yare River valley, and doubling back cost me a full day. 'Twas as I tracked him down the wide, fertile valley the Yare had cut through the surrounding mountains that I finally remembered the peddler had asked Fisk if he'd lived in Ruesport and realized where he must be going.

Knowing Fisk's destination let me travel faster, but one thing still slowed my pace—the need to earn money on the road. Fisk's method for doing this involves betting a tavern crowd that they can't figure out the mechanism of a particular card trick. Once he convinced me it wasn't cheating, I had to own the convenience of it, for it took under an hour and could be done after dark when our day's journey was over. But the only way I know to earn traveling money is to stop and work for it. Once I turned north, the weather was too bitter to spend even a relatively mild night in the open, and paying for lodgings and food took its toll on my thin purse.

I started trying to find half a day's work for room,

board, and a few silver roundels as soon as I passed into the Yare valley. The first few times I had no difficulty, for I've done this before. But one afternoon I was helping build stalls in a new barn, and I grew so warm that I rolled up my shirtsleeves.

The broken circles on my wrists had long since ceased to startle me, even the way the magica ink made them glow to my sight—for when Lady Ceciel dosed me with her foul potions, she changed something about me, mayhap the nature of my sensing Gift. Before, like all others with that particular talent, I could detect the presence of magic only by reaching out till I felt its energy tingle against my skin. Ceciel had not, thank goodness, turned me into some sort of magic-using freak, but once her potions began to work, I started *seeing* magica, as a sort of light that glowed around the creatures, plants, and items that had it. 'Twas most disconcerting, and I'd told no one of it, not even Fisk, for I hoped 'twould pass off in time.

So when I rolled up my sleeves, as half the men in the barn had done already, and saw the others staring at my wrists, for a horrified moment I wondered if they too could see that whitish glow. Then I realized that the circles themselves accounted for their shock and dismay.

I'd told Fisk I would not conceal my shame, and I meant it. I might no longer consider myself some sort of knight, but a man's honor is in his own keeping, and even being unredeemed didn't change that. The details were too wearisome to recount. I stood straight and told them that I'd had some trouble with the law and incurred a debt I couldn't, with honor, pay.

They seemed to accept it and we went on working, though now they eyed me askance, and the casual conversation that had passed among us was silenced. But when the day ended and 'twas time to collect my wages—five silver roundels promised—the master carpenter gave me only a few copper fracts. When I protested, he grinned and said 'twas all my work was good for—a base lie, for I am handy with tools—and if I had any complaints, I could take them to the law, which of course I couldn't.

I must confess my thoughts turned to Rosamund that night. She'd always been outside my grasp. Beautiful and Gifted, she was destined to wed far higher than a baron's fourth son. The gulf between us had always been uncrossable, so its widening shouldn't have troubled me. But it did.

The next time the circles on my wrists were revealed in the course of a day's work (my hands and arms were filthy with the oil I'd worked into some leather strapping, and I had to wash them), the saddler fired me on the spot, quite perturbed, for he'd never have hired me if he'd known. At least he paid me for the work I'd done.

Thus it went all through the journey, and I soon found I could place men into one of two categories: the honest, who wouldn't hire me at all, and the dishonest, who'd hire me but not pay. The longer this went on, the more dismaying I found it, and becoming Rupert's steward began to look better to me . . . which I found more dismaying than all the rest. If I gave up the freedom for which I'd paid so high, I would truly lose myself.

My knowledge that Fisk was going into some difficulty and would need my aid kept me traveling onward—though my doubts about whether an unredeemed man's presence might prove more disaster than aid were growing. Still, if he wanted me gone, he could tell me so. After the trouble I'd gone to chasing him down, he owed me that much truth.

Despite these tribulations I was only half a day behind him when I finally reached Ruesport. As I said, I'm a better winter traveler than he, and Tipple was the slower of our horses even in good weather. I stopped Chant on the last hill before the road descended and looked over the city. 'Twas a bright day, mild enough that the snow, about six inches deep here, would be crusted tomorrow morning.

The old town of Ruesport had been built in the arms of the Y formed where a small busy river (the Nighber, I later learned) rushed out of the mountains and into the Yare. Cities being what they are in these peaceful days, the buildings had long since outgrown the walls of the Oldtown, especially on the lower, flatter land on the Yare side, though a surprising number of buildings perched among the rough hills from which the Nighber raced.

Past the turbulence where the two rivers met, the Yare, already large, became great. Wharves lined the river's pregnant curve, and even in the month of Pinon dozens of ships rested there.

I saw no sign of cultivation in the flat sweep of land beyond the docks, though I knew the sea was still some leagues farther on. This seemed odd, for the land south of town was heavily farmed. Rising in my stirrups to see better, I caught the glimmer of sun on standing water and realized that west of the town, before it reached the sea, some part of the river spread out into a vast marsh.

The most outstanding features of the city itself were the several sweeping bridges that spanned each river. The ones that overleapt the Yare were particularly impressive, for the bluff on which the Oldtown rested was about forty feet higher than the other side of the riverbank, so the bridges not only spanned the river, they also rose to the higher ground on which the old walls sat. What kind of timber was strong enough to span . . . Ah. Peering at the distant beams, I saw a faint, telltale glow in the shadows beneath the bridge and whistled softly. To harvest magica trees that size without incurring the Green God's wrath, they must have made an incredible sacrifice.

I'd be riding Chant over those timbers soon, for somewhere in that spread of humanity my errant comrade lurked. The end of my journey should have made me feel triumphant, but what if he didn't want me? It seemed far more likely now than it had when I'd first set out, and dread made my heart heavy in my chest. But putting it off would make it no better, and I was cursed if I'd run from Fisk after traveling all this way just to confront him. Lifting the reins, I urged Chant forward with some care, for the road was busy this close to town, and the snow was packed and slippery.

As we passed among the buildings, the snow turned to dirty slush, which did little to enhance the looks of the place. The buildings had more wood in them and less stone and brick than I was accustomed to, and the roofs were topped with wooden shingles instead of thatch. 'Twas only five days before Calling Night, and folk were setting out greenery and affixing torch brackets to their homes and shops.

I was interested to see lampstands, which even in the daylight glowed with magica's eerie gleam, along the main streets. Those who live near swamps have always used phosphor moss as a temporary light source, though it fades in a few hours. Breeding that much of the magica form of the species, and keeping it alive in streetlamps, bespoke a plentiful supply and great care on the part of the lamp tenders.

With the holiday coming the townsfolk were merry, and the road was full of the amusing pageant humanity makes of itself. I passed a coach stopped dead between two inns, both of whose landlords had run out to entice the passenger to stay with them. A brisk quarrel broke out between a housewife holding a broken bowl and a potter—though they broke off arguing to watch the best show of all, which was picking its dainty way through the slush.

He wore a doublet of delicate blue silk, slashed in so many places it couldn't possibly provide any warmth, and a stylish short cape slung across one shoulder. The lace that trimmed his collar dripped halfway down his thin chest, and the feathers in his hatband (the hat was blue, too) fell halfway down his back. The real sport came from his tall walking stick, from which blue ribbons, ending in white tassels, dangled almost to the ground. The tassels had attracted a tiny, scruffy dog, which charged at them, yipping, and then scurried away when the dandy struck at it with the staff. But the staff's movement made the tassels dance, and the mutt leapt in for another assault.

The dandy cursed, swung at the dog, minced a step or two, and repeated the process—evidently never thinking to wrap the ribbons round the stick until the dog lost interest. Or mayhap he was too proud to do so. I pulled Chant to a stop to watch and so had a perfect seat for the next act of the farce, which began with the cries of a carriage driver to make way as he tried to maneuver his coach through the crowded street.

The dandy obviously recognized the carriage, for he turned to the street and struck a noble pose, one hand on his hip, one foot lifted to the base of a convenient lampstand. His long-nosed face lifted to gaze into the distance—which fixed his eyes on the window of a butcher's shop where several fat, plucked geese hung by their necks.

He'd quite forgotten the dog, which seized a tassel

and began to worry it, growling fiercely. Color rose in the dandy's cheeks, but he held his pose, smiling grimly for the passing lady. I couldn't see inside the coach, but surely only a lady could inspire such a performance.

And all for naught. Just before the coach reached him, the traffic cleared. The coachman snapped the reins, the horses broke into a trot, and the coach rolled by so briskly that the wheels sent a wave of slush over the fellow's boots up to the knees of his blue silk britches.

The dog yelped at the drenching and scampered off, and the street erupted with smothered guffaws. It seemed I wasn't the only one watching the show. I tried not to laugh, for 'tis never pleasant to look a fool, but I couldn't restrain my grin.

The dandy, who'd been brushing at his knees and cursing, raised a face red with ill temper. His gaze passed over a pair of sturdy, laughing carters and passed me before it settled on a snickering apprentice, mayhap twelve or thirteen, with thick steel-rimmed spectacles and an apron full of wrapped packages.

The dandy strode forward, splashing in the slush, and grabbed the boy's jacket. "How dare you laugh at me, you snotty whelp."

Merriment vanished from the boy's face. "I'm sorry,

Sir. It was only— Here! I said I'm sorry!"

The dandy had yanked him around and slammed him into the shop wall. The boy made a move as if to free himself, then glanced at the packages in his apron, which would fall if he released his grip. "I'm sorry!" The boy's voice rose to a wail, but no apology could lessen the dandy's humiliation.

"I'll teach you to mock your betters." He lifted the tasseled staff to strike.

I have no memory of dismounting, but my hand closed around the staff before it could fall—just as the smith's hand had saved me in Toffleton, a good turn that surely deserved another.

The dandy tugged on the staff, but I didn't let go. "No God looks after mankind, Sir, but that's not to say you may mistreat this lad."

He released the wide-eyed boy and turned to me. The boy took to his heels. Gazing into that furious face, I didn't think the boy cowardly in the least.

With a contemptuous sneer, the dandy looked me up and down, and opened his mouth to speak . . . then his knee shot upward, aiming for my groin. Thankfully he missed his target, striking my upper thigh instead, but the mere thought of that blow connecting made me bend protectively.

The dandy's free hand cuffed my ear, and I was

sufficiently distracted that this time he wrenched his staff away. He lifted it to strike as I straightened, and I caught it as it whistled down. The blow stung my palms smartly, but I was too angry to care. I pulled the staff from his grip and tossed it aside.

"You, Sir, need a lesson in manners far more than that boy does." I grasped his doublet as I spoke, and thumped him into the same wall where he'd held the young apprentice. He didn't resist, mayhap knowing that not many will fight a man who isn't fighting back, but his eyes glittered with malice.

"A gentleman, Sir, accepts the small misfortunes of life with good humor and good grace." I suddenly realized that I was quoting my father, who had often lectured my brothers and me on gentlemanly behavior. The irony stung, but I had fallen into the rhythm of it and would not be stopped.

"A gentleman does not use his strength against those weaker than himself—don't slide your eyes away like that. Those carters were laughing harder than the boy, but they were bigger than you, you contemptible bully. A gentleman—"

"Help!" the dandy shrieked. He came to life in my hands, struggling to free himself, though not very hard. "Help! Murder! Brigands! Help!" He sounded just like Fisk.

It should have warned me, but I was quite startled when two husky men tackled me to the muddy cobbles and began to pummel me. I squirmed, kicked, and pummeled back, but I was getting the worst of it when the sound of tramping feet heralded the arrival of half a dozen leather-aproned workmen, led by the young apprentice with steel-rimmed spectacles.

They hauled my assailants off me, and it might have ended there but for the arrival of some seven or eight young men, robed like law clerks, who pitched in on the dandy's side.

I cried out, "Wait!" but no one listened, and the street erupted into a maelstrom of flying fists and boots. I must confess I wasn't entirely sorry for it— after all the frustrations of the last few weeks, I'd enjoy bashing someone.

Honest pedestrians scattered like pigeons. The nearby merchants closed and barred their shutters, then came out to join the fray. The potter, alas, failed to get his shutters closed in time. A black-robed clerk hurtled into a pile of pots, then broke even more crockery righting himself and struggling clear of the shards. Although most of the merchants took whatever side they fancied, the potter's wife rushed out the door on our side—and she wielded a wicked broom.

I worked my way through the chaos in determined

search of muddy blue silk and finally reached the dandy, though I acquired a bruised eye and a bloody nose in the process. He was prancing around the edges of the brawl, striking at my supporters with his ridiculous staff, which he'd somehow reacquired.

I took it from him again and landed a solid blow to his stomach. When he doubled over, I lifted my knee to meet his unmarked face. He fell then, and I was turning in search of a more worthy opponent when I was stunned by a washboard breaking over my head. I went to my knees and stayed there for some seconds, so I missed the deputies' arrival. But the hands that helped me to my feet and then kept hold belonged to a man whose scarlet cloak bore the crossed swords and town crest that indicate a minion of the law.

For a moment I was sorry, but looking at the shambles we'd made of the tidy, prosperous street, mayhap 'twas time to stop.

I was cheered to see that all involved were on their feet, none seriously injured. I put a handkerchief to my bleeding nose and saw the blue-clad dandy who'd started all this talking earnestly to the deputies. With a sinking heart, I noted they didn't restrain him (though one of them still gripped my arm) but listened with respectful expressions. 'Twas only then that I remembered I was unredeemed, and my heart sank so low that not even the discovery of the dandy's hat, trampled to muddy ruin, could cheer me.

I was at this man's mercy, and from what I'd seen, 'twould prove a scant commodity.

The deputies let me lead Chant over the great bridge to the older part of town, and then down a short, straight street lined with tall stone buildings to the Council Hall. 'Twas six stories high and had once been a fortress, I judged. The banners of the town's guilds flapped on its walls, their brave display only slightly faded by sun and weather. The sheriff's office, down several flights of narrow stairs, was near the old dungeons, windowless and lit by several oil lamps even in the day. But a small charcoal brazier in the fireplace warmed the room well enough—even before a dozen men crowded in.

The dandy had asked the deputies to bring only me, but the potter, a man I took to be the apprentice's master, and several others had come along, all of them quarreling and gesturing. Pulling my guard with me, I made my way to a corner and stood quietly. My nose had finally stopped bleeding, so I put my kerchief away. I could do nothing about the bloodstains or the mud, and I knew how disreputable I must look—even if no one saw my wrists.

The sheriff put up with the din for mayhap two minutes before roaring for silence. When he got it, he turned not to the dandy, whose lower lip was quite swollen, but to the potter.

The potter launched into a detailed account of his broken wares, their quality, their worth, and the necessity that he be instantly compensated for their loss. It took the sheriff a while to work through these mercantile concerns, though when he got round to it, the potter gave a fair description of the events. He'd been watching the dandy, whose name was Thrope, and had seen the whole affray.

His tale gave me a chance to study the sheriff, a man in late middle age with a neatly cut rim of hair embracing his baldness. His features were blunt and rough, and the arms under his plain shirt were thick with muscle. By this, and the small scars on his face and hands, I judged it likely he'd once been a man-at-arms. Such men are often chosen as deputies and sometimes rise to sheriff—though more often that job is given to someone higher up the social ladder. This man made no pretense of rank or wealth, for his clothes were as rough and serviceable as my own, though a great deal cleaner.

When the potter finally finished, the sheriff, whose

name, coincidentally, was Potter, looked around the crowded room and picked out the principal players.

"Master Thrope, come forward if you please. And you, Sir." He gestured for me to come too. "You're a stranger to Ruesport?"

I wiggled through the crowd, trying to display more courage than I felt. "I was just riding in when all this started."

"I see. Check him out, Ferrin. And unless the rest of you have something to add . . ."

'Twas a clear dismissal, and most of the men shuffled from the room, but the man I'd guessed to be the apprentice's master stepped forward instead. "Stranger he may be, Rob Potter, but he did a good thing this day. The Lock Makers' Guild will remember it." He glared at the dandy, but I paid little heed, for one of the guards had taken my wrist and was undoing my cuff buttons.

"I can see why the judicar'd be angered," the lock maker went on. "But he'd no call to beat an honest boy, and if this . . ." His voice trailed off, for no one was listening.

They were staring, frozen, at the broken circles on my wrists.

The silence stretched for a long time, and it was Judicar Thrope who broke it. "I don't believe I need to say another word. You know your duty, Sheriff." He turned and minced out.

The lock maker looked at my wrists, then at Sheriff Potter as if to speak, then at my wrists again. He turned and followed Thrope without another word. *If any hand be turned against thee, thou mayst claim no redress from thy fellow men.*

Sheriff Potter was watching me. "You're a bit young for this, aren't you? Pull his shirt down, Ferrin."

I flushed with shame and anger, but 'twas useless to protest, so I undid my doublet and removed it, and the deputy pulled my shirt from my shoulders. He whistled, long and low, turning me so Sheriff Potter could examine the scars on my back, which he did for an absurdly long time—it took no more than a glance to see I'd been flogged.

'Twas by a half-mad shipmaster for spilling a pail of paint, and had nothing to do with the law. But no one would ever believe that, and I was fuming at the injustice of it when the guard finally let me turn round again.

"So, stranger." The sheriff rounded his desk and sat down. "What's your name?"

"Michael Sevenson." He didn't ask me to sit. I felt as if I was standing before my tutor's desk, or my father's, waiting to be scolded for some misdeed, and set my teeth over simmering resentment. The man was only doing his job.

Potter signaled all but two of his guardsman to leave the room, and I pulled up my shirt and put my doublet back on, trying to keep my fingers from quivering as I did up the buttons.

"What brings you to Ruesport, Michael Sevenson?"

This would surely bring Fisk more trouble than any help I could give him would be worth.

"Does it matter?"

"I think it might."

Then he waited, as if he'd all the time in the world, until I shrugged and said, "I'm seeking a friend."

"Does this friend have a name, Michael Sevenson? Or is it Sir Michael?" He'd caught my noble accent, even in the few words I'd spoken.

"Not anymore," I said, and one of the guards snorted contemptuously. When a noble goes unredeemed, 'tis usually for a crime that would have hanged a humbler man.

They thought my family had bought off some judicar. My cheeks burned, but the sheriff asked patiently, "Your friend's name?"

He would persist until I gave it. "Fisk."

A slight frown creased the man's brow. "Is he a stranger here too?"

"Yes. No. That is, I believe he lived here once, but he doesn't anymore."

"Fisk, Fisk," the sheriff murmured, in the manner of a man trying to remember. Then his eyes widened. "Maxwell let him come—" He broke off the unguarded exclamation, and sat silent a moment, factoring new information into some equation. "So." His gaze returned to me. "You're a friend of young Fisk. I'd hoped he'd do better for himself, but I suppose it was too much to expect."

"You know Fisk?" Somehow, I never thought of anyone knowing Fisk, though he must have encountered many people in the erratic course of his life. And now an unredeemed man was claiming him as friend in a town full of people whose opinion he might care about.

"I'd not say I know him. I was only a deputy when he cleared out, but I remember the story well enough. A pity."

A pity Fisk had ended up consorting with a scoundrel like me. I said nothing.

"However, I do know Yorick Thrope." Neither his face nor his voice revealed more than the bare words, but the clear implication was that to know the man was to hate him. My heart lifted, cautiously. "I know Master Maxwell, too."

Decision made, he rose to his feet and put on the brown woolen jacket that had hung on his chair back. "I've a notion that you're trouble, Michael Sevenson, but if Horatius Maxwell will give warrant for your good behavior, I'll release you into his custody."

So much confused me in this speech that he had time to dismiss the remaining guards and haul me halfway up the first flight of stairs before I found my voice.

"You're not charging me?"

"For getting involved in a brawl? I'd have to lock up twenty others with you. I haven't heard a single word to say you started it—indeed, I've heard testimony to the contrary."

"But the dandy, Thrope, *Judicar* Thrope, expects you to lock me up. Or worse."

"What makes you say that, Michael Sevenson? He said I knew my duty, and I believe I do. You don't like my decision? I can always change it."

We rounded the landing and started up the second flight of stairs. Sunlight gleamed at the top.

"But . . ." What was I arguing about? "No, it's fine with me. But who's this Maxwell you speak of?"

The sheriff stopped, pulling me to a stop as well. Standing on the same step, he was half a head shorter than I. "Maxwell is your friend Fisk's brother by marriage. You didn't know that?"

"No, I . . . He once said he had sisters, but Fisk seldom talks about himself." Fisk had been returning to his *family*. No wonder he'd left his unredeemed companion behind!

"Well." The sheriff started to climb again and I followed. "He'd better be willing to talk to Maxwell about you. If Max won't give warrant for you, you'll have to spend the night in a cell and get out of Ruesport first thing in the morning."

The daylight was red-gold, crimsoning the stones of the Council Hall's antechamber—the sun was setting. I had no desire to spend the night in a cell. "Fisk will vouch for me, but surely you don't need to bring this Maxwell into it? If you'd ask to see Fisk alone . . ." He might yet be spared the shame of having known me. And then I would go.

The sheriff snorted. "I'd not take young Fisk's word on the good behavior of a rabbit. It's Jud— Master Maxwell who'll vouch for you. Or not. And Michael Sevenson?"

We topped the stairs and stepped into the light.

"Yes?"

"I said I've a notion that you're trouble. If you make trouble here, those stripes on your back'll seem like a maiden's slap. You clear on that?"

"Quite clear." You woodenheaded son of a sow. I only hoped the mysterious Master Maxwell would take Fisk's word for me. If Fisk would give it—for I now realized that he'd sneaked out on me like a thief and fled across a dozen fiefdoms simply to avoid the very humiliation that I was about to bring upon him.

CHAPTER 4

Fisk

I chose to wear my second-best doublet for the "quiet family dinner with just one guest" for which my sisters had been preparing frantically all day. Even Michael's brother Benton's plainer giveaways might highlight the fact that my sisters' gowns were beginning to wear. And while I might have enjoyed showing up old Max, I wouldn't deliberately embarrass my sisters. I told myself yet again that I couldn't have brought Michael, that he'd be fine without me. If I repeated it often enough, someday I might come to believe it. I couldn't have brought him—I was going to embarrass them enough just by being there myself.

I'd arrived in Ruesport that morning, and the familiar scents of smoke and winter-wet wood carried me back to my childhood. I must have run through these streets thousands of times, carrying Mama's sewing, or running errands for a few fracts. Great Fallon Road enters Ruesport through the Yarelands, and the small, neat house I'd grown up in wasn't far from the road. Some craftsman's family probably lived there now, and I wished them better luck than my family'd had. Though luck, really, had nothing to do with it.

I stifled the surge of anger with the ease of long practice, and I turned and rode Tipple briskly over Newbridge, which is higher than Highbridge and hasn't been new since before I was born. My memories of the Oldtown's streets were darker, and not nearly so enticing. The stews and slums on the other side of Trullsgate Bridge from the Oldtown held even worse memories, but they were few.

I made my way through the Oldtown's twisting streets to the tall, narrow house where old Maxwell had lived. The current owner's manservant told me he'd moved east shortly after his marriage. His expression was a bit odd as he gave me directions to Maxwell's house, but I ignored that in my pleasure at my sisters' good fortune. I knew the old man had money, but even a modest house in the neighborhood outside the east wall was something I'd had no idea he could afford. Unless he couldn't afford it and was only trying to impress his young bride.

A woman can pay a high price for a fine house and silk petticoats, but it shouldn't be too high in this case. Before I had let Anna marry a man nineteen years her senior, I'd checked his reputation with every whore in town. It turned out he almost never went to whores, but they'd heard enough to tell me he was normal in his tastes and kind, even to women he hired.

Anna looked relieved when I told her that, though she shook her head. "I told you, he's a good man. And he seems to love me quite a lot. I won't mind . . . that is, I want to marry him."

She didn't, but the alternatives were worse, for her, for Judith, and someday for Lissy, and neither of us could accept that.

It was the price he'd demanded of me that bothered Anna.

So it was with some foreboding that I located my sister's house in the east part of the city. It was small-ish for the east, which meant it was large for anywhere else: a three-storey redbrick manor, with windows of the new, thin, diamond-paned glass which is so easy to break in through.

The wrought-iron gate in the high wall surrounding the house was stout enough, but it squealed when I opened it. The small front garden was tidy, and the fountain had been shut down for the winter, so it took

me a moment to realize why the place felt neglected—
no greenery. Every other house in town was trimmed
with garlands of juniper, or holly from the marish. In
this neighborhood some houses were already wrapped
with ribbons, despite the fact that they'd be ruined if
it snowed. But Maxwell's house was bare.

Perhaps they were gone. Perhaps I was too late, and
the unnamed catastrophe (curse Anna, why couldn't
she write a straightforward note?) had swept them all
away.

My heart pounded as I tied Tipple to a tether ring
on the empty fountain and climbed three steps to
knock on the door. Anna opened it herself.

She'd grown plumper in five years, and wore a servant's stained apron and a white cap, from which frizzy
brown curls escaped. For some reason, our hair had
always been similar and not like that of either of our
parents. Her eyes widened with recognition, then lit
with joy.

"Nonny!" It was a shriek to split eardrums, but I
didn't care—the crushing hug that followed it would
have made up for anything, although . . .

"You know, Annie, I've been asking you to call me
Fisk since I was nine. I'd think you could manage it
by now."

"I know." She stepped free of my arms and wiped

her cheeks, looking me over anxiously. "It's just I don't think of you that way." Her arms went round me again, not only hugging but pulling me over the threshold. "Oh, Judith, look. Non— Fisk is here."

"So I heard." Judith too wore an apron, and smelled of silver polish. She was thin as a rail and hatchet-faced, with Father's lank hair. "Hello, Fisk. I see nobody's hanged you yet."

Anna gasped, but the sardonic grin that went with the words was surprisingly companionable, and I found myself grinning in return. "Hello, Judith. I see nobody's married you yet." It should have pricked, at least a little, but her grin only twitched a bit wider.

Max came out of a room to the left of the entryway, probably his study. He was a small, neat man, and if his hair was a bit thinner, and his face a bit more lined, that was only to be expected. The anger hardening his expression was new, for he'd had the cursed gall to be sorry for me the few times we'd met.

Anna stepped forward and said firmly, "Stop look-ing like that, Max. He only came because I wrote and asked him to. I think he might be able help us. And you know we need it."

Confusion washed over his face, and when it receded, he looked tired. "Without consulting me? I'd think, my dear . . ." I lost track of what he was saying, for a girl—no, a young woman—was peering out of the study behind him. I knew who she had to be, for her resemblance to Anna was marked, though her hair was darker and more softly curled. If I'd passed her on the street, I wouldn't have known her. Ten to fifteen is a long time, and when I'd imagined her growing up, it had been as an awkward schoolgirl, like Michael's sister, not a young beauty.

"Lissy?" I asked, still not quite believing it.

"Oh." Her eyes were wide. "Oh, Nonny!" She rushed forward and kissed my cheek, suddenly the impulsive little girl I remembered. But her shape as she hugged me was not at all familiar, and I held her away and looked her up and down incredulously. "You grew up!"

It shouldn't have surprised me, and Judith snickered. But Lissy laughed, and the flirtatious sparkle in her eyes stunned me further. "So did you. You were only a boy when you left."

There was an awkward pause as all eyes turned to Maxwell, and I felt my hackles rise. Lissy was the only one of my sisters not wearing an apron, and if this was how he kept *his* part of the bargain . . .

"Oh, very well." His exasperated sigh left him thinner than before, as if something in him had deflated. "The way things are now, they could hardly get worse.

You're welcome to stay, young Fisk." He held out his hand.

I folded my arms. "What, exactly, is going on here?"

"Mistress Anna!" A slamming door and a clatter of feet heralded the arrival of an oldish woman in the good gray gown of an upper servant. "Mistress! The pots on the stove look to boil their lids off. Who's this?" Her dark eyes were sharp as a crow's.

"I still want to know—" I began.

"Oh, dear!" Anna started toward the rear of the house, where the kitchen presumably lurked. "This is my brother, Non— Fisk, Mrs. Trimmer. He'll be staying with us."

"I didn't know we had company staying. I suppose you'll want me to ready a bedchamber, fetching out sheets, hauling a mattress about, clean—"

"Thank you, that would be splendid," said Anna gently.

Mrs. Trimmer's mouth shut with a snap and then opened, but before she could speak, Maxwell cut in. "I'd like a word with you, my dear. If you don't mind."

Anna, who hadn't paused for my question or Mrs. Trimmer's hectoring, hesitated in the doorway. "But we've a guest for dinner. If I don't—"

"I still want—"

"I'll take care of dinner." Lissy darted in and untied

Anna's apron, whisking it over her own head.

"Thanks, Liss. Add the onions to the cream as soon as you get them chopped. And stir—"

"I want—"

"I'll be fine." Lissy smiled and swept out, and Anna followed Maxwell into the study.

Mrs. Trimmer turned beady eyes on me. "Humph. I've heard of you. I suppose you've gotten clever and come home to batten on the leavings. Serve you right there aren't any. I hope you're prepared to work."

If Mrs. Trimmer had been wearing an apron, I might have taken that more kindly.

"I never work." I smiled blandly. "If you're clever you don't have to. Are you a hard worker, Mrs. Trimmer?"

"That I am," she announced. "And an honest woman to boot." Then the insult caught up with her and she glared. I smiled back, and she turned and stumped up the stairs muttering, not quite under her breath, about gallows bait.

I made a mental note to check my bed tonight and turned to Judith, who was the only one left in the hallway.

"Not bad," she said judiciously. "A little heavy-handed, but if you'd been subtle, she'd have missed it."

"Why in the world do you keep that harridan?"

"Because she and her husband are the only ser-vants who didn't quit when we stopped paying them." Judith's eyes glinted. "Lissy considered it an act of betrayal when they all decamped, but I found it reas-suring to learn we hadn't hired idiots." She went through an open door as she spoke, and I followed her into what turned out to be the dining room. "I think Trimmer would have quit, too, but no one in their right mind would hire Mrs. Trimmer, so he's stuck here. And she does work. Just don't let her bully you."

"Don't worry." The dining room had paneling halfway up the walls, and plaster leaves and flowers around the ceiling. The blank white upper walls were designed to hold pictures, but there were none. Looking closely, I could see the holes where candle sconces had been taken down.

Judith, who'd followed my gaze, gestured to the heap of flatware gleaming on the long table. "This will be the next to go, so we decided to have one last din-ner party before it's sold. At least that's the excuse. I think Max may have broken down and decided to ask for a loan." She went to the buffet, dug inside for a moment, and tossed me an apron.

"Judith, what *happened*?" I laid the apron aside but sat and picked up a rag. You don't need an apron to polish silver unless you're careless, which I'm not.

"I thought Anna wrote you. She said she was going to try. You took your time getting here." She rubbed a fork briskly.

"I got the letter only a month ago. I came as fast as I could. And if you don't tell me what's going on right now, you'll be washing silver polish out of your hair!"

"Didn't Anna explain—"

"You know what Annie's letters are like. She didn't say anything except that some hideous disaster had befallen you and I had to come at once."

"But she's gotten much better about . . ." Judith frowned, and my suspicion stirred.

"You think she was that vague deliberately? Why?"

"I'm not sure. She might have reverted to old habits under stress. Or . . ."

"Or?"

"She may have thought you wouldn't be willing to come just to help Max."

I snorted. "Just to help Max I wouldn't, but my family's fate is pretty well tied to his. What happened?"

Judith's eyes were distant. "It really started with the fire. . . ."

It took the rest of the afternoon to get the whole story. It seemed old Max, along with most of the merchants in the city, was heavily invested in a convoy of ships that was setting off to trade in Tallowsport. The ships hadn't even left the dock when a fire started in one of the shipyards, burning a shed full of pitch kegs, which then exploded.

"The fire went everywhere, Fisk. Dozens of people were burned and three men died!"

Eight ships had burned to the waterline, among them the ships Maxwell had invested in.

"So we lost a lot of money, but Max hadn't borrowed—it was just his savings." We'd finished the silver by this time and were spreading the heavy linen tablecloth. It, too, Judith said, was to be sold after tonight. "I don't suppose you've acquired a fortune over the last five years?"

"No, but at least I didn't lose one. Go on."

The real disaster occurred almost a month after the fire. Maxwell had judged a murder, an ugly case where two drunken tanners had raped and killed a traveling player who'd beaten them at a shell game. It was horrible, but it seemed clear-cut. There were two witnesses; one of them, a woman too ill to rise and go for help, actually saw the crime committed. The other had seen the two men enter the alley where the girl was killed. Both of them identified the tanners, whom Maxwell, quite properly, ordered hanged.

Then, over a month after the trial, the invalid killed

herself, leaving a note that she could no longer bear the guilt of lying two men to their death, and that she'd been bribed to identify them . . . by Judicar Maxwell. The Judicary Guild ordered an immediate investigation. They had complete confidence in Max's honesty—though that wavered a bit when they discovered that the other witness had left town a month before the woman's death. The guild audited Maxwell's books and bank account and found nothing suspicious until some bright young clerk had the notion to search Max's study. In a hidden compartment beneath a window seat they found another set of ledgers, for a bank account in Fallon. They were in Maxwell's handwriting and showed he'd received a large sum of money not long before the hearing, and paid out several smaller sums of money, one of which exactly matched the amount the woman's suicide note claimed she'd been paid.

When Judith told me the sum that was left, I whistled. "It sounds like old Max recouped his losses."

Judith's eyes flashed. "If you'd been here, you wouldn't joke about it."

I wasn't joking. At least, not entirely. But Judith went on, "He lost everything he cares about except his family. Not just money, but the respect of the community, his position. His . . . place. He was framed, Fisk.

And they did a cursed good job, too." Her expression was grim.

"Judith, are you sure of that? Anyone can be—"

"Not Max. I've lived in his house for five years. I'm certain. He was framed."

If Anna had said that, I wouldn't have paid much attention, but Judith had sat through the same lessons I had—a scholar was trained to evaluate the facts. And Judith was Judith. Putting compassion above truth wasn't one of her virtues, but if Max had been framed . . .

"By who then? And why?"

"That, dear brother, is the mystery Anna called you home to solve."

"Me? The Judicary Guild already investigated. What does she think I can do that they didn't?"

"You can talk to people who won't talk to the law. It must have been some criminal who framed him, since he has no other enemies. And you have criminal connections in this town."

Truth above compassion, all right. "That was a long time ago. For all I know, they've all been hanged by now. By Max, probably." In truth, the criminals I'd associated with hadn't been the kind to commit hanging crimes, but I was in no mood to make concessions.

"You can't know that until you ask around, can

you?" Judith didn't need to tell me how urgent the matter was. We were setting the table with silverware that was about to be sold. "I know we have no right to ask you for help—not anymore. Though in fairness to Max, I can see why he didn't want to end up in a position where he might have to hang his brother by marriage."

"It wasn't that. I embarrassed him."

Judith's eyes fell. "He did offer you money, to get started somewhere else."

"So he did." I smiled at the memory. "Quite a lot of money." I had dumped it on his desk and walked out without a backward glance.

Judith winced. "Will you try anyway?"

"Do I have a choice?"

To say that I wasn't looking forward to dinner was an understatement. I straightened the lace on my cuffs as I walked down the hall toward the stair. The hall was dark, since lamp oil is expensive, but the landing that overlooked the entryway glowed with a blaze of light from below. As I drew nearer, I heard a babble of voices. Acrimonious voices. I quickened my steps. When I reached the landing, I looked down, and stopped dead.

Michael.

The small crowd surrounding him included Maxwell and all my sisters, but it was Michael I looked at. His rough clothes were stained with blood. His hair, now grown back to shoulder length, was dirty, and the small scar on his jaw, not to mention the swelling bruise under his left eye, completed the picture of a particularly scruffy bandit. Or maybe it was the hard, closed expression on his face.

Michael had followed me . . . for a full month? In midwinter? Why?

The man beside him wasn't actually gripping his arm, but the attitude was there. ". . . in a brawl, so he came to my attention." The man was speaking to Maxwell. The details of his clothes, scars, posture, and words added up to just one total—sheriff.

I seriously considered backing up into the shadows. My jacket was a dark red-brown and would conceal me nicely. No one had seen me yet. I still had time to avoid the worst of the humiliating scene that was doubtless about to occur. What in the world did Michael think he was *doing*?

"He claims he's looking for your brother by marriage," the sheriff went on, almost as if he was answering my thought. "Says he might be in trouble. I hadn't heard young Fisk was back, but I figured you'd know, and that you might want to take charge of this fellow.

I need to tell you, Max, he's unredeemed."

The onlookers gasped, and Anna shrank closer to her husband. Michael's face set harder. Had he come all this way, exposed himself to this, because he thought I might be in trouble? Even after I'd run out on him? Of course he had. And I'd abandoned him. Because I was afraid of being embarrassed. Just like Max had disowned me.

I must have been out of my mind.

I stepped forward, letting my heel thump on the first step. "I'm Fisk," I told the sheriff. "Can I be of some assistance?"

He took his time looking me over, and Maxwell rushed into the breach. "Sheriff Potter claims this . . . this person knows you." His nose was pinched with distaste—his eyes begged me to deny it.

"Well, he does. Hello, Michael. How come you're the one who always needs rescuing?"

Michael's controlled expression shattered—for a moment I was afraid he might cry. But he took a deep breath and summoned up a shaky smile. "Mayhap 'tis that I try harder." His voice shook too.

The sheriff had followed this with considerable interest. Now he turned to Maxwell. "So he told me the truth. Will you give warrant for him? I'm not just going to turn him loose."

Maxwell's "no" and my "yes" clashed in midair. Our eyes met.

"I won't have an unredeemed man in my house." It was firm, final, and dignified. I didn't give a tinker's curse.

"Why not? You've already got me, and Michael's a much better person than I am. Though I must admit"— I cast a glance at my employer—"he doesn't look it."

"No," said Maxwell.

"He goes, I go."

"No!" Anna stepped forward and caught my arm. "We're your family. You can't leave us for . . . for . . ."

"He claims me and you don't. Who do you think I'm going to choose, Annie?"

She flinched, then took a deep breath and turned to Maxwell. "We need Nonny's help. Give the warrant, Max."

"No!" But it was more protest than refusal, and the tension along my spine eased, even before Maxwell went on, "He's unredeemed, Anna. The Gods alone know what he's done—or what he'll do! I can't just—"

"I thought we needed criminal types," said Judith. "Isn't that why we sent for Fisk?"

"*I* didn't . . ." Maxwell looked at the faces of his

women, and his will crumpled. "Oh, very well. Yes, Rob, I'll give warrant for this Sevenson's behavior. I only hope I don't live to regret it. I've enough on my conscience as it is."

Anna's arms went round him. "You won't regret it, dear. Nonny vouched for him."

"I did? I don't remember doing anything of the kind."

"Fisk!" Michael muttered though clenched teeth.

Maxwell looked pained. "What is your relationship to this person, Fisk?"

"He's my . . ." They were all waiting. For the first time, I noticed several strangers in the crowd. Michael was no longer my employer. My debt to him was paid. It was guilt, combined with the beaten misery on his face, that stung me into the reply I made.

"He's a knight errant and I'm his squire."

Their faces went blank with astonishment. It was probably the bravest thing I've ever said, and Michael—the coward, the rat, the traitor—gave me the same incredulous look as everyone else.

It was Judith who finally broke the silence. "Well, if you're going to bring him to dinner, you'd better wash him, whatever he is. I must say, Fisk, life's a lot more entertaining since you came home. If this is the drama, I can't wait for the farce."

◇ ◇ ◇

I took Michael upstairs to wash and change while the others got rid of the sheriff.

"Why did you say that?" Michael hissed as soon as we were out of earshot. "Now they think we're both crazy."

"So? It's better than what they were thinking before. Besides, you are crazy. What are you doing here, Mike?"

"I knew you must be going into trouble or you would have told me. You *should* have told me . . . Nonny."

I winced. "It's short for Nonopherian. After that idiot philosopher who went around pulling crooked petals off flowers."

"I know who Nonopherian was, and striving for excellence in all things doesn't make him an idiot. Though I admit, 'tis a mouthful."

"I prefer to be called Fisk . . . Michael."

"Then I will never call you anything else." The nobility of his words was undermined by the wicked satisfaction in his eyes. I reluctantly banished "Mike" from my vocabulary, even as he went on, seriously, "You really should have told me. You know I'd not let you face a problem alone, whatever it might be. Though it seems"—his voice became grimmer—"that I may do you more harm than good."

The anger of shame hardened his face, and I wondered, suddenly, what his journey had been like. At least I could do some mending on his tattered pride.

"Well, I told you to keep your shirt on. But I'm glad you're here. I'm going to need all the help I can get." I told him Maxwell's story, as briefly as possible, while he washed.

Mr. Trimmer, a willowy old man who'd been one of the strangers in the entry, brought up Michael's pack and assured us he'd stable Chanticleer with Tipple. I wondered if my family could afford to feed two horses, and concluded that Michael and I should buy some hay. I hoped he had the money for it.

Dinner was an anticlimax.

The second stranger I'd noticed in the entryway was the dinner guest, Benjamin Worthington. His long buttoned vest and jacket were tactfully subdued, but of excellent cloth and cut, and his manner had the subtle confidence that comes from knowing you're the wealthiest man in the room. He was clearly an old friend of Maxwell's and a favorite with my sisters, and as dinner commenced, I began to see why.

The addition of Michael demolished whatever seating plan Anna had intended. Maxwell sat at the head of the long table, with Worthington to his right and Anna to his left. As hostess, Anna should have been seated on Worthington's right, but instead she set Lissy between Worthington and me, and Michael between herself and Judith. Watching her shrink from Michael's presence, it wasn't hard to figure out that she'd rearranged the seating to keep the unredeemed man from sitting next to Lissy.

Trimmer served the soup, cream with onions and potatoes. The conversation would have been stilted, but Worthington started an intense discussion by telling Max that the Shipbuilders' Guild had petitioned for permission to tear down the North Tower to expand the wharves. This caused an immediate outcry, for the towers were the lower town's oldest landmarks.

I'd been gone long enough not to care, though I understood the fervor it roused in the others. As Trimmer replaced the soup bowls with various vegetables and a roast goose stuffed with apples and onions, I took the time to study Worthington more thoroughly. Beyond his clothes, he was a large man, though not overly given to fat, passing into that unnamed time between middle and old age. He must have been ten years Maxwell's senior, and his hair, now half gray, would have been plain brown in his youth. Indeed, plain brown described him well—his speech and manners were those of a well-to-do craftsman with no pretensions. Was his wealth self-made? If so, it betrayed a degree of ambition that nothing else about him showed. Watching him steer the awkward conversation into comfortable channels, I could see why my sisters liked him.

When the North Tower conversation died a natural death, he brought up the subject of shipping goods from the new mining towns. This was clearly a hobby-horse of Maxwell's, for his quiet manner became quite impassioned as he spoke of manufacturers who used unskilled men to produce shoddy goods, bringing down the reputation of the town. He hadn't been that ardent when he asked to marry my sister.

"Make a good profit, do they?" I put all the interest I could into my tone, though I admit I said it only to annoy him. Max looked appalled and opened his mouth to reply—then he realized he'd been gulled and scowled.

"They don't make as much as you'd think," Worthington interposed smoothly. "But they've cut into the Smiths' Guild's profits enough to make them howl."

"Not to mention the fact that their workmen have no guild to offer them security," Maxwell put in, his voice determinedly level. "They hire men off the farms with the promise of good wages in the mines, and when they fail—and without the support of a guild, they often do—the men come here instead of going home. When they get no work, they take to begging, or even crime, and the expense of that falls on the whole town, not just the smiths."

"'Tis difficult," said Michael, "for men in the countryside. If a farmer has more than two sons, he'll be hard put to find a living for them, and apprentice fees come high."

Everyone stared and he blushed—he'd become so involved in the conversation, he'd forgotten his own situation.

Anna, who seemed to have forgotten it too, flinched away, but Lissy fixed her bright gaze on him. "Sheriff Potter said you got involved in a brawl, Master Sevenson. How did that come about?"

"'Twas foolish," said Michael shortly. But Lissy's pretty, curious face would have thawed a glacier, and he relented and told of a dandy, a ribboned walking stick, and a dog. Both stick and man were evidently known to my family, for soon they were chuckling and, by the end of the tale, laughing aloud.

"Well, I think it's unfair that you should meet Loves-the-Rope Thrope as soon as you rode into town," said Lissy, still giggling. "And I promise you Mi— Master Sevenson, we're not all that spiteful."

"Please, call me Michael," said Michael. Then he

realized they might not want to call an unredeemed man by his first name and fell silent.

"I must admit," Maxwell put in quietly, "I used to think Thrope a pleasant person, despite his poor taste, but now . . ." He was staring at Michael's downcast face, probably realizing that Michael hadn't been unredeemed very long. Old Max was never a fool.

"Ah, but that was when you outranked him, Max," Worthington said comfortably. "I may not be an educated man, but I've traded from Landsend to D'vorin, and I've seen his sort before. Besides, you were a better judicar than he'll ever be, and he knows it."

His voice grew gentle on the last words, but even so an uncomfortable silence fell. Someone should have found a tactful way to break it, but I wasn't feeling tactful—at least, not toward Max.

"Is Thrope the one who got your job?"

"The town had to appoint someone." Maxwell sounded resigned. "And Thrope was best qualified. I hold no grudges. Frankly, I'm lucky I didn't end up before my fellow judicars."

Anna's hand shot out to cover his. "No one believed you were guilty, my dear. It was just that the scandal was so great, the town couldn't keep employing you."

"That's not precisely true," said Maxwell dryly. "They didn't think it was just to convict me on the evidence of a woman who couldn't be questioned. And I had friends. Have friends," he amended, smiling at Worthington. "A few of them haven't deserted me."

He turned to me so suddenly, I was startled. "I don't know if you've been told, Fisk, for Anna didn't know this when she wrote to you, but Councilman Sawyer came to see me the other day. He's councilman for the Ropers' Guild," he added to Michael. "I worked for the ropers as a clerk before my appointment to judicar. Sawyer said that they couldn't disregard the scandal, but if any doubt could be cast on the evidence against me, he'd hire me back in my old capacity."

"As a clerk?" Worthington's mouth was tight. "That's a cursed insult, Max."

"On the contrary, it's a generous gesture of trust and a good position. I started my legal career as the notary in charge of the ropers' charities."

"You were about to be appointed to the governing *board* of the ropers' charities," said Anna. "Ben is right. It's an insult, even if Sawyer means well."

"I am on that board," said Worthington glumly. "Believe me, you're not missing anything."

But no one believed him, and the silence that fell this time was even more awkward. It was Trimmer who broke it. "Mistress? Mrs. Trimmer is ready to put the children to bed, if you'd like to see them now."

Children? Nobody'd said a word about children.

Mrs. Trimmer led them in, and what followed seemed to be an evening ritual, for the boy went straight to Anna and scrambled onto her lap while the girl went her father. They both wore nightgowns, with bed robes over them and thick woolen stockings, but there the similarity ended. The boy, perhaps two, was the younger, with his father's serious gray eyes and thin face. He cuddled against Anna and looked at the rest of us curiously, but he was hardly noticeable with his sister present. Where had she come by that hair?

It was redder than a copper pot, and it roared around her freckled cheeks like a nimbus of flame. Hair darkens as a person grows older—my mother's chestnut hair might have been that color once. But frankly, my first thought was to wonder if Annie had played Maxwell false, and I *knew* she wasn't the type. Still, I hoped old Max had a trusting nature.

It seemed he did, for the girl climbed into his lap as if she owned it. "Mrs. Trimmer made me play with dolls *all* afternoon, Papa, and I don't want to tomorrow, so you tell her to stop. I want to go all the way to the marish for holly, and *not* buy it in the market, 'cause that's boring. And I want maple cakes for breakfast and *not* porridge."

I choked on a laugh and began to cough, and her determined gaze turned to me. "Who's that?"

"This is your Uncle Fisk." Max was clearly relieved to put off dealing with the rebellion for a moment. "He's going to stay with us for a while, along with his friend, Master Sevenson. Say how do you do, Becca."

"Howdoyoudo." Uncles obviously weren't very interesting. "Papa, you have to tell Mrs. Trimmer—" Something connected in the young brain, and her gaze shot back to me. "*You* have *horses*."

"I do?"

"The ones in the stable. Thomas and I want to ride them, but Trimmer said we couldn't 'cause we didn't have the owner's permission, but you own them so you have to tell Trimmer we can ride them 'cause we want to *really* bad."

The owner was clearly in for either a fight or a horseback ride, so I took the sensible way out. "They aren't my horses. They belong to Michael, ah, Master Sevenson here."

The intense gaze switched to Michael, and the boy, who'd been talking to Anna, added a garbled plea. Michael didn't appear in the least flustered. "'Twould be an honor to take you riding, Mistress Becca, and Master Thomas, too, if your parents say you may."

"Papa, you have to tell him—"

"We'll see, Firebug. Not tomorrow, anyway, since you have to go to the market for juniper boughs."

Becca recognized a bribe when she heard one and considered it. In the silence I heard Thomas murmur that the gray horse was big and the little one had spots all over, just like Cory Seaton's dog.

"Can we go get holly in the marish?" Becca had decided to bargain.

"No, it's too dangerous for children. We're not going to have holly this year."

My mother had told me the marish was dangerous, too—every parent did. To go down to the end of the road and creep among the weedy hillocks was a dare every child in Ruesport accepted, sooner or later. But none went in too far, for the silence was eerie. I'd been certain the rustling in the cattails was caused by poisonous frogs, even though my father said quite firmly that there were no such things.

"But *everyone* has holly. And if we go to the marish and cut it ourselves, it won't cost *anything*."

Max winced, and I realized he'd tried to keep the children from learning of his financial troubles. Not a chance. Children always know everything.

"No. If we went to cut it ourselves, we might end up taking some magica holly. And you'll eat whatever your mama fixes for breakfast."

"But—"

"No, Rebecca."

A crafty look stole into her eyes. "All right. Thank you, Papa." She smacked a kiss on his cheek and got a hug and a kiss in return before sliding from his lap and heading for Anna. I wasn't in the least surprised that her first words were "Mama, you have to fix maple cakes for breakfast tomorrow."

"Master Maxwell." It was Trimmer's lugubrious voice. "Master Tristram Fowler has called to ask Mistress Elissa if she would care for a stroll in the orchard. I said I'd inquire—"

"Oh!" Lissy jumped to her feet. "I'll get my cloak."

"With dinner not finished and the night as dark as the inside of an egg?" Mrs. Trimmer demanded. "No decent young man would dream of calling at this hour."

The young man who'd followed Trimmer into the room was meant to hear it, and color appeared on his prominent cheekbones. He was tall and gangly, no older than Lissy, with a beaky nose and a determined chin. His eyes met Maxwell's steadily, but it was Lissy who replied, "He has to work during the day—when else can he call? We'll keep to the orchard, so it's perfectly safe. Uncle Max?"

Max looked helplessly at this wife.

"You'll freeze, Lissy," Anna began. "And—"

"I'll wear my warmest cloak. Thank you, dearest!"

Rebecca should have taken lessons from her aunt—it would be almost impossible to say no in the face of that warm gratitude. But young Fowler's eyes remained on Max's face.

"Oh, very well." Max sounded harried.

"Thank you, Sir." Even Fowler's smile was steady and determined, but the light in his eyes as he turned to my sister roused brotherly instincts I hadn't felt for years. Just how private was this orchard? I had no right to ask—Lissy's well-being was Max's responsibility. The knowledge revived an old ache, and I sat silent as Lissy whisked the young man out.

"Well," said Mrs. Trimmer. "You know your own business best, Master Max, but if you ask me, that's trouble with a capital T."

It might have been an indication of concern, but Mrs. Trimmer's dress was newer than my sisters'.

"But no one asked you, did they?" said Judith, beating me to it by half a breath.

Mrs. Trimmer opened her mouth, but Anna cut in briskly, "Bedtime. And if you go with Mrs. Trimmer quietly, I'll make you maple cakes in the morning."

The children were led off by their grumbling

nursemaid; Thomas looked sleepy and Rebecca looked satisfied.

"You know, Max, as things are, she could do worse than young Fowler." It was Worthington, plain and sensible. "He may not be rich, but he's sound and honest. There are worse things than starting from scratch."

"I know." Max sighed. "I suppose I should be grateful she has any suitors left. It's just that, pretty as she is, she could have married anyone before . . ." His voice trailed off.

"So what?" said Judith, with more than her usual tartness. "Things are what they are. Frankly, she's lucky he's willing to lower himself to wed her. Besides, Max, you're in no position to lecture anyone about marrying beneath himself for love."

I still hadn't forgiven her half an hour later when Anna dragged Michael and me out for our own private conversation in the orchard.

"Max did marry beneath him," Anna said placidly. "And you know it, Nonny, so stop fussing. Judith was about to become engaged to Henry Darrow. He's a craftsman already, in the Woodworkers' Guild, with a good chance of becoming councilman someday, and when the scandal broke he backed out. Judith was . . . not heartbroken, but disappointed. It soured her a bit on marriage."

"Rubbish," I said shortly. "She's always been like that."

There were two gates leading out of the kitchen garden; one led to the alley behind the house, and the other opened into acres of winter-bare, tangled apple trees. Our breath made silver puffs before our faces.

"Annie, do you own all this land?"

"No, it belongs to the Seatons, but they let us walk here."

This orchard was big enough to be *very* private, and I wondered where young Fowler and Lissy were. I'd have wondered more, but fortunately, it was a cold night.

"It's a wonderful place for the children to play," Anna continued. "It's walled all around, so they can wander off for a moment or two and I don't have to worry. Even if they climb the trees, they can't get too high."

When did you have children, Anna? I wondered. *And why didn't I know?* But I knew the answers to both those questions, so instead I asked, "Do you want us to take them riding? They're going to plague you until you say yes."

Anna's eyes flicked to Michael, then away. "I'll think about it."

Was the presence of his young children one of the reasons Max had tried to keep Michael out? Not necessarily. Max cared a lot about respectability. He'd probably have acted the same if he'd been a bachelor.

But Michael didn't know that—he moved away from Anna even as she said, "This isn't about the children. We sent for you because of what happened to Max."

"I know, I know—you want me to prove his innocence. And I'll try, but it may not be that easy. It may not even be possible. Though if all you need for Max to get a job is some doubt cast on the evidence, I can probably arrange it."

Michael winced, and I knew I'd have an argument on my hands if it came to that. But for all her soft heart, Anna was a realist. She'd had to be.

"I don't care about the job," she answered. "We can go to another town if we have to, Max could get some sort of work, and I could too. And Judith could come with us, and Lissy can marry Tris Fowler if that's what she wants. But before we can do anything, you have to prove it to Max."

"Oh, come on. He has to know he's innocent." Unless he wasn't, but I wasn't about to say that to Anna.

"He knows he didn't bribe anyone. But Nonny, the woman who saw the killing, Ginny Weaver, she was a *good* woman. She really might have felt guilty enough to kill herself if she'd been bribed. And there was no sign of a struggle—she wrote the note, then drank too much of her pain medicine, so it does look like suicide. After the hearing, he was so sure he did right. It was a horrible case, of course, and it troubled Max. He hardly ever orders hanging. And when she died . . ."

"Now he's wondering if he hanged two innocent men."

Anna nodded miserably. "It's eating at him. He goes over the notes on the hearing, again and again. He has nightmares. If you can't prove that those men were guilty, I don't think he'll ever get over it. That's why we haven't left yet. I don't think Max could start over with this on his heart. And I don't think some trumped-up proof will do. Max would see through it. He questions everything these days."

I sighed. "It was a thought. I'll hunt up some of my old acquaintances and see what they say. Come to think of it, Anna, do you know of anyone who hates Max enough to do this?"

"No one I know of." She shook her head. "He talked about his cases sometimes, but I didn't pay much attention. He must have angered many criminals.

People who might have done this."

She was probably right, though Max used to have a good reputation in the criminal community. Smart enough, but lenient when he could be—Merciful Max was the judicar you hoped would hear your case, if you ever got that unlucky. I wondered how Loves-the-Rope Thrope had earned his nickname, and shivered. "I'll try to track down Jo— someone I knew, tomorrow night." Anna might not know who hated Max, but Jonas knew everything. Everything criminal, that is.

"And tomorrow during the day we could talk to this Ginny Weaver's family," said Michael. "If she was as frail as you say, she might not have been able to fight if someone wanted her dead. There are ways to force someone to drink things. Or befool them into it. And we should talk to the family and friends of the other witness, the one who vanished."

"Ren Clogger," said Anna. "He was a tanner, too. But he didn't vanish; he left town. Right after paying off all his gambling debts. He told people he'd finally gotten lucky."

"If he was a gambler, mayhap he'd have been easy to bribe," said Michael.

"That's what everyone thought," said Anna. "Unfortunately."

A short silence fell, and I pulled my cloak tighter against the chill. "I was thinking about that ledger they planted. It has to have been forged."

"Of course. I thought . . . I'd hoped you might know some forgers."

"And I'm sure they'd be delighted to tell me all about it. What did you think, Anna? That I'd know . . . wait a minute . . . Judith said the ledger was found in a secret compartment in Max's study. How many people could have known about that? The compartment, I mean."

"Quite a few. It wasn't a secret compartment, just a cupboard under the window seat. Anyone who moved the cushion might have seen it. Max never used it."

"Still, that ledger must have been planted by someone who knows your house. The servants would know?"

"The indoor ones, certainly. They dusted in there. But I can't believe . . ."

"One of your servants almost has to be involved. Someone had to steal a sample of Max's writing for the forger and plant the ledgers."

"But I know them, Nonny. They're good people and they were sorry to leave us. They believed Max was innocent."

"One of them probably knew it for sure."

"You may be right," she allowed, but she clearly didn't like it. She clutched her cloak closer, stamping her feet on the cold ground.

"We'll also speak to your old servants," said Michael thoughtfully. "If one is richer than he should be, or has left town, that might tell us something."

"I know where most of them went," Anna said. "But really, anyone who's been in Max's study might know about the window seat."

"So you'd rather blame a family friend? I suppose—"

"I was talking about Max's business associates," said Anna with dignity. "Although I don't imagine they'd have any motive."

"Why stop with friends and associates? You've got a brother who's a known criminal. Or better yet, I think Judith did it. She has access to Max's papers. She'd know about the window seat. And she's smart enough to come up with something this complex. It fits." I'd have to put that theory to Judith and see what she said.

For just a second Michael took me seriously—a wave of protest swept over his face. Then Anna snorted. "I thought you'd have grown up more than that." Her tone of big-sisterly rebuke sent me straight back to the nursery. "If you're going to be like this, I'm going to bed. Good night, Master Sevenson. Nonny . . . it's so good to have you here." She hugged me, then turned and went back through the orchard gate.

I was still staring after her when Michael said, "We should go in, too. We've more than enough to do tomorrow."

He didn't sound enthusiastic about it, and this was the kind of task Michael-the-crazy-knight-errant should have been overjoyed with. I was worried about Michael. He'd been so subdued, almost surly, during dinner. The only time he'd brightened up at all was when we'd started talking about Max's problem. I'd intended to write to Lady Kathryn that he'd turned up safe and sound . . . but now I wasn't so sure about the sound part. And I had no idea how to help him, either. He was unredeemed. There was nothing I could do to change that, or make it easier.

"Yes," I said absently. "I suppose . . ." But the sound of voices and laughter coming down the orchard path was more interesting than what I'd been about to say.

Young Fowler and Lissy looked as if they didn't feel the cold. There was a glow about them that would have made an ice age seem trivial. They wished us both a pleasant night before passing through the gate, and Lissy kissed my cheek, though more shyly than she had this morning.

As they walked off, Fowler put his arm around her shoulders.

"I don't think he had to do that. Do you think he had to do that?"

Michael was staring after them too. "I think," he said slowly, "that some motives are more complicated than revenge."

CHAPTER 5

Michael

I was still thinking about motives next morning, though not about young Fowler's. Both Fisk and I agreed that that fine, honest, upstanding young man couldn't have had anything to do with framing Max, and I still don't know which of us sounded more sour about it. This troubled me. I didn't want to become so small-spirited as to resent those whose luck in life had been better than mine, and I resolved not to let my misfortunes affect me so.

Besides, helping Fisk's family appeared to be something even an unredeemed man could do. This thought cheered me so much that I didn't resist when Fisk went through my pack this morning and selected one of my better doublets. We had agreed on the need to present a respectable appearance, though all we wanted was ask a few questions. I feared to intrude on

Ginny Weaver's grieving family, and I think Fisk dreaded it too. That was why we went first to the shop owned by Ren Clogger's brother; we'd gotten his name and directions from Master Maxwell at breakfast.

Fisk's eyes were bright as he rapped on the door. Indeed, the farther we got from his family, the more cheerful his manner became. He'd been subdued yesterday—at least, subdued for Fisk—and the pained look that came over his face when the children were first mentioned made me want to bash someone. Probably Master Maxwell, who seemed to have been responsible for Fisk's estrangement from his sisters. But Maxwell had enough trouble already, and knocking him down wouldn't help the small family Fisk so clearly loved.

Fisk knocked again, and when no one answered, he stepped back into the street to peer through the windows of the wheelwright's shop, where we'd been told Master Clogger lived and worked.

"Mayhap he's away," I said reluctantly, for I'd no desire to confront Mistress Weaver's kin sooner than need be.

"At half past first bell on a workday? I doubt it."

"First bell?" I asked curiously.

"The work bell. It rang about two hours ago. Surely you heard it."

I'd been hearing bells since I came into Ruesport but had taken no notice of them. In most cities bells were part of the perpetual din, and every city seems to assign different meanings to them. But before I could ask, Fisk went on, "In Ruesport the guilds ring the work bell for the beginning of the workday, mid-meal, afternoon break, and the workday's end. It gets so you run your life by that bell, even if you don't do shift work."

I shook my head. "I'd never make a city man. I'd hate to have my time so ruled."

Fisk laughed. "I know what you mean. They even call the journeymen and apprentices 'bellmen' here. But it's unlikely that Clogger would be far from his shop this time of day, and even then his workmen should be here."

A rhythmic thumping sounded from the barrel maker's shop across the street, and I raised my voice. "Mayhap he didn't hear us."

'Twas all too likely to my mind, for this section of Ruesport was dedicated to the heavier and nosier forms of manufacture, and the pleasant scent of cut lumber overpowered all other odors, though horse manure was a close second.

Fisk seemed less familiar with this neighborhood, which made me aware of how easily he'd guided me through the other parts of the city. Now he led me through an alley to the back of the building, where we found Master Clogger in his work yard. He was directing two journeymen in fitting a wheel hub onto an axle, obviously in charge, though he wore a leather apron filled with clever tool pockets just like his workmen.

When Fisk said he wished to speak to him about his brother, Master Clogger led us off to a private corner of the yard near a long water trough.

"I'm sorry, but I can't help you. I told Ren a year ago that I'd paid the last I was going to. Whatever he lost you'll have to get it from him. He's a full adult, responsible for his own debts." Clogger was large, with arms and shoulders like an ox, and he sounded more angry than sorry.

Fisk said hastily, "He doesn't owe us anything. We've never met your brother, Sir, and we don't want money. We just want information."

Master Clogger thought this over, dipping a kerchief into the trough and wiping his face with cold water. "Why?"

We'd discussed how to answer this question, and Fisk had finally agreed that 'twould be better to tell the truth. But looking at his face now, I saw that resolve waver and cut in swiftly. "We're friends of

Master Maxwell, Sir, and we don't think your brother was paid to lie. We're trying to prove it."

Clogger's brows shot up. "Who are you two? I didn't think anyone would dare defend Maxwell, after what happened."

"Fisk is Master Maxwell's brother by marriage, and I—"

"Michael's a knight errant," Fisk said smoothly. "And I'm his squire."

Clogger's eyes widened, then narrowed in predictable amusement. I glared at Fisk. What had possessed him to say that? We had agreed to try to appear respectable today.

"A knight errant." Clogger's lips twitched. "That might account for it, after all. I'm sorry gentlemen, but I still can't help you, for Ren never told me what happened. After I refused to pay any more of his debts, we . . . we still spoke from time to time, but it was awkward between us."

Fisk frowned. "Surely he spoke to you about testifying at the murder trial."

"Hoof and horn, yes! A terrible thing, that killing. The whole town was appalled. Especially Ren, for he knew those men. Not well, not friends or anything, but they were all tanners. That's why he was so sure of their identity, because he knew them." Clogger's big jaw firmed. "And debts or no, Ren wouldn't have lied men to the gallows, no matter how much he was paid. He was a gambler and a bad one—not that there's any such thing as a good one. But to give false witness in a hanging case? No, that just wasn't in him."

"What kind of gambling did he do?" Fisk asked, perching on the edge of the trough. 'Twas a clear indication he intended to spend some time on the conversation. Master Clogger reached around and seated himself on a nearby keg while I leaned against the trough beside Fisk.

"He'd gamble on anything," Clogger admitted ruefully. "Cards and dice, mostly, but he'd bet on a horse race or a cockfight if it came his way. The sad thing was, he was a good tanner. He made this for me." He held out the apron he wore, and the craftsmanship, especially in the styling of different pockets for particular tools, was admirable.

"That's his mark, here on the corner," Clogger went on. "He said the light circle was his good luck, so he put it on top of the dark one. That was Ren all over, a good tanner and a cursed fool. But not a killer, even by lies. I'd stake—" He stopped and shook his head. "I don't wager, not after seeing what happened to Ren. And even though I don't believe he'd do it, I have to admit . . ."

"You don't know where he got the money?" Fisk asked. "We heard he paid his debts before he left."

Clogger snorted. "Well, he didn't pay me back, but I suppose that was too much to expect. He did come to say good-bye. Said he'd finally got lucky. He was going to another town, to start fresh. I argued some. You can't run from yourself, and his work was known in Ruesport. But maybe he was right—new friends, friends who don't gamble . . . I don't know. He said he'd write when he settled, but he's been gone only five months. I might not hear from him for a while yet. That was one of the things that made it look bad, that he left just a few weeks after the hearing. And before you ask, he never said where he was going. I don't think he knew. It'd be just like Ren to get on the first ship he saw and trust to luck."

"But he did pay off his debts?" I asked.

"I can't swear to it, but no one's come dunning me since he left." Clogger rose to his feet. "The judicars asked me that, too—where he'd gotten the money. They couldn't find anyone who admitted losing money to Ren, and the whole city knew about the scandal. If it was true, you'd think someone would have come for-ward. I hope you succeed, Sir Knight, Squire. My brother wasn't an evil man, for all his faults, and if you clear Maxwell, you'll likely clear Ren's name, too. But I don't know how I can help you—he didn't tell me anything."

We stayed a little longer but learned nothing more except that Ren Clogger had no other family, and, according to the judicary investigators, he'd told his friends nothing that he hadn't told his brother.

"That didn't help much," I said. We had passed back over the bridge Fisk told me was called Drybridge, although today 'twas icy with the spray that rose from the churning river, and were now in the midst of a big market square, full of bustle and life. A running patterer passed by, his musical singsong informing us that Mara Mitchen had birthed twin boys, the stout ship *Bumblebee* was taking on cargo, and Glover Spices had a sale on nutmeg. Every shop, stand, and barrow was selling juniper and holly, and some had ribbons, candles, and torches as well. Calling Night was only four days away.

"We learned a few things," said Fisk. "We learned that somebody bribed Ren Clogger for something. I've never met a gambler who won big—or lost big— who wouldn't tell everyone he met each turn of the card or roll of the dice."

"Hmm. And whatever it was, it happened only weeks after the hearing. But it doesn't add up to much."

"We've just started. Maybe if we track down who-ever planted that forged ledger in Max's study, things will start to add up." Fisk grinned. "I still think Judith did it."

"And what motive might she have?" I asked with elaborate patience.

"General meanness. When I was, oh, five or six I think, she put pepper into my custard for almost a week. *Pepper.* And she told me we were economizing on spices and I had to eat it all and not complain or I'd hurt Mama's feelings."

I laughed. "And what was her motive for that? Or shouldn't I ask?"

Fisk suppressed another grin. "It wasn't my fault. Or at least, it wasn't *deliberate.*"

"I suppose she was bigger than you were, too."

"She still is," said Fisk. "Father always said that Anna got his eyes, Judith got his height, and I got . . ."

"What?"

"His brains," Fisk finished coolly.

We had passed from the big market square into another square, much smaller. The shops here were older, and the shoppers wore rough, even ragged clothes. 'Twas only the crossing of one street that made the difference, but I took a closer grip on my purse and Fisk saw it.

"The council's been talking about tearing down the old market for years," he commented. "They say it'd cut crime in the Oldtown by half, but I think they're being naive. All tearing down this market would do is force the poorer folk to shop in the slums—they're just across Trullsgate Bridge," he added informatively.

"And Trullsgate Bridge is beyond Trull's Gate?" I was only trying to orient myself, since it seemed we'd be in Ruesport for some time, but Fisk grinned again.

"No, Trullsgate Bridge is by Sutter's Gate."

I sighed. "When the council pulls down the old market, mayhap they should consider renaming some things."

"Saying 'when the council pulls down the old market' is like saying 'when pigs fly,'" said Fisk. "They've been planning to do it for decades, but the guilds can't agree on what to build in its place. Half want a university and half want a hospital. The whole city is divided into university wishers and hospital wishers, so here the market sits."

"Which side are you on?" I asked, though I'd already guessed the answer. Fisk's education and love of learning have often surprised me.

But he surprised me again. "Hospital. It'd be more useful to more townsfolk, and the only reason they want a university is because Fallon has one."

We went up a straight street where the guildhalls were, which for a wonder was actually called Straight Street. Then we passed out of Crowsgate over Newbridge into the spread of shops, work yards, and houses on the other side of the Yare. Ginny Weaver's family dwelled toward the southern end of town, where the buildings began to thin into large gardens and farmed fields. As we approached it was easy to see why, or rather to smell why, for no one wants to live too near a tannery.

Ginny Weaver's daughter, who opened the door to us, didn't seem to be aware of the stench. She was in her thirties, a trim woman with red hair tucked into her cap and flour on her hands and apron.

We apologized for interrupting her baking, and Fisk once again introduced us as knight and squire. I was still wondering what ailed the man when he per- suaded Mistress Skinner to let us in, for she seemed to want to settle the matter on the doorstep. Indeed, I think 'twas the interested face of a gray-haired lady peering through a window across the street rather than Fisk that finally convinced her to admit us. Her husband, Den, was working. The grubby seven-year-old hunched over a slate of staggering sums was Ricky, the wide-eyed toddler clinging to her skirt was Sara, and she asked us to call her Lenna. She didn't introduce the baby in its basket near the stove.

It took some time to convince her to go on working while we talked, but finally we settled at the kitchen table, sipping hot tea in thick mugs, and she went back to mixing dough.

"I don't know what I can tell you. Ma's dead now. So're those men. Like Den says, nothing can change that." Her eyes filled, and she blinked back the tears. The boy, Ricky, laid down his slate and departed.

"She felt bad about being so sick, what it cost the family. She was a fishmonger. Worked all her life, and she hated using money instead of bringing it in. Den told her not to be silly, she'd done lots for us, but she still hated it."

"Medicine comes high," said Fisk. "Especially magica."

Lenna shook her head. "She said not to waste it on her; she knew she was dying. But sometimes magica was the only thing that could stop the pain. Her guild helped out, and the tanners' too, so we were getting by. It's not like—"

She turned away abruptly, dumped her dough onto

a floury cutting board, and started to knead, composing herself.

Fisk looked around the room, and something in the way his eyes narrowed made me look, too. I saw nothing extraordinary.

"Lenna, do you really believe your mother would send two innocent men to their deaths for money?" Fisk's question was so blunt that I winced, but Mistress Lenna only shrugged.

"That's what her note said. And I can't see her lying when she was about to die."

"You think she wouldn't lie to you, but she'd help hang two innocent men because she felt bad about costing her family?"

Lenna spun. "I told you—"

The door opened and a dark-haired man in a tanner's apron came into the kitchen. "These men bothering you, Lennie?"

So much for introductions. The boy, Ricky, tagged at his heels.

"No." She wiped her eyes swiftly, leaving flour smudges on her cheeks. "They just came to ask a few questions about Ma. They're trying to help Jud— Master Maxwell."

The man scowled. "That murdering bastard doesn't deserve help."

We had both risen and I grasped Fisk's arm, but not in time to silence him. "It seems he had several helpers, your mother by marriage among them. I'd think you'd want to clear her name, along with his."

Skinner stepped forward, clenching his fists.

"We're leaving," I told him hastily. "Come on, Fisk."

He let me pull him out to the street, which I did quite firmly. "Well, that was tactful. What were you thinking of, badgering that poor woman?"

Fisk smiled. "They kept the money."

"What?"

"You saw that kitchen—even the stove was new. The children's clothes, the dishes . . . they couldn't possibly afford all that after a long illness in the family unless they kept the money."

"But a bribe is ill-gotten gains. The judicars would have awarded it to the hanged men's families."

"Ah, but you're forgetting, old Max was never convicted. Never even went to a hearing. How can they take away the bribe if they don't convict the briber? No wonder the Skinners aren't talking. If we clear Max, if the truth comes out, they'll probably have to give it back. And they're already spending it. They must be delighted with the way things worked out. I'll bet our investigation gives them nightmares."

I considered this. "They may have accepted the way

things turned out, but I don't think they're delighted. I think Mistress Lenna would rather see her mother cleared."

"Maybe," said Fisk, "but she's still wearing new shoes."

We strolled between the busy work yards in silence.

"There's another thing that comes to my mind," I said after a time. "Have you noticed how many tanners are involved in this? The killers, one witness, another witness's son by marriage. All tanners."

Fisk frowned thoughtfully. "If Ginny Weaver saw it from her window, the crime must have taken place near a tanner's yard, but still . . . I don't know what it means."

"Me neither. I just—" A clear, mellow bell pealed, and Fisk looked startled.

"Mid-meal already? We're going to be late. I hope they save us something."

"What are you going to do after mid-meal? Track down your old acquaintances, or start looking for the servants?"

"I'm going to take a nap," said Fisk. "Or try to. My old acquaintances are nocturnal types. I'll be up half the night looking for them, so I'll probably sleep late in the morning, too."

"'Tis no matter. I'll start tracking down the servants

tomorrow. This afternoon I'll buy some feed for Chant and Tipple and give them a brush. Trimmer did his best, but . . ." When I'd looked into their stalls this morning, I'd been relieved to see that Trimmer had attended to the horses, and I appreciated his efforts. Still, 'twas not his work, and I'd resolved to take up their care myself.

Fisk and I parted then, for this was a good part of town in which to purchase hay, oats, and straw. At least that was what I told Fisk, and 'twas true, if not quite all the truth. The part I didn't tell Fisk was that I wasn't sure I could face another cozy family meal, with Mistress Anna shrinking from me and Maxwell wondering what crime I'd committed. Yet I might be able to help the Maxwells out of their predicament, and if there was anything else of worth that an unredeemed man could accomplish in this world, I didn't know what it might be.

This thought brought back the bleak mood I had all but forgotten in the interest of the morning's work, so I resolved to go on working. I arranged for the delivery of stable supplies and bought a couple of pork pastries at the market, after which I had nowhere to go but back to the Maxwells'.

Once there I mucked out the stable and curried both horses. The box stalls were large enough to keep them comfortable for a few days, especially after a long journey, but soon they'd need some exercise. I wondered if the Seatons would let us turn them out into the orchard. If it was walled all round 'twould be safe enough, and horses won't harm a well grown tree, though they'll graze on saplings.

I was heading for the orchard to inspect the walls, largely for want of anything else to do, when the kitchen garden caught my eye. Last night in the dark I'd not noticed much, but now the loss of the Maxwell's gardener was apparent, for the dead growth hadn't even been cleared. The ground was frozen too hard to mulch the brown leaves into the soil, but at least I could haul them off to the midden. The idea of doing something else to earn my keep in this house, where I was so clearly unwelcome, appealed to me.

I located a shed full of tools and selected a hoe, a rake, and a pitchfork to load the small wheelbarrow, and soon I was busy. Being raised on a country estate, one learns much about growing things. 'Twas not the work of a country steward I objected to, 'twas the rootedness of it, being forever tied to one small piece of the Green God's earth.

I'd cleared the dry cornstalks and started on the vines when I heard young voices and turned to see Mistress Anna and Mrs. Trimmer leading the children out of the orchard. Their cheeks were red with cold and laughter. 'Twas distressing to watch Mistress Anna's expression freeze when she saw me and clutched the children protectively to her skirts. That was the impulse of instinct, for she collected herself immediately and sent them off with Mrs. Trimmer—to weave juniper garlands, according to their shrill, excited cries.

Making Calling Night garlands is a family task, so I was surprised when, instead of following, Mistress Anna walked carefully across the muddy ground to where I worked. Her expression was neither shy nor frightened but fell somewhere between. There was nothing an unredeemed man could do to make her comfortable, so I simply nodded and hoped my own expression wasn't as stiff and unfriendly as it felt. "Mistress Anna."

"Master Sevenson." She clasped her hands as if she didn't know what to do with them. Then she turned toward a wooden bench, tucked under a bush that might be lilac, and sat down with the relieved air of a person who's found a way to make an embarrassing situation seem a bit more natural.

Intrigued despite myself, I leaned on the rake and waited.

"Nonny talked to us at mid-meal. About you."

"I see."

Her gaze dropped, but she went on determinedly. "He told us how you rescued him. How he might have been flogged, or even worse. I wanted to thank you. It's been hard for Nonny, and I . . . well, I wanted to thank you."

"You needn't. Fisk has long since repaid any favor I did him. Indeed"—I offered her a wry smile—"he's proved a most excellent squire."

Her lips twitched at that, but she still looked nervous. "I wondered . . . You seem to be a gentle sort of person, and Nonny is so loyal to you. I wondered . . ."

"What I did?" I swept the rake over the ground and lifted a load of withered vines into the barrow. "Fisk didn't tell you?"

She shook her head. "He said that was your prob—decision."

"How nice of him." The complexity of the past fell heavily on my heart, and I stole an old line of Fisk's. "'Tis a long story."

I turned back to the garden, hoping to end the discussion, but she went on: "It wasn't that so much. I just wondered if—if Nonny had dragged you into trouble," she continued in a rush. "He's a good person, the best brother anyone could have, but he is . . ."

She thought 'twas Fisk's fault I was unredeemed.

"No, nothing of the kind. Fisk has *saved* me time and again. Indeed, as far as dragging people into trouble goes, I'm afraid it's the other way round."

Her eyes were full of hope and doubt. I couldn't let her think badly of Fisk, so I told the whole story after all. 'Twas as long as I feared, for she asked many questions and insisted on hearing each twist of the tale. The sun was dropping by the time I finished, and I was sitting beside her. She'd lifted her feet onto the bench some time ago, curling up like a child, with her cloak wrapped around her knees. Her eyes were bright with interest, and she'd laughed much throughout my account. And though she sobered when I told her how I'd been declared unredeemed, she no longer shrank from me.

"Well, I think it was quite rotten of Nonny to creep away without a word, though you're probably right about why he did it. I'm glad you followed him."

"Truly?" I couldn't meet her eyes. "I'd wondered if I'm not bringing him more trouble than my help is worth."

"Truly," she said firmly. "Nonny hasn't had much luck with friends. Or family. I think your friendship is worth more to him than any trouble you could possibly bring."

I met her eyes now, very directly. After all, I'd told

my tale—an exchange was due. "You say Fisk has been unlucky. Will you tell me how?"

She looked startled. "Hasn't Nonny told you?"

"He hardly ever talks about himself. Before I came here, all I knew of him was that he had sisters, and a criminal past. He also seems to be well educated, though he never talks about his schooling."

"Oh, that was Papa. He taught both Fisk and Judith, since they had the brains for it and he had to teach. It was . . . Oh dear, I'd better start at the beginning." She looked off a moment, ordering her thoughts.

"I think the beginning is actually before the beginning. My great-grandmother was a noblewomen, but born without Gifts. She had hopes for her daughters anyway—sometimes the Gift does skip a generation."

And sometimes it breeds out of a line for good and all. Remembering the eerie glow of some of the apple trees last night, I could think of worse things than being Giftless. But I could see where this was leading and nodded for her to go on.

"Unfortunately her children were Giftless as well, and all her descendants. My grandmother married a merchant in a small town called Coverton, and Mama married the local schoolmaster's son. She could have done better; my grandfather was well off. But Mama loved Papa. He wasn't handsome, but he was smart and gentle and merry. We weren't rich, but our house was always happy when Papa was there. He adored Mama, too, and said a scholar had no need of a Gifted wife.

"Papa had big dreams, you see. His own father had a university education, and though he couldn't afford to send Papa, he taught him well. Papa planned to write a thesis good enough to be accepted on merit and then go on to teach. To be part of a great university, shaping the world with knowledge. It consumed him, I think." Her eyes dropped to her knees and she fell silent.

"'Tis a worthy ambition," I said. So this was where Fisk's odd erudition came from—he was the last of a line of scholars. So how under two moons had he ended in manacles on a judgment scaffold?

"Yes." She smiled sadly. "I suppose it is worthy. But not practical. Papa's father died, and he took over the school, working on his thesis at night. I was born, then Judith, and Mama was carrying Fisk when he finished it. He quit the school, moved the whole family to Fallon, and submitted his thesis to the university there."

She stopped again, lips tight. The light around us

was golden with sunset, and 'twould soon be too cold to sit out.

"It was rejected?" I guessed.

"They said it wasn't original enough. The scholarship was fine, but . . . It's the only time I ever saw my father drunk. I was just three, but I still remember it.

"He took odd jobs around the outskirts of the university—tutor, printer's helper, things like that. And he started another thesis, but Fisk had been born by then and money was tight. So when he heard Ruesport was planning to build a university, he packed up the family again and we came here."

I remembered the small, dingy shops and alleys of the old market. "But they never built it."

"Not to this day. If they had, coming here wouldn't have been such a bad idea. Even if his new thesis was rejected, he could have gotten work as a librarian. That would have suited him. He spent every spare fract on books. His study held the biggest library in Ruesport, and he had books shipped to him from all up and down the coast."

"Books can be a good investment; they sell for almost as much used as new."

"I suppose. But it made no difference. He took odd jobs again, mostly tutoring other men's university-bound sons. He could have taught in any of the guild schools, but he said he needed the time to work on his thesis."

"Was his next thesis rejected too?"

"He never finished it. He didn't want to finish it, Master Sevenson—he was afraid to. He'd change a paragraph, throw out a chapter, find a new line of reasoning, get another source. It went on and on. Mama kept it for years after he died, hoping to get it published, but when she died . . ."

"What?"

"Nonny burned it." Her voice dropped almost to a whisper, and her eyes held the memory of those flames. I was about to ask why, but she shook herself and went on. "Mama didn't care that we weren't rich; she loved Papa. We all did. He worked enough to keep us, and Mama took in a bit of sewing. Fine embroidery, like a noblewoman, for that was a skill her family had passed down. We used to help with the plain stitching when she had a big job, and we were happy. But then, when Lissy was six, Papa died."

Her expression held both sorrow and amusement.

"He was reading a book at a market stall and it started to rain. He moved the book into the shelter of the building's eaves and went right on reading, with the rain running down his back. He caught a chill and it went to his lungs and killed him—just like that.

Nonny and Judith were devastated, and Mama . . ."

She took a deep breath, her eyes shimmering in the glowing light. "She pulled herself together after a while. She had to. She turned her embroidery into a business, taking in mending as well, and even laundry. Non— Fisk and I helped sew. He was nine then, and I was thirteen, with Judith a year younger than me. Judith tried to help, but she's a terrible needlewoman, so she kept house and looked after Lissy instead. Lissy threaded needles for us, and Fisk ran errands for shopkeepers, too, and did any job they'd pay him for. But he couldn't pay an apprentice fee, so he couldn't make much no matter how hard he worked. It was strange, to be sewing without Papa reading to us. Then, a year later, the influenza came to Ruesport."

My breath caught, but she went on without prompting. "It was terrible. Hundreds of people sickened, and there was barely enough ordinary medicine, much less magica. The prices soared. When Mama got sick . . ." She wiped her eyes impatiently. "This is silly. It was years ago. You'd think I could talk about it now, but it was . . . I had my hands full, nursing her. Judith took off for Coverton, hitching rides, walking. She had to sneak past the road guards, for they'd quarantined the town, but she did it. She went to our uncle to ask for help, but he wouldn't even let her in for fear of the sickness. He said Mama went against his advice marrying Papa, and if the influenza came to Coverton, they'd need every copper for themselves. I'm afraid none of us have ever forgiven him, though it wouldn't have mattered even if he'd given Judith all the money we needed. Mama was dead by the time she got home. Nonny and I . . ." Her voice shook and she took another deep breath.

"Nonny did everything he could to make money, but it wasn't enough. So one night, when she was very ill, he broke into an herbalist's shop to steal magica medicine. And he got caught, though not by the law. Some burglar had realized that herbalists were making a lot of money these days. He blacked Nonny's eye for trying to cut into his territory. But when Nonny tried to fight back, when he explained why he needed it, the burglar let Nonny stay and even helped him look for magica medicines. But it was all for nothing. They found a waiting list, and learned that the herbalists were all out of magica—they were making it up fresh as soon as the herbs were found and taking it straight to the next customer on the list. He couldn't steal it, for it wasn't there. Mama died two days later."

This time I let the silence stretch, though the light was fading now.

"After she was buried, Judith, Nonny, and I piled all the money we had left on the kitchen table and counted it. There wasn't enough for next month's rent on the house, so we moved to some rooms in the Oldtown that were cheaper. A lot cheaper.

"Selling the furniture kept us for a while, but we couldn't handle the sewing business without Mama. Judith took in washing, Nonny went back to running errands, and I got a job serving in a tavern—a decent place near the guildhalls, where the council clerks went. We scraped by for a year. Then one of the customers wanted to bed me—tried, in fact. When the tapster found us scuffling in the back alley, the man said I'd lured him out there, and I was fired. The next tavern wasn't as nice, and it didn't pay as well, either. That was when Nonny went and found the burglar who'd caught him in the herb shop. He talked the man into taking him on as an apprentice. Burglarly's the one profession where no fee is required, and this man often trained boys. He made a bit more, and we managed for almost two years, but we were barely getting by among the three of us. Winter was coming, and food prices always rise then. Sometimes the tavern customers would make me offers, and I was beginning to think I'd have to say yes. Nonny and Judith both said not to, that we'd work something out, but I knew they were lying, and I think they knew it too. Then Max came."

A serene smile lit her face. "He'd seen me working in the first tavern, and when I was fired, he followed me to the second. He hadn't said anything before, because I was only seventeen and he was almost twenty years older. But he said he loved me and wanted to marry me, even though he knew I didn't love him. And he said he'd take in Judith and Lissy and give them dowries. But he was a judicar, and Nonny . . . He hadn't been caught, but the deputies knew about him. It was only a matter of time, Max said. But he'd give him the money to leave and start fresh somewhere else."

She met my eyes now, despite the discomfort I read in them, and I understood why Maxwell loved her. 'Tis rare to find a woman so courageous.

"We talked about it, Nonny and I, almost all night. He didn't want me to marry Max. I didn't want him to leave. But we both knew what the alternative was, for me, Judith, and someday Lissy, too. Nonny was only thirteen, but he'd seen a lot in the last few years. More than a boy should. So he left. And Max kept his word. He's an honorable man, Master Sevenson. Kind. Good."

"So is Fisk," I said, "when given the chance."

Color flooded her cheeks, but she had no answer.

CHAPTER 6
Fisk

A damp wind was blowing in from the sea, so the warm fug of the Irony Tavern was very welcome, though I blinked at the flaming banks of candles that adorned the sconces, shelves, and rough timber wheels that hung from the rafters.

I'd taken a nap after lunch, and then spent the late afternoon helping Judith, Lissy, and the children make juniper garlands and speculating about why Michael and Anna had come in late, actually looking comfortable in each other's presence. Max had promised to hang the garlands and put out torch brackets tomorrow, so the house would make a respectable show for the neighbors.

Calling Night was only four nights off and the Irony hadn't put out any greenery at all, but the blaze of candlelight was more in keeping with the holiday night than the cozy dimness I remembered in the old days. I strolled over to the counter and said, "Hello, Ham. What are you trying to do? Call the sun back early?"

The tapster looked me up and down, and a grin split his doughy face. "Well, well, if it's not the teacher's boy. I'd heard you was back, and a bold lad, too, bringing bad company with you so open like."

"I see the sheriff's office still leaks like a sieve. Honestly, it's a wonder they ever catch anybody. Michael is my . . . guard." I could have said he was my great-grandfather, my rich lover, or the High Liege and been equally disbelieved. I gestured around. "What's with the candles?"

"Ah, I was told keepin' the place all dark made it look like a robbers' lair, like my customers had something to hide. And I have to say, the lights do cut down on the riffraff."

Riffraff was the kindest term that might be applied to most of the Irony's patrons, and we both grinned.

"Actually," I went on, "I'm looking for Jonas Bish. Does he still come here?"

Ham chewed his lower lip. "Maybe, maybe not." He'd have said the same if Jonas was two years buried, but I knew how the system worked, so I ordered an ale and chatted with Ham until another customer pulled him away.

Moving from the bar to a sit in a corner that used to be dim, I watched the ebb and flow of the tavern's life and mentally timed the progress of the kitchen boy who was making his way to Jonas's lodging at the moment. If he was there and wanted to see me, he'd be here shortly. If he was working tonight, he might come late, or not at all.

It was about three hours later that I saw him coming through the crowd toward me. He stopped at my table, gazing down at me like a fond uncle. "Fisk, lad! You look downright prosperous. I may have to pay you a visit some night."

I laughed and clasped his hand without reservation, for Jonas was a decent man, despite his preference for having boys take the risks for him. As he used to say, they never hang children. Almost never.

He seated himself and I signaled Ham to bring a cup of tea, for Jonas has one of those stomachs that can't tolerate alcohol. We chatted about the last few years, in careful euphemisms that avoided any confession of crime, but it wasn't long before he smiled and asked, "So, lad, why have you come looking for old Jonas on your second night in town?"

"I'm trying to help Max," I said. I wouldn't have

been so frank with most, but when it didn't concern himself or his trade brothers, Jonas was a civic-minded sort. For a burglar.

"Good luck to you," he said sincerely. "Those lads he hanged were a nasty lot. I was glad they were respectable tanners and not criminals. But then . . . You really think Merciful Max didn't do it? The evidence against him was pretty strong—that fire left him scraping. Though he wasn't the only one," he added glumly.

"You had shares in that cargo, too?" I wasn't surprised, for I knew Jonas invested when he could.

He snorted. "Every man in Ruesport with a roundel to spare lost out when those ships burned. It was a sweet venture, likely to return twenty-two percent by my figuring, though they were touting it at thirty or higher. But at least the town got pumps out of it."

"Pumps?"

"You haven't seen them? Well, you might not have noticed, but when you see what looks like a boarded-over wagon in a square or alley, that's one of the new fire pumps. There's pipes beneath 'em that run into a river or a nearby well, and they haul up more water than four bucket lines. Tears up the street something awful when they lay the pipes." Jonas shook his head. "But after that fire no one complained. You can tell which guild has the most pull with the council just by seeing where the next pump goes in."

"Do you think Max did it?"

Jonas looked thoughtful. "Hard to say. The evidence was strong, but circumstantial for the most part. And it's hard to believe that Merciful Max would hang innocent men for any price. Now Loves-the-Rope Thrope, it's right in *his* style. But if it wasn't Maxwell, it's a cursed nice frame, I'll give 'em that."

"So who could have done it? Or would have done it? Any ideas?"

"Ah, that's what you wanted old Jonas for. Well, if it'll get Thrope off the justice scaffold, I'm all for it. Let's see." He sipped his tea and I waited. "Yes, there's a few who hate Maxwell that much. Not so many as you'd think, for he erred on the soft side, but there's a few. George Little hates him enough to do most anything, though I'm not sure he's . . . not so much not smart enough, but he's not subtle enough to rig a frame like this."

"George Little?"

"He was a blacksmith whose brother was a craft brother of ours—though I hate to call that one brother in any way. A cutpurse, with a nasty habit of beating his marks. A couple of 'em died, later. George had nothing to do with the beatings, but he melted and recast the loot, so when they were caught, Max had the cutpurse hanged and the smith flogged. Little swore vengeance with every cut of the whip, till he started screaming. Yes. He hates Maxwell enough." Jonas sipped his tea.

I made a mental note of the name. "Who else?"

"Well, this 'un had less cause, but I've heard a bit about Nate and he's not . . . he's not crazy, but he doesn't think like other folks. Nate Jobber. He was a forger."

If I could have pricked my ears like Tipple, I would have. I was looking for forgers.

"A good one, too, but he didn't think of himself that way. He thought he was an artist, who'd someday paint pictures to hang in all the great lords' palaces."

"Was he that good?" Jonas would know—a burglar has to know about art.

"Nah, just a dabbler. But he didn't see it that way, so . . . But I'm getting ahead of myself. Nate forged some documents for an embezzlement scam, and his comrades got greedy and bankrupted their mark. The man's wife left him, too, though I don't know if that was because of losing all the money or other things. But the long and the short of it is, the mark killed himself."

A chill ran through my flesh. One of the things a man whose name wasn't Jack Bannister had taught me was never to take so much that your mark might become desperate. Death is a debt that can't be repaid in coin.

"Now, Nate had no part in the scam beyond making up the documents, but his confederates had the sense to ship out to another fiefdom before it all came out, leaving Nate to face the judicars alone. Maxwell said Nate's craft was a menace to honest folk and ordered the tendons in his hands cut. Had 'em healed, too—the doctors standing right there to do the cutting and stitching both, and used magica to get 'em to knit. But you know how a tendon is once it's been severed. Nate's hands are stiff now. He can do most jobs, but he can barely write, much less forge another man's name. Course his victim no longer breathes, so some'd say he got off light. I don't think it bothered him to give up forgery, but he can't paint neither. Frankly, I'm not sure Nate wouldn't rather have hanged. No spine to him, that one."

Jonas had finished his tea, so I signaled Ham for another cup and waited until he'd poured it and left. If Jobber was no longer an able forger, he was less interesting to me, but he might have friends who were still in the business.

"This last one I'm not so sure about," Jonas went on slowly. "I don't know much of him. And if he ever said a word against Maxwell, I haven't heard of it. But he struck me as a mean 'un, and I think he's that kind, to smile and talk meek and plot revenge.

"Erril Kline was a law clerk, on the side of the righteous and all, till one day he took a bribe to keep a man's name out of some testimony he was taking down. Not a hanging offense, but the Judicary Guild took a dim view of it. It was the guild's council who ordered him disrobed, but it was Maxwell who'd found out what he'd done and brought it to the guild's attention. They rule their own with a tight hand, the judicary."

"That was all? He just got disrobed?"

"There was no victim to be repaid," said Jonas comfortably. "I know it's not a lot, but talk to him. See what you think."

"I will, if you can tell me where to find him."

Jonas knew all three men's whereabouts, or at least where they worked. I was wondering how I could get men who hated Max to talk to me when the tavern door banged open and a man thrust his head in. "Fire at Morna's place!"

Jonas and I rose to our feet, and I dropped half a dozen fracts on the table even as I asked, "Why isn't the fire bell ringing?"

"Give it a bit." Jonas made for the door, along with

every able-bodied man in the room. We'd barely turned into the maze of streets that led to Trullsgate Bridge when the fire bell began to ring, shrill enough to pierce the soundest sleep. I followed the crowd, since I'd no idea where or what "Morna's place" was. As we passed though Sutter's Gate, I saw a column of orange-tinted smoke rising over the ramshackle roofs of the stews and swore. The elderly buildings there were pushed closer than in any other part of Ruesport, and the wells were fewer here. There couldn't be a worse place for a fire to start.

"I don't suppose I'm going to see one of those new pumps in operation?"

"Not a chance. It's cursed shortsighted, but the brothel keepers don't carry much weight with the council. It's the bucket line for us, lad."

I grimaced, for like any townsman I've been on bucket lines before, and on a night this cold it's an unpleasant experience.

Jonas and I ended up part of a line that went down to the Yare. Young, healthy types like me always end up on the full-bucket side of the line. At first I tried to keep dry as pail after pail sloshed through my hands, but it wasn't possible, and soon I was working too hard to feel the wet or the cold.

Several twists of the narrow street obscured my

view of the fire, though its light flickered on the roofs above my head and enough smoke blew down to make my eyes smart and set me coughing.

Information passed up and down the line along with the buckets. The fire had started in an attic. One of the girls' leaving a candle burning was the best guess as to cause, though there were other guesses, some surprisingly inventive. Everyone had gotten out in time.

The local fire team pulled down the walls of the burning house as fast as they could, despite Morna's protests, and enough water was splashing around that none of the neighboring buildings caught fire. Even so, it was over three hours before they declared the danger over and dissolved the lines. The muscles in my arms quivered with strain and my back was sore. But as I made my way back to Max's, growing colder with every step, I felt a kind of contentment. It'd been a long time since I'd been sufficiently part of a town to go to its defense.

I was surprised, when I reached the house, to see light in Max's study window. The bell rouses everyone, but the east was beyond the area where citizens would be called to fight a fire in the stews. If Max was still up, there might be a fire in the fireplace—or was there a stove in that room?

I let myself in quietly. All I had to do was cross the hall and knock on Max's door, and I'd find out if the room had a stove or a fireplace. I was freezing in my wet clothes. But I stood in the hall and stared at the crack of light under the door for so long that I jumped when it opened.

Max carried a lamp, and blinked in astonishment when its light reached me. Then his nose twitched. "You were fighting the fire?" He sounded surprised, and my pride was pricked.

"I tried to get out of it, but they were watching too close. Luckily the fire got bad enough to distract them later on and I was able to slip away."

For a second he looked like he was going to buy it; then his disapproval dissolved in a sigh. "You must be cold. The stove's quite warm." He opened the door wider and stood aside.

I hesitated for a moment, but I was chilled to the bone. I went through the door and over to the stove, which radiated heat like a smith's forge, unbuttoned my jacket with cold-clumsy fingers, and held it wide. If Max hadn't been there, I might have stripped to the skin and gone up to bed in just my cloak, but he came in behind me and perched on the edge of his desk.

I moved around the stove so I could face him. The lamp cast eerie upward shadows, and I noticed that he wore a bed robe and slippers. "The bell woke you?"

He nodded. "Once I saw the smoke over the stews, I knew I wouldn't be called, but I couldn't get back to sleep, so I decided to do a little work." He gestured to the ledgers spread out on his desk, and a sudden thought occurred to me.

"How come they let Ginny Weaver's family keep the bribe and not you? If your money was declared ill-gotten gains, surely hers would have been too."

Max shrugged. "I didn't know they'd kept it. Maybe the council was being merciful—the family had already lost Mistress Weaver, and the official ruling was that the case was too uncertain to bring to a hearing. Though frankly, if it had been my decision, I'd have charged me. I think Worthington, Sawyer, and some others interceded on my behalf. I was lucky just to be disrobed. The money . . ." A tired smile twisted his lips. "I'd like to say it doesn't matter, but I've been trying to figure out how I'm going to pay the door tax. I don't think I can."

He looked depressed. No, worse than depressed—he looked beaten. All desire to quarrel left me. "What's the difference between a tax collector and a bandit?"

He answered automatically, "I don't know. What?"

"The tax collectors take more, and you can't fight back."

He snorted, but he also seemed to recognize the joke for the peace offering it was. "I don't suppose you learned anything today?"

It was my turn to snort. "This is our first day investigating—give us a week, please. Seriously, I did learn a bit." I recounted what Jonas had told me, and he nodded, for none of it was news to him. But when I finished, he was frowning.

"I wouldn't have been able to pick those names out of all those I've sentenced over the years. Was your friend sure about Kline? He was only disrobed, and while it's even more embarrassing and uncomfortable than I'd suspected, I wouldn't kill an elderly invalid just to take revenge for it."

"Then you think Ginny Weaver was murdered?"

"If the note was forged, she must have been, and I find that more tragic than anything that happened to me, even if she was dying. She was a splendid old lady, outspoken and courageous. It's her testimony that still lets me believe . . . So tell me, why was Master Bish willing to help me out?"

My surprise almost distracted me from the sentence Max hadn't finished, since I hadn't given him Jonas's name. But I already knew that he was struggling to believe that the men he'd hanged were guilty, and I had no desire to invade Max's privacy. If I did, he might try to invade mine.

"Jonas doesn't like your replacement. He'd rather have you back, right or wrong."

"Poor Thrope." Max shook his head. "Not that the approval of the criminal community is anything to brag about, but no one seems to like the man."

"From what Michael said, there's reason for that."

"Yes, but there are reasons Thrope's the way he is. His mother was noble born, but she—"

"Wasn't Gifted," I said. "There's a lot of that going around."

Max remembered my own background, and color rose in his cheeks. "Then you should understand the man. He was born to a rich merchant, but his goal is to rise high enough to marry back into the nobility."

"The lady in the coach," I said, remembering Michael's story.

"Indeed, I'm afraid so. That will make him all the angrier with your friend."

I bristled defensively, but Max's face didn't have that pinched look he'd assumed before when Michael's name was mentioned. I wondered again what had passed between Michael and Anna. She'd repeated it to her husband, whatever it was. I resolved to ask Michael, but for now . . .

"Even if I do uncover something, it probably won't

happen before the door tax comes due." It wouldn't, for the first day of the new year falls right after Calling Night.

"Oh, I knew that. I'll probably 'borrow' the money from Ben Worthington. Though why I say borrow I don't know, since I've no way to pay him back. But he's the biggest philanthropist in Ruesport—he can afford to give money to his friends as well as to strangers."

He didn't sound happy about it.

"That's interesting," I said. "Most self-made men don't give much away." They were cursed hard to gull, too, but I saw no need to mention that to Max.

"Ben gives a great deal, in money and time, to the community. He's on both the merchants' and the ropers' charity boards. He started as a rope weaver and still owns the shop. He once told me a man should never forget his roots. It seems to work for him." But Max was staring at me now, and the knowledge that he'd cut off *my* roots was clear in his eyes. "I'm sorry," he added softly.

We weren't talking about Worthington anymore.

"Sorry for failing to keep your end of the bargain?"

Take care of them, old man, or I'll come back and make you regret it. It was the last thing I'd said to Max before dumping the money he'd offered me on his desk and walking out. I could see he remembered my words, for he winced.

"I suppose I have failed. But you should know, I've never regretted marrying Anna. I can't. Not even now, for her sake."

He clearly meant it, even though marrying a richer wife might have enabled him to pay his door tax without begging charity.

"Have you told her that?"

A smile wiped the weariness from his face. "Often."

Which accounted for the core of serenity Annie carried about with her these days. I was glad she was happy, but that wouldn't pay the door tax. And I was no more able to support my sisters now than I'd been at thirteen, so it all came down to clearing old Max.

"Don't worry," I told him gloomily. "I'll think of something."

CHAPTER 7

Michael

Fisk still slept when I left the house next morning, but I held no grudge. After having my sleep disrupted by that shrill bell, I thought it a wonder anyone roused early. I'd recognized it as some sort of alarm and gone to the window to see if the neighborhood answered to it, but when no one surged into the street, I concluded that it didn't involve this area. There was a time when I might have gone to help anyway, but whatever the emergency was, assisting might reveal the broken circles that glowed softly on my wrists. So I went back to bed, though I had to put a pillow over my head to sleep, for the bell rang on and on.

Since I could be of no use talking to Fisk's former associates, I was eager to make a start on the rest of the investigation. Anna knew the current whereabouts of all the servants who'd left the Maxwells' employ. Three of the six were still in this neighborhood. I decided to begin with them, then return to the house at mid-meal for Fisk's company and guidance in tracking down the rest.

The nearest was the cook, who'd gotten work in a house not three streets from her old job. She was astonishingly thin for one in her profession, but pleasant and cheerful, and she invited me into the steamy, bustling kitchen and told me all she knew—which was of no use whatsoever.

She believed in Maxwell's innocence and became quite heated about it, for he'd been a good employer. But she was a working woman, with her own folk to support. Without pay . . .

I haven't Fisk's habit of pricing everything I see, and know little of women's clothes, but her plain gown didn't look new and her shoes were quite worn.

A sensible bribe taker might not spend the money openly, but I consider myself a fair judge of character, and this woman spoke, looked, and gestured as if she had nothing to hide.

The groom, who was next on my list, was of the same stripe, though not so fond of the Maxwells as the cook. He thought Master Max a good enough man, but with a townsman's poor eye for horseflesh. I'm not a townsman. We chatted for some time, surrounded by the comforting scents of horse and hay, and he showed off his charges—including a foal, born to a perfectly ordinary coach mare, who'd turned out to be magica. Someday, he bragged, she would outrun the wind. Indeed, the lively filly glowed so bright to my changed sight that I jumped when I saw her, and left the stable with chills at the freakishness of it rippling up my spine. I had some hope that the ability would fade with time. I prayed it would.

But I judged the groom to be as innocent of concealment as the cook. So was the housemaid I spoke to next. She wasn't happy to be interrupted in the midst of her morning's work, so I helped her make beds and dust furnishings as we talked.

Soon I stood in the street again, with three servants interviewed and naught to show for it. 'Twas too soon to expect Fisk to wake, for mid-meal was some hours off. The sun shone, snowbanks dripped, and water chuckled in the gutters. Unless a new storm came in, we'd not have a white Calling Night, which would be a pity, for the holiday lights are splendid reflecting off the snow. But now it felt like spring had begun three months early, and my adventuring spirit roused. I had Anna's directions and had traveled about the town with Fisk yesterday. I could find the other servants on my own.

I ran into a bit of difficulty after crossing the Yare, but I found the bakeshop Anna had described without having to ask directions more than twice. It seemed Nettie, the kitchen maid I was seeking, had quit her job there over a week ago. "To set up as an herbalist's apprentice, fancy that, and her with no more Gift than Hobby Martin's favorite pig."

'Twas indeed unusual. Herbalists charge a high apprentice fee, and their training is long and demanding, especially for someone with no sensing Gift.

But Nettie was working in the shop to which the baker directed me. She was fresh faced and attractive, and answered my questions willingly, though she continued shaking ground herbs into labeled paper packets and sealing them with wax and the shop's seal as we spoke. Like the other servants, she said she thought it very unlikely Master Maxwell had done such a brutal thing, but my suspicions grew. Her blue gown was of better cloth than a kitchen maid could readily afford, with lace edging her collar and ruffling at her elbows, and lace is never cheap.

"This is quite a step up for you, isn't it?" I asked, gazing at the tidily labeled pots, packets, and jars. 'Twas not an intrusive question, but she stiffened as if I'd insulted her.

"Why yes. I've always been interested in herbs and such. I had to save a long time to afford the fee, but Mistress Dackett is a good teacher."

Her expression was guarded now, and her smile had vanished.

I struggled to keep my suspicions from my face and sought for some question or comment that would soothe her sudden nervousness. Then the door banged open and a rush of crisp air swept Mistress Dackett into the shop. She was a large woman, as plump as the cook had been thin, with dark curls escaping her cap. She was already speaking as she entered.

"Sorry I'm late, girl, but you can go now and— Ah, what can I do for you, Sir?"

"Nothing, Mistress. I came to speak to Mistress Nettie, though I was careful not to disrupt her work. I'm a friend of Horatius Maxwell and seek to help him clear his name."

I was grateful for Fisk's absence, for at this point he would probably have introduced us as knight errant and squire—why he was doing that, when he'd always thought it lunacy himself, escaped me. But even my new, sensible introduction failed me now.

"Then you should choose your friends better, Sir. He should have been the one hanged!"

Her eyes were bright with outrage, not grief, so I dared ask, "Were you acquainted with the tanners who were executed?"

"No, but it turns my stomach to see a judicar bought off and then get away with it because of his fancy friends in the ropers and judicary. It's a crime, Sir, and nothing will make me say otherwise!"

I wouldn't have had the nerve to try. I slid from my stool and edged around her toward the door. The wrath of the righteous is a terrible thing, but Mistress Nettie had defended Maxwell, so I glanced back to see how she reacted to her employer's vehemence.

She was gone.

'Twas the work of a moment to dash around the building to the back entrance, and for once my luck was in—a cloaked, beskirted figure was just vanishing around the corner. She carried a basket on her arm.

I ran to the corner and peered cautiously down the alley in time to see her turn into the street, walking with the brisk stride of someone who knows where she's going.

There weren't many people about, and a hood might look suspicious on so mild a day, but I pulled mine up and followed her, prepared to turn aside the moment she looked back.

I might have spared myself the trouble, for she

never looked back, which must surely be a sign of a clear conscience. Fisk spins around like a top when he's up to something, and I fear I've caught the habit from him. But if Mistress Nettie was innocent, where did she get the money for that good blue gown? And the cloak that covered it was the deep red of fennet root, which is an expensive dye.

Eventually she turned west onto a wider, busier street. 'Twas crammed with carts, both horse-drawn and hand pushed, and also folk on foot and ahorse, and a few leading laden mules. I pushed back my hood, for the chances of her recognizing me in this crowd were slight. I had to weave and dart closer lest I lose track of her.

She continued walking west, where the shops and inns gave way to drab warehouses and the stacked, canvas-covered crates of the loading docks. The foot traffic had thinned, and now the carts began to drop away as well.

I crossed to the other side of the street and fell back again, though I didn't bother to raise my hood—if she hadn't looked back in all this time, she probably wouldn't now. But where under two moons was she going?

The warehouses grew smaller, and vacant lots appeared between them. Then the cobbles stopped.

Beyond lay a muddy lane passing between stubbled fields that would carry hay in the summer.

Nettie stopped as abruptly as the paving stones and sat on the corner of a water trough. I darted back and ducked behind a storage shed. I was glad for a chance to see her face, even from the side, for the thought that I might be following the wrong woman had crossed my mind. But it was she, and now she pulled a pair of tall wooden pattens from her basket and strapped them over her shoes, obviously intending to go still farther west—but there was nothing there!

The bell for mid-meal tolled and she looked up, her hands moving more quickly as she tucked her skirt into her belt so it wouldn't be splashed with the mud. Had she arranged to meet someone for mid-meal? In a hay field? The horrid thought that it might be a suitor crossed my mind, for I'd no desire to spy on a lovers' tryst. But Mistress Dackett had approved her absence. *Sorry I'm late, you can go now.*

I also remembered that I'd planned to meet Fisk at mid-meal, but I couldn't abandon the chase. I lingered in the shelter of the buildings until she'd passed through the open field and behind a grassy hillock; then I dashed after her. I was instantly sorry, as the oily mud swept my feet from under me in a splattering fall. At least 'twas not face-first. I clambered upright, wiped my hands on my britches, and proceeded more carefully.

At the end of the field the cart track turned to a footpath—it was this Nettie had followed behind the hillock. Following in turn, I passed into the marshland I'd seen when I'd first overviewed the city.

'Twas not so flat as it appeared from a distance, for the track wove around a series of grass-covered humps, ranging in size from small hills to something the height of a shed. Between them lay irregular ponds, dense with cattails and brown marsh grass. The scent of decaying plants overcame even the chill freshness of the winter air, but 'twas not unpleasant. Small birds hopped, chirping, among the reeds, and I heard a flock of geese muttering as they fed. In summer this place would teem with birds, frogs, and water life, but in this fallow time 'twas sufficiently quiet that I heard the voices in plenty of time to slow my approach.

Peering around one of the smaller hillocks, I saw that some long-ago flood had swept a tree to rest on its far side, and now the log made a dry bench where Nettie sat with an older woman. Though I had to look twice to be certain of her gender, for she wore britches and boots like a man, and her tunic barely reached her thighs. Her hair was gray, going white, and she wore no cap but braided it into a coil atop her head like a fine lady—a style most incongruous with her rough clothes. Could she be a Savant? She looked wild enough.

Not much is known of Savants, but I've never heard of one enjoying a picnic with those who've sought their aid, and that's just what Nettie and the stranger were doing. The basket yielded sandwiches, pickles, and a flask of something that steamed when they poured it.

I realized they were going to stay a while, and eased back along the trail. It took some time to work my way around the hillock where their log had fetched up, and longer still to climb it without a sound. Well, without too much noise, anyway.

Even when I reached the top and could peer down at the two women, to my considerable frustration I still couldn't hear what they said, so I settled in to watch. I was already muddy from my fall, and lying on a hillock in a bog on a thawing day is neither warm nor dry. Fisk would complain about having to clean my clothes, though he was the one who claimed care of my wardrobe as one of his duties—I'd never asked it of him.

Nettie and the old woman finished their meal and sat chatting for long enough that I became bored and began to feel my own hunger. I'd no thought of giving up, but I was delighted when they finally rose, Nettie laying a burlap-covered bundle on the useful log and the woman pulling a sack from behind it, which went into Nettie's basket.

Nettie kissed the woman's cheek, hugged her, and then turned and started back toward town.

I itched to follow her and discover what was in that basket. On the other hand, I knew where to find Nettie; once her companion vanished, she'd be gone for good. I crept back a bit, preparing to scramble down the slope and follow the old woman, but instead of leaving she sat down once more, with her back to me, and opened the bundle.

It contained a number of cloth bags, of the kind that usually hold flour or beans, and what looked to be a whetstone. I observed this in a glance, but the woman spent some time contemplating her new property. I had just began to wonder why when she stood, put her hands on her hips, and turned and looked straight at me.

"If you're not going to follow Nettie back, or jump me, then you may as well come down and state your business." She sounded very calm and a touch critical, like a nursemaid pointing out a child's silliness, and my face was hot as I scrambled down to face her.

"How did you know? I'd have sworn Mistress Nettie wasn't aware of me."

"Ah, she's a town girl."

Up close I saw that her skin was deeply scarred from the pox, and her eyes were blue and keen. I wondered if she was younger than I'd first thought.

"Are . . . are you a Savant?" I felt shy asking, though I'm not sure why.

"No, I'm not," she said. "And now my turn. What are you, young man, and why were you following that girl?"

She may not have been a Savant, but there was something about her . . . Introducing myself as a friend of Master Maxwell, instead of in the old way, felt like a lie though it was cold truth. "Have you heard about that?" I added. "What happened to him?"

I wouldn't have had to ask anyone else in Ruesport that question, but I was surprised when she said, "Oh, yes. Nettie worked for him, remember? She doesn't think he did it. But then, she's young." 'Twas simply said, but her eyes were suddenly ancient, and now I wondered if she was older than I'd thought. "Why were you following her?"

I explained that too, circumspectly, and she watched me intently till I stammered to a halt. Then she loaded the contents of Nettie's bundle into her sack and hoisted it onto her shoulder. "You can come along, if you've a mind to."

She strode off so quickly, I had to scramble to catch up. Her path went roundabout as a gopher's tunnel. I've a good sense of direction, but I don't think I could have retraced my steps to the log even before we reached a small raft, dragged up onto the bank of a pond. She pushed it off and stepped aboard, dainty as a fox, and took up a long pole. She looked at me inquiringly. I probably should have feared her. She might not attack me, but I'd no doubt of her ability to get me lost in the marish and then vanish like a mist wraith. But I stepped onto the raft without hesitation, for 'tis a very long time since I believed the tales of witches, who pervert the Savants' ways and sacrifice others to gain power over magica. And there was something about the directness of her gaze that demanded trust.

I wasn't as skilled as she and the raft rocked. I sat down quickly near the center, and she nodded approval, planted the pole, and leaned into it.

She didn't speak as she punted us through the twisting maze of pools. Being accustomed to the silence that sometimes overtakes country folk, I didn't trouble her. Nor was I fool enough to try to take the task of poling from her, despite the difference in our age and gender.

For the most part I simply enjoyed being under the sky instead of cooped up among buildings. The rustling grass and shimmering water held a sere beauty, even in winter. Only a few of the ponds were frozen over, and I realized that the two rivers' currents must twist through them.

I earned my passage by dragging the raft over several narrow spits of land. One place was obviously used often, for the tracks of dragged rafts almost looked like a road. The last raft over it had been several feet wider than ours. She saw me looking at the trail and nodded. "Aye, there's a fair few live in the marish. The town says criminals come here to hide from the law, and that's true enough. If they don't flee into the hills and take the road to Fallon, they mostly die, for we seldom help 'em. And though I'm not one, there's three Savants here."

"Three? In a place this small?"

"I think maybe it's because the six elements are stronger here." We floated the raft again, and she pushed off.

I looked about. The six elements? Water, yes, and earth mayhap. Life certainly. And magic . . . Yes, I could sense it. Dormant now, with winter brown settled over the marish, but there. I shouldn't have been able to sense it, and I shivered, pulling my mind back to her statement. Air is everywhere, but . . . "What about fire?"

She smiled. "You should be here in a lightning storm."

Shortly after that we reached our destination. I dragged the raft well up the bank, while she carried her sack into a wattle-and-daub hut that resembled a water rat's nest more than any human habitation. But the open door was made of planks, with a blanket tacked over them to keep drafts from flowing through the cracks, and when I stepped inside, I saw the shutters had been similarly treated. 'Twould be snug enough, I judged, for the earthen floor was dry and no light showed between the rough, woven sticks of the inner walls. There was no stove, but braziers of several different styles and sizes sat in the corners, and there was a proper stone-lined fire pit, with a smoke hole above it and a kettle hanging from a nearby tripod.

One whole wall was lined with peat bricks, and I eyed them curiously—I'd never used peat, though I'd heard it burns almost as hot and slow as charcoal. A smaller pile of peat beside it glowed with magica's strange light. With three Savants in the area, no doubt the proper sacrifice had been made. A low pallet heaped with blankets, one chair, and several tables crowded with sacks, boxes, and pots made up the rest of the furnishings. It was the bunches of dried and drying herbs hanging from every inch of the ceiling that made the small hut seem so cramped. The scent of earth and smoke made the herbs less pungent than in my mother's herbery, but 'twas still a familiar scent.

She waved me to the chair and went to the kettle, dishing thick stew into a smooth wooden bowl. "You missed mid-meal"—she handed it to me—"so you may as well eat while you ask your questions."

The stew held potatoes and carrots as well as rabbit, and was seasoned with herbs, but my attention was mostly on the questions flooding my mind. It seemed rude just to blurt them out. She saw my hesitation and snorted. "What did you come for, if not to ask?"

This was true, so I said softly, "I think what I most want to know, Mistress, is what *were* you?" Her life now, as hermit and herbalist, was spread before me.

Her lips twitched. "You've a gift for truth, haven't you? For seeing what's important. I was a prostitute."

I stopped chewing and stared, for of all the answers I'd expected, that was the last. She grinned mischievously. "That's how I got this." She gestured to her scarred face. "I couldn't work after. Too proud to beg help from friends. I didn't even want to be seen. So I gave my little girl to a friend who'd married out of it, and I came here to die."

There was a story that would take up hours behind the simple words, but she obviously had no mind to tell it, so I focused on the relevant fact. "Mistress Nettie is your daughter?"

"Aye, I'm Nettie's Ma. She doesn't tell folk about her birth—says she's an orphan, and small blame to her, poor tyke. But I kept track of her as she grew, and she's never forgotten me. I'm grateful to have a chance to do her a good turn, and maybe make up a bit for all the ways I failed her."

Realization dawned abruptly. "She got her apprentice fee from you. She sells your herbs and keeps the profit."

"Not all the profit, young man. Braziers and blankets don't grow in a swamp. Nor flour, salt, and beans. She buys what I need, and if there's enough left to pay for an apprenticeship and a decent gown, it's little enough for a mother to do. Especially given all that I couldn't do for her before."

"I see." And indeed, only one question remained. "But why do you tell me this? Why bring me here?"

She laughed. "You should have seen your face coming down that slope. I never saw anyone so like to burst with curiosity. You'd have spent days pestering poor Nettie, and like as not got yourself frozen or drowned trying to track me. Now you've seen what there is to see, you know all there is to know, and you'll leave us both alone."

I was suddenly shamed, as I'd not been even when they tattooed the circles on my wrists. "I am most sorry for disturbing your peace."

She smiled at that, and the serenity in her face said more plainly than words that her peace was too deep for me to trouble.

Which being the case, I summoned the nerve to ask one more question. "What's your name?"

And that seemed to be the most personal question of all, for her eyes lost focus as they gazed into the past. "That's a rude question here in the marish, youngster. I've had no need of a name for years. Think of me as Nettie's Ma. It's truer than any other name I could give you."

'Twas midafternoon when Nettie's Ma returned me to the trail that led back to Ruesport, and after the quiet of the marish, the city's raucous bustle was shocking. I wished I had managed to learn more. Nettie's suspicious behavior had cost me most of the day and turned out to be nothing but a matter of family helping family. Even Fisk, who claimed to be so cynical he'd do nothing unless there was something in it for him, had run to help his family the moment they wrote of their need. And that despite the way Maxwell had betrayed him. If my father should need my aid, would I offer it so unhesitatingly? I sighed. My father had never needed anyone's aid in his life, least of all mine.

Back at the Maxwells' I found Fisk, acrimoniously helping Mistress Judith beat the dust out of some rugs. Standing in the doorway and watching them bicker, I remembered that their father had tutored both of them and wondered which had been the better student. It appeared their rivalry was a fierce one, and no victor had yet emerged.

When I stepped forward, Fisk broke off his quarrel, and his eyes widened. "What have you been doing? Pig wrestling?"

"I've been in the marish. 'Tis a lovely place."

"Lovely." Fisk eyed my boots, which were coated with mud well above the ankle. "Agues, fevers, poisonous snakes, poisonous frogs, and mud that will swallow an oxcart. I bet you just adored it."

I had to laugh, for though sailors tell of frogs whose skin is poisonous, I know there are no such things in this land—and no frog whose bite is poisonous anywhere. We helped Mistress Judith take down the last of the rugs before Fisk hauled me up to my room to put on clean clothes. I told him the tale of my day's adventures, and though they held some interest, we were forced to conclude that naught had come of them.

Then Fisk told me what he'd learned last night, and I thought that sounded promising. "Though if they all hate Master Maxwell, it may be hard to persuade them to talk to us."

"It will be, if we tell them we want to help him." Fisk eyed me warily, for he knows my views on lying. "Speaking of helping, what did you say to Anna last night?"

"I told her the truth," I said, and watched in amusement as he rolled his eyes.

"Well, Max's enemies are tomorrow's problem. Today we ought to talk to the last of the servants. One of 'em has to be guilty—surely something will show it."

"I'd swear all those I spoke with were as honest as sunlight. And if any had wealth they couldn't account for, they've been too clever to display it."

"It's been only four months since those ledgers were planted, and maybe two since the fuss over Max began to die down. They might be waiting to spend the money—that'd be the smart thing to do." Fisk thought a moment more. "Almost no one is that smart. Come on, Michael. I want to talk to the last two servants before dark."

The sun was low when we located the house on the Yareside where the second kitchen maid had found employment. 'Twas the house of a brewer and vintner, a sprawling place with a large work yard and storage sheds in the back as big as some barns. I wasn't surprised they had servants, but when we tapped on the back door, it was the mistress herself who answered. No servant wears inch-long lace about her collar, cap, and sleeves, and no servant would have mastered the art of looking at folk in such a way as to make them feel like a pair of bedbugs.

"I heard you might be coming." She folded her arms under the shelf of her bosom and glared. She wasn't tall, but the doorway was several steps higher than the yard where Fisk and I stood. She was glaring down at me.

"It's just like that hanging fiend to send criminals to harass folk, but you'll get nothing to help him from *my* household. My servants don't consort with *unredeemed* men."

She cast me a final, scorching glance and slammed the door. Scorching was the right term, too, for both my face and the tattoos concealed by my sleeves seemed to burn.

"Well," said Fisk blankly. "That was . . . different."

"I'm sorry." My voice sounded stiff and strange. "I should go."

"Don't be ridiculous." Fisk took my arm and pulled

me from the yard. "She wouldn't have let that poor girl tell anyone anything."

"What girl?" We had reached the street, but my heart still pounded with rage and shame, and I had trouble concentrating on his words.

"The girl hovering in the hallway behind the dragon. I got a good look at her while you were being flame roasted. Not that I needed to see much, for no one with a copper to spare would work for that harridan. Which was what we came to find out, and we have, and quickly, too, so stop looking like that."

I don't know how I looked, but what I felt was a gratitude deeper than when Fisk had rescued me from Lady Ceciel. My heart steadied and my mind began to work once more. "How did she know about me?"

"One of the people you talked to this morning probably spread the word. Gossip runs fast in towns."

"Yes, but the people I spoke with today didn't know I was unredeemed. They greeted me courteously and we parted the same."

Fisk's steps slowed. "The sheriff's deputies know about your legal status, and they gossip too. Both Ham and Jonas had heard. But for the rumors of our investigation and your status to both reach Yareside in the same afternoon . . . I don't know."

Nor did I, alas.

◇ ◇ ◇

The sun was setting when we located our last stop, a carpenter's workshop where the Maxwells' gardener and handyman had gone to work for his older brother. He came out onto the steps when we knocked, and I saw at once that he, too, had heard of me—his gaze held both horror and fascination.

"I'm sorry, masters, but I can't be letting you in. This is my brother's house."

And mayhap this brother had children, who should not be exposed to one such as me. My voice had fled, so it was Fisk who explained our errand and introduced us—as knight and squire, which was ridiculous now, and painful, too. An unredeemed man could never be the hero I had once so foolishly imagined myself. And Fisk had always thought it folly, so why was he doing this? If he persisted, I would have to speak to him about it, though my heart cringed at discussing the death of my youthful dreams.

The gardener looked startled but did not laugh, and answered willingly and swiftly. 'Twas plain that he believed Master Maxwell innocent and wished to help him, but he also wished me off his brother's doorstep. The more Fisk asked, the shorter his replies became, and he cast a harried glance at the neighbors' windows.

"One last question," said Fisk, and I watched sourly as relief lit the gardener's face. "How did you know we were coming?"

"A man stopped by the shop—about mid-meal, it was. We didn't know him, but he'd heard your friend here was asking questions and thought we'd like a warn—ah, to know."

He cast me another wary glance, but this revelation was so curious, I found my voice returning. "What was his name?"

"He didn't give it." The gardener frowned, noting this omission for the first time, and went on without prompting. "He was of middle height with brown hair, what there was of it. Almost bald, and he was youngish. Thirty or thereabouts."

"Was there anything else unusual about him?" Fisk asked.

"No. At least . . . Under his cloak he was wearing a short leather vest. The kind that doesn't button, you know?"

The kind that poor folk who do hard work often wear. Fisk and I nodded and he went on.

"I didn't think much about it at the time, but as I look back, his britches didn't match the vest. Good cloth, not too worn. And his shirt was clean." He cast another glance at the houses along the street, and indeed, I could sense many pairs of eyes upon us.

"Thank—"

He shut the door, cutting off the rest of Fisk's courtesy, and Fisk smiled. "And that was informative. I don't suppose any of the people you talked to today matched that description?"

"No." This time 'twas I who hauled him away, for the nosiness of the neighbors preyed on my nerves. "Mayhap 'tis just some public-spirited citizen."

"Who just happened to hear of you from a gossiping deputy, and then just happened to find out that you've been questioning the servants? No. Someone you spoke to today is trying to stop us from asking more questions—which means one of them is guilty."

"Then they've not revealed it." I sighed.

"Hmm. Speaking of coincidences, I've got another for you—Judith tells me Tristram Fowler is a law clerk employed by the Tanners' Guild."

I moaned. "We have enough tanners—we don't need any more. You don't really think . . ."

We looked at each other and spoke together. "No."

"All the same," Fisk went on, "things are stacking up against him. Before Max was disgraced, he'd never have been considered as a suitor for Lissy. And I doubt she'd have looked at him twice, before he showed such dedication in the face of adversity."

"That's preposterous. He's too . . . too forthright. There's a devious mind behind this tangle."

Fisk's expression lightened. "Judith has a devious mind."

"Be serious."

"Why couldn't it be Judith? She has access to Max's study, too, remember?"

Fisk will argue nonsense simply for the pleasure he takes in debate, and I knew better than to let him suck me in. Still . . . "What about motive? She has no reason to harm her own family."

"Maybe she didn't want to marry what's-his-name, and did it to make him back out. Or maybe what's-his-name did it because *he* didn't want to marry Judith! Now that's a motive!"

I had to laugh, and Fisk allowed the discussion to return to serious matters. But although we discussed these puzzles all the way back to the house, we found no answers.

My second dinner in the Maxwells' household was more comfortable than the first. Fisk told me there was no need to dress for dinner—and when I saw the thick brown pottery and tin flatware that had replaced porcelain and silver, I realized why. Our pretense of not noticing the changed dishes was aided by the presence of the children, who were evidently accustomed to dining with the family at casual meals.

Mistress Lissy hurried in just as the meal was about to start, and even a stranger could see she'd been with young Fowler, for her whole face was aglow. But the first subject that came up for discussion was horseback rides. Mistress Becca's imperious demands for a precise date were finally squelched by her father's statement that we'd tell her when we were ready, and if she pestered us anymore, he'd decide she was still too young and withdraw his permission.

With so lively a start the conversation flowed easily, and I was pleased to see that even lost in the rosy fog of first love, Mistress Lissy cared enough to draw out the brother she hadn't seen since she was ten.

Trimmer served us, but only to the extent of bringing the pork roast, vegetables, bread, and pickles to the table. All too shortly Mrs. Trimmer took the children off to bed. Then Anna served tea while Mistress Judith and Lissy cleared the table.

'Twas then, with the children gone, that Maxwell cleared his throat and said, "I should probably tell you that I went to see Ben Worthington today and borrowed enough to keep the household till the end of Hollyon. After that . . ." He sighed, and Anna's hand shot out to cover his.

"We'll be all right, whatever we do."

Mistress Judith nodded sharply and said, "Very practical."

Mistress Lissy said nothing, no doubt wondering how best to explain to her suitor that he had only a month to propose.

Fisk and I said nothing either, but our eyes met across the table in the realization that we'd been given a deadline. "I suppose if we're making any headway, he can borrow more," Fisk murmured. "Though if we haven't figured it out by that time, I doubt—"

"Sheriff Potter to see you, Sir," Trimmer announced gloomily. "Again."

The sheriff, as seemed to be the custom in this informal household, had already followed Trimmer into the room. Lamplight gleamed on his bald pate as he smiled, but the casual glance he cast over the company missed nothing, and my lips tightened in dislike.

Maxwell's brows rose, though he smiled in return. "If you continue to show up at dinnertime I'll start thinking it's a hint. Sit down, Rob. Anna will get you some tea."

"Thank you, but I'm here on business tonight. I actually wanted to speak to Master Fisk and his friend."

'Twas clearly a request for us to go somewhere private with him. We all stiffened except for Fisk, who leaned back in his chair, as relaxed as a cat. "Well, you've found me. Ask away."

Sheriff Potter took off his cloak and sat down. "I think I'd like tea after all. It's bitter out." He didn't fake ease as well as Fisk did. The rest of us didn't even try, but exchanged worried glances. Anna made no move for the teapot. "I wondered if you could tell me where you were last night, Master Fisk."

"I probably could." Fisk stopped there, hoping Potter would leap in with a revealing question, but the sheriff was a master of the strategy of silence. 'Twas Fisk who finally asked, "What time are you interested in?"

"Oh, about one or two hours after midnight."

A puzzled crease appeared between Fisk's brows. "Before the fire started? I was in the Irony from just after dark to the time the bell sounded."

"And have you witnesses who'd swear to that?"

"Several." Fisk sounded even more cautious. "Ham, the tapster at the Irony, for one, if the sheriff's office still takes his word like you used to."

Potter nodded, and I felt my shoulders sag with relief. Whatever it was, Fisk had an alibi.

"And Master Sevenson." Potter nodded to me. "Can Ham swear to your whereabouts too?"

"No," I said. "I was—" Fisk's boot connected with my shin beneath the table, hard enough to make me wince.

Potter's lips twitched, but his smile vanished as Fisk demanded, "Why do you want to know?"

"Some men my deputies spoke to saw a man with a scar like your friend's hanging around Morna's place before the fire." He touched two fingers to his jaw, in the place where a collision with a broken branch when I was twelve had left me with a scraping scar. "Morna never saw him, but when we found those empty oil casks in the rubble, well, I started wondering."

He sat back with the smooth smile I was coming to hate, laying his little trap of silence. But I didn't blunder into it this time, for my blood had chilled.

I had no alibi. And Potter had trapped Fisk into admitting it, for the witnesses who would clear Fisk would swear I'd not been with him. My scruples against lying vanished, and my mind raced frantically for something, anything, to say in my defense. Not that it would help. An unredeemed man has no legal rights. If Potter chose to think me guilty, his deputies could drag me out and hang me from the nearest tree. My pulse beat thick and sluggish. "I was here—"

This time Fisk's kick was even harder, and I grunted and glared at him. What use to delay? I had no alibi, and—

"This was before the fire started?" Mistress Anna's voice broke the tense stillness. "Then I can testify to

Master Sevenson's whereabouts, though I can't name the exact hours."

A ripple of astonishment passed around the table, and Potter's eyes narrowed.

"It was windy last night, you'll remember?" she went on. "One of the shutters came loose and was banging against the wall downstairs. Very annoying. After a while I went down to close it and encountered Master Sevenson on the same errand. Since we were wide-awake by then, we fell into conversation and talked, oh, an hour or more, I'd guess. Then we went up to bed, and the fire bell started ringing just as I was dropping off to sleep, maybe fifteen minutes after I left him. And it kept me awake, too. So Master Sevenson couldn't be the man your witnesses saw, could he?" And she smiled—not at me, but at her brother, whose answering smile held a lifetime of love and conspiracy.

The thundering rush of relief all but deafened me, and I barely heard Potter speak, though his voice was no longer soft. "What room was this shutter in, Master Sevenson?"

"In Max's study," Mistress Anna inserted swiftly. "The one on the far right. The latch has been loose for several months."

"And can your husband confirm any of this?"

Maxwell had looked increasingly flustered as he

watched his wife lie to the law. Now he opened his mouth to reply, but Anna cut him off too. "No, he was asleep till the bell woke him. He got up and went downstairs then, but Master Sevenson and I were both abed."

Maxwell, helplessly, nodded confirmation. Lissy was wide-eyed but silent, and Mistress Judith's face was set like stone.

Potter knew Anna was lying, but as long as she stuck to her story, there was little he could do. "Then I've wasted your time." *You've wasted mine*, his tone said. "I'll leave you now." His voice was smooth again, and 'twas quite clear he'd no intention of abandoning the matter.

"Wait a moment," said Fisk.

I considered kicking him, for I wanted the sheriff gone, but before I could launch the blow, Fisk continued, "As it happens, I have a few questions. These men who identified my friend—did they describe anything else about him? Height? His hair? His clothes?"

"No." Potter hesitated, then glanced at Max and went on. "In fact, I wanted to talk to them, but when my deputies went back to question the men further, they couldn't be found. Sailors, maybe, who went back to their ships."

"Maybe you should investigate that, Robin Potter,"

Anna put in. "Instead of persecuting my brother and his friends."

"Or," said Fisk, "men paid to implicate Michael, whose stories wouldn't stand up to close questioning. Frames are fashionable in Ruesport this year, aren't they?"

"Speaking of investigating"—Potter's glance included both of us—"I've had a complaint that you two are bothering people."

"Complaint from whom?" 'Twas Maxwell who asked, honest surprise in his voice.

I assumed 'twas the kitchenmaid's mistress, but Potter replied, "Yorick Thrope."

"Thrope? What business is it of his?" Maxwell demanded.

"Maybe he doesn't like Master Sevenson." Potter rose to go.

"Or maybe," said Fisk, "he likes his job. He must have pretty good connections to have heard about our asking questions so fast. Did he order you to stop us?"

"Yes," said Potter. "He did." But he said nothing more.

The grin Fisk cast him looked almost sincere. "Just one more question. Do you have a deputy or clerk who's in his early thirties and going bald? Brown hair?"

"Yes." Potter pulled on his cloak. "I can think of three men who answer that description. And no, I won't give you their names. Good night."

And he departed, leaving behind him the kind of silence that comes after some shattering crash. Silence . . . and complicity.

CHAPTER 8

Fisk

M ax took one look at Mrs. Trimmer's avid face hovering in the slightly open doorway that led to the kitchen and began talking about the town's preparations for Calling Night—firmly.

Anna and Lissy helped him change the subject, but Judith sat silent, her face creased in thought, and Michael was still chalk white with fear. That was something of a relief, for I'd begun to wonder if he had the sense to be afraid of anything.

As soon as the tea was finished, Max announced that he and Anna were going to bed, "Since we got so little sleep last night." His voice was dry enough to turn mud to dust, but Anna only smiled and said she'd come as soon as she rinsed the teapot.

Michael said he'd help her, with considerable determination. If Anna could cope with Becca, she could handle Michael with no trouble at all, so I yawned and went upstairs to bed.

Michael was still fuming next morning. "How under two moons does a man that hard come to have a name like Robin Potter?"

We were on our way to visit George Little, the smith whose brother Max had ordered hanged, and the weather was just right for such an errand. Yesterday's warmth had vanished, and the puddles had turned to sheets of ice that reflected the bulging clouds. It was bitter cold, and the Millside's steep streets were treacherous, but working folk can't yield to weather.

"Probably his father, or his grandfather, or his great—"

"Was a potter. But Robin? His parents were insane."

"He was only a baby when they named him. He was probably cute."

Michael snorted. "That man was never a baby. And he could never, ever be cute."

I grinned, stretching cold muscles. But as Jack Bannister once told me, men need to talk about things that frighten them. The Gods know I do it. "He's new since my day—and frankly, we're lucky. Old Sheriff Havermen was a senile toady. He'd have followed Thrope's orders and told us to clear out."

"'Twas curious"—Michael sounded more reasonable now—"that he didn't even ask us to stop, much less . . . what he could have done." He pulled his cloak closer, and I wondered again what his journey here had been like. I found I disliked seeing Michael learn fear, no matter how badly he needed the lesson.

"I think it's several things. One, he doesn't like Thrope. Two, he likes Max and hopes we'll find something. And three . . ."

"What."

I hesitated, for this is something I seldom say, but . . . "I think maybe he's a fair man. We haven't done anything to be thrown out of town for. Which should cheer you up, because it means he probably won't hang you without cause. If he liked Thrope and hated Max, it might be different, but as it is, I think he'll cut us a bit of slack."

"Just enough to hang ourselves, no doubt." But Michael smiled as he said it, and I was glad to see him regaining his usual spirits.

"What I don't understand is how whoever it is found out what we were doing fast enough to set up a frame. That fire happened the *second night* we were in town. They know too much."

Michael looked thoughtful. "Many people know we're here. The sheriff's office. The servants we questioned.

Mayhap one of them is guilty, and took the news to whoever framed Max. Hire an arsonist, bribe a few 'witnesses,' and the thing is done. We never spoke to the other kitchen maid. I think we should."

I hadn't spoken to any of the servants Michael had interviewed, and if nothing came of our investigations today, I would. Michael wouldn't recognize a lie if it was marked with a signpost and announced by the town crier. But I only said, "Most arsonists won't work with only one day's lead time. Not unless you pay them extra. A lot extra."

Michael shrugged. "So someone paid them more."

"Hmm. Given the size of those bribes, whoever's behind this has lots of money. But the timing still bothers me."

"'Tis the fact that he's trying to frame me for arson that troubles me. If not for Mistress Anna, I might be facing flogging or worse right now. None died, but a debt that can't be paid in money is sometimes paid in blood. And I can't even pay the price of a cowshed."

Michael's expression was shadowed again, so I answered lightly. "It's more often repaid in labor. How do you feel about working for a brothel keeper for the next twenty years?"

He laughed, and I went on, "Next time you warn me that your Gift for sensing ambushes isn't reliable, I'm going to listen. You sense matchmaking aunts, but not people trying to frame you for serious crimes?"

"I told you 'twas so." Michael sounded unreasonably cheerful about it. "At least our activities are worrying someone. Mayhap we're getting closer to the truth."

"If someone is worried about us, then I take back what I said about him knowing too much. We haven't learned anything."

We rounded a corner and the smithy came in sight.

"That may be about to change," said Michael softly.

I understood why his voice had dropped. The neighborhood wasn't a bad one. The other buildings on the street were made of the same rough dark timber and gray stone. But the smithy had an aura of its own—ramshackle, though I saw no signs of neglect. Melancholy and malevolent at the same time.

"Maybe it's the weather," I said. "Depressing."

"Mayhap," said Michael.

I shrugged my fancies aside and rapped on the door's thick planks. It opened without sinister creaking, and a man with rough-cut black hair and a smith's apron stood before us.

"This is Michael Sevenson, a knight errant, and I'm his squire, Fisk. We're looking for George Little."

The man stared. "You're what?"

"He's a knight errant, and I'm his squire," I said

patiently. Saying it was still embarrassing, but I was beginning to get used to that. I had to do something to bring Michael around, and crazy though it was, this looked to be my best bet. "His name is Sevenson, mine is Fisk. Are you Master Little?"

He stared some more and slowly reached a conclusion. His massive shoulders rose and fell. All of him was massive, which is no surprise in a smith, but the prospect of asking him questions he might not like held little appeal. I resolved to be tactful. I also resolved to squelch Michael when he wasn't. Looking at this man's huge arms and lowering brows gave me lots of motivation.

"Aye, I'm Little. Come in. You've got work for me?"

At least he hadn't heard of us.

Heat billowed from the doorway. The coals in the forge were dull red, but the bellows beside them were large enough to bring them quickly to white heat. The workbench was littered with tools I didn't even recognize, except for the anvil and a set of hammers that ranged in size from one a carpenter might use to one I'm not sure I could have lifted.

"So, masters, what do you need? Horses shod? My rates are low, 'less they're biters—I get bit, the price goes up."

"Actually," said Michael, "we wanted to ask you

some questions about your brother.'"

Little's eyes widened; then his brows sank into a suspicious glower. I cursed Michael's inconvenient candor.

"Phil's dead. What do you want to know about him for?"

"We're interested in the truth," said Michael.

"Would you tell us the truth about your brother?" I asked hastily, before Michael could go on to say precisely why we wanted it. "I'll bet not many people heard your brother's side of things. And yours, too. You were flogged, weren't you?"

"Ah, that didn't matter. They'd no call to hang Phil, though. We paid the money back. And he didn't mean for anyone to die. They'd no call—" He turned abruptly to his workbench, fidgeting with a lethal-looking awl. "What are you here for? Nobody cared about Phil but me. And nobody cared about me except Phil."

Michael opened his mouth, but I managed to speak first. "It must have been hard to lose a brother like that. Especially if you were close."

"Phil looked out for me." The look he cast Michael and me was almost pleading, and I knew he'd go on now without prompting. It's not only things that frighten them that people need to talk about. A brighter, more imaginative man would have been suspicious, but the dull-witted are easy to lead.

"Was he older than you, or younger?" The sympathy on Michael's face was patently sincere, and the last of Little's hesitation vanished.

"He was older. Small and scrawny, so I got the smithy when Pa died, but he didn't care. Said we'd look out for each other, just like always. And we did, too. He gave me an equal cut of everything he got. There wasn't no call—"

His eyes shifted away.

"He hurt a lot of people." Michael's voice was gentle.

Little's sigh could have moved a twelve-ton ship on a windless day. "Phil wasn't quite . . . It mostly wasn't worse than Pa used to do to him. To both of us, though Phil kept Pa off me when he could. He didn't mean to kill anyone."

"But you knew what he was doing?" I asked.

"Yeah. I didn't mind being flogged. Figured I had it coming. I tried to tell Phil to take it easy, but he . . . The ones he beat, they were men who looked like Pa. And we paid the money back. There wasn't no call to hang him." His grief was giving way to sullen anger, and I decided I didn't want to be around when he thought to ask again why we wanted to know.

"Thank you, Master Little, that's what we needed.

Come on, Michael. We're leaving."

Out in the street I took several deep breaths—the cold, fresh day seemed brighter. "Well, scratch one enemy. He hates Max enough, but he doesn't have a devious bone in his body."

"'Tis piteous," Michael murmured. "With a different brother he'd have been an honest citizen. With a different father they might both have been all right."

"And if good old Phil hadn't been so crazy, several innocent men might still be alive. I can't scrape up much sympathy for Phil."

"No, but 'tis still piteous. And you're right; Little could never come up with so complex a scheme."

"Well, Kline, from all accounts, is a very bright lad. Jonas says his rooms are in the Oldtown."

I was pleased to see Michael turn toward Trullsgate Bridge without further prompting. I'd make a townsman of him yet.

"If Kline is bright," he said, "you might consider changing the way you introduce us. Or even if he isn't so bright. What are you about, Fisk? You thought I was mad to claim knight errantry. You hated it."

Michael's eyes were bright with indignation; he gestured as he spoke. Much better than the crushed wariness he'd displayed when Sheriff Potter dragged him into Max's hall.

"I'm coming to see the advantages. When people are wondering if you're crazy, they're not as likely to wonder what you're up to. And it's better to have them wonder than to know the truth."

"That I'm an unredeemed man, you mean." Michael's expression closed again.

"No. The truth is that you *are* crazy. Come on, there used to be a good bakeshop by Sutter's Gate—if it's still there, we can eat mid-meal before we face the clever Master Kline."

LEGAL ADVICE. CONTRACTS DRAWN UP. PROMISSORY NOTES. WILLS. ACCOUNTING. DEBTS COLLECTED. LETTERS WRITTEN OR READ. COPYING.

The neatly lettered sign in Erril Kline's window told the full tale of what he'd come to.

"I didn't think a nonguildsman could practice law," said Michael.

"He can still draw up documents, but his clients have to go to a judicary member to get them ratified. I'll bet he makes most of his money from debt collecting. If he's not a brawny type, that's a hard job."

"What about copying?"

"Copying pays one copper roundel per page." I'd tried it myself, once, and cursed the father who'd taught me to write so neatly with every stroke of the pen. "If he's trying to make a living copying, he's starving."

Far from being brawny, Erril Kline, who opened the door at our knock, was shorter than I am and slight, with curly, pale brown hair, wide-set eyes, a charming smile, and freckles. He had to be at least in his mid-twenties, but he looked almost as young as Michael and I.

Then his eyes narrowed, and though his smile didn't change, he didn't look young at all.

"Masters Sevenson and Fisk, no doubt. I heard you might be calling." His fingers were ink stained, and looking past him I saw a paper-cluttered desk. He was wearing threadbare fingerless gloves, even indoors.

"We'd like to talk to you," I began carefully.

"About poor Master Maxwell's sad predicament? Alas, I don't know what I can do for you. And since I'm rather busy . . ." He smiled again and started to close the door.

"How much?" said Michael abruptly.

The door stopped. "How much what?"

"How much for half an hour of your time?"

The door swung open. "Ten gold roundels."

Michael opened his mouth. "Do—"

"No!" I yelped. Not only was that an outrageous price, we didn't have it. Michael had bought feed for the horses just two days ago. How could he be so oblivious to our financial state? "Three silver roundels is more than you're making at anything else, and I'm not paying your top price. One silver roundel."

"I get six for drawing up documents, and I can't lower my rates, even for you gentlemen. Think of the delay to my other clients' work. Five silver for half an hour."

Michael started to speak again, and I jabbed an elbow into his ribs. "You don't have to work, just talk. One, for fifteen minutes."

We settled on one and five octs for ten minutes, to be timed on the guild tower clock which was visible from the window. Kline also insisted on being paid in Ruesport coin, and that was just to be annoying. All towns mint pure coin—otherwise their money would be worthless for trade. Fortunately, Michael had gotten change from the grain merchant, so we had some Ruesport coins mixed in with all the others.

Kline was smiling when he let us in. The room was so small that the meager coals that glowed in the fire-place almost heated it. In truth, meager was the word for everything from the thin blankets on the bed to the single small lamp on the desk. The cluttered desk wasn't meager, but it was so battered that most would have broken it up to assist the struggling embers.

"Very well, gentlemen, my next ten minutes are at your disposal. What do you want to know?"

How much do you hate the man who took you from a promising law career to copper-a-page copying? I looked at Michael, who made a show of rubbing his ribs and said nothing.

"What actually happened between you and the Judicary Guild? We'd like to hear your side of it."

"My side? Surely the facts are the facts. But it's your ten minutes." Kline replaced his smile with a thoughtful expression. "Let me see. It began when one of our local fences retired to another town—or more accurately another fiefdom, where Sheriff Potter's writ doesn't stand. Our good sheriff had been showing considerable interest in his activities, and he decided a change of address might be salubrious.

"Nothing daunted, Sheriff Rob entered into correspondence with the man and persuaded him to offer up his client list—something about what our good sheriff would or wouldn't tell the authorities in the town where the fence had moved. In fact, I believe Potter threatened to hire an artist and a printer and send the poor man's portrait and an account of his activities to every sheriff in the realm. You must admit, Rob Potter is a veritable badger when he sets about catching someone. I've known him to—"

"We've met the sheriff," I said. "Go on."

"Well, the fence was understandably intimidated.

The judicary, at the sheriff's request, sent a clerk to take his deposition, and that clerk chose a promising young notary, myself, to accompany him and do the actual writing. I was flattered"—the smile returned—"because when the guild starts tagging you for these errands, it's usually a sign of promotion to come. And since the judicary offered the Saddlers' Guild one of their notaries to replace me, they had no objection to letting me go. Would you care to hear why I was working for the saddlers?"

"No," I said firmly. I wondered if he could stretch his story for more than ten minutes. "Get on with it."

"Just before the clerk and I set off, a man named Tocker called at my rooms—late at night, and with considerable stealth. He was a burglar by trade, quite a harmless little man. He'd heard that the fence was giving up his clients, and as one of those clients he was understandably concerned. Being brighter than his fellows, he'd hit on the idea of asking the notary who was to take down the names to exclude his. So simple, not to write those few small words. He offered me fifty gold roundels for this bit of nonwriting, and I said yes."

He was still smiling.

"And did you?"

"Don't rush me. The clerk and I took ship and had

a very pleasant voyage. Only a month to get all the way to Lambington, where the fence had taken up residence. It was a lovely town, nestled amid rolling hills, the leaves just beginning—"

"Did you exclude the name?" Michael spoke this time, and he sounded as annoyed as I felt.

"Of course. I try to give value to all who hire me. There were over sixty names on that list and poor Tocker was near the end. The clerk never noticed my omission. Master Tocker went about his business untroubled by Sheriff Rob, and I was promoted to clerk myself. I went from the Saddlers to the Smiths' Guild, which was much more interesting, because—"

"So how did you get caught?" I demanded.

"With my new station I felt the need to improve my appearance. A few new doublets. New boots. Rooms in a better neighborhood. My salary was larger, but when the bills came due, it wasn't sufficient, and I went to my good friend Tocker for the difference. After all, I'd done him a considerable favor."

"So you blackmailed him."

"I did." Kline's smile seemed to be engraved on his face. "Mind, I wasn't excessively greedy, having seen what happens when a blackmailer pushes his, ah . . ."

"Victims," Michael supplied coldly.

"Victims too far. I asked only a bit here and there,

and Tocker paid quite amiably. But I fear I must have angered him more than I realized, for one night he was working in a cobbler's shop . . . or was it a haberdasher? No, I think—"

"Let me guess," I interrupted. "He got caught."

"As you say, he got caught. And was so irritated by my modest demands that he ratted me out to Sheriff Rob. He then set off for parts unknown—working passage, poor man, for after paying back all his victims, he was very poor indeed. But it was summertime, and I understand sailing then isn't—"

"Did the judiciary just accept his word for it?"

"By no means. I denied it with great indignation, and the clerk honestly didn't remember Tocker's name being mentioned. But Maxwell, who'd heard Tocker's case, didn't accept the guild's ruling. He sent two more clerks, at his own expense, all the way to Lambington to talk to the fence, who did remember mentioning Tocker. He'd made notes before we came, so he wouldn't forget anyone Sheriff Rob might already know about. When the clerks checked his notes against my list, it was the same in every particular except that Tocker's name wasn't on it. So I was convicted of bribe taking and had to pay the money back—to the Judiciary Guild, since Tocker had gone by then. And I was disrobed, of course. Is there anything

else? You still have"—he went to look out his window—
"two minutes left."

"Thanks, we've got what we came for." He'd told us
nothing we couldn't have learned elsewhere. I only
hoped my smile was as annoying as his. "Michael?"

"Just two questions. The name of the fence, and the
clerk you traveled with."

"Names? My dear gentlemen, I said I'd tell you what,
not who. Names cost another silver roundel each."

Michael flushed with anger. "We have two minutes
left."

"But not for names. Names are extra."

"Forget it," I said. "We can get the names anywhere.
Come on."

Michael sputtered for ten minutes after we left
Kline's rooms, even after I pointed out that we could
get the names from Max for nothing. And we had
learned what we wanted to know.

"He's devious enough," I said. "But I'm afraid he's
not rich enough to have paid to have Max framed.
Though the shabbiness could be an act."

"He hates enough, too," said Michael. "Beneath
his smiles, he burns with it. Mayhap he was blackmailing others, and so amassed enough to buy his
vengeance."

I cast Michael a surprised look, for I hadn't sensed

hatred. But Michael was Gifted, however erratically those Gifts worked. And it wasn't a bad theory.

"We'll ask Max tonight, about the names and the possibility that Kline was blackmailing others. Though Max might not know. Blackmail victims almost never come forward to claim redress." Maybe I should consider taking it up?

Nate Jobber, the forger who was next on our list, wasn't at the tavern where he worked nights. The tapster gave us directions to his rooms, but he wasn't there either. The elderly lady who lived below him didn't know where he was.

Michael and I gave up and went home to dinner, resolving to catch the elusive Nate Jobber at work that evening.

We arrived home late and found Benjamin Worthington present and the children absent. I was disappointed, for I'd trade Becca's conversation and Thomas's shy giggles for the presence of any guest. On the other hand, I wasn't the one scrounging for money to pay the door tax. And I had to admit he treated pork stew, bread, and applesauce as if it was the finest meal he'd ever eaten. Indeed, he claimed that his servants were readying his house for Calling Night and his only other recourse was a tavern. "And you know how I hate eating in taverns." From the conversation I gathered he opened his house to friends every year, which can run from expensive to ruinous depending on how many friends you have. It seemed Worthington had a lot of friends.

As the meal finished, he asked Max if they could talk a bit of business over tea, in the study perhaps, ". . . and if they don't mind, I'd like Fisk and Sevenson here to join us."

Business? With us? Michael, Max, and I exchanged startled glances.

"We'd be most gratified," said Michael politely.

We'd be cursed curious! And we weren't the only ones. Anna brought the tea herself, and took so long serving it that Worthington finally laughed and said, "You can get it out of him later, Anna. You always do." She crinkled her nose at him before she left.

The study was cozy, with the lamps lit and the warmth of the stove. Michael, Worthington, and I pulled up straight chairs to sit before Max's desk, and something about the way Worthington glanced at his made me wonder if once there had been cushioned chairs for visitors in this room.

"I'm not sure if it's worth making a pother about," Worthington began as he picked up his teacup, "but I wanted to warn the two of you—all three of you—that the most interesting rumor in town right now is that Sevenson here started that fire in the Oldtown last night."

"That's quick for gossip, even from the sheriff's department," I said. "Potter seems more competent than old Halverson. You'd think he could stop those leaks, or at least slow them down."

Worthington laughed. "You'll never stop gossip, lad. It's like trying to stop the moons from circling. But I thought you should know it's stirring up a lot of the feeling against you. You'll want to be careful."

"We will," I promised, wondering how I could keep Michael from leaving the house.

Worthington rubbed his chin. "Well, it wasn't entirely intended for your benefit. The fact that you're living with Max, and investigating the crime he was accused of, is being talked about as well. In fact, more people are talking about that than about the arson. To put it bluntly, your investigation is making people remember the accusations against Max, and that's not a good thing. I'm afraid it might stir up the same kind of trouble he had before."

Max sighed. "I'll stay in. Thanks for warning me, Ben."

"Trouble?" I asked.

"There were some . . . difficulties when I was first disrobed." Max sounded more embarrassed than indignant. "The townsfolk were unhappy, and rightly so in my—"

"Unhappy?" Worthington snorted. "He was beaten by one mob, and might have been killed if the deputies hadn't arrived. And there was vandalism here at the house, stones thrown through windows, manure dumped in the fountain, that kind of thing. And the fact that Sevenson's accused of arson can only make it worse," Worthington added. "Since the docks burned, that's a very serious crime. The whole town suffered from that fire, one way or another."

He didn't bring up the fact that Michael was un-redeemed, but Michael understood the implication anyway. His gaze had fallen to his hands, which were clenched in his lap. In about five more seconds he would offer to leave.

"But the only reason Michael's being accused of arson is *because* we're investigating!" I said hastily. "Someone's trying to stop us, and we can't afford to let them win."

When I said "afford," I meant more than just money, but Max's gaze strayed to his ledgers. "I was a fool to invest so heavily in one venture, no matter how sound it looked."

Worthington smiled comfortably. "You've got plenty of company. I'd have been in it to the teeth, but when you trade from Landsend to D'vorin, you don't always have cash on hand. At the time I was upset that I couldn't invest more. It wasn't your fault, Max. Just bad luck."

"Well, luck has nothing to do with what's happening now," I said. "If someone's trying to stop us from investigating, then we must be on the right track." I wished I knew what track it was. Whom had we spoken to, what had we asked, that had frightened our enemy into taking steps? "And if they want Michael gone, then that's the best reason I've heard yet for keeping him around," I added firmly.

"That's ridiculous." Michael's voice was quiet enough to make me nervous that he might leave town altogether. I'd have to watch him day and night, which was impossible. I'd have to convince him that his presence would be better for Max than his absence, and that might be even more difficult.

"Maybe Fisk could contact some of the town's arsonists," Max said thoughtfully. "If you could discover who started those fires, Sevenson would be cleared, and it might give you a link to my enemy."

"No," I said firmly. "It's one thing to go poking around an old case, but Potter's deputies are investigating the fire. They'll do a better job than we could."

The last thing we needed was to have the house burn down, especially with two small children and my sisters in it.

"Potter's a sound man," Worthington assured us. "I'm sure he'll find the real culprit. But until he does, you should all watch your step."

"We're always careful," I said. "No, that's wrong. *I'm* always careful. Michael's a lunatic."

Michael still wasn't meeting my eyes, but he nodded farewell as Worthington took his leave. And with no company to put on a brave face for, Max looked almost as depressed as Michael did.

"Speaking of investigating," I said determinedly, "we talked to Erril Kline today. Michael was wondering if he was, or is, blackmailing people other than Tocker."

"I wondered about that myself," said Max wearily. "But I can't give you an answer. A dishonest clerk has chances to commit all sorts of crimes. Everything of importance flows through the law clerk's hands: contracts, marriage settlements, wills. Even charitable contributions. As the clerk in charge of the ropers' charity accounts, I learned more about the private affairs of the wealthy guildsmen than years of gossip could have told me. Not directly, mind you, but it's all in the

ledgers. A change in the timing or amount of a dona-
tion, especially combined with a bit of rumor . . . The
possibilities for abuse are unbelievably vast. That's
why I took the possibility of Kline's malfeasance so
seriously. But he could have been perfectly honest
right up to the moment Tocker bribed him. There's no
way to know."

"Mayhap his poverty is genuine, then," Michael
murmured. At least he was talking again. Trying to
solve Max's problems pulled him out of his own
more than anything else could have—a born knight
errant. I stifled a sigh.

"We'll talk to the last of Jonas's suspects tonight," I
said. "We can catch Nate Jobber at the tavern where he
works. After that . . . we'll see."

We were almost out the door when Michael turned
back to Max. "Just two more questions, Sir. Kline
would give us no names beyond Tocker's unless we
paid him extra. Who was the fence who gave up his
client list, and who was the clerk who went with Kline
to get it?"

Max snorted. "Typical of him. And he only did it to
annoy you, for that's a matter of public record. The
fence was a Master Pritchart, and the clerk was an old
friend of yours."

"My friend?" Michael looked baffled.

"A small irony." Max smiled. "The clerk was Yorick Thrope."

"Yorick Thrope!" Michael exclaimed for the fourth time. Or possibly the fifth.

The icy breeze tugged my cloak. The glowing moss lamps only made the shadows around them darker, and the twisting Oldtown streets were full of memories of danger and fear. I'd done a lot of "work" in the Oldtown—in fact, we'd already passed four shops I'd robbed. I'd hated being a burglar.

"It doesn't prove anything," I said, also for the fourth or fifth time. "He couldn't have known he'd replace Max—there are always dozens of clerks in the running for judicar. It doesn't prove—"

"But Thrope knew we were in town before anyone else, which solves your timing problem. And as a law clerk he might well know how to find an arsonist for hire. As to his not knowing he'd be appointed, he was acquainted with a blackmailer! Mayhap Kline pressured someone on the appointment committee. He's in the perfect position to have framed both Max and me! It all fits!"

My steps slowed as I considered it. Right or wrong, giving our enemy a face and a name had done wonders for Michael. He might have been willing to run from some faceless villain, if it would be better for Max and his family, but he wasn't about to run from Yorick Thrope. "You really think he'd kill Ginny Weaver and frame Max, just for an appointment he'd probably get anyway the next time a judicar retired?"

Michael's steps slowed to match mine. "Mayhap he needed the position now, for some reason we don't know about. But you may be right. It seems a paltry reason for murder."

"Most murders," I said grimly, "are committed for reasons that seem paltry to everyone but the killer. We'll keep Thrope in mind. The tavern's here."

It wasn't actually there, but halfway down a narrow side street. There were no streetlamps, and only the light cast by the tavern's small windows marked it.

The place was about half full when Michael and I went in. It seemed to cater to craftsmen and laborers from across the river; some of the patrons still wore the leather or canvas aprons of their trade and smelled of wood, or wool, or printer's ink.

The two men behind the bar broke off an animated conversation when we entered. I wove between the tables and stepped up to them. "Good evening, Sirs. My name is Fisk, and this gentleman is a kni—"

"We know who you are," said the shorter of the two tapsters. He was a plump fellow with dark hair, longer than his rank entitled him to, and intense dark eyes. "And I've no mind to do any favors for the kind of scum that'd help a murdering bastard like *Judicar* Maxwell. Now get out—I have work to do."

Well, that told me which of them was Jobber. The other tapster, a narrow-faced ferret of a man, nodded firm agreement, and I guessed he was the tavern's owner.

"What makes you so sure we want to help him?" I bluffed.

Jobber blinked. "But I heard—"

"You always believe everything you hear? If you give me a bit of your time, I can tell you a thing or two about good old Max that I'll bet you haven't heard."

Jobber's firm expression wavered, and he glanced at his employer. "I'm working—"

"I'll pay twice your night's wages for an hour of your time." I had no qualms about making this offer—it would probably be less than we'd paid Kline that morning.

"No," said the tavern owner. "The evening crowd's coming in. I can't—"

"I'll take Jobber's place while he talks to Fisk," Michael offered. "I've worked in taverns before."

I had long since ceased to be surprised by the skills Michael had picked up in his travels, but the tavern owner gave him a startled glance. "I thought you were supposed to be some sort of crazy knight or something."

Michael smiled grimly. "Errantry involves mastering many skills these days. If my work dissatisfies you, say so, and we'll leave."

And so it came about that Nate Jobber and I sat at a table in back of the room, and Michael, wearing Jobber's apron, took his place by the kegs. He did seem to know what he was doing. I watched him draw three mugs of ale for a group of thirsty candle-makers, judging by the splashes of colored wax on their sleeves. Calling Night was only two nights away. I was surprised they weren't working the clock around. Perhaps most folk had already bought their candles.

"What do you mean, you're not trying to help Maxwell?" Jobber demanded. "Your sister's married to him!"

I'd never said that I wasn't helping Max, but that had been to appease Michael, who was now safely out of earshot. "Yes, but do you know how he came to marry my sister?"

The version I gave him of Max and Anna's courtship would have horrified both of them. In fact, if it came to Annie's ears, she'd probably never speak to me again, for Max emerged as a veritable villain, preying on a poverty-stricken girl.

Watching Jobber's eyes, I could see I'd hit the right note. Those eyes were red rimmed, and on a hunch I held up my hand to summon Michael to our table. Jobber ordered neat gin, and I took the same. I wished that Michael was sufficiently crafty to serve Jobber a double and water mine, but I knew the thought would never even cross his mind.

"And then," I finished my tale, "Max ordered me out of town. He couldn't afford to have someone like me as a brother by marriage, he said. You ever hit a strange town without a copper fract in your pocket? Believe me, I have no reason to want to help Max." I was a little alarmed at how easily the bitterness seeped into my voice.

"But why leave town just because he said to? You'd never been caught. He couldn't just throw you out."

"Well, he didn't hire thugs to beat me up. But the idea of staying, with every deputy in town devoting close attention to my affairs, didn't hold much appeal. A judicar has a lot of power." Again, I'd said the right thing.

"That's straight." Jobber took a stiff drink, and I sipped mine. "Old sanctimonious Max has the law on his side and that's that. No one cares about anything else. No one cares about . . ." He stopped and drank again.

"Ho, server! I've spilled my beer!" The shout was loud enough to draw eyes from all over the room. A broad-shouldered man in a brown wool doublet had indeed spilled his beer, and as Michael snatched up a dry cloth and made for the table, other calls for service erupted.

"Hey, I've spilled mine too. Server!"

"Well, hang me, so've I. Server, over here!"

This sudden outbreak of clumisness was obviously staged, and the calls for service turned, predictably, to complaints about how slow the new help was. It seemed Jobber and the tavern keeper weren't the only ones who'd heard about Michael and me—though this crowd clearly hadn't heard the arson rumor, or their harassment would have been a lot worse. I wondered how Worthington had learned of it, since it didn't seem to be too widespread.

"So, Master Jobber, I understand old Max treated you even worse than he did me."

"It wasn't me," said Jobber confusingly. "He committed a crime against all mankind. If the Gods looked out for man, Horatius Maxwell would never know peace again." He lifted his glass, and I sipped while he drank, my attention sharpening. Had Jobber decided to make up for the Gods' negligence?

"Tell me about it."

As Michael found dry cloths and mopped up the tables, Jobber told me his story. He'd been approached by a group of con men to forge documents and deeds. He'd worked with them before and saw no harm in it. "It was only supposed to be money—not a blood debt. I'd no way to know that fool would kill himself."

"You couldn't know. I'll bet Max never even considered that."

"Actually he did," said Jobber, surprising me. "That was one of the reasons he opted for a lesser penalty. Lesser!" His choked laugh was almost a sob, and I took advantage of the fuss made by someone tripping Michael to pour some gin from my near-full glass into Jobber's.

Michael had fallen to his knees but succeeded in keeping the glasses on his tray upright. I have to admit that as Jobber went on, my attention was divided—a full tray was an invitation to tripping feet, and the strings of his apron didn't stay tied, no matter how tight he knotted them. I thought the tavern keeper's scowl would keep the horseplay to a decent level, though he was probably more concerned for his furniture than his staff, and his customers were enjoying the game. I hoped I'd have time to finish with Jobber before he got rid of Michael to put a stop to it.

Michael was coping well—his expression was open, and merely annoyed.

". . . so the rest of them took their shares and ran, and left me to take the blame. The punishment." Jobber shivered.

"How did the judicars find out about your part in it?"

"Oh, that was Sheriff Potter. I'd put my mark into the company's seal, and he noticed it. He has a good eye, Potter, and he'd seen my paintings."

"You *signed* a document you were forging for a *con?*" It wasn't tactful, but the insanity of it startled me into truthfulness. A very rare occurrence, I might add.

"Of course," said Jobber. "It was my work, and well done, too, even if it wasn't . . . art." His voice dropped almost to a whisper, as if it was the first time he'd said the word.

"I bet Max didn't even—"

A full mug of ale was launched into the air from a table behind us and just missed Michael as he leapt aside. His expression had passed from annoyance to anger, and red mantled his cheekbones as he went for a mop. I was glad to note that some of the patrons laughed good-naturedly at his escape. If part of the crowd was on Michael's side, or at least neutral, it should keep the tricks from getting too nasty before I finished here.

Jobber turned to watch, and I took the opportunity to pour the last of my gin into his glass. Unfortunately, Jobber had a head for drink. His tongue hadn't even begun to trip, and though his eyes were reddened, that could have been from emotion as much as alcohol.

"What were you saying?" he asked.

"What? Oh, ah, I hope they paid for your expertise. Not many can forge a document well."

"They paid enough, but I didn't care about the money. It wasn't for me."

I blinked in astonishment, but he went on without prompting. "The money was for my art. But Maxwell didn't understand. Didn't care. So he took my talent from the world." He held out his hands and flexed his fingers—they worked, but you could see the stiffness. "It'd have been kinder if he'd killed me. I was sorry that man died, but it wasn't worth taking away my talent for. And not just from me, either. Someday the world will discover my paintings and my early work will be remembered—prized! Art is immortal, but all my future paintings have been slain, like—"

"Ho! I've spilled my beer!"

This time a mug had found its target. Michael's apron dripped. He stared down at it, his face alarmingly expressionless.

"You know, this place has really gone downhill," the red-faced loudmouth who'd thrown the beer went on cheerily. "The help can't even keep themselves clean."

Michael's gaze rose slowly. His eyes weren't expressionless now. I had waited too long. I leapt to my feet and started toward him, though I knew I couldn't make it in time. The tavern keeper was about to lose some furniture after all, which didn't trouble me, except that Michael and I would no doubt have to pay for it.

But for any injury Michael sustained there would be no redress, so I was never more grateful to hear the piercing clang of the fire bell.

Everyone in the room jumped. I grabbed Michael's arm and pulled him away from the loudmouth, though even he had been distracted.

The tavern keeper left Jobber to guard his liquor and hurried with the rest of us into the street to look for the fire. It was only six or seven blocks away, and flame-lit smoke guided the crowd that rushed toward it.

The fury had faded from Michael's eyes, though his lips were still pressed tight. I tried to distract him by wondering aloud if we'd get a chance to see the new pumps in action. In fact we did. As we drew near the fire, I saw a stream of water leaping into the air like a huge fountain, waving back and forth to splatter gallons of water against the buildings nearest the one that blazed so merrily.

The fire-team leader was shouting volunteers into order, for bucket lines would still be needed—though that pump was a near miracle. Only eight men worked the long brass bars on either side of it, one side up, the other down, while four more aimed the turret-mounted tube from whence the fountain of water came.

"'Tis like a giant pissing." There was laughter in Michael's voice, but I could see he was as impressed as I. "I wonder if Seven Oaks could afford . . ." His voice trailed off, but for a moment I glimpsed the young noble who'd been trained as an estate steward.

"My office! My paintings! My otter cloak! Save them!" The earsplitting shriek parted the crowd. Yorick Thrope hurtled over to the men who rotated the tube and tried to force the stream toward the burning building.

They resisted, and if two more men hadn't grabbed Thrope's arms and pulled him off, there might have been trouble. But our fire-team leaders are well trained, and hysterical property owners are something they often contended with.

The two husky men kept hold of Thrope even after he stopped struggling. As the business of organizing the town's defense went forward, I noted that Thrope's shouted offers of reward were for the saving of his clothes and knickknacks and not for his legal files. Though if he kept his office on the lower floor and lived above it, those files were already ash. Would the whole ground floor be ablaze that way if the fire had started accidentally? I know nothing of arson, but it seemed unlikely. I was about to say as much to Michael when a full bucket was thrust into my hands.

This time I was assigned to the front of the line. Michael and I were separated by several men, but there would have been little time to chat in any case. Aided by the bucket line, the pump's stream kept the neighboring buildings from burning, but Thrope's office blazed like the bonfires that would be lit in just two nights to call back the waning sun.

The smoke choked me, and the odd gusts of wind eddying around the great blaze carried clouds of stinging sparks. The cold splatters raining from the pump stream felt good on my heated skin.

Soon Thrope's roof began to blaze, and the pumpmen cranked their tube upward to send water streaming over the neighboring roofs. Then the ox team arrived to pull down the burning building. I was surprised to see only two of the great sturdy beasts. I looked behind them for more, but there weren't any, and I suddenly understood the hush that had fallen on the crowd—these oxen were magica. They looked quite ordinary, stamping and snorting at the smoke, though their handler kept them half a block back and his assistant dragged chains from their hitch to the fire. When I was a boy, they'd used a ten-horse team to do this job. Now we all stepped back as two men, clad from head to toe in thick, water-soaked wool, ran forward and fixed chain-linked iron hooks into the timbers around Thrope's front door.

The handler urged the oxen to pull away, the irregular clang of shod hooves almost lost in the fire's roar. The chains tightened and I held my breath. Sometimes the doorframe pulls out of the wall, but if the building is constructed right and the fire has weakened it . . . Surely only two beasts, even magica, couldn't possibly . . .

But they could.

Timber squealed and began to crack. I backed up again, though by now I was well out of range of anything that might fall. The handler shouted and the oxen leaned into their collars, muscles swelling. The stressed chains twisted, glittering in the brilliant light. Then the house tore open, a huge section of the front wall hurtling into the street, splattering burning timber and hot stones. Fire erupted inside the building; then the roof caved in, sending sheets of flame billowing in all directions.

We all cried out, a howl of excitement that sounded puny beside the fire's great voice. Now we could reach it; now we could fight. The stream from the pump shot into the scarlet cavern and vanished in a hiss of steam. Bucket after bucket flowed through my hands, but the smoke was less suffocating now, and the flames didn't sound as greedy.

My throat was raw and my back ached, for this was my second bucket line in two days. Eventually the fire sank low enough for the pumpmen to move closer. They directed the stream over the flaming ruins of the front wall, and Michael and I were among those summoned to pull charred rubble out of the pumpmen's path. The timbers might look black, but they weren't all cool—a lesson I learned painfully the first time my grip fell on a hot ember.

The fire's heat was decreasing. Looking at the growing patches of darkness in the fire's heart, I saw that we were winning. I grinned at Michael, who smiled back, teeth flashing in his grubby face.

It took another two hours of fierce work before the fire was out. I sat down with my back against a neighboring building, its walls still warm from the fire's heat. I didn't know where my cloak was—it had probably become one of the soaking rags that those like Michael, who still had a bit of energy, were using to drench a few remaining embers in the blackened ruin that had once been a home and office. The cold began to reach through my exhaustion. Time to go home.

It was hard to pick Michael out of the blackened wraiths working in the charcoal pit of the inner walls. The Creature Moon was riding high, but the Green Moon had set, and the oil lamps the local householders brought out shone feebly in the reeking darkness. Finally I saw him, seated on a bit of charred stone. His eyes were closed. His face was so dirty I couldn't read his expression, but the slump of his shoulders told the tale.

"Michael, we'd better go. It's—"

"You!" The voice was a vicious rasp. Yorick Thrope shouldered past me, his fine clothes tattered and filthy, his face twisted. This had been his home and place of business. I felt sorry for him . . . for about three seconds.

"You did this!" He stood before Michael, panting with rage, his hands clenching and opening.

Michael rose and stumbled back, bumping into the corner behind him. Seeing that he was trapped, I moved forward, intending to grab Thrope if he tried anything stupid. But Thrope was a law clerk—they fight with words.

"Get Sheriff Potter. I accuse this man of arson. He's unredeemed. I want him hanged."

The tired, dirty men around us simply stood for a moment. Then a rumble of angry comment rose, and I felt a surge of relief I never expected to feel at the sight of the law as Potter pushed through the crowd— I hadn't known he was here.

"Steady on, Master Thrope. What makes you think Sevenson is responsible?"

Mentioning Michael's name was a mistake. The hiss of indrawn breath echoed off the stone, proving that at least some of those present had heard the rumors that Michael was an arsonist.

"I talked to Master Alvern earlier. He saw a man answering this man's exact description, coming out of my office just before the fire started. Alvern knew I was gone and called to him, but the man hurried off."

"Aye, it's true." Another man came forward. He had a round, mild face, and his gold-rimmed spectacles were as grimy as the rest of him. "I was going to tell you, Sheriff, as soon as we finished here. I didn't dream he'd have the nerve to stick around. He acted so suspicious when I called out that I went over to check on the building. The shutters were closed, but I heard flames and saw firelight through the cracks. I tried to get in, but he'd locked the door behind him. His having a key to Master Thrope's place was one of the things that made me suspicious. I'm the one who raised the alarm."

"He's unredeemed," Thrope snarled. "He has no rights. Hang him now, at the scene of his crime, before the whole town goes up in flames."

The sound that came from the crowd then resembled a growl more than any human comment, and several men moved through the ruins toward Michael, though it was clear he couldn't escape.

"Wait!" Potter and I yelled together. But it was the ring of command in the sheriff's voice that made them pause, so I fell silent and let him continue. "No man will be hanged without a hearing, unredeemed or not. We're all tired and in no condition to deal with this rationally. I'll keep Master Sevenson locked up tonight, and we'll settle this in the morning."

"Sheriff, he has an alibi for the time before the fire." I spoke as loudly as my raw throat would allow. "He was working in a tavern several blocks away for an hour before the bell rang, and there are witnesses to swear to it."

"Then you can bring them forward in the morning," said Potter. "I'll hear their stories then, and I'll be the judge of their reliability." He took Michael's arm and waved several deputies forward to escort him through the angry crowd.

"But that's impossible." Master Alvern's dirty spectacles flashed. "I saw him."

"You couldn't have." A blackened scarecrow, the tavern keeper, stepped forward. "Both of 'em were in my tavern for over an hour before the bell sounded, and there's dozens can swear to it. If you sounded the alarm at once, it couldn't be him you saw."

"That's true."

"I was there too—I saw him spilling ale all over the place."

I blessed the bullies who'd made Michael so conspicuous from the bottom of my heart.

Confusion marked Potter's face. He hadn't believed I could actually produce witnesses. "You're all certain of this?"

It was hard to make out individual voices in the babble that followed, but the gist was clear—they were certain.

Potter turned to Alvern, whose mouth opened and

closed like a fish. "But I *saw* him. He was wearing a cloak, with the hood low over his eyes, but he had a scar on his chin, right here." Alvern touched the side of his jaw, where Michael's scar was. That scar was invisible now, under the soot, and Potter's eyes narrowed.

"You didn't see his face, Master Alvern? Just the scar?"

"Well, I suppose. But I saw the scar plainly. There's a lampstand right there."

"Scars can be faked." I tried to say that loudly, too, but my voice cracked and I started to cough.

"So they can," said the sheriff. "It seems you're right, Master Fisk. Frames are in fashion these days. Take your friend home and keep him there."

I put an arm around Michael's shoulders and pulled him away. He was shaking. So was I.

"But he's unredeemed," Thrope yelped.

"True, but I'm not going to hang him for something he couldn't have done. You should go somewhere too, Master Thrope. A friend's home, perhaps? There's nothing more . . ."

Potter's soothing voice faded as Michael and I rounded a corner. Out of sight of the crowd we picked up our pace. We'd have run if we hadn't been so tired.

"That was close." Michael's voice was rough with smoke and fear.

"Well, you were right about one thing—we're making someone nervous. Unfortunately, he's returning the favor. But you may be right about something else. Tomorrow, Noble Sir, we're going to start investigating Yorick Thrope."

CHAPTER 9
Michael

Late-morning sun streamed through the small kitchen windows and lit the work-worn table where Fisk and I broke our fast. And in the clear light of morning, my conviction that Yorick Thrope was guilty had undergone a change.

"No man could fake such distress as Thrope showed last night," I said. "Besides, why would he burn down his own home just to be rid of two amateur investigators who don't know anything? I don't like the man, but this is nonsense."

Without our cloaks, we'd been half frozen by the time we reached Maxwell's house. Heating wash water and the remains of the stew we'd had for dinner took so long, 'twas nearly dawn when Fisk and I reached our beds. Thus 'twas almost time for mid-meal now, but after dining so late, toasted bread, cheese, and a few wrinkled, still-sweet apples suited me well. And the urgency of the conversation banished my persistent desire to yawn.

"Maybe he has a motive we don't know about. Maybe there was something incriminating in his office that he wanted to destroy."

"Even assuming he kept some incriminating paper in the first place, why not just burn it in the fireplace? Thrope is the one person who could destroy his own documents without having to burn the whole building."

"Hmm." Fisk wielded the toasting fork, and the bread at its tip was turning evenly golden on both sides. 'Tis a rare talent, and I was somewhat envious, though 'tis the only culinary skill he possesses. "Maybe he had something that someone else expected him to keep, and he needed an excuse for it to be destroyed."

I snorted. "Even if that was true, 'twould be far cheaper to fake a burglary. 'Tis ridiculous on the face of it."

"If it wasn't Thrope, how did the arsonist get the key?"

"How should I know? Mayhap he stole it and had a copy made. Mayhap he bribed a locksmith. Mayhap he is a locksmith."

"But who'd want to hurt Thrope, Max, and you? None of Max's enemies had anything against Thrope, and the man Alvern saw by that so-convenient lampstand had faked your scar, which proves they meant you to take the blame."

It did, and my guts clenched to think how nearly they'd succeeded. When I awakened this morning in Maxwell's comfortable guest bed, my first thought was that it wasn't a cell. And it could have turned out worse than that.

"You're assuming that the person who burned Thrope's home is also Maxwell's enemy," I said. "He might simply have wanted to hurt Thrope, and an unredeemed man, already suspected of arson, made a convenient scapegoat."

My being unredeemed had already attracted Maxwell's enemies—why not Thrope's, too?

"I don't buy it," said Fisk stubbornly. "It's too coincidental if everyone in Ruesport suddenly decides to frame you for arson. It all has to be connected. Somehow."

"But we've no way of knowing who might wish to harm Thrope, or why," I said. "He's a judicar now. Mayhap he ruled against the Furniture Makers' Guild, and someone was hurt thereby. Mayhap he just kicked someone's dog. Motive is the least of it."

A spark of mischief lit Fisk's eyes. "Well, in that case, Judith did it."

"Fisk!"

"But she's connected to the Furniture Makers' Guild—the former husband-to-be, remember? She has access to Max's ledgers. And she knows what we've been doing for the last few days, which solves the timing problem. It all fits."

"Which shows how absurd your reasoning is. Besides, she doesn't have any connection with either an arsonist or a forger, and we know this man does."

"I wouldn't put it past her." Fisk pulled the hot bread from his fork and laid a slice of cheese on it, and his expression grew serious once more. "Max was a judicar, Thrope is one now. Maybe they ruled against the same person at some point."

"Thrope's been a judicar for less than a year," I pointed out.

"Still, the law is a connection between them," said Fisk. "And as a law clerk Thrope probably met lots of arsonists and forgers. Or someone who'd know them. He could have given his key to the arsonist, and then gone out to establish his own alibi. He had a motive to destroy Max. And using you to keep Max down would probably bring him endless joy."

"Not a very good motive." I took up the toasting

fork, though my bread tends to end up burned in some places and cold in others.

"Either way, Thrope's connected," said Fisk stubbornly.

"How? You keep saying our enemy knows what we do—Thrope has no way of knowing that. If our enemy knows so much of our activities, it's surprising he couldn't manage to set a fire at a time when I've no alibi."

"Now that's where you're wrong. Think about it. When the first fire was set, he knew that I was out among witnesses and you were home in bed. He framed you *because* you didn't have an alibi."

"And also because I was unredeemed, and wouldn't have a hearing where the truth might come to light." Fisk could dance around the fact if he willed, but it should be acknowledged.

"Anyway," Fisk went on, "Annie foiled that plan, so for the second fire he picked a night when he knew we were both out. He was trusting to luck that we wouldn't be talking to anyone just before the bell sounded, but we were the ones who got lucky. No, he knows what we're doing, and I'll be hanged if I understand how. Unless it *is* Judith."

I was too discouraged to respond to jests. "I wonder what he'll try next."

"No way to know. Though I think we'll follow Sheriff Potter's orders and keep you home from now on."

"I think not."

"Michael—"

"'Twill not stop our enemy, and your family are less convincing witnesses than strangers. Why should I stay in Ruesport if I can't do anything to help?"

I held Fisk's eyes for a long moment, and he finally sighed. "I'm your squire, not your keeper. Though Potter probably will kick you out of town if there's any more trouble, and that won't do any of us any good."

"Being outside the law, I see no reason to obey a sheriff's orders."

I wondered why the sheriff hadn't kicked me out already, but as long as I might still do some good here, I had to try.

Fisk shrugged. "Well, if you're determined to do something stupid, you can go back to Clogger's brother and Lenna Skinner and see if you can find a connection between them and Thrope. There's got to be a motive around here somewhere. But wear a cloak and keep your hood pulled up—it's cold enough that no one will think twice about it. The way rumor flies, I'll bet half the town has convicted you for every fire set in the last thirty years."

"But I'm only eighteen."

"Doesn't matter. Not to most people."

I contemplated my half-burnt bread gloomily. "What will you be doing?"

"I," said Fisk, "am going to look up some old friends and see if they know anything about Master Thrope beyond the obvious. A stronger connection between him and Kline would be interesting."

I had no better ideas. "I still don't think Thrope burned down his own home. But mayhap there is someone who wants to hurt him, as well as Master Maxwell."

"Maybe it's someone who just hates the law," said Fisk. "Forget about Judith, it's probably us."

I couldn't help but smile. "Well, don't look to me—I'd have burned Sheriff Potter's house, given the choice."

We argued about the sheriff's character as we donned our doublets, then borrowed cloaks from Maxwell's closet under Trimmer's dour guidance. Master Maxwell had gone to the Oldtown on business, despite his promise to Worthington. It seemed no one cared to obey orders today.

I was especially pleased with my disobedience when I stepped out into the bright, frosty day. Fisk, on the other hand, drew his cloak closer.

"Pull your hood up, Noble Sir, and don't speak to anyone. The whole town will have heard about your scar, and there's no reason to take chances."

"I have a clean handkerchief, too," I told him. "Stop fussing. I can hardly discover a connection between Ren Clogger or Ginny Weaver and Thrope without talking to people. I'll also try to find out if anyone has a particular grudge against judicars, or the law in general."

"They probably all hate the law," said Fisk, finally setting off toward the gate. Several people walked down the street beyond the gate, and they paid no heed to Fisk's and my emergence from Max's house, which cheered me further. "It'd be finding someone who doesn't that would be hard."

"That's too cynical," I said. "Most folk respect the law, and those who enforce it."

"Most people don't . . . What's the difference between a law clerk and a bandit?"

Most folk weren't addicted to those stupid jokes. "I don't know," I said patiently. "What?"

"I can't think of any difference either," said Fisk. "That's why I asked you."

We parted with laughter, though my merriment soon died. As I walked, I tried to think of any way to discover if Mistress Weaver or Master Clogger had some connection to Thrope other than by asking their kin straight out. After a time, I decided to ask their kin straight out. Even the Skinners, who'd kept the bribe, had no reason to lie about anything else, and Clogger's brother had no reason to lie about anything at all.

I kept my hood up and found my way to Clogger's wheelwright shop with only two wrong turnings. I was prepared to go around to the yard to find him, but the door opened moments after my knock.

"Good morning. What can I . . . You!"

"I've a few more questions, Master Clogger, if you can spare a moment."

He cast a hunted look up and down the street, but there was no one in sight. "I told you all I know. I don't—"

"'Tis for your brother. Surely you want his name cleared, even if he's not here to know about it."

"I don't . . . Ah, hang it." He grabbed my arm and pulled me into the shop's front room, shutting the door behind us. The shop seemed dim after the sunlight, but it smelled of fresh-cut wood and oil, and the wheels leaning against the walls were bright and new.

"They say you're unredeemed, Master Sevenson. They say you're a fire setter."

My heart pounded, but I lifted my head and said, "Then they speak half the truth, for I am unredeemed. But I'm no fire setter, and my only business in this town is to help my friend clear Master Maxwell."

"And that'll clear Ren?"

"As I don't yet know the truth, I can't promise that; but if Maxwell is innocent, surely your brother is too."

"But if that's true, where did Ren get the money?"

"That's one of the things we hope to find out."

He fell silent a moment, then nodded slowly. "My brother wasn't a killer. What else do you want to know?"

"Did your brother have any association with a law clerk named Yorick Thrope?"

Clogger's brows lifted. "The man whose house burned last night? None that I know of."

"Think on it a moment," I urged. "He might have mentioned the name quite casually."

He frowned in thought. "Thrope . . . He's the hanging judicar, isn't he?"

"Yes." My heart beat quicker.

"Ren never mentioned him. Not that I remember, anyway."

"Do you know who handled your brother's legal affairs?"

"I don't think he had any legal affairs, but if he did it'd probably be one of the tanners' clerks. When Ren and I were on speaking terms, we had other things to talk about."

His face was hard, but regret roughened his voice. I

asked for the name and direction of some of Ren Clogger's friends. He might have told others things he kept from the brother who disapproved of him.

I would have forgotten to pull up my hood, but before he let me out, Clogger stepped into the street and looked both ways to be sure no one would see the unredeemed arsonist leaving his premises.

My heart was heavy as I walked toward the Skinners' tannery. Would it ever be thus, with respectable folk unwilling even to be seen with me? I feared it might, and the memory of Seven Oaks came wistfully to mind. Folk there knew my circumstances and I'd be accepted, after a time at least. As each year passed, 'twould grow easier and more comfortable. And more tedious, and more suffocating, and the only change would be the endless cycle of the seasons, and the world and life would pass me by. No thank you, Father.

It took almost an hour to reach Mistress Skinner's home, at the outskirts of Yareside, but I found it with so little difficulty that I began to fear Fisk would succeed in making me a townsman. Like Clogger, Mistress Skinner answered my knock, and like Clogger she recognized me instantly—but there the similarity ended.

"Go away." The door started to close and I thrust

out my foot to block it, an act of rudeness I have ever despised.

"I want only a minute of your time, Mistress Lenna. And if we're lucky, my friend and I, 'twill help clear your mother's good name. For I don't believe she'd lie men to their death, and I think you know that too."

She froze, staring, and I pulled my foot back, giving her the choice. She bore no flour smudges today, but the fine lines around her eyes cut more deeply than they had before.

"My husband told me not to let you in." She cast a harried look at the neighbors' windows as she spoke, and my stomach clenched at the growing familiarity of it.

"Then I'll stand here and we'll speak as we are now. Don't worry, I'll keep my hood up," I added bitterly. I could hardly blame her, for most folk would feel the same—but it still hurt.

Irony glittered in her eyes. "If you think that'll make a difference, you don't know my neighbors." But it seemed she had some courage, for she folded her arms and leaned against the doorframe. "You know my mother was ill—dying—when she heard that girl scream for help?"

"Yes, I knew that." I'd no notion where she wished to go with this, but I was willing to let her steer the conversation as she would. Indeed, some stirring in the corners of my mind, where my Gifts lurk, told me this was more important than the question I'd come to ask.

"She couldn't walk by then. Too much pain in her joints. Den and I had taken the children over to his brother's house that night, so she was alone. She said she'd be fine, and we left her medicine right beside the bed. She should have been all right."

"I'm sure you did well by her." But Lenna waved this aside; 'twas not reassurance she sought.

"Ma told me she yelled out the window for them to stop, that they'd been seen. But when no one came after them, they realized she was alone. Thank goodness the house was locked! She tried to go for help, Master Sevenson. She dragged herself out of her bed, and down the hall, and down the stairs. She almost made it to the front door before she passed out. We found her there when we came home, Den and me, so cold I thought I'd never get her warm again. But all she cared about was that girl. That she hadn't been able to save her."

Lenna came by her courage honestly.

"'Tis hard to believe, is it not, that a woman so brave would lie about who committed that crime."

"Very hard to believe."

"Do you think she took her own life?"

For the first time indecision showed on her face. "She was in a lot of pain. And she knew her illness was costing us. I don't know about that. But I do know . . ."

She looked past me and her expression changed. "You have to go now."

But the door didn't close. I looked over my shoulder. Half a dozen folk, both men and women, stood by a neighbor's doorstep, watching us.

"Just one thing, mistress. Did your mother have any connection to a man named Yorick Thrope?"

She blinked in surprise. "Not that I know of."

"You're certain of that?"

"Positive. I heard his name for the first time this morning, and it struck me as an odd one. . . . I'd have remembered hearing it before."

I'd no need to ask in what context she had heard it. "Then who handled your mother's legal—"

A snowball exploded above the door, making both of us jump. The crowd had grown to eight and moved closer. One lad, in his early teens, was reaching down to a patch of dirty snow.

When I turned back, the door was closed. 'Twas obviously time to move on, and I did, but not running—nothing better encourages a predator to the chase.

I would have preferred to make my way to the open fields beyond the town, for I had no doubt of my ability to outrun these city folk on rough ground. Unfortunately they stood between me and the countryside, so I walked townward, hearing the soft thud of their footsteps and sometimes a muffled comment or giggle.

They'd followed me for over a block when the second snowball shattered over the road at my feet. Suddenly the absurdity of the whole thing struck me—this was a group of respectable craftsmen, and I was fleeing them in broad daylight on a public street.

I turned to face them, pushing back my hood. "Good Sirs, let us—"

It wasn't a snowball that tugged the side of my cloak and rattled on the cobbles. It seemed they weren't good sirs. I spun and took to my heels. As Fisk has explained to me at some length, there are times when running is the right thing to do.

They were less than half a block behind me, and I couldn't get out of their sight no matter how many corners I turned. But I soon settled into my stride, my heartbeat hard and steady, my breathing even.

I increased the distance between us a bit, but I couldn't outdistance the stones that whizzed past me, one going on to crack a shop window. I heard the owner's outraged shouts as I ran past and hoped, briefly, that he could check my pursuers. But their blood was up, and the next stone struck my back quite painfully. Fortunately, loose stones are hard to come by on a city street.

Their shouts outdistanced me as well. A shopkeeper who'd been sweeping her doorstep thrust her broom into my path, but I leapt it with barely a break in stride.

The wheelbarrow full of coal shoved before me was harder to deal with, for 'twas too tall to leap. I rammed the lip of the barrow with my thigh as I darted round it, and staggered.

Each stolen glance over my shoulder revealed a larger crowd. Those eight folk had grown to a good-sized mob, and fear lent speed to my racing feet.

I saw the lad with the bloody butcher's apron and yoked buckets ahead of me but judged him little threat, even when he stepped forward at the mob's shouts. 'Twas not until he hurled the contents of his buckets over the street that I saw the danger, and then it was too late—the chips and shavings of slippery fat turned the rough cobbles into a skating pond and brought me down with a bruising crash.

The pain that shot through my right wrist was the worst of it—bad enough to paralyze me for several precious seconds. I might have crouched there, clutching it and moaning, till they laid hands on me, but the feral roar that rose when they saw me down sent the strength of panic flooding through my limbs. Unfortunately, it made the fat chips no less slippery, and I slithered among them for far too long before I thought to lie down and roll till the street beneath me was clear.

I'd lost all my lead, and they were almost upon me as I clambered to my feet and raced away. They would have seized me if the fat chips hadn't had the same effect on my pursuers that they'd had on me.

I heard the startled shouts and risked a glance, just in time to see the main body of the mob fall over the leaders, who'd already gone down on the slippery stones. By the time they got clear of the mess I'd gained over a block, and many, either injured or discouraged, had fallen out of the chase. But the men who ran behind me now were the most deter-mined. They'd gained in ferocity what they'd lost in numbers.

And I was tiring. My wrist ached even through my fear and I'd bruised one knee. The cold air chilled my lungs with each tearing breath—if I got a stitch in my side, I'd be done for.

I took to darting down the side streets, hoping I

could get out of their sight long enough to find some hideout, some shelter.

The next few blocks afforded naught but stone walls and stonier stares. Then I turned a corner, for the moment beyond their sight. A narrow alley opened on my right. I waltzed around a scrawny boy with steel-rimmed spectacles whose startled face looked strangely familiar and sped down the alley. I'd run halfway down that accursed lane before I saw it was a dead end, mayhap in more senses than one.

I could hear the voices of the mob. If I went back, I'd likely run out into the midst of them. The only objects big enough to hide a man were the rain bar-rels, full of icy water. I leapt behind one and crouched against the rough wall, my pulse beating so loudly I barely heard the young voice shout, "That way! He went that way!"

I froze, like a rabbit with a wolf's eyes upon it, but the mob boiled past the alley without even glancing aside. My mouth fell open. I was still crouched there when the scrawny lad came into view and waved one hand in a gesture I read as *All clear, come out.*

'Twas the apprentice I'd saved from Thrope's be-ribboned cane.

I came painfully to my feet, pulling my hood well over my face and my cloak tight around me. By the time I reached the alley's entrance the lad had gone, walking down the street ahead of me, not looking back. I hoped he knew my gratitude went with him. Fisk once said that a good deed carries a stiffer sentence than most crimes; I wondered what he'd make of this.

There was no sign of the mob, but I set off in the direction opposite the one they'd taken and walked several blocks before doubling back toward Highbridge.

The journey back to the Maxwells' was uneventful, except for a few encounters with dogs, who found the scent of fat that clung to my cloak and clothes wonderfully intriguing. Animal handling is one of my more reliable Gifts, and after allowing them to see for themselves that I'd no bones concealed in my pockets, I persuaded them to go their way.

My reek was not so obvious to humans, and my face was unmarked, but Mistress Judith must have shared Fisk's ability to read folk. When I stepped into the Maxwells' front hall, her first words were "What happened to you?"

Even before I explained how I'd fallen, Mistress Judith led me to a chair in the dining room, calling for Max and Anna and insisting I sit down. Mistress Lissy brought me a cup of tea. I kept the story as short as I could, for I'd no wish to distress them, and my wrist and bruises ached. But when I finished, Anna's eyes were sparkling with indignation.

"What a wicked thing. I hope those brutal folk never have another sound night's sleep. Could you identify them for Sheriff Potter?"

"No," I said. "I was running too hard to attend to their faces, and even if I could, 'twould serve no purpose. I'm unredeemed." I had never seen more clearly what that meant. For a moment, more than my bruises ached.

"But that's . . . that's . . ."

"He's right, Anna." Max sounded tired. "There's nothing Rob can do. A mob is a terrible thing. I suppose it can happen in any town, but it's worrisome to see one here."

"But—"

"But whatever happens, Master Sevenson's wrist needs some arnica," Mistress Judith interrupted. "Go up to your room, Sir, and we'll come up shortly."

I thanked her and managed not to wince as I stood, or limp too much as I walked away.

The first to enter my room were Trimmer and Maxwell, who carried a bathtub between them. They were followed by the women of the household with buckets of hot water. They made several trips, paying no heed to my protests, then left me alone with a tub of warm water and stinging eyes. It felt good to be cared for.

'Twas painful to fold my bruised knees to fit in the tub, but as my muscles warmed and relaxed, I began to feel better. I'd left the tub and started to dress when Fisk rapped on the door, then entered before I could say yea or nay. He carried a roll of bandages and a bottle of arnica. My bizarrely enhanced sensing Gift showed me 'twas not magica, which would be far too expensive for this impoverished household, but its coolness was welcome on my sprained wrist.

Fisk wrapped the bandages tight, as I told my tale yet again and watched his frown deepen. But the first thing he said was "That'll teach you to keep your hood up. Or at least it should."

"You told me so, yes, I know." The hands on my wrist were gentle. "Actually, I did. When I spoke with Mistress Skinner, my hood was up the whole time." How had that mob known who I was?

Fisk and I gazed at each other in baffled frustration, and 'twas he who broke the silence. "This is ridiculous. The only ones who knew where you were

going today were you and I. And we didn't tell anyone. At least I—"

"Nor did I. I told you, I spoke to no one."

"Except Clogger. Could he be working for our mysterious villain?"

I could see Fisk didn't believe that, and besides . . .
"I didn't tell him where I planned to go next, either.
Could someone be watching the house?"

"Maybe. Yes. I've cased houses myself—most people
are amazingly blind to things like that. But watching
the house wouldn't tell anyone where you were going.
Even if they followed you, they still wouldn't have had
time to prime the mob."

"Are you sure the mob needed priming?" I asked
wearily. "An unredeemed man is—"

"Outside the law, yes, I know," said Fisk impatiently.
"But they wouldn't go to such effort to kill you just for
being unredeemed. And I asked around: Most of the
people who'd heard that you were accused of arson
last night had also heard that you had witnesses who
swear to your whereabouts. They also think the witnesses were probably paid off, but still . . . No.
Someone followed you and then stirred up that mob.
I just don't understand how they did it in such a
short time. It would take at least an hour to find that

many homicidal idiots, surely?"

The idea that someone might follow me all day without my noticing was unpleasant; but I had no more sensible solution to offer, and the baffled silence fell once more. This time I broke it. "Well, I've learned one thing: There are more reasons to follow a sheriff's advice than the desire to be law-abiding."

Fisk grinned. "I thought you didn't like Potter."

"I don't, but I have to admit he was right in this instance. Fisk, I should leave this house."

I still wanted to help the Maxwells, but after today there was no way to deny the danger my presence might cause them.

"And put up at an inn, handy for mobs, assassins, and framers?" said Fisk. "What a wonderful idea! Why didn't I think of it?" He gathered up the remaining bandages.

"Your sisters are here. And the children."

"So am I, but I see you're not worrying about that."

"Fisk, think—"

"No. We'll leave together, when we've finished here and not before. And my sisters will say the same. We'd better go down—it's dinnertime."

'Twas a quiet meal, or it would have been except for Mistress Becca, who'd decided she wanted her own horse "since no one *ever* takes me riding."

Mrs. Trimmer poked her head out of the kitchen door at that. "Someone better take her," she told us. "Yesterday she sneaked into that gray monster's stall before I caught her. If you're not going to throw that gallows bait out, Master Max, you might as well put 'em to use."

The time had obviously come, and I promised to take Becca and Thomas for a ride in the orchard tomorrow. Max and Anna agreed, and Becca left the table with victory lighting her face. The words "Remember, you *promised*" drifted down the stairs, and we all smiled.

True to form Sheriff Potter arrived at the end of the meal, with Trimmer's announcement preceding him by mere seconds.

I'd expected some repercussion from the day's events, so I decided to strike first. "Good evening, Sheriff. Have you come to arrest me for almost getting torn apart by your peaceful, law-abiding citizens? Or are you looking for the real guilty party for once?"

Fisk's jaw dropped. I suppose I sounded more acerbic than usual, but I was tired of being abused.

Sheriff Potter only smiled, curse him. "Don't be so

twitchy, Master Sevenson. I might think you have something to hide. I came tonight in response to a householder's request."

Max looked startled. "But I didn't—"

"I sent for him," said Anna. "I wanted to report the assault Master Sevenson suffered today and find out what he's going to do about it."

"As it happens, I've already heard about it. In fact, half Yareside came to my office to complain about a mob disturbing the peace. I did warn you," he added to me.

His voice was genial, but the newly familiar chill of fear silenced me. Disturbing the peace is a legitimate charge. 'Twould hardly apply to this case under normal circumstances, but my circumstances weren't normal.

"So what are you going to do about it?" Anna demanded.

"Nothing," said Potter mildly. He pulled out a chair and sat, but made no move to take off his cloak.

"What? A bunch of thugs chases a man through half Yareside, throwing stones, and you're going to do *nothing*? Sheriff?" The edge in Anna's voice on that final word could have sliced bacon.

Potter's lips compressed briefly, but his voice was

mild. "He's unredeemed, Anna. I have no writ to inter-
fere with anyone on his behalf. You know that. And if
you don't, Max certainly does."

"Yes, but I know you, too, Rob Potter. I can't believe
there's nothing you can do."

"Oh, I could do something. I could lock Master
Sevenson up and throw away the key. It's a tempting
thought."

"Are you going to succumb to temptation, Sheriff?"
My voice was steadier than I'd expected. I had been
prepared to be asked to leave town. But with so many
who wished me ill abroad, the thought of being
penned in a cage appalled me.

Potter tipped his chair back. "It'd please Yorick
Thrope. He wants you restrained 'for the good of
Ruesport and all its citizens.' He says you probably
hired someone to set the last fire, while you estab-
lished an alibi to take suspicion off yourself. But then,
he says, you couldn't resist showing up to watch it
burn. His theory is that you're one of those who can't
help setting fires; that that's what those circles on your
wrists are for, to warn folk about you even if you did
pay enough of your debt to escape the rope. It's a
pretty good theory. I work for the judicary, you know.
Yorick Thrope is one of my bosses."

"You have our sincere condolences," said Fisk. "What are you going to do?"

"Restrain Master Sevenson, of course. Master Sevenson, I forbid you to leave town without reporting to my office. There. Consider yourself restrained." He rose and nodded. "Good night, all."

"But what about—"

He shook his head and Anna broke off, flushing with frustrated outrage. He smiled again and left. A man could come to hate that smile.

"Well," said Mistress Judith as the door closed behind Potter. "He dislikes being ordered about by Thrope, doesn't he? What is the man about?"

"He's fishing," said Fisk. "He figures if Michael and I stir up enough mud, the fish he wants will be forced to the surface."

Despite my dismay, my lips twitched, and I added fishing to the list of things I must someday teach Fisk. At the first sign of trouble fish go to the bottom and wait till the danger passes. I should probably do the same. And yet . . . Maxwell's enemy was more foolish than the fish, for Fisk's and my floundering *had* made him take action. On the other hand, none of those actions had revealed him. If he was so aware of our movements, surely he also knew how little we'd discovered. So why was he trying to be rid of us? Could he have another motive for setting those fires?

After we'd gone upstairs to seek our beds, I decided to share my speculations with Fisk. He might know little of fishing, but he knew far more about criminals and their motives than I. I'd already put on my nightshirt, so I pulled my cloak over it and put on my slippers to pad down the hall to Fisk's room. I doubted he'd be asleep so soon, and when I reached his door, I saw lamplight shining beneath it and knocked.

Fisk called for me to enter. He too had put on his nightshirt, but he sat on his bed, leaning against the headboard with a pillow behind him and his knees pulled up.

I sat at the bed's foot, imitating his posture, and considered his thoughtful scowl. "You think I should leave the house too, don't you?"

The scowl deepened and I saw I'd guessed right. "In truth, I can think of a couple of advantages that might outweigh the drawbacks. And it's *we*, not *I*, if you please—I'll be hanged if I'll let you skin out and leave me to cope with this mess alone. If we go to an inn, whatever means he's using to find out what we're doing might not be available to him. And as you pointed out, strangers make better witnesses than family. The downside is that we'd be more vulnerable in a public inn. And finally, this man is Max's enemy, not ours. I'm not sure I want to leave him alone with four women, two children, and an old man. Especially on Calling Night."

I hadn't thought of that, but now I pictured streets athrong with revelers, some masked, some drunk, and all carrying torches. Not that that mattered; with torches mounted on every wall and post, there'd be no shortage of flame. And our enemy had no scruples about using fire, whoever he was. "But this is such a quiet neighborhood."

"Yes, and Max's house is at the very end of this quiet street and backs onto an orchard. Unless one of the neighbors opens their house, we might as well be alo—"

The sharp rap wasn't overly loud, but we both froze, listening.

"Downstairs?" I asked softly.

Rap! Wood on wood or stone on wood, but so muffled by walls and distance, I couldn't be sure.

"Downstairs," Fisk replied, and seized the lamp.

Mistress Judith was already in the hall when we

opened the door, and the Maxwells emerged from their room as we passed. Fisk's lamp was the only source of light, so we trailed after him, whispering speculations. The women wore nightcaps, and their nightgowns covered more of them than the dresses they wore during the day, but I was the only one wearing something warmer than a nightshirt, and I was the only one not barefoot.

We were halfway down the stairs when the crash of shattering glass broke the stillness. Fisk began to run, with me after him. We crammed ourselves through Max's study door in time to hear the sound of racing feet on the courtyard path, and the slam of the front gate.

"Quick!" Mistress Judith spun to Fisk. "Go after them!"

Fisk cast her an astonished glance. "Are you out of your mind?"

"You are the youngest, fittest man in the house. You might be able to catch them."

"That's what I'm afraid of." Fisk set the lamp on Maxwell's desk and picked his way carefully among the shards of glass to lift a chunk of broken brick that lay under a chair. "Three tries just to hit a window. I'd say that makes them two thirds drunk, but it might be more. Three quarters?"

Mistress Judith snorted. "Three quarters drunk, they couldn't have run like that. Half to two thirds."

Fisk laughed, but there was a note in it I disliked.

"Stop it, Nonny." Anna curled against her husband's side, her face pinched with anger and fear. "We'll have the windowpane replaced tomorrow."

"With what? Glass is expensive. You and Max don't even have enough to pay the door tax."

"True." Max spoke gently, but Fisk flushed and bit his lip. "I'm afraid it will come off the price of the house when we sell. In the end, it makes little difference."

A silence fell as we all struggled with raw nerves, and I was the one who broke it. "I'm leaving tomorrow."

Fisk hesitated a minute, then nodded. "That might be best. We'll get a room in the Oldtown—it'll be cheaper."

"But Nonny . . ." Anna bit her lip, concern for her children warring with concern for her brother. Mistress Judith simply watched, through thought-narrowed eyes.

"No," said Max.

"What?" said Fisk.

"I said no." The ghost of a smile touched his prim mouth. "I might throw you out myself, but I'll not let anyone be driven from my house. This happened before"—he gestured to the shattered window—"when I was first disrobed. I didn't yield to intimidation then and I won't now. Come back to bed, Anna. We can patch the window in the morning."

And he departed with his wife, looking amazingly dignified for a barefooted man in his nightshirt.

"The judicar has spoken." Mistress Judith sounded amused, but I saw she'd started to shiver and laid my cloak over her shoulders. The draft from the shattered window was cold. The glance she gave me in return was more ironic than grateful, but she pulled the cloak tight. "Should you go, Fisk?"

"I don't know. What do you think?"

"Hmm. Good and bad each way. I'll feel better when Calling Night's past."

"No lie. Judith, what will happen? Financially?"

"Max will sell the house, pay off his debts—there aren't many—and we'll go somewhere else and start over. Though Anna's right—Max would have more heart for it if . . ."

"If he was sure those men were guilty. Don't worry, Judith—that's the one thing I'm certain of."

"Certainty," said Mistress Judith, with the air of someone quoting an authority, "is all very well. But can you prove it?"

Her smile held an edge I didn't understand. She handed me my cloak and departed, leaving me wondering what she'd said to strike Fisk white and mute with anger.

CHAPTER 10
Fisk

Next morning we had to tell Lissy what had happened, for she slept on the top floor and had heard nothing. The issue of whether or not Michael and I should move to the inn was still undecided. Max's firm no was pitted against Michael's firm yes, with my sisters and I uncertain. I thought Michael would win; Max couldn't keep him by force and I've never seen anyone who could outstubborn Michael. Though if Judith quoted any more of Father's maxims to me, *I'd* be the one leaving.

We squabbled over the matter through breakfast. Then Michael went to give Becca and Thomas their horseback ride, and I went out to do something stupid. I had to wake Ham up, since tavern keepers have late hours, but I finally talked him out of a list of the town's forgers. He refused to name any arsonists, as taverns are susceptible to fire.

The day might be the shortest of the year, but the weather was cool and clear, promising a perfect holiday night. Folk twined red and gold ribbons around the garlands that decorated their homes. The scent of cooking came from only about one house in five, but no one went hungry on Calling Night, when the rivers burned and the whole world blazed, calling the sun back from its annual decline. The tradition of burning lights on Calling Night was older than the realm itself, and modern astronomical theories about planetary rotation didn't affect it.

I managed to find three of the men Ham had named. To no one's surprise they denied being forgers and were quite shocked that Ham would play such a wicked prank on me. That out of the way they were willing to talk, for in giving me their names, Ham had also vouched for me, and most of the Irony's patrons accepted his judgment. As far as I could tell, they all disliked Thrope—again no surprise—though none seemed to have any close connection with him. Their feelings about Max were divided. They'd respected him before he was disrobed, though none entertained a liking for any judicar, but if those lads he hanged really were innocent . . .

I went home for mid-meal no wiser than I'd been

that morning. If one of those three had forged the ledger used to frame Max, they'd never reveal it to their victim's investigator, which was why the whole idea was stupid. Unfortunately, I didn't have a better one. The knowledge that I might fail had been growing these last few days, and I'd been trying to ignore it. I didn't care much about Max, though I'd come to like him better than I thought I could, but I hated to disappoint Annie.

I noticed the air of tension the moment I entered the house, and deciding to forgive Judith, I pulled her aside to find out what had happened. It seemed that several householders had come to express their "concern" over what might occur in their respectable neighborhood with an unredeemed man living here. Michael was in the orchard and Max dealt with them, but . . . "He was upset, Fisk. These men weren't drunken rabble, and Max cares about his reputation. What's left of it."

I snorted. "Tell me about it." But in truth, trouble from the neighbors was the last thing we needed.

We sat to eat mid-meal in the warmth of the kitchen. The only reason Michael wasn't instantly aware that a secret was being kept from him was that Becca monopolized the conversation. She hadn't fallen off once, or Thomas either, so it didn't matter that Master

Michael's wrist was all sore. *And* her legs didn't hurt in the least, so he was wrong and she *could* have another ride tomorrow.

"That's because your muscles haven't had time to stiffen." Michael had to swallow a mouthful of leftover pork sandwich in order to speak. "'Tis when the morning comes that we shall see."

"Phooey," said Becca. "You said Thomas wouldn't hurt, and he's younger than me."

"Master Thomas had the good sense to stop when I recommended it."

"Yes, but *I'm* older, so I can ride longer."

"Alas, Mistress Rebecca, I fear you'll find—"

"Master Maxwell." For the first time since I'd met him, Trimmer sounded less than gloomy, though excited would be too strong a word. "Master Lewis Sawyer, councilman for the Ropers' Guild, has called. I escorted him to your study. Perhaps—"

"Lewis? What in the world?" Max rose hastily, abandoning his sandwich. "We should ask him to dine."

"Not in the kitchen!" Anna leapt to her feet. "Stall him for five minutes, then bring him to the dining room. We can pretend we're just ready to start."

Max nodded and left so quickly that Lissy had to run after him to pull his napkin out of his belt.

Mrs. Trimmer picked up the children's plates and

took Becca and Thomas to the nursery. Judith slapped together new sandwiches, and uneaten soup was poured back into the kettle. Anna, Michael, and I headed to the dining room and whisked dishes onto the table, while Lissy forked pickled beets into a serving bowl and Trimmer carried food to the table.

Then we heard the study door open. Anna stuffed her apron into an empty vase and pasted a gracious smile on her face as Trimmer dove for the kitchen in a most undignified manner. The dining room looked perfect when Max led Councilman Sawyer in, and Lissy and Judith made their calm and tidy entrances, just as if we were sitting down for the first time. I never cared for burglary, but I love a good con. I smiled at Max's introduction and shook Councilman Sawyer's hand.

The councilman was broadly built, and someone should have told him that men with high complexions shouldn't wear red. But since the buttons on his dou-blet appeared to be made of solid gold, I doubt that anyone told him anything he didn't want to hear.

If he was disturbed to meet Michael, he didn't show it, and he spoke civilly with everyone through-out the meal. He said he'd been glad to hear about the investigation to exonerate Max and asked how it was going. I told him we had several promising leads and then reached under the table to pinch Michael's knee. A pinch is far less obvious than a kick in the shins, but it's possible only when your victim is sitting beside you.

Councilman Sawyer ignored Michael's startled glance and said he was glad of it. He went on to re-iterate the ropers' offer to employ Max as their charities clerk, if he could clear his name.

Max thanked him, though as Sawyer moved the conversation smoothly on, his expression grew more and more puzzled. The councilman lingered for tea after the meal and then departed, leaving us gazing at each other in bafflement.

"Max, what did he want?" Anna demanded.

"I have no idea."

"But earlier, in the study . . ."

"He said nothing. Well, he offered me a loan, but that's been a standing offer for some time and I'd rather borrow from Ben. He repeated his personal belief in my innocence, and his offer to employ me if I could clear my name and, ah . . ." His eyes slid away from Michael and me. ". . . put my household in order. He didn't—"

"I bet I know!" Judith exclaimed. "But I'll have to see his horse to prove it."

She threw down her napkin and raced up the stairs

in a way that brought our childhood forcibly to mind. Anna, Lissy, and I chased after her, and it seemed Max and Michael had once been children, too, since they were hot on our heels.

We fetched up at the window in the sewing room, which had the best view of the street.

"Yes!" Judith's voice was a hiss of satisfaction.

Councilman Sawyer's gold-buttoned doublet was too rich for an afternoon call, but his horse put him into the shade. It was draped in old-fashioned barding, with looping ropes of gold thread embracing the ropers' crest. I'd seen it before, during the parade of guilds that takes place in Birthingtime, but never outside of a parade.

" 'Tis very, uh, impressive," said Michael. "But I still don't understand."

"That," Judith told him, "is the ceremonial tack of the ropers' councilman. And I'll bet he tethered his horse in the street, so it's been standing in front of our house for over an hour. He's just made it plain that Max has the full support of the Ropers' Guild without ever saying a word. *That* for the neighbors!"

Max blinked rapidly. "I didn't know . . . I didn't . . ."

Anna touched his arm. "They're only returning the loyalty you've always given them. Just as you'd have volunteered to serve on their charity boards, they're—"

"Now what?" Judith demanded.

Ben Worthington was riding down the street. He turned in the saddle to stare after Councilman Sawyer's horse.

"Does this mean we have to have mid-meal again?" Anna sounded just a nudge from hysterical giggles.

"Surely not," said Max. "He must have eaten by this time. I wonder what he wants."

Happily, Worthington had already dined, so Anna offered him tea. It took him a while to get to the point, but he'd heard about Michael's run-in with the Yareside bullies. He'd also considered the risks of Calling Night, and what he wanted was to move everyone into his house for as long as they cared to stay.

"I've got more room than anyone could use, and so many servants, I sometimes think I should fire half the lazy idlers. And the children would cheer the place up. I know you think I'm overreacting, and I probably am, but humor me on this one. Please?"

The answer was already plain in Max's relieved expression, but he said, "I thought you were opening your house this year."

"I am, and a cursed nuisance it is. Anna could do me a great service if she'd play hostess—especially if Judith and Miss Lissy would help out. Or if you'd rather not party all night, you can hide out in the west wing and never set eyes on the festivities. Frankly, Max, I want the lot of you out of here tonight, and you know I'm right."

Max nodded. "I accept your offer gratefully, for the others, but this house is the only valuable property I own, and I can't leave it unattended. However—"

"No," said Anna and Michael together. Judith laughed.

It took over an hour to reach the sensible agreement that Michael, Trimmer, and I would stay to watch the house while the others went with Worthington. Once it was settled, a frenzy of packing broke out. Worthington, gazing in dismay at the growing mound of baggage, sent for his carriage. Finally Mrs. Trimmer herded the children out the door. Anna grabbed my arm and started to give me all sorts of complicated directions concerning the chicken she'd set to roast before Sawyer arrived.

I grabbed Michael, who'd been helping the groom strap bags onto the carriage roof, and told Anna he was the one who could cook. Michael started to say he only did camp cooking; then he remembered what my attempts at cooking turned out like and paid attention to Anna's instructions.

I stood back to enjoy the chaos and caught sight of Lissy stuffing a warm scarf and her thickest cloak into one of her bags. She meant to go out with the revelers tonight. With young Fowler? I frowned, for a whole night spent wandering about in Fowler's company was different from a short stroll in a cold orchard.

But then Anna kissed me and told me to take care, and the coach rattled away before I could decide whether or not to rat Lissy out. It had been too long since I'd been a brother. I was out of practice.

Michael, Trimmer, and I spent the afternoon doing what every household in town was doing—pulling buckets of water from the well and filling barrels placed at strategic locations. There hadn't been a serious Calling Night fire in Ruesport for two hundred years, and no one wanted to break that record. We dropped three empty grain sacks beside each barrel, and our precautions were complete. Then Michael offered to leave again, thus removing the worst danger.

"And how do you plan to get word of your absence to every thug in the city before nightfall? Well, don't worry. When they show up with their torches, I'm sure they'll be happy to believe Trimmer and me when we say you're not home."

Michael gave me a dirty look and said no more about leaving.

I thought we were all overreacting. A couple of drunks throwing a brick through a window is one thing; coming in force to assault a house is quite another, especially since all the deputies patrol on Calling Night. I was even more reassured when we saw that a neighbor two doors down was opening his house, for that meant plenty of witnesses and help, if it should be needed.

Michael must have managed to follow Anna's directions, for the roast chicken was delicious. We worked out a watch schedule that called for Michael to patrol the house early, and for me to take the middle hours and Trimmer the predawn, when most of the revelers had gone home to bed. But I was too tense to fall asleep—and anyway, nobody sleeps on Calling Night.

Michael and I made the first round at dusk, lighting the torches in the wall brackets. Trimmer lit the candles in the windows after pulling the draperies well back.

The quiet street glowed in the torchlight, and the ribbons twined through the garlands glittered with gold embroidery, for this was a rich neighborhood.

The first group of revelers, half of them masked, appeared at the end of the street. They made their way to a house whose gates stood open for friends to stop by and while away the wait for the sun with good food and good cheer. The light from the revelers' torches glinted like laughter on the women's satin skirts, and the plumes in the men's hats rippled.

The sewing room window provided the best view of the spectacle, and if I couldn't see the burning of the rivers, well, that was the fate of those who stood house watch. It would be childish to whine about it, even if this was the first time I'd been home in five years.

We watched folk come and go for an hour, made a second round and replenished the torches, and had just gone to the kitchen to brew a pot of tea when Trimmer came in through the dining room door.

"A note for Master Sevenson. A boy just delivered it."

The paper was folded but not sealed, and Michael frowned as he reached for it. "I didn't hear anyone knock."

"He came to the back," said Trimmer, edging into a position where he could read over Michael's shoulder. He did it so casually that I might not have noticed if I hadn't been trying to do the same thing. He beat me to the best place, curse him.

Michael cast us an amused glance and read the note. His brows lifted and he read it again. I hadn't decided whether to pull Trimmer away and take his place or simply snatch the note from Michael when he looked up and gave it to me.

I know who started those fires. Come to the Old Ropers' Home tonight, at the second hour after midnight. Alone, or I won't be there. I got to talk to someone. I'm afraid.

Needless to say, it wasn't signed. I read it a second time, though there was hardly any need. My thoughts raced.

"A trap?" Michael asked softly.

"Of course it's a trap. The question is, what do we do about it?"

"Excuse me, Sir, but why are you so certain it's not genuine?"

I'd forgotten Trimmer was there. It was Michael who replied, "Think about it, Master Trimmer. If the man who wrote this truly fears for himself, why would he go to a disgraced stranger instead of Sheriff Potter? No, I've received an invitation. And I believe I'll accept. You and Fisk can watch the house, can't you Trimmer?"

He was absolutely out of his mind, which was nothing new. But I had to admit I wanted a chance to get ahead of our enemy.

"Trimmer can watch the house. If there's any trouble, he can go to the party down the block and get all the help he needs."

"'Tis foolish for you to come with me." But Michael sounded more resigned than anything else, and I smiled.

"It's foolish to go at all. But we don't have to be completely stupid about it."

"I thought you didn't trust the law! Besides, they won't help an unredeemed man. And besides—"

"You just don't like Sheriff Potter," I replied. "Keep your voice down."

I'd chosen to take side streets to the Council Hall, for the markets were so crowded with revelers, it would have taken longer to cross them than to go around. Not that the side streets were empty; groups of laughing, chattering folk went from house to house, the acrid smoke of their torches stinging the eyes. But at least these folk were going somewhere, and not as likely as the market crowd to mischievously pull down a hood. If we'd had a mask Michael could have worn that as well, but if Max owned one, Trimmer didn't know where he kept it. We carried torches—with so much light around they weren't necessary, but not to have them might have made people wonder. Michael had quietly switched his from his right hand to his left soon after we set out, so I knew his wrist still bothered him. He didn't complain about it, though—he was too busy complaining about my plan. I didn't care what he said; if I was going to walk into a trap, I wanted Sheriff Potter along to quell the riot, and maybe even arrest someone if we got lucky.

"But I keep telling you, he won't help an un-redeemed . . . Horn and hoof, what's that?"

No torches illuminated the ragged black gap between the two houses, but I knew where we were. "That's Potter's house. Or at least it was. No relation to the sheriff. He used some magica boards to lay down a floor even though an herbalist who had the sensing Gift told him what they were, and the weeds grew up and tore the house apart. It was . . . Michael, what's wrong?"

"Nothing." He drew a shuddering breath, his eyes on the empty lot. I saw only shadows. "Nothing. Come on."

Not for the first time, I cursed Ceciel Mallory, but he'd tell me when he was ready. Or not. If I started pushing Michael to answer personal questions, he might return the favor, an idea I didn't much care for. The destruction of Potter's house had fascinated my father.

Michael was so distracted he stopped complaining, and we soon reached the Council Hall. There, however, my plan went to pieces.

◇ ◇ ◇

"I told you, Sheriff Potter's not here tonight."

The deputy was in his early thirties and balding. I wondered if the man who'd roused the mob in Yareside would have answered his description.

"So where can we find him? Is he out with the street patrols?"

"I don't think the sheriff's whereabouts are any of your business, Master Fisk." He said my name, but his eyes slid to Michael. His cohorts, who were watching with interest, grinned. Michael sneered at them. I sighed.

"Look, I told you about the note, right?"

"Aye, and I told you the sheriff wasn't here and that I'd no men to spare for chasing greased pigs."

"But it's a trap!"

"So don't go."

We glared at each other, but I had to try. "Look, if Potter's out with the patrols, just tell us where, and he can make up his own mind about whether he wants to come."

The deputy rubbed his chin. "I suppose there's no harm in telling you. He's off duty tonight."

"Off? The whole town's parading around with torches, he's got two cases of arson, and he's going to *parties*?"

"It's Calling Night. He's got a right to some time off.

But he set up the street patrols, and left me here with just two men to hold any troublemakers the patrols bring in. And I can't spare either of them, so . . . Wait a minute. I might give you Jimmy."

The deputies who were too busy holding up the wall to come with us grinned again. I didn't even want to ask. "Who's Jimmy?"

"He's the lad who . . . Here, I'll fetch him." He took several steps and called down the hallway. "Jimmy!"

Light footsteps hurried toward us. "Yes, Sir?"

The boy who skittered into the room couldn't have been more than thirteen and maybe younger. His joints seemed too big for his lanky form, and a cowlick twisted the crown of his thick, fair hair. His first job, no doubt—probably his first week.

"No." It was the first time Michael had spoken. "This could be dangerous."

"You wanted the law." The deputy gestured to the astonished boy. "He works for the law. He takes prisoners their meals and cleans the cells, makes up the cots, things like that. Real reliable. He's got a good head on his shoulders."

For a kid. But I didn't say it aloud.

Jimmy, who had no idea what was going on, stood up straight and tried to look older than he was. I stifled another sigh. "You say he's smart and reliable. Would you accept his word as a witness to our whereabouts and activities tonight?"

It was the deputy's turn to look Jimmy over thoughtfully. He couldn't stand straighter, so he puffed out his chest.

"Yes," said the deputy slowly. "I'd take his word. He's smarter than he looks."

Jimmy turned crimson and the other deputies snickered. Sometimes, you have to settle for what you can get. "We'll take him. Come on, Michael—it's almost the second hour now."

Michael explained the situation to Jimmy as we wove through the crowds. The burning of the rivers usually takes place around the third hour, and Trullsgate Bridge was already so full of spectators that we had to shove our way across.

"Will I have to arrest anyone?" Jimmy's eyes were round with excitement. "I don't . . . I better tell you, I don't know how to do anything like that. I've seen the deputies do it, but—"

"No," said Michael. "You're here as a witness to Fisk's and my actions. So if a fire is started, or some such thing, you can swear we didn't do it. Whatever happens, 'tis very important that you keep yourself safe. You understand?"

Jimmy nodded, as well he might—it was probably the sixth time Michael had repeated that particular instruction. He'd objected to bringing Jimmy at all, and I admit I'd have preferred Potter. But the boy was an independent witness whose word the law would accept. And if the villain had been sincere when he'd told Michael to come alone, Jimmy probably wouldn't frighten him into changing his plan. On thinking it over, I didn't find that entirely consoling, but we arrived at the Old Ropers' Home before I could come up with a better idea.

It was a rambling structure built in the old style—more wood, less stone—and it had added so many wings, rooms, and levels that it was hard to tell its original dimensions.

At the open houses in the poorer parts of town, the hosts set out barrels of sand to hold their guests' torches. The Old Ropers' Home wasn't open, and we had to go back half a block to find a barrel to abandon our torches in. Not that we needed them—even in this nonresidential district, half the windows blazed with light.

The ropers had hung garlands over their front door, but the ribbons were faded and frayed. Some windows held candles, but there were no torches in the wall brackets.

"Someone didn't feel like celebrating," Michael murmured.

"More likely someone's economizing." I stepped up to the door and rapped the knocker briskly. "Torches cost money."

"Only a few copper roundels," said the rich man's son. "Surely the Ropers' Guild could afford it. Are we late?"

"A bit. Second hour rang when we were crossing the bridge. But if it's a trap, he can hardly spring it without us."

"Then why isn't anyone opening the door? Knock again."

"Here, I'll do it." Jimmy stepped forward and banged the knocker. The door snapped open.

"No need to break it! We're not all deaf, you know. Well, Lenny is, and Davis and Hardy and Stam, but I'm not."

White hair bristled around the old man's crumpled face. His skinny form was covered with a nightshirt and boots, topped by a short cape of deep crimson that he clutched around his shoulders like a shawl. "If you're out partying, it's no use—we don't have a party here. Least, not now. Mistress Mapple shut it down at midnight and sent us off to bed. Like kids or something." A sparkle lit the aged eyes, and he glanced over his shoulder and dropped his voice. "But we fooled her. We got dice . . ." He stopped, eyes narrowing in sudden suspicion. "What are you doing here? We got no party, like I said. You take yourselves off." He started to shut the door. I pushed my way in and then caught him as he tottered, holding him up till he regained his balance.

"I told you to be off! You can't come bargin'—"

"Be easy, good Sir." Michael smiled, an innocent smile that could have lulled the most suspicious mark. "We've no desire to betray your dice game. Earlier this evening I received a note from someone asking me to meet them here, and I've come to do so."

"Meet someone here?" The old man was astonished. "Who?"

"The note was unsigned."

"Unsigned? Then why'd you come?"

A very good question. I wished I had an answer. "Look, could we talk to Mistress Mapple? Is she the one in charge?"

"She's in charge, all right. A bossier wench never donned cap and apron. I suppose I can fetch her, but you don't go telling her about our dice game, now, or . . ."

He led us upstairs to an office full of ledgers and wobbled off to fetch Mistress Mapple.

"Why do I think this isn't going to work?"

It was a rhetorical question, but Michael replied, "'Tis too ordinary. You expected assassins hiding in the shadows, not old men playing dice. But *he* must have known what we'd find."

"Yes. So this is part of his plan. Do you think he just wanted us out of the way so he could burn down Max's house?"

The possibility was so alarming, I started to pace. Michael perched on a clerk's high stool, and Jimmy tucked himself into a corner, the better to witness things.

"Why should he?" Michael didn't even look worried. "It's not like we have evidence against him stored there. 'Twould be a foolish risk for no benefit."

"That's just what he's been doing, taking foolish risks for no benefit. At least, none that we know about." I scowled at the shelves of ledgers. "I've seen moneylenders with fewer books. How could one old men's home—"

"It's not just one old men's home, young man. This is the office for all the Ropers' Guild's charities. They're good and responsible men, as these accounts attest."

They paid her salary too, but I wouldn't have dared say it aloud. The elderly doorman's comments had led me to expect a massive matriarch, but the woman who confronted us was shorter than I and pleasingly plump. Or she would have been pleasing if she hadn't been so stiff. Apron, cap, spine, and expression were all so starchy, they looked as if they'd crack if she bent. I doubted Mistress Mapple ever cracked anything, and my sympathy for the old ropers increased.

"My name is Fisk, Mistress, and this is Michael Sevenson, a knight errant and associate of mine."

Mistress Mapple blinked, unsure how to take that mad statement. Michael looked resigned. Jimmy suppressed a grin.

"Master Sevenson received a note earlier this evening, asking him to meet someone here at the second hour."

"A note? From whom?"

"'Twas unsigned, Mistress." Michael handed it to her, and her eyes widened as she read.

"Those fires? Someone knows who set them?"

"So they say," said Michael. "Do you recognize the writing?"

She frowned over it. "It looks a bit like Joe Spinner's. I'll go wake him. This is a serious matter—it must be resolved." She sailed off to do so, and I hoped Joe Spinner wasn't at the dice game.

"If this Spinner wrote the note, then we've something

new to deal with," said Michael. "We've not come across his name before."

"No, but every sixth name in those books is probably Spinner. Or Weaver. Lots of rope makers go by one or the other."

A distant eruption of shouting made me wince—the dice game had been discovered.

Sure enough, when Spinner finally appeared in Mistress Mapple's stern wake, smelling of rum and clad in a bed robe and worn boots, he was surly and obviously blamed us for spoiling his sport. But he answered our questions readily.

No, he hadn't sent any notes this evening. Why would he do a fool thing like that? He blinked in surprise at the writing, and said it looked like his but he hadn't written it.

He didn't know anything about the fires.

He'd never heard of Yorick Thrope.

He'd heard of Max, of course, but had never dealt with him and had no personal feelings one way or the other.

Michael asked if he knew a balding man in his early thirties, and Mistress Mapple shifted impatiently from foot to foot. It was clear that we *were* chasing greased pigs, and I was worrying about what might be happening back at Max's house when Jimmy said, "Sir?"

His voice was soft, but something in it froze us in our tracks. We stared at him, but he was staring at the fireplace. Smoke wisped over its back wall and up the chimney, which it obviously shared with a fireplace in the room beneath us. Where there was a fire. Obviously.

"It's been getting bigger for several minutes," said Jimmy. "I just wondered . . ."

"The downstairs parlor is off-limits," said Mistress Mapple. "If they've started a dice game there . . ."

A puff of smoke too large for the chimney to handle burst into the room, and the soft crackle of fire came with it.

Michael ran for the stairs, Jimmy behind him, followed by Mistress Mapple and me with Joe Spinner bringing up the rear.

When he reached the front hall, Michael paused, unsure which of the doors concealed the room he wanted. He turned to the first and threw it open on darkness and silence.

Mistress Mapple knew where she was going. She came off the stairs like a charger, yanked open the third door, and leapt back as heat and light poured into the hall. Fire flowed up the walls, up the draperies at the long windows, over paintings and shelves, but the floor was not ablaze. There was no way it could have started at the base of every wall like this unless it was set, and in the second before Michael slammed the door shut, I saw several oil kegs lying empty by the hearth.

"Mistress Mapple," said Michael crisply. "How many servants sleep here?"

"Just two men and the kitchen girl." Mistress Mapple backed away with little, mincing steps, as if someone else controlled her feet. Her eyes were fixed on the smoke puffing under the door. "We had to let two of them go, when the rev—"

"Fine. I want you to wake the men to fetch us buckets from the well, while you and the girl get everyone out. Jimmy can raise the alarm. We may be able to keep the fire in check till help arrives."

"That's good. But I'll go." Her steps grew more decisive, as she headed toward the front door. "I'll raise the alarm. Go for help, yes, go for help, that's what . . ." She ran into the street and vanished.

Michael clutched his hair. "All right, Jimmy, you go get everyone out. Find—"

"I know where Croft and Marky's rooms are," Joe Spinner volunteered. "I'll fetch them, and some of the stouter lads, and we'll make you two a bucket line."

He hurried off, and Michael looked less harassed. "Jimmy, you get folks out. Start at the top floor, open every door, and don't let anyone stop to dress or pack anything. Get them *out*."

Jimmy nodded. He looked frightened, but there was sense and purpose in his face as well. He took the stairs two at a time. Michael turned to me, but I was already heading out the front door, looking for . . . yes, there it was, with worn blankets piled beside it. Everyone sets out water barrels on Calling Night.

Unfortunately, it was outside, and the fire wasn't. The full barrel was far too heavy for the two of us to lift, and there was no lid, though we threw the worn blankets in to contain its splashing. The only way we could move the barrel was to tip it onto its edge and roll it. Once we figured that out it moved fairly quickly, but it took all our strength to roll it up the two steps to the front door, and a wobble on the second step cost us a quarter of the contents. We took a moment outside the parlor door to wet our doublets and dip our heads in the barrel to drench our hair.

The blankets were completely soaked. We used my knife to cut strips off one of them to tie over our mouths, and Michael had the sense to cut another to wrap his hand in before he touched the doorknob.

I was surprised when it didn't hiss.

Water trickled from Michael's flattened hair. He took a deep breath and opened the door, and the fire inhaled and belched out a wave of heat that seared the exposed skin around my eyes like a sunburn.

Flames rippled over the walls. The empty oil kegs by the hearth sent up a pillar of fire, and golden ghosts flickered and vanished in the carpet fringe. But the floor was still clear and the ceiling was just beginning to burn.

Michael grabbed an unburned section of the carpet's fringe and started to roll up the rug, denying the fire easy access to the floor. I left him to it and attacked the blaze around the door, for I'd no mind to put out the fire on the far wall only to find our escape cut off.

The flames hissed and vanished when the wet blanket struck them, and hope flared in my heart. I put out the flames on one side of the door and turned to the other side, but by the time I'd finished that, orange tongues were licking up the wall I'd first drenched. I remembered the empty oil kegs and swore.

My blanket was drying, so I stepped into the hall to wet it again. The coolness of the air made me realize how hot the burning parlor was. My eyes itched. I plunged my blanket into the barrel, then my head. I was blinking water from my eyes when Michael backed from the room, coughing, and I went back in to tackle the walls again.

I made some progress, but the blanket didn't hold

enough water and I was wondering if we had any chance at all when a stranger ran into the room and pitched a bucket of water at the flames. I forget the two menservants' names, but I'll never forget their faces. With four of us wielding buckets and blankets, we actually did some good until the water barrel was emptied.

Then the servants organized a bucket line with a few of the strongest inhabitants, drawing the heavy buckets from the well, but they didn't come fast enough, couldn't come fast enough, and the fire was gaining on us.

The whole ceiling was ablaze. While water thrown at a wall runs down to douse the wall below it, water thrown at the ceiling douses little but the thrower . . . except when Michael threw it.

The first thing I noticed was that he had frozen, staring up at the ceiling. My immediate thought was that it was about to come down—a persistent fear that kept me ready to leap for the door at the slightest creak of timber. I grabbed his arm to drag him out, but there wasn't anything wrong with the ceiling. In fact, the fire had died in the blackened patch he stared at.

His muscles were hard as wood under my hand.

"Michael?" He couldn't hear me over the roar of the

flames. "Michael!" I shook him and he turned slowly, his reddened eyes dazed and . . . fearful?

Not that fear wasn't an intelligent reaction. I was terrified. But Michael wasn't usually that sensible.

I shoved a full bucket at him. He took it with his right hand and almost dropped it—he'd been using his left hand to spare his wrist. But then he turned and hurled the bucket's contents into the flames above him, and another black patch appeared.

Bucket after bucket came through the door, and we pitched them up. In my case it wasn't much use, but Michael's buckets worked better. Too much better. So much better that even as my hair dried and began to scorch, and the flames crept down the walls, I noticed and wondered.

Michael worked like a man possessed. When I heard the crack of timber I'd been waiting for, I grabbed his arm again to pull him from the room. He actually fought me for a moment, but then the ceiling creaked and he heard it. We leapt to the door and stumbled out together, slamming it behind us.

The hall was no longer cool, and the top half was full of smoke through which nightshirted old men drifted like wraiths. The fire bell tolled in the distance.

"You can't go back!" Jimmy perched on the bottom stair, barring the way up. His voice was hoarse. "You gotta go outside. Outside, gaffer. Out!"

"But I want to get my whittling knife. You hustled me out so fast, I didn't have a chance—"

I gripped the old man's shoulders and shoved him toward the door. "Out!"

"Humph. No respect these days." He wandered off into the smoke, muttering.

"Did you get them all out?"

Jimmy took a breath and coughed. "We cleared the upper floors, but we can't get 'em out of the building. They can't see the fire, so they don't—"

The crash of the falling ceiling shook the room. The parlor door exploded open, and fire billowed into the hall. The old men scattered, then shuffled for the street door. Michael stood, staring into the blaze.

"Can the ropers get upstairs anywhere else?" I had to shout now, to be heard over the flames.

"No," Jimmy yelled. "Joe and the kitchen girl are on the other stairs."

The last of the old men filed through the door. "Come on, then."

I grabbed Michael's arm on the way past, and this time he didn't resist as I hauled him into the raucous cold of the night. The fire bell was louder out here, and the local fire-team leader had arrived and was shouting chaos into order. We tumbled down the steps and moved to one side, pulling the clean, sweet air into our lungs.

Fear still sang in my blood, but I now had time to realize that my face, hands, and arms stung, and my throat felt as if someone had taken a file to it. I also realized that I was holding a full bucket of water, though I'd no memory of picking it up.

The room next to the parlor started to burn, light welling from its windows. Half a dozen of the fire crew had stopped working and were staring at me. No, not at me. At Michael.

Michael stood, firelight glaring on his exposed face as the gazed into the burning room.

"Michael."

He didn't move, but a low growl rose from the men who'd seen him, and they started toward us.

"Michael, run!"

I shoved him away. His astonished glance took in the men coming toward us, and for once in his life he did the sensible thing and fled.

I used the only weapon I had, dousing three of them with a sheet of cold water as they passed. It was more effective than I'd expected, for all three forgot about Michael and turned on me. I knew better than to resist.

Unlike Jimmy, who sprinted after them and

grabbed one of the leaders. "He didn't do it! Listen to me! I was with—"

The man tried to shake him off, then grabbed Jimmy's shoulders and shoved him away. He stumbled back, and his head hit the building behind him with a thud that made me flinch. But his hands clutched the bricks as he slid down the wall, which I hoped was a good sign. The chase had taken him away from the burning building, so he was in no danger of being trampled.

The road Michael had taken sloped down, and I thought I saw an eddy in the crowd several blocks away.

Standing on tiptoe, I could see all the way to the river. On any other night it would have made little difference, but on Calling Night the streets were almost as bright as day. Michael was ahead of the pack, but he was still bruised from his last encounter with a mob, and the work he'd put in this evening had taken its toll—they were gaining on him.

If it had been dark, he might have slipped away, but with torches and candles blazing from all sides he didn't have a chance. So he ran for the river. And the river began to burn.

I could see only a thin wedge of it between the buildings, but I grew up in this town. When the first small raft of blazing, pitch-soaked timber came floating past, I knew what would follow.

Michael reached the bank as the first wave of flaming rafts burst into view, and the spectacle froze him in his tracks. Perfectly silhouetted against the luminous water, the idiot.

The mob responded with a hail of stones.

He staggered, almost falling, and my heart contracted with fear. Then he recovered and ran, splashing, into the river, which glittered at the disturbance like liquid gold.

He slowed to dodge a burning raft, and another hail of stones found him before he reached the deep water and began to swim. Michael was a strong swimmer.

The leaders of the mob raced into the river, then waded back out. A few more people hurled stones, but as the magnificent flotilla swept down the current, shuddering and jostling, the ripples of Michael's movement were lost.

Michael *was* a strong swimmer, but given the temperature of the Nighber this time of year, he might have been better off to take his chances with the mob.

I settled back and unclenched my teeth from my lower lip. The chaos was finally getting organized, and one of those miraculous pumps was rolling through the street. The fire didn't seem to have made too much headway. I was more concerned for Jimmy, who still lay in a crumpled heap against the wall across the street. Not a good sign.

Scanning the scene, I noticed another man doing the same thing. His face was turned away, but firelight gleamed on his bald crown. I sighed—and went to tell Sheriff Potter to send someone to tend young Jimmy.

Michael was on his own.

CHAPTER 11
Michael

By the time the implacable current swept me past the last of the buildings, I was so cold I could barely force my legs to carry me onto the shallow bank. For a time I simply lay there, shudders racking my body. Then, blinking water-fogged eyes, I saw that the fire had followed me. One of the burning rafts that had made the swim so hazardous spun lazily along the shore I'd washed up on.

I'd thought I couldn't move, but now I saw that fire was life, warmth was life, and I wanted it the way some men crave rum or a woman's body. I crawled several yards before I found the strength to stagger to my feet and into the shallows. One hand under a joint of the logs that formed the raft's base sufficed to drag it out—four feet across and blazing like a bit of fallen sun. Another raft had come to rest half a dozen yards downstream. 'Twas a long way over the mud, and the buried stones bruised my numb feet, for I'd pulled off my boots in the river. I dragged it over by the first one. Then I dropped between them, the fire so close, 'twas almost like being back in the burning parlor. But even that memory had no power to overcome my exhaustion; within moments I fell asleep.

The next time I woke the sun was rising, its light a benediction over all living things. The fire rafts smoldered sullenly, and the ground beneath me leached heat from my chilled flesh. Frost rimmed the brown grass, making it beautiful. I realized that I might die, but the thought held no urgency, and the aching cold that had roused me seemed distant. In fact it might be better if I died, freakish thing that I'd become. With a little groping my mind found the magic that had risen last night in response to the fire. Sometimes 'twas centered in the core of my body, sometimes it seemed to fill me to the extremities of my skin. If I opened my eyes, I knew, my changed sight would see its radiance about my flesh. I didn't open my eyes.

I did try to use the magic to warm myself, for I sensed, or thought I sensed, that I might be able to do this. But it refused to respond to my will, and I didn't know how to make it. Yes. Better to die.

I felt the hands that grasped and shook me and

heard a voice babbling, but it was too much trouble to respond. I wished whoever it was would go away, for I wanted to sleep.

But soon I was dragged onto something soft, and sensed wood beneath it and to the sides. Soft cloth fell over me; then I felt the shifting instability of water. A boat. 'Twas as good a place to sleep as any.

My next awareness was of warmth. Too much warmth. I lay on a pallet covered with silky fur, with more fur above me—a lot more, judging by the weight. I stretched, enjoying the softness against my bare skin, even when my bruises protested. Then I felt a smooth stone against my belly, and my knee bumped another. Why were there rocks in my bed?

I opened my eyes and saw rows of sticks, well chinked with mud, like an orderly beaver's den. The soft fur was rabbit, and atop that layer on layer of sheepskins. The stones, no doubt, had been heated and thrust beneath the furs. No wonder I was hot. Then I remembered where I'd seen such walls before.

I sat up, scattering pelts, and Nettie's Ma, who was crouched beside her kettle, looked up and smiled. "Decided to stay with the living, I see. Good choice."

I was suddenly aware of my nakedness and clutched a sheep pelt to my torso. It prickled after the rabbit fur.

"Who undress— Ah, where are my clothes, Mistress?"

Her laughter was warm and rich. "Your clothes are outside drying, for I just finished washing 'em. And I undressed you, wicked old woman that I am. But I promise you, young Sir, there's very little *I* haven't seen."

'Twas no doubt true, but that didn't stop me from blushing so hard, it warmed me better than fur and hot rocks.

She laughed again and brought me a bowl of stew. Hunger overcame my embarrassment, though I tried to keep the pelt wrapped round me as I ate.

"You must be hollow as a drum, but don't make yourself sick. Your friend's kept this long, he'll keep a bit longer."

"My friend?" I asked though a mouthful of stew. It was mostly barley, and I didn't recognize the meat.

"He's been walking the marish since just after dawn, looking for you."

"How do you know he's looking for me?"

"Because every few minutes he calls out, 'Michael.'"

The stew no longer tasted so good. "How do you know he's a friend? There might be a number of people looking for me."

The creases around her eyes deepened. "I figure he's a friend, 'cause every now and then he calls,

'Answer me, you stubborn son-of-a-bitch.'"

"Fisk." My mouth stretched in a smile. "He must be frantic by now. Mistress, I need my clothes. Will you guide me to him?"

"Aye, I'll take you, but you can't have your clothes—they're wet. Finish your stew; I'll come up with something."

So it came about that I went in search of Fisk wearing nothing but a few old blankets—wool, not the precious fur. The day was cold but gloriously bright, and birds sang their welcome to the sun the townsfolk had called back last night. I was glad Nettie's Ma did the poling, for there was no way I could have assisted and kept my decency. Despite my sore wrist, and her undoubted skill, it still felt strange to sit, blanket-wrapped like a babe, while an old woman carted me about.

Fortunately, Fisk wasn't far off. We heard him before we saw him, and the voice that called my name was rough with shouting, smoke, and mayhap worry as well.

I called back as soon as he came into view. He went rigid, hands lifted to shield his eyes, and I waved and called again. He sat down then, quite suddenly, right where he stood.

By the time we drew near, he had seated himself

more comfortably on a grassy mound, and his expression was sardonic. "Good morning, Noble Sir. Which do you want first, the bad news, the bad news, or the worse news?"

His voice sounded even rougher when he spoke, and I smiled. "Let me think about it. If you come aboard, I'll introduce you to Nettie's Ma, the captain of this craft."

Fisk eyed the raft dubiously, and I remembered that he couldn't swim. But he stepped aboard and balanced himself, at least as well as I had the first time. He carried a pack, and I reached for it eagerly. "Clothes? Bless you, Fisk!"

"What else is a squire for? Mistress, you have my sincere thanks. I know how much looking after he needs."

"Squire?" Nettie's Ma cocked her head like a curious crow.

"He's a knight errant. That's why he gets into so much trouble."

"That'd do it." Her eyes laughed but I stiffened, realizing for the first time that she must have seen the broken circles tattooed on my wrists. She clearly didn't care, but I wished, quite passionately, that I could dress and hide them. Ridiculous, for on this small raft to dress to hide my wrists would reveal all the rest of me. I clutched my blanket tighter.

"You may as well start with the worst news, for it can't be too— Wait! Nothing's happened to your family, has it? Worthington had them safe!"

"No, they're all fine, and since the house is still standing, they decided to come home today. But two men died in that fire last night."

A chill twisted through me. "So Mistress Weaver's not the only one he's killed. But how? I'd have sworn everyone got out."

"Most did. Jimmy and the kitchen girl cleared everyone out of the upper floors, and the fire team cleared the ground floor. These two had got hold of a jug of rum and decided to celebrate Calling Night in the traditional way. They hid themselves in a room in the cellar and got dead . . ." Fisk grimaced at the trap his tongue had set, but went on ". . . dead drunk. The smoke killed them. From the look of things, they never woke at all. Still . . ."

"Yes. Our enemy has a lot to answer for."

"That's what the town thinks too, except . . . Are you ready for the bad news now?"

"Go ahead." His face told me 'twas serious, despite his light tone.

"The townsfolk don't think it's some mysterious arsonist. They think it's you."

"But I have an alibi for Thrope's office, and last night. Surely Jimmy . . ." The look on his face stopped me. "What happened to Jimmy? You said everyone got out!"

"He did get out. Stop wiggling like that—you're rocking the raft. The doctor says he'll be fine. When the mob went after you, he tried to stop them, got shoved aside, and hit his head. He's awake and alert this morning, though he's got the mother of all headaches, but he doesn't remember much after midday yesterday, and nothing at all of the three or four hours before the blow. The doctor says it's often that way with head injuries, and that most of his memories will probably come back over the next few days or weeks, though probably not the time right before the accident."

"And what does Jimmy say about almost being dragged to his death by a couple of strangers?"

"Not much, since he doesn't remember it." Fisk smiled suddenly. "He's a bit embarrassed, to be regarded as a hero when he doesn't remember doing anything. But you should see the way the kitchen girl looks at him."

I had to laugh. "He's really all right?"

"So the doctor says."

"Then the worst is that I've no alibi? Wait a minute,

what about Mistress Mapple?"

"She could only testify as to what we did after she arrived. And *we* have no alibi. But that's just the beginning. The sheriff's looking for you."

I tensed, but Nettie's Ma, who'd been listening with interest as she poled us along, snorted. "He's welcome to try. No one finds anything in the marish if we don't want them to."

"Mistress, 'tis a courageous offer, but enough men—"

"No," said Fisk. "She's right. No deputy's ever gotten anything out of the marish but fever and snake bite. And having looked for you, I'm beginning to see why. I was trying to follow the riverbank, such as it is, and I've no idea where I was when you found me."

"You weren't far off," Nettie's Ma told him. "When the river wanders into the marish, it gets lost too. With folk, depends on what they've done. Some we help. Some we even let stay. The others find their way out and circle around to the Fallon Road. Or they don't." There was no change in her serenity as she said it.

"So why are you helping me?" I held out my wrists so the sun shone on the tattoos.

"Those are just marks, boy. One fool judicar's opinion. I make my own judgments."

"And very well, too," said Fisk cheerfully. "But how did you find him? How did you even know to look?"

I hadn't thought to ask those questions, and the gaze I turned to her was full of wonder.

She laughed. "No, I'm no Savant. I didn't find him, Dibby did. He was out gathering rafts—the riverburning keeps the marish in firewood for half a year, for the frames hardly burn at all. He brought you to me because my house was closest, and you were so cold it was a near thing."

It sounded simple, but I still wondered.

"All things considered," I said to Fisk, "I'm surprised Sheriff Potter didn't hold you."

"I think he thought about it, but he decided to leave me at large so I could lead him to you. There was a very healthy beggar sleeping by the back gate, and the street sweeper has Max's street just about spotless."

"Where are they now?" I asked with some fore-boding.

"Watching the house," said Fisk. "Don't worry, Noble Sir, I was dodging deputies when you were in the schoolroom. They think taking those red cloaks off makes them invisible. The reward bothers me more."

"Reward?" I began to feel beleaguered.

"For your apprehension. The city, at the judicary's request, put up two hundred gold roundels. The Merchants' Guild, out of civic concern, added another two hundred, and Yorick Thrope threw in fifty for spite. Not bad, for an amateur."

"I'm flattered. I suppose it's dead or alive?"

"The writ doesn't say. Why bother? You're un-redeemed—no need for a hearing. But rumor has it you're a very dangerous man, and dead would be safer. And that's enough money to ensure there'll be more than deputies hunting the marish."

Nettie's Ma *tsk*ed. "Poor dears. They'll get all muddy."

Fisk laughed, but I didn't. "I have to go. I won't bring danger here." I should never have followed Fisk in the first place. I had wanted to help the Maxwells, to prove that even unredeemed I might still be of use in the world. Now I saw that was impossible, that no one who cared for me could remain untouched by the disgrace that marked me. I had to leave. But go where? Despair clutched my heart.

Nettie's Ma started to protest, then paused. "If you have to go, then you may. But I promise no one will find you here, for even magica hounds can't track through water for more than a hundred feet or so. At least stay till the search has stopped."

"And until I can get you a disguise," said Fisk. "And some boots. We also need to agree on a place to meet. Fallon perhaps? I can elude the deputies myself, but it'll be harder to get Chanticleer and Tipple past them."

I opened my mouth to say I'd leave the horses . . . and couldn't say it. Chant and Tipple where the only friends who wouldn't be condemned just for traveling with me, and Fisk, curse him, knows my weaknesses.

"Then it's settled." His eyes gleamed at having out-maneuvered me. "You'll stay here till it's safe to leave. I'll come again this afternoon with a disguise, and we'll get you ready for the road."

I wondered what ruse he would come up with next, to keep me here till he could clear Max, for Fisk was too loyal to abandon either his family or me. Whatever it was, I couldn't allow it to succeed—yet even as I resolved to flee, a part of my heart rebelled. My presence had brought danger with it, but I *had* assisted with the investigation. If Maxwell's enemy hadn't used my status against us so cleverly, I could have helped them . . . just like a real knight errant.

I was pleased to be clothed once more, though the slippers Fisk had brought were far less sturdy than my lost boots. Nettie's Ma gave Fisk breakfast, then carried him off to a place where he could escape the watery maze. She said she'd return for him that afternoon, after she'd gathered some firewood for herself.

Fisk eyed me strangely when I didn't volunteer to help her, and my claim to be too weary wasn't far from true. But there was something I needed to do more than resting, or working at a debt that could never be wholly repaid.

I'd intended to start as soon as the raft vanished, but when I returned to the cottage the weariness I'd feigned claimed me, and I slept for several hours. Then I made another stew for dinner, and biscuits as well, for I hated to be completely useless.

Nettie's Ma had a coal box. I raked a bit of the hearth fire into it, gathered up a few bricks of the non-magica peat and an armload of wood from the pile out back, and set off over the chain of small hillocks behind the house. I also carried a plain clay cup.

It didn't take long to find a sheltered hollow with a pond in its bottom. I pulled the grass from a small ring of earth and built my fire.

It took some time to burn down to the bed of embers I needed. I took a few steps to the pond and sank the cup into the tangled grass base first, so the clear surface water flowed over the rim. 'Twas cold and wet, as water should be.

I sat before my fire pit and tossed some onto the coals. A hiss, a puff of stinking steam, and after a moment the coals began to brighten. I hadn't used much.

I closed my eyes, trying to ignore the unsteady

pounding of my heart, and sought within me for magic. It was there, coiled in my guts like a snake. I commanded it to touch the water, and nothing happened. I willed it. Nothing. But last night . . .

I took a deep breath and remembered—the fire flowing over the walls, its heat on my skin, the raw, steamy air that came though the cloth over my mouth. I needed a weapon, and water was my weapon. I'd wanted it to work, to eat the fire, to slow it, crush it, *wet* it, so the old men would have time to flee their beds. I'd *wanted* it, and now, at the memory of that fierce desire, the magic stirred.

My heart clenched. My only desire now was to run away and forget the whole thing. The magic settled back into itself. I opened my eyes, swore, then began to laugh.

It took half a dozen attempts, but finally, in answer to my fearful wanting, the magic crept down my arms to the water in my hands, which I wanted to be more, to be stronger, to become a weapon against the fire. The water in the cup began to glow.

'Twas hard to see in the sunlight, but I knew what I was looking for. I quelled my shock, letting the magic flood into it till it seemed to stop of its own accord.

I let the magic retreat, thankfully, then took the glowing water and cast a bit of it on the embers. A hiss, a puff of steam, and the embers blackened. And stayed black. And stayed.

"Interesting," said Fisk's voice behind me.

I must have jumped a foot into the air. The cup flew up and would have spilled if Fisk hadn't leapt to catch it.

"Sorry." He gazed at the water in fascination. He didn't look sorry. "Is it still . . ."

"Yes," I said shortly. Even in his hands the water glowed, as nothing but the plants and animals the Gods have Gifted should glow, as no normal person should be able to see.

My stomach heaved, and I scrambled away and was thoroughly sick. Fisk, for once, had the tact to leave me alone. After a few moments I wiped my mouth and returned to the fire pit. Fisk had poured a long *S* in the embers, and 'twas still damp and dark. So was the spot on which I'd poured the magica water several minutes ago. I couldn't see the place I'd drenched with ordinary water at all.

"I've never heard of magica water," Fisk said. "I didn't know there was such a thing."

"There shouldn't be," I said, trying not to let him see that I was shaking.

"Why not?"

"Why *not*? What do you mean, why not?"

"Why not? Why shouldn't there be such a thing as magica water?"

"Because it's unnatural! Magic is the province of nature, given by the Gods only to plants, animals, and those poor folk who've little more wit than animals. And them it slays before too long. It—"

"Do you think it'll harm you?" Fisk sounded serious but not alarmed. The knot in my stomach began to relax.

"I don't know. How can I? This didn't come from the Gods, Fisk, it came—"

"From Lady Ceciel's potions, just as she hoped. I knew she was a clever bitch. Was it like this from the start?"

So I told him the secret I'd kept so many months, of my fear when I'd realized that I could see what others only sensed with touch, and finally of last night, when a monster reared up within me to fill bucket after bucket with eerie light and ate the fire before my eyes. I was still trembling when I finished, but it felt good to say it, to share the horror.

Fisk didn't look horrified. "So what magic does with water is to . . . to enhance its nature. Like it does with plants and animals. Magic just makes water more itself, right?"

"So it seems, but I can't say for certain. It might turn

oxen into toads, for all I know."

"Then I probably shouldn't taste it?"

"Don't you dare! It might kill you. It might change you into some sort of unnatural freak, like me."

"Humph. That's the problem, isn't it? Have you thought about this?" He sounded critical, curse him.

"I've thought of little else," I snarled. "How could I—"

"I said thought, not felt. Have you *thought* about it?"

"What's to think about? It is what it is."

Fisk rolled his eyes. "Didn't they teach logic in that university of yours? Or weren't you paying attention that day? You say you're an unnatural freak. Anything made by man is un-natural. A house is unnatural. A blanket is unnatural. A sword is unnatural, and it can kill. Those things don't frighten you."

"No, but—"

"And 'freak' is just an unkind way of saying someone is different. In case you haven't noticed, everyone is different. I learned to read when I was four, so I'm a freak. Judith is tall, so she's a freak. Lissy is pretty, so she's a fre—"

"And you think working magic is no different?"

"Well it is, in that most of the things that folks call freakish are, in fact, natural."

I wondered if Fisk could hear his scholarly father in his voice as clearly as I could.

"Your . . . ability is not from nature but manmade," he went on. "Like a house, or a blanket, or any other tool."

"You think this is a *tool*? Something to *use*?"

"Why not? You used it very effectively last night. Though I doubt that'll come up much. How often do you really need to make water wetter?"

My lips twitched. "I suppose it's generally wet enough. I can't use this, Fisk. 'Twould be . . . 'twould be monstrous. Unfair to those who can't."

"Most people can't read when they're four years old, but that never stopped me. A man on his own, Noble Sir, needs all the tools he can lay his hands on. But it's your choice."

"It is, and I choose not to use it. Mayhap 'twill fade, eventually." I wished I believed that it would. On top of my unredeemed status, this must make my presence doubly dangerous to those around me.

"As I said, it's your choice," Fisk remarked. "But stop looking so appalled. So you can make water wetter? So what? It's not going to destroy your enemies or enrich your friends. Unfortunately. We could use help in both those departments right now. I don't suppose . . ." His hopeful expression was patently false.

"No, I know of no way to use magic to find Master Maxwell's enemy. Or to make you rich. Sorry."

He returned my wavering smile. "You see. You make water wetter, but nothing else changes. And water's wet enough."

Which he proceeded to prove by dousing the remaining embers with plain pond water. Was Fisk right? For all its strangeness, was making magic so terrible a thing? It had *saved* folk last night, buying precious time for Jimmy to clear the building. Mayhap Fisk had some logic on his side after all, though I still felt freakish and frightened as Fisk led me back to start working on a disguise. But I no longer felt so very alone, and for that I was grateful.

I'd not have thought that donning a disguise could distract my thoughts, but the way Fisk deals with disguise could distract a man from a toothache.

"Try limping. All right, forget the limp. Maybe an eye patch."

"One wouldn't be enough to make a beggar, and I refuse to go about blinded. Mayhap 'tis—"

Fisk moaned. "How about mute? It's the only way you'll pass as anything but noble if you can't lose that accent."

"You're the one who wanted me to pass for a beggar. Why can't I—"

"You haven't seen the writs. They describe you

down to the holes in your socks. The scar's the biggest problem." Fisk gazed at my face as if he was thinking of amputating it. "A beggar has an excuse to grow a few days' stubble. I wish beards weren't so unfashionable now; that would solve the problem completely."

"I don't care about fashion. I can grow a beard."

"Yes, but the object is to *keep* from attracting attention."

"You'll never pass him as a beggar." Nettie's Ma had been vastly amused by the whole process. "He's too . . . too . . ."

"I know," said Fisk grimly. "But no one looks twice at a beggar. It was worth a try."

"Too what?" I asked.

"Do you have any ideas?" Fisk asked Nettie's Ma.

"Traveling bookseller? Some of them have noblish accents, and it's a good excuse for being on the road. I've even got a pack that'll do." She rose and went to pull a crate from beneath her table.

"You know, that might work. Max hasn't sold his books yet, so there's even stock to hand. But what about the scar?"

"Too *what*?" I pulled off the battered hat that Fisk had forced on me.

"Here it is!" Nettie's Ma pulled out a pack and held it up. The leather was crumpled from long confinement, but it looked sturdy and in good repair.

She gave it to me to straighten while she and Fisk argued on. Hoping to discover some clue as to why I'd make so poor a beggar, I paid more attention to the argument than the task, until I came across a tanner's mark on the bottom corner of the pack, a light circle over a dark one. *He said the light circle was his good luck, so he put it on top.* Master Clogger's remembered voice drowned out Fisk's, and my heartbeat pounded in my ears.

"Mistress, where did you come by this?" I thought my voice sounded normal, but they broke off to stare at me.

"Dibby got it off a corpse," Nettie's Ma replied. "Washed up about where you did. Most things that go into the river hit that beach—the current slows there. Dibby lives up channel from it, and goes there most days to see what's come down. It's not like that lad had any more use for it. Does it bother you?"

"No, 'tis only . . ." I passed the pack to Fisk, pointing out the mark.

His eyes widened. "When? When was the corpse found?"

"Last summer." Nettie's Ma looked from Fisk to me, baffled by our intensity. "Why? Did you know him?"

"No," said Fisk. "But if he was who I think he was . . .

When in the summer? Please. It may be important."

Her brows lifted. "Then you're out of luck. I don't keep track of the days. I know I got the pack in summer because I used it to gather herbs, but that's all I can tell you. Dibby might know more. He buried the man."

So we set out to find Dibby.

"It could have been anyone," I told Fisk. "Clogger sold his work in this town for years."

"Yes, but the timing's too close—it has to be Clogger. We should have thought of this before. We knew our enemy killed the other witness."

Fisk's expression was grim, but excitement lit his eyes. I must confess I felt the same, except when I thought of the wheelwright's grief. Besides, it might not be Clogger. Or there might be no way to identify the corpse. Or there might be nothing to tell us who killed him, after all this time. I said as much to Fisk, who snorted.

"The way our luck runs, this Dibby will be off to visit relatives for the winter."

Nettie's Ma laughed.

And Fisk proved wrong, for Master Dibby was there when we arrived at his ramshackle hut. 'Twas built half of wattle and daub, like Nettie's Ma's cottage, and half of scavenged timber. Master Dibby's scrounging was apparent in his furnishings as well, all bits and pieces that might have been fine when they were whole. Master Dibby himself was small and spry, despite the hump that lifted one shoulder, and his dark eyes were bright with intelligence. But when we asked him for the date he found the corpse, he gave us a glance of amused astonishment.

"I'll just have to check my calendar. You want the date? No one here cares about things like that. It was late summer, if that helps, and the tides were high."

Fisk sighed. "A man vanished from town around the time you found that corpse. A tanner, whose work this is." He showed Dibby the mark.

"Then you've likely got the wrong man. We send a listener into town when a body turns up, and no one was looking for this 'un."

"They wouldn't have," I said, realizing how clever our enemy had been. "If it's the man we think, he told his kin he was leaving for another town. Do you have anything else of his, Master Dibby?"

"His belt, which has the same mark." He sucked in his stomach and turned the leather to display it. "I traded off most of his clothes. They didn't fit me." Indeed, he'd be hard put to find clothes that would, but he went on without self-consciousness, "Tanner, huh? I thought he was a sailor, though the clothes were wrong."

"How'd he die, Dib?" asked Nettie's Ma. "You never said."

I should have thought to ask that myself.

"Knifed," Dibby replied. "And it looked like he put up a fight, poor fool. That's one of the things that made me think he was a sailor. They go that way, sometimes, and not many captains'll hold a ship to look for 'em."

My pity for the dead man grew, whoever he was, but Fisk went on doggedly, "If he had two things with Clogger's mark, it's even more likely he was Clogger. Why did you think him a sailor, Master Dibby? They don't carry this kind of pack."

"No, nor wear boots like this 'un had. I told you the clothes were wrong. It was the spread of his money that made me think sailor."

"The spread of his money? You mean he wasn't robbed?"

"Oh, he was robbed. Least his purse was gone. But he'd sewed a couple dozen gold roundels into the hem of his jacket, and whoever killed him missed them."

"The jacket hem is the third place a thief would look," said Fisk. "Right after the boots."

Dibby shrugged. "I didn't find 'em till his jacket was dry and I started wondering why it was so heavy. He had coin from all over the realm, and sailors often have purses like that. Though not usually so full. I'd have said merchant, but they don't end up knifed in the river. Here, I'll show you."

Fisk's eyes widened. "You still have the money? After five months?"

Dibby smiled. "Where would I spend it? You say he had kin? I'd appreciate it if you'd see it back to 'em."

He went to the back of the room and dug into a battered chest. "It's most all here." He poured a small sack of coins onto the table.

The rest of us bent over the glittering heap. "I see what you mean," murmured Nettie's Ma. "Here's one from Horncastle. That's to the south, isn't it?"

The coin's design was worn, but the name and crest of the city where it was minted were clear enough on the "town" side, as was the face of the liege whose fiefdom held that city on the "heads" side.

"Horncastle's south," said Fisk. "But Bawden is north."

"He went far afield, whoever he was." Dibby stood back from our gathering since he'd already examined them. "There's several coins from Tallowsport. Nothing from Crown City, though. Not much from any inland city, which was another reason I thought him a sailor."

"Where's Kemit?" Nettie's Ma asked curiously.

"Very far south indeed," said Fisk slowly. "At the tip of

the great desert. But even Kemit isn't as far away as this."

The coin glittered on his palm, but the anger in his eyes was brighter.

"D'vorin? 'Tis a long way indeed, but I don't see . . ." Then I did see, and my mouth went dry. "That's preposterous! He's a rich man. Powerful. He's a friend, for pity's sake! There's no motive!"

"D'vorin? I've never heard of it." Nettie's Ma looked from one of us to the other.

"D'vorin, Mistress, is a very small port, to the very far north, on the other side of the realm. Most ships never get that far. Most never pass Tallowsport. But we know of one merchant who trades there, oh yes, we do. I think we've found our connection."

"It couldn't be Worthington," I said. "He has no motive."

Nettie's Ma was taking us by raft to a place from which Fisk could find his way back to town, for he was afire to investigate his absurd theory.

"How could a local tanner get D'vorin coins, except from a man who trades there?"

"He could have won them from a sailor who's been there."

The truth of it silenced Fisk for five full seconds.

"All right. But if it's Worthington, that solves the

timing problem. *He* learned we were going to try to clear Max the night we arrived. The first fire was set the very next night. And Worthington has enough money to pay someone to take that kind of risk."

"Yes, but he didn't know I planned to visit Mistress Skinner day before yesterday, so he can't be the one who set the mob on me."

Fisk scowled. "No one outside the household knew about that. So unless it really is Jud—"

His jaw dropped. His eyes widened. And curse him, he said nothing about the revelation that had so obviously occurred.

"Fisk? Speak to me. Fisk!" The blow I launched at his shoulder was harder than it need have been, but he made no complaint. And instead of communicating, he closed his eyes and began pounding his palm against his forehead.

"We're stupid. We're so stupid. Even being amateurs doesn't excuse this. We're *stupid.* "

"I should probably warn you that if you don't tell me what you're talking about, I'm going to throw you overboard."

"Stupid, stupid, stupid."

"You can't swim."

"There's no excuse for idiocy like— No, all right, take it easy, you're rocking the raft. Michael, think! We knew a servant had to have planted those forged ledgers, right?"

"It seemed like a logical possibility, but I talked to all of them and—"

"Who knew you were going to talk to Lenna Skinner? List them."

"You," I said pointedly. Fisk grinned. "Me. The rest of the household: Maxwell, Anna, Mistress Judith, Mistress Lissy, the children, the Trim— No."

"Trimmer. Right there, listening to all our plans as we made them. No wonder Worthington knew everything we did!"

"But he stayed! He was loyal!"

"Stayed, without pay, for four months. That should have made me suspicious from the start. No servant can afford that kind of loyalty—especially not a man whose wife's dresses are in better repair than my sisters'. " He fell silent, awaiting my next argument, but now 'twas my turn to remember.

"The note."

"What?"

"The note that led us to the Old Ropers' Home. He said a boy delivered it, and when I said I hadn't heard the knocker, he said the boy had come to the back. But Trimmer came into the kitchen from the dining room.

From the front hall. There was no boy. He had the note in his possession all the time. You're right, Fisk—we're fools."

There was a moment of silence while we contemplated this unfortunate fact. I broke it. "If Trimmer was bribed, by whoever it might be, what do you mean to do about it?"

"Lie," said Fisk. "I'm tempted to strangle the truth out of the him, but that might warn Worthington—oh, all right, whoever it is—that we're on to him. They already know you're alive; the girls were worried, so I told them this afternoon, and that means that Worthington knows it too. Hmm. I'll tell everyone I'm working on a plan to smuggle you out. Maybe it'll give me a chance to check a few things out without every building I enter going up in flames."

"And if 'tis not Master Worthington? Then what?"

"Then I'll strangle the truth out of Trimmer. Why are you so convinced it isn't Worthington?"

"Because—" The raft grated on the bottom near the bank. I started and looked at Nettie's Ma, who gestured for me to continue. "Because I can't imagine what his motive might be. And I think his liking for Maxwell is genuine. Worthington kept him from being prosecuted. Lent him money and support."

Fisk rose to his feet. "I'd feel guilty enough to do those things if I'd set up a friend. Mistress, you already have my deepest gratitude, but I'm afraid I'll have to impose on you further. How can I let you know to pick me up?"

"You can't," said Nettie's Ma. "I'll meet you here tomorrow night at dusk, and you can tell us what you've learned."

Fisk frowned. "I probably won't be finished by tomorrow. Maybe the next night would—"

"Tomorrow!" Nettie's Ma and I spoke together, though my voice was sharper. I suddenly realized that Fisk had found a way to keep me from fleeing without him—there was no way I could leave now! "Tomorrow, Fisk," I repeated firmly. "Or I'll think something has happened and come in search of you."

"Don't do that! You're not safe in this town. I'll come tomorrow night." He stepped off the raft and splashed through the shallows to the bank.

"Fisk, be careful. Whoever this man is, he's dangerous. If he suspects—"

"Why should he? I told you, I'm going to lie."

"Then lie well," I commanded, and wondered at the strange smile that lit his face.

"I always do," he said. "But in a way, I hope it isn't Worthington."

"'Twould be hard for Max," I agreed, "to know his friend betrayed him."

"Friendship be hanged." Fisk grinned. "I still want it to be Judith." He strode off before I could caution him further, which was mayhap as well, for my nagging sprang more from my own worry than from any likelihood that Fisk would fail to take care.

I talked Nettie's Ma into letting me take the pole for a time—sore wrist or no, I could no longer endure sitting idle. I pushed off into the shallows, and Nettie's Ma sat crosslegged where her weight balanced mine and neither laughed nor complained as I steered us in circles.

The sun was setting, its mellow light flashing on the ripples produced by my clumsiness. The chill of the winter day was giving way to real cold, and the birds had retired. The loudest sound was the splash of my pole, and the peace of the place settled into my heart and eased it. When Nettie's Ma spoke, her voice was so soft, it didn't even make a ripple in the stillness.

"You like the marish, don't you? Most find it muddy and drab, but it touches you."

"Yes. 'Tis a subtle beauty, but I think it as lovely as any place I've seen."

She nodded, and the silence returned as I steered

us around a bend, overcorrected, and spun us lazily until I got the raft straightened and moving forward again.

"Have you thought what you'll do when you and your friend are finished here? When this Worthington, or whoever it is, is discovered?"

"Move on," I said, trying to fight the chill that touched my heart. Once the crime was solved, it should be possible to persuade Fisk to stay. He loved his family, and having cleared Max, he'd have earned his place. If he failed, and they had to leave, they'd need him even more. Even more than I would. The raft started to spin again and I swore.

"You could stay here."

"In the marish?" I stared at Nettie's Ma in amazement.

"Aye. It's not as harsh a life as you might think. And those marks on your wrists would matter no more to the human folk here than they do to the birds and the otters."

"I always wanted to travel," I said slowly. "To see the sun rise over a different hill each morning. But you're right. Out there, 'twill be hard to be . . . I don't know how to say it. Unchanged?"

She nodded. "It's almost impossible not to become what folks think you are. In all my life, this is the only place I've been able to be who *I* am. You already know the shape they'll be pushing you into. Think on it, that's all."

I did. And I shivered.

CHAPTER 12

Fisk

It was dinnertime when I reached Max's house, even though I went straight there. I didn't bother to elude the deputy, disguised as a ratcatcher, who picked me up shortly after I emerged from the marish. Potter was no fool—he knew where Michael would wash up, and when I didn't resume my search first thing tomorrow, he'd know he was alive. Potter was no problem, for Nettie's Ma was right about the marish. It was Worthington who worried me.

Michael still had his doubts, but I was certain the moment I saw D'VORIN embossed in the soft gold. He'd been too close, too kind, too cursed *nice*—why I hadn't suspected him before?

But the law wouldn't act without proof, and I had no proof. I wouldn't be getting any tonight, either. In the last twenty-four hours I'd fought a fire, tramped through a swamp, uncovered a murderer, gotten no sleep, and worried a lot. But I wasn't too tired to enjoy the expression on the face of the street sweeper in front of Max's house when I strolled past him. He fell into a spirited argument with the ratcatcher who'd followed me from the marish, and I was so amused by the two of them that I forgot Trimmer would be opening the door. I barely had time to conceal my expression with a yawn.

Over dinner I assured the others once more of Michael's safety. With Trimmer hovering unobtrusively in the background (the urge to throttle him was amazingly strong), I mentioned Michael's reluctance to leave the horses, and that it would take some time to come up with a plan to smuggle them out. I added that it would also be wise to let the search die down and went to bed without so much as glancing at Trimmer, congratulating myself on having won several days to investigate.

After breakfast I noted the positions of the beggar in the back alley and the chimney sweep, whose handcart had broken down within sight of Max's front gate, and then went through the orchard, over the outer wall, and down the road into town.

Tradition held that the worst of the winter storms

waited till after Calling Night. It didn't always work that way, but this year it looked like tradition was right on target. Gray clouds marched in from the sea, and the wind that carried them was cold enough to make me clutch my cloak tighter and wish I'd brought a scarf.

No one seemed to be following me as I made my way over Drybridge to Master Clogger's wheelwright shop, though with everyone bundled up against the chill, it was hard to be certain. The poor fools watching Max's house were going to freeze.

I had to go round to the yard to find Clogger, but he let me without hesitation, announcing that he didn't hold with mobs no matter what anyone said. He glared at a neighbor's windows as he spoke, but I already knew what the townsfolk thought. As long as Michael was safe, it didn't matter—though if a mob came after me, that would change in a hurry. I wondered why Worthington had chosen to frame Michael alone and not both of us. It might be because Michael wouldn't be granted a hearing, where our suspicions could be publicly aired, but still . . .

When Michael had turned up on Max's doorstep, with his self-esteem battered almost beyond recognition, I'd been forced to desperate measures to shake him back into himself. Now I was trying to balance that against the need to keep him alive, and it wasn't easy—but at least I was no longer worried that he'd abandon me for my own good. With Michael, curiosity was a stronger bond than chains.

Clogger wasn't as indifferent to the neighbors as he pretended, or maybe he just wanted to get out of the cold, for he led me into his shop. I told him, as gently as I could, about discovering the pack, and anguish twisted his blunt face. I hardly needed to ask, "You'd recognize that pack, wouldn't you?"

"Yes. I watched him load it. It was a good piece of work. One of his best. He was a good tanner, a good man. If he'd just . . ." He stopped to take a deep, shaking breath. "How did it happen?"

"He was knifed. Very quick, very clean. He'd barely have had time to realize what was happening," I lied.

Clogger sighed. "I wish . . . He was so angry with those bastards. What they'd done to that girl. Angry and sad. I can't believe he'd lie about it, even to pay his debts. But if someone killed him to keep him silent . . ."

"He could have been killed to keep him silent even if he didn't lie—to keep him from denying it when the scandal about Maxwell broke."

"And that old woman too? You think they killed her?" He went to his cluttered workbench and sank down on a stool, as if standing was suddenly too much effort. He picked up a wheel spoke from a pile on the bench, turned it, and put it back.

"Two people could have sworn that Max didn't bribe them to lie. Both are dead, one murdered and one 'committed suicide.' What do you think?"

"But if that's true, where did Ren get the money? I thought about what you said the other day. I talked to some of his friends. The ones he paid off. All of them told me that Ren wouldn't say where the money came from. A few said he told 'em that 'a very generous man' was helping him out. That was all they knew." He picked up a plane, caressed the smooth grip, and replaced it. He picked up a chisel.

A very generous man. A philanthropist perhaps?

"Did anyone mention a name? Or anything else Ren said about the man?"

"No. One of them had the impression somebody had hired Ren to act as his agent—broker some kind of deal. But Ren was being discreet, for once in his life." He abandoned the chisel and picked up a hatchet, thumping the blunt end into his palm. "You think that's what he did? Promised Ren a good job in another town, so his departure wouldn't raise suspicion, and then killed him."

"Yes," I said quietly. "That's what I think. I'm sorry."

Thump, thump, thump. The hatchet seemed to satisfy him, for he kept it.

"You're sure no one mentioned anything that would give me a clue to the man's identity?" I asked.

"Nothing. 'A very generous man' was the only thing Ren told 'em. Who do you think it is?"

Thump. Thump.

I didn't dare mention Worthington's name. "I don't know. But when I do, your brother will have justice."

I left him gazing into space, pounding the hatchet softly against his palm.

Having no desire to repeat Michael's mistakes, I went round to the tannery's back gate to see Mistress Skinner. I succeeded in avoiding the mob but not the husband, who flatly refused to let me in. But there's more than one way to lift a purse.

I walked down the street Mistress Skinner would take to the nearest market, found a sheltered nook beside some high steps, and settled in to wait . . . and wait . . . and wait. . . .

My buttocks became numb, and I rose to pace. I was so cold, I started to feel sorry for the deputies watching Max's house. I waited some more. Mid-meal came and went. I got hungry. I paced again. I waited.

I was questioning the wisdom of this strategy for

about the hundredth time when Mistress Skinner came down the street carrying an empty basket. She wore a man's coat and a long scarf, which was a lot more practical than a cloak in this wind.

I rose from my shadowy corner as she passed. "Mistress Skinner? May I speak with you a moment?"

She spun, her eyes widening. "You! Den said he ran you off."

"He did." I smiled. When I want to, I can look *very* harmless. Actually, I look harmless even when I don't want to. "But I really need to speak to you. We can stay here on the street if you wish. Or there's an inn over there—we could have tea. Whatever you'd like."

She settled at this reassuring speech, but her eyes were thoughtful. I wondered if she'd noticed that not talking to me wasn't among the options I listed.

"I don't know which would be safer," she said. "I'm sorry about what happened to your friend. The mob, I mean. I'd have let him in if I'd realized they'd chase him like that. I'm glad he escaped. Both times."

I forgot my reassuring act and frowned. "How do you know he escaped the second time? That he's still alive, I mean?"

She smiled. "Because if he wasn't, you'd have a very different expression on your face today. If you want folk to think he's dead, you'll have to—"

"I don't," I said. I might have if I'd thought of it. The search would die quicker. And I could have circled back from the marish and done my investigating while the deputies thought I was looking for Michael's body in the swamp. Why hadn't I thought of it?

My irritation must have shown, for she laughed softly. "The inn, Master Fisk. Den's less likely to find us indoors."

A brisk fire blazed on the hearth, but the mid-meal crowd had gone and we had the place almost to ourselves. I took the opportunity to order a sandwich with my tea.

"So why is it so important for you to talk to me, Master Fisk? I told you all I knew that first day. If Ma didn't kill herself, I don't know it. Or at least, I can't prove it." Irony tainted her bleak voice, and her eyes were dry. I began to hope a rational conversation was possible. I also thought I might be able to trust her. Her husband, on the other hand . . . Maybe a roundabout approach would be wiser.

"I have some new questions today. Have you ever heard of a man named Yorick Thrope?"

"Your friend asked me that. I told him the truth—I never heard that name before his office burned down."

"How about your mother? Did she know him?"

Lenna Skinner shrugged. "Not that I know of, but

it's possible. 'Specially if he bought fish."

"Everybody buys fish," I said. "How about Benjamin Worthington?"

"Oh!" She smiled. "Of course I know Master Worthington. Ma did too. He's a fine man, and he's been a good friend to us."

I schooled my well-trained face to hide my sudden surge of interest. "How do you know him? In what capacity, I mean?"

She smiled again, a little sadly. "You mean how could we be friends since he's so rich." It wasn't a question. "I suppose it is a bit one-sided, but if he ever needs our help, he's got it. My pa was a rope maker. When Ma got sick, the Fishmongers' Guild paid out, of course, but only magica medicine eased the pain when it took her bad. As a roper's widow Ma was entitled to their guild's aid as well, and they did help. But Master Worthington was more generous than the guild, and not just with money. He'd come by from time to time, to be sure she didn't lack for anything. Bring her a bit of fruit or a warm shawl and talk awhile. Ma used to flirt with him. I hear he visits most on the ropers' sick list. He's on the charity board, you see. But most charity board members just meet once a month to have a good dinner and glance at the ledgers. They don't really care about the people they're helping. Not like

Master Worthington. Why do you ask?"

"His name came up and I wanted your opinion of him, that's all." This wasn't the first time a con had taken a dangerous turn, but that didn't quench the fear leaping along my nerves. If she went to Worthington . . . . I smiled easily. "What do you think of Sheriff Potter?"

"We've had no dealings with him, except when he looked into Ma's death. The writing on the note was hers, and enough medicine to kill her was gone from the bottle. There was no sign of a struggle. He asked a lot of questions, but those were the things that mattered. That, and the money in her chest."

"Her chest? I thought she had a bank account."

Lenna snorted. "She was a fishmonger, not a rich merchant. She kept her money in the chest at the foot of her bed, in a lockbox. Except the money for . . . the money they say she got from Maxwell. That was just there, in the chest under her clothes. Bags and bags, and her box with only a few fracts in it. More money than Den and I had ever seen in one place." Her mouth flattened unhappily. "She was dead. Den says that you don't scuttle the ship that carries your own cargo." She drew a shaking breath. "But that's blood money, Master Fisk, and it's my ma's blood. She felt so bad about that poor girl being murdered. She'd never lie about a thing like that—I don't care what the writing on that note looked like. I know she was dying, but it shouldn't have happened so sudden. No time to . . . to say things." She wiped her cheeks angrily. "Anything else you want to ask me? I'll tell you whatever you want to know if it helps catch the man who did that to Ma. I don't care what Den says."

"All right. Have you heard of a man called Josiah Marcher?"

I made up more names, and asked her about two members of the Tanners' Guild Council, so when I left Worthington was only one of several upright, honorable men that I'd inquired about.

When I thought about Ginny Weaver chatting with the good friend who carried her suicide note in his pocket, and that incriminating money in his saddlebags, I regretted having eaten the sandwich. But Worthington hadn't had the key to her lockbox, and I was surprised that hadn't caught Potter's attention. Even if it had, there wasn't much he could do about it. The evidence that her suicide was genuine was overwhelming, and I still had no proof. But speaking of keys . . .

"Good afternoon, good Sir. Can you tell me where I might find Yorick Thrope?"

The tailor, who sat crosslegged on the floor, blinked

up sympathetically through gold-rimmed spectacles. "Client of his, were you, Sir?" He rose from his place beside the half-clad dummy as he spoke. "I'm afraid I don't know where he's staying—the judicary could tell you. But if you're hoping your papers survived, I have to warn you they didn't get anything out. Not that Master Thrope . . . Ah, that's to say, the fire was too fierce."

"Not that Thrope concerned himself with his clients' papers," I said dryly.

"Well, it'd be hard to think of work with all you owned going up in flames." He didn't sound convinced, and I suppressed a smile. It was no surprise to learn that Thrope's neighbors didn't like him either. Still . . .

"I suppose it would be hard. He must have had most of his savings in that building, for property in this part of town comes high."

The tailor snorted. "He didn't own the place; he was renting. All Thrope's money went . . . Well, let's just say that I value him high as a customer." His eyes sparkled, and I had to laugh. But he went on, "It's Master W takes the loss for the building. Though he'll likely have been insured."

"Master W?" I stifled an urge to grab his vest and shake him. "That'd be Benjamin Worthington?"

"Of course. He owns quite a bit of property around here—he's a good landlord, too. Made me a fair price when I saved up enough to buy. Not a cheap price, mind, but a fair one." He looked around his little shop with pride.

It was no trouble to extract the information that Master Worthington had a manager who handled his rentals, a harder man than Master W, but honest. I couldn't think of a way to bring keys into the conversation without arousing suspicion, but the manager almost certainly kept duplicate keys to all the properties in his office, and Worthington would have access to that office. It wasn't proof, but the number of connections I was amassing should convince even Michael.

Passing over Trullsgate Bridge took me almost to the doorstep of the burned-out brothel. The neighbors all knew where Mistress Morna had relocated—she was just two blocks away.

The ramshackle, half-rotted buildings of the stews held memories I didn't want to examine, and the sour, musty smell of Morna's new place brought the past back even more sharply. She'd just awakened when I arrived, and her bed robe was her real one, warm and worn, not a working garment. "Bit early for a social call, isn't it, mate?"

"This isn't a social call, Mistress. I just want to ask a few questions."

"Why?" Her gaze ran over me, placing my station and pricing my clothes as expertly as I could have done it. "You're no deputy."

"Do you care why?"

She grinned at that. "Not at all, but I warn you, my time costs."

"I'll gladly pay your usual price for half an hour, deservedly high though I'm sure it is." I bowed, suppressing a wince at the thought of how thin my purse was growing.

"Ah, but questions are something special, and special, as everyone knows, costs extra."

I gazed into the clouded mirror that hung over the mantel. "Have I suddenly started to look like an easy mark? I didn't when I shaved this morning. . . ."

We settled on a gold roundel for the inconvenience and a silver one for each question, which was perfectly outrageous, but she was a shrewd bargainer. And even at a silver roundel each I didn't dare let her guess my purpose—if she scented further profit, she'd be on Worthington's doorstep in an instant.

Somewhat to my surprise she hadn't heard of Thrope until he became known as a hanging judicar. She knew nothing of Worthington. She'd never heard of my imaginary folk either, though one of the tanners' councilmen was a regular.

I paid her off and left her to her breakfast, feeling amused, sad, and frustrated. No help there.

The Old Ropers' Home was only a few blocks away. Though I saw daylight through the window of the room that had been next to the burning parlor, the front door was still intact. I rapped hard and prepared to wait, remembering the elderly doorman from Calling Night, but the door was opened almost at once by Mistress Mapple herself.

"You!" She started to slam it, and I swiftly inserted one foot, which was promptly mashed into the door-frame with bruising force.

I yelped, shoved the door open, and limped, swearing, into the hall. Part of the parlor wall had burned away, and the gap was filled with wide boards. The scent of burning lingered, but the hall had been cleaned. Mistress Mapple, starchy as ever, folded her arms and lifted her chin.

"How dare you, Sir! I'm amazed—"

"How dare *you*, Madam. Of all the ungrateful . . ."

We wrangled for several minutes before she conceded that neither Michael nor I had had any opportunity to start the fire and that we had, in fact, helped fight it.

I, in turn, conceded that I shouldn't have tried to push my way in—though that didn't give her the right to assault me!

She liked confrontation, especially if she won, and soon we were on such comfortable terms that she was happy to sit on the steps beside me and gossip about the fire's aftermath. Aside from the deaths, which sent grief skittering over her stiff face, the damage could have been much worse. And Master Worthington had personally offered to help them rebuild since the Ropers' Guild wasn't in great revenue at the moment.

"I haven't heard there's anything wrong with the rope-making business," I said leadingly.

"The guild lost a lot when the docks burned. Everyone did. Then that silly young man messed up the books, and the charity fund's been in dreadful shape ever since."

It seemed that on top of their losses, the guild had been foolish enough to put one of their councilman's wastrel sons in charge of the charity fund's bookkeeping. Not an uncommon practice, for it was a soft job and paid well. The young wastrel, however, hadn't done even the minimal amount of work required. When he'd been promoted, and shipped off to wreak havoc on the ropers' bureau in Allenston, the books were a mess and the home had been on short funds ever since. "Though Master Griffin says we'll be back on our feet within the year, and *he* is a very competent young man."

"Not another wastrel son, then?"

"Oh, no. Master Griffin is Master Worthington's own secretary. A very respectful young man, though not married, which just shows you how blind girls are these days."

I already had plenty of connections between Worthington and this fire, so my curiosity was completely idle when I asked, "So why are all the girls blind to Master Griffin?"

She snorted. "The most ridiculous reason imaginable. I mean, who cares if a man has hair or not? It's what's under the hair that counts. It's not his fault he's gone bald so young, poor lad. I swear, girls today . . ."

My own hair was still prickling on the back of my neck when I took my leave.

"So you think 'twas Worthington's secretary who warned folk not to speak with me?" Michael asked.

"And probably set the mob on you as well. It all fits."

Nettie's Ma handed me a haunch of roast rabbit, which I accepted with a grateful smile. There was only one chair at her table and I sat there, while Michael perched on the bed and she sat on the tiny stool by

the fire. I appreciated the courtesy, but I'd have preferred to trade places with her—I was still half frozen
from the journey across the marish.

When I left the Old Ropers' Home, the wind had
acquired a raw bite that made the simple cold of the
day look balmy, and I had only a few hours left before
my promised meeting with Nettie's Ma. I hurried back
to Max's house and slipped over the orchard wall with
some caution. Sooner or later even the dullest deputy
would figure this one out, but they hadn't yet. They
were still at their posts outside Max's gates, and one
had had the good sense to disguise himself as a seller
of hot nuts, which gave him an excuse for a brazier on
his cart.

Anna came in and sat on my bed as I changed into
the warmest clothes my pack provided. She used to
come and sit on my bed when I came back from a
night of thieving, to assure herself of my continued
well-being and, I sometimes thought, to assure me that
my sisters cared, no matter how indifferent the rest of
the world might be. The impulse to confide everything, as I used to, was strong. I steered the subject to
the honorable Master Worthington and gritted my
teeth as she exalted his kindness to everyone from his
disgraced friends to "that worthless mutt he rescued"—which didn't impress me, as I've known several

villains who were kind to animals and even more who loved their mothers. Before I left, I borrowed Max's warmest cloak for Michael and took an old one of Lissy's to offer Nettie's Ma.

I was late reaching the marish, and spent the voyage through the chained ponds and channels telling Michael and Nettie's Ma what I'd learned and trying to keep my teeth from chattering. As we glided over the dark water, the wind died, and snow began to fall in thick, determined flakes. At least the mud hut was small enough that the hearth fire warmed it.

"Mayhap it does fit," Michael replied now, "but all you have is a series of vague connections. Worthington has a good, no, an admirable reason for everything he's done. And he must be sincerely charitable, at least in part, for he befriended Ginny Weaver long before that poor girl was killed. If they laughed at your theory and hanged me on the spot, I couldn't blame them. He has no motive, Fisk, and you have no proof."

"We just started asking the right questions. Look how much I learned in one day, once I knew enough to ask about Worthington."

"But why? Master Maxwell is his friend. I'd swear to it."

"Yes, that's another link. He's connected to Max, too."

"So? He has no reason to destroy him."

"He must have a reason. We're just not seeing it."

Nettie's Ma had been quiet so long, I jumped when she spoke. "Were they connected in some other way? How did they become friends?"

"I don't know how they met," I said. "But it was probably through the Ropers' Guild. Worthington got his start as a rope maker, and he's still involved with their charities. Such a charitable man."

"Well, you can't condemn him for that," said Michael.

"Oh, can't I? A cursed hypocrite is what he is. He's probably selling the orphan girls to brothels."

Michael laughed. I didn't. I try not to hate people, because Jack Bannister taught me that hatred clouds your judgment. But with the honorable Master Worthington it was a hard fight.

"What's Maxwell's link with the ropers?" Nettie's Ma asked. "Nettie said he was a judicar."

"He is," Michael told her. "But he began his career as the ropers' law clerk. 'Tis likely how he and Worthington became friends, for they must have dealt together often."

"Wait a minute!" I sat up so briskly the chair wobbled. "That's another connection! The fire in the Old Ropers' Home killed two old ropers. Maybe they knew something, or . . . or something."

Michael snorted. "If they knew something, why didn't they go to the law?"

"Maybe Worthington bribed . . . No, I suppose not. No one with a fract to spare would live under Mistress Mapple's thumb, and . . ." The idea surfaced slowly, like a bubble through mud. The mud of my own stupidity, for watching the pieces click neatly into place, I couldn't imagine why I hadn't seen it before. Unlike Michael, I understand what motivates men.

Rough hands locked on my shoulders and shook me. "Fisk, if you don't tell me, I swear I'll—"

"All right, all right, let go. You're going to break the chair."

"I'm going to break your head if you don't—"

"*Money*, Michael."

"I don't have much. Why? Do you need—"

"No, money is the motive!"

"But Worthington's rich."

"Maybe. Oh, all right. But it has to be money. The old ropers died by accident. If they hadn't been hiding, drunk, they'd have gotten out with everyone else. What's the other thing that fire accomplished?"

"Well, it—"

"It burned up the ledgers! The ropers' charity books that Worthington so generously offered his own secretary to keep. It was probably the ledgers he wanted to destroy all along, and the other two fires were set to keep people from looking for a rational motive for the one at the Old Ropers' Home. His arsonist probably had the whole thing planned—they were just looking for someone to take the blame. Then you showed up, a stranger, and unredeemed to boot."

Michael's mouth had opened and closed several times during this speech. "You think he was embezzling from the ropers' charities? But he's rich!"

Nettie's Ma stirred. "A lot of rich men got poorer last summer when the docks burned. You could see the flames from all over the marish. Did he have cargo on those ships?"

"He did," I said. "But not much. He had too many ships out to invest heavily."

"Or so he told us," said Michael thoughtfully. "But I don't think a man like Worthington got rich by letting opportunities pass him by. My father would have borrowed, in a situation like that. Mayhap Master Worthington did too."

There was a long, speculative silence. But . . . "Hard to believe the local bankers weren't suspicious when he paid off his note. Especially if he had ships out. Bankers pay attention to things like that."

"He likely borrowed in Fallon," said Nettie's Ma. "Everyone around here with a fract to spare had it on those ships, including the bankers."

"He owed money," said Michael. "And he had no way to pay it. So he takes it from the ropers' charity fund, which he controls since his secretary does the books."

"Mistress Mapple said they'd been short of funds since the dock fire."

"And he plans to pay it back when his ships come in. But that will take months, and—"

"Maybe it occurs to him that if he scrambled the books well enough he might not have to pay the money back."

Michael's gaze was fixed on nothing—I'm not even sure he heard me. "And then he learns his friend Maxwell is about to be appointed to the charity board."

"What?"

"Don't you remember? They talked about it at dinner that first night."

All I remembered about that dinner was seeing Becca and Thomas for the first time. But Michael went on, "Maxwell, who'd actually *kept* the ropers' charity books when he was a clerk. He'd have noticed the discrepancies. And he's not the kind to quit when he sees something suspicious. So Worthington had to stop Maxwell's appointment. Maxwell had just hanged two

men, and Worthington knew one of the witnesses personally, and the other was a gambler deep in debt. . . .
You're right, Fisk. It fits."

The crackle and pop of the fire was the only sound.

"Can you prove it?" Nettie's Ma finally asked. "If he's
burned up the ledgers and killed the witnesses, he's
covered his tracks."

"I'll bet anything you name he hasn't burned all the
ledgers." I love the predictability of humankind. "He's
a merchant. They're compulsive about ledgers. He'll
have his own books, true ones, tucked somewhere in
his office, just waiting for a team of judicary auditors
to look them over. All we have to do is extract them."

Nettie's Ma frowned. "That's crazy. This man kills
when he's crossed. Call in the law."

"We can't." Not that I would if I could. I've never
met a law officer I'd trust with a delicate affair like this
one. "Worthington's too powerful. Potter's head would
roll if he didn't find those books. He couldn't risk it."

"But it sounds like a perfect task"—a lunatic grin lit
Michael's face—"for a knight errant and his squire."

There were three inches of snow on the ground when
I went through the orchard gate into Max's garden, and
it showed no sign of stopping. That was good, for if it
didn't cover my tracks by morning, even the most foolish

deputy would know how I was getting in and out. My escape route had to work for only one more day.

Both moons were buried in the clouds, but the colorless light of snowfall was enough to guide me to the back door without mishap. I eased it open with barely a sound, for I'd taken the precaution of oiling the hinges right after Calling Night. But no one had oiled the alley gate—its squeal was shockingly loud in the stillness. I leapt into the house and closed the door, leaving only a crack to peek through.

Two cloaked figures stood, framed by the gate posts, one shorter than the other. So much shorter that the tall one had to lean down to kiss her, and her hood fell back. It was Lissy. The man must be young Fowler, and judging by the length of that embrace, not to mention the lateness of the hour, they must be lovers. I hoped the deputy on duty enjoyed the show.

They finally released each other, and she closed the gate and crossed the garden, snow catching in her hair. Her expression was dreamy, but when I opened the door for her, she shrieked softly and jumped several inches.

"Come in, little sister. We're letting in the cold."

"Gracious, you startled me! And you can stop looking like that, Nonny, because it's none of your business."

A night candle burned in a small holder on the wall; I lit one of the candles I'd left on the shelf beside the door, then another for Lissy. "I suppose it would be foolish to play the protective brother after all these years. But it is Max and Anna's business."

"That's not what I meant. It's no more their business than it is yours." Her face in the golden light was composed, and so lovely I had to fight down a fresh urge to go after young Fowler and punch him out.

"You're underage, and—"

"Legally, yes. But I didn't think you cared much about law. And speaking of the law . . ." Her eyes ran over my wet coat and muddy boots. She didn't have to say another word.

"You wouldn't."

"Not unless you forced me to. And seriously, Nonny, there's no reason you should worry. I know what I'm doing."

"Playing the . . ." I couldn't say it. "Playing games with young Fowler?"

She grinned. "Playing the slut, you were going to say? Don't be silly. He wanted to ask Max for permission to marry me months ago—I'm the one who insisted we wait. I can't run out on Annie while this mess is unresolved. But I promise you, his intentions are honorable. Does that make you feel better?" She took her candle and turned toward the stairs.

"You're too young. I ought to call your cursed bluff." But I didn't dare, and we both knew it. The last thing I'd need tomorrow night was a pile of deputies underfoot.

She laughed, and I suddenly realized that she was only ten years old in my own mind. It was time to start seeing her for the woman she was, instead of the child she'd been. That young woman was a near stranger, and I'd no right to take her father's role. Not that *he'd* have done anything, even if he'd been alive.

But the loss of my ten-year-old sister hurt, even when her older self hugged me and bid me good night.

CHAPTER 13

Michael

The storm continued through most of the next day, leaving over a foot of snow in its wake. I didn't envy Fisk the task of scouting Worthington's home. Meanwhile Nettie's Ma and I sat snug in her hut, composing the note that would lure Master Worthington away for a few, crucial hours.

I found the tanner's body and I know you killed him. I don't want much. Just food and other stuff, delivered to the marish regular. Meet me tonight . . .

The note was simple. 'Twas harder for her to convince me she'd be safe. I'd wanted to leave her out of it, and just burgle the place in the middle of the night. But Fisk said merchants frequently worked late, and that we needed to get in before the night watch started making rounds. Nettie's Ma had laughed and said that she could keep Worthington chasing her in circles till dawn. Given her skills and her knowledge of the marish, I knew she was right. But this was a man who killed when he felt himself endangered, and the snow would make it all but impossible to hide her trail.

Unfortunately, I had no better plan. As the Creature Moon rose higher, I set out to meet Fisk in the shadow of the Eastgate as we'd agreed, and a strange, half-painful elation filled my heart. I don't know what impulse had seized me, to claim this bit of madness as knight errantry—my last act of errantry, no doubt. I broke my wrist when I was nine. When the bones finally knit, and the healer freed me from the splint, for a time moving my arm was agony . . . but to finally be free of the binding of cloth and wood had felt so *right*. As if I was whole again, no matter how much it ached.

'Twas still early, so there were folk on the streets, but I'd stitched some unnecessary patches onto Max's cloak and wrapped an old scarf around my face. Fisk's first words were an approving "You'll do."

His own face was red with cold.

"Don't you own a scarf? I'd offer you this one, but—"

"Don't you dare! If I had my way, you'd be safe in

the swamp, helping that wily old fox dodge a killer. Though now that I think about it, she's probably better off not having to look after an amateur."

I sighed. "I reached the same conclusion. But it's hard to let an old woman fight our battles for us."

"Nonsense—she loved the idea. I'm just glad she got you wrapped up properly."

"'Twas not her idea," I admitted, "but mine. Remember when I told you that I'd not conceal my shame? I've changed my mind—I'm going to conceal it for all I'm worth. 'Tis too hard, Fisk. Folk see only the tattoos, not me at all."

I was not the man those marks proclaimed, and I'd not let others force me into becoming that man. Neither would I court a punishment I hadn't earned, and if that was cowardice, so be it.

Fisk was staring at me. "I think . . . I'm not sure, but I *think* that's the first sensible thing I've ever heard you say. We should celebrate!"

I had to laugh, which was no doubt his purpose. "We're setting forth on a noble adventure—what better celebration could there be?"

Fisk sighed. "I take it back. You haven't changed a bit."

I smiled behind my concealing scarf, but my smile soon faded. I had changed. Indeed, I'd all but lost myself in other folks' fear and disdain. And 'twas Fisk who'd restored my spirit, a piece at a time, whenever he introduced me as a knight errant.

Worthington's house lay at the outskirts of town where the largest, newest houses are built. In this wealthy neighborhood the snow had been shoveled off the streets instead of trampled down. It made for easier walking.

The manor and its grounds covered an entire block, surrounded by a stone wall eight feet high. We walked right past Worthington's gate, and I was about to ask where we could hide to watch it when Fisk tugged me, into the shallow shelter of one of the neighbors' gates.

"We're going to watch from here? What if the folk who live here come out?"

"It's the only cover I've found, and I spent most of the day walking around these walls. This house is empty except for a caretaker, and we can see Worthington's front gate without being too obvious."

"But what if someone passes and sees us lurking here?"

Fisk shrugged. "If we see anyone, we'll step out and walk past them talking about how cursed high the price of this house is. Which reminds me, take those patches off your cloak. They stand out in this neighborhood."

I drew my dagger and did so, my sore wrist a little stiffer in the cold. "What if Worthington goes out the back gate?"

"We'll wait an hour after your messenger comes out, assume he's gone, and go in. You told the boy to give the note to Worthington personally, didn't you?"

"Just as we planned."

"Then that's the best we can do. Life's not perfect— if Judith had done it, I'd be a lot warmer now. You know, she could still be involved. Maybe she's Worthington's inside man, instead of Trimmer."

"And what's her motive supposed to be now?"

Fisk grinned. "Maybe she and Worthington are lovers—she's smart enough to look to the money."

"He's old enough to be her father!"

"So? It didn't stop Max. Maybe . . . Is that the boy you hired to bring the note? So soon?"

"I told him to wait half an hour before he set out. Why stand in the cold longer than we must?"

"Um."

We watched from the clinging shadows as the boy rang the gate bell. He was admitted so quickly, I blinked in astonishment.

"Does Worthington have some poor gatekeeper standing out in this cold?"

"Don't feel too sorry for him. He's got a little hut

with a brazier, and I think the menservants take it in shifts. They spent the day a lot warmer than I did."

"How do you know all this?"

"I managed to deliver a package earlier and become completely lost when I tried to find my way out. I got a pretty good look at the grounds. I didn't get a chance to count the staff, but Lissy's best guess was about two dozen."

"Lissy?"

"Why not? She'd just spent the night here, and a bit of blackmail ensures discretion wonderfully well. She even drew me a rough floor plan."

"Blackmail? You're black—"

"Shh! Here he comes."

The boy I'd paid to carry Nettie's Ma's note emerged from the gate and hurried down the street. By now 'twas almost too dark to see him go; only a hint of sunset colored the western sky, and the moons had not yet risen. It was very cold.

"The dance commences," Fisk said softly. He sounded as if he was quoting someone, but before I could ask, he went on, "I wonder how long it will take Worthington to— Is that him? I'll be hanged! I didn't expect him to move so fast."

Worthington stopped to talk with the gatekeeper, who passed him something—almost certainly the key.

'Twas considerate, not to keep his servant waiting in the cold while he was out disposing of inconvenient witnesses. I began to share Fisk's dislike for the man, especially when he locked the gate behind him.

"Are you going to pick the lock?" I whispered, watching Worthington's cloaked form stride briskly down the street toward the marish. He carried a long walking stick—something I'd never seen him use before.

"To keep him from slipping in the snow, no doubt," Fisk murmured.

"Nettie's Ma knows what she's about." I tried to sound more confident than I felt, but I doubt I succeeded.

Fisk grimaced. "No, I'm not going to kneel on cold stone for ten minutes while every neighbor peers out his window and wonders whether he should fetch the sheriff. We're going over the back wall, which will take about ten seconds."

And so it proved, for in this tidy part of town they'd placed bins for the midden outside the back gates. They made a most convenient stepping stone.

Once we were sitting comfortably atop the wall, Fisk glanced at the dark back windows of the nearby houses. "Stay here a moment, will you? I'm going to scout the grounds, and if I have to get out in a hurry you can pull me up."

I gazed over the empty expanse of the gardens. "Why should you need to escape? There's nothing here. I don't even see a privy."

"All inside, according to Lissy. Nice on a night like this. I don't know why I'd need to escape in a hurry. You never know until it happens. Why is it everything I do with you ends up in burglary? I hate burglary. I retired from burglary!"

I grinned. "Mayhap 'tis your destiny."

Fisk gave me a black look, lowered himself till he hung from his hands, then dropped into the snow.

He crouched low, going from one clump of barren bushes to another, but his every step left a trail a babe could track, a matter I resolved to mention to him. But I wasn't too concerned as he made his way along the side of the house, for 'twas far too cold for anyone to wander outside.

In fact, I thought his caution a waste of time. 'Twas also too cold to perch on a stone wall like an overlarge gargoyle. I was about to descend and follow him, despite his instructions, when he stiffened, turned, and raced for the wall—the sleek shadow on his heels gaining with every leaping bound.

Fisk must have known he wasn't going to make it, for he changed course and raced toward a nearby tree. The dog was all but on his heels when he jumped for a low branch and swung up onto it—not quite in time.

The dog leapt, his jaws closing on a foot. Fisk's balance on the branch wasn't secure, and my heart surged into my throat as he tottered. Then his boot slipped off. The dog fell into the snow and shook his prize fiercely, making sure it was dead. Fisk scurried up three branches and perched there, clutching the trunk and rubbing his stockinged foot.

Seeing him safe, I became aware of two strange things. The first, that I was halfway across the garden with no memory of climbing down from the wall. And the second, even stranger, that this whole drama had taken place in silence—the dog wasn't barking.

Not that he didn't try. Now that the boot had been killed, he frisked beneath the tree, and his jaws moved but no sound emerged. I could hear the creak of snow-weighted branches and my own soft steps, or I might have feared for my ears. 'Twas not till I drew near that I heard his rasping gasps and realized the truth—the beast was mute. It was good of Worthington to keep him, for an animal born disabled is in the opposite position of one born magica. Few folk would have cared for him, and he'd be unlikely to survive in the wild.

I'd no fear for myself—animal handling is one of my more reliable Gifts, and I'm fond of dogs. Knowing it would be foolish to surprise him, I called softly. At first he was so excited, he didn't hear; then his head snapped around and he ran toward me. I waited till he was about ten feet off before telling him to *Sit!* in a quiet, masterful voice.

He understood the tone, the command, and the lifted hand, and he skidded to a stop before me, haunches tucked beneath him and a comical expression of confusion on his face.

He looked to be a cross between a hound and one of the larger breeds built for running. 'Twas now full dark and hard to judge his color, but he'd long, floppy ears, a ropy tail, and a lean build. His short fur was soft, especially his ears, which I tugged gently as I told him what a good dog he was. His tail lashed the snow.

He was a fine fellow, not long past puppyhood, I thought, and we were on the best of terms when I finally led him back to Fisk's tree. Fisk hadn't budged an inch, not even to descend to a lower crouch, and his whisper was full of indignation. "I looked for dogs. I listened for a dog the whole cursed day and never heard a bark. Who ever heard of a mute watchdog? It's insane."

"'Twas charitable of Worthington to take him in."

Fisk snorted. "Not that charitable—with three-inch teeth, who needs a bark? Lock it in a shed or something."

"If I pen him up, they might miss him—especially if

they call him in later, which I think likely on such a cold night. Once you've been properly introduced, he'll be fine. Come down."

Fisk eyed the dog, who sat at my side panting happily at his erstwhile prey. Dogs love to tree things.

"Thank you—I think I'll be introduced from up here. How do you do, mutt? My name is Fisk. And yours?"

I laughed and he shushed me, even though I did it softly. "Well, 'tis your fault. For pity's sake get down here."

Fisk descended reluctantly. The dog wagged his tail as he dropped to the ground, to show there were no hard feelings.

"This is Fisk," I told him. "He's a friend of mine, so you mustn't chase him." I knew it was my tone that mattered, but dogs understand us so well that you can't help but speak sensibly to them. And actions matter as much as tone.

"Hold out your hand, Fisk, and let him smell you."

"The way I'm sweating, it can do that from here." But he held out his hand and permitted the pup to sniff his fingers, only pulling back when the soft tongue flicked out. "What did it do that for?"

"He's just saying he accepts you. You can pet him now."

"Humph! Seeing if I taste like a late-night snack,

more like." He stroked the dog's head rather clumsily, and I made note of yet another thing to teach my squire. But the pup took the effort for the deed and beat the snow with his tail again. Indeed, after Fisk retrieved his boot, he followed us to the house, only going about his business when it became clear we weren't going to play anymore.

And creeping along the mansion's wall, thrashing through prickly junipers as Fisk sought a window frame loose enough to yield to a narrow knife blade, was far from play. The ground floor windows were dark, but some of the attic windows cast gold squares onto the snow. The servants, who rose early, were beginning to retire.

"Shouldn't we do this later, when everyone's in bed?" I whispered.

"One, it would have been hard to deliver a note to Worthington after he'd gone to bed. Two, he'd be a lot less likely to go haring off to the marish in the middle of the night than at dusk, even if it is dark by now. Three—"

"All right, all right. I just—"

Fisk's knife slid through a window frame, and he hissed in satisfaction as the latch twisted free. The window swung out without a sound, warm air breathing over us.

Fisk knocked his boots together to shake the snow off before climbing over the sill. I followed his example and then stood still, for the room was darker than the night outside.

"Wait a second for your eyes to adapt," Fisk whispered.

I've sometimes wondered if my squire is part cat because of his love of comfort and sleep, and when he ghosted forward after only a few seconds, I was certain of it.

Candlelight from the hall spilled in as Fisk opened the door. I joined him without knocking anything over, though my boots sounded louder than I liked when I stepped off the carpet.

Fisk stood in the open doorway for a long time, and I realized he was listening, though for what I couldn't say.

I heard only a soft clatter from the back of the house—it sounded as though someone was washing the dinner dishes—and an occasional creak of settling wood.

Finally he was satisfied and we crept down the hall, making little noise, for there was carpet here too. Even the stairs were carpeted, and we stole up them like . . . well, like burglars.

Fisk counted doors on the left, and Lissy's floor

plan must have been accurate; when he finally opened a door the light from the hall sconces revealed a large, paper-piled desk.

A small fire still flickered on the hearth, and the first thing Fisk did was to hurry across the room and draw the draperies over the tall windows. Then he dragged the rug that lay before the desk over to the door and folded one corner under so the roll of carpet blocked any light that might seep into the hall. Only then did he deal with the desk lamp, a chore that consisted of clipping up its side panels. Worthington was rich enough to light his study with magica phosphor moss. Its clear, white light made me glad for the thick curtains.

The furniture was made of richly grained wood with padded leather seats, and the big chair behind the desk had a padded back too. But even the elaborately patterned rug that covered the elaborately parqueted floor (or had before Fisk folded it against the door) was less expensive than the shelves of books that covered the entire wall opposite the fireplace.

"Hoof and horn! I've never seen a private library this large. And Master Worthington doesn't strike me as a scholar, either. What do you think they cost him?"

Fisk glanced at the books without much interest—strange, since books usually draw him like a magnet draws iron. "About six thousand, seven hundred gold roundels, give or take a few hundred."

His voice was soft but not a whisper. I assumed he knew what he was doing and replied at the same volume. "How do you know? You haven't even counted them."

"I don't have to. My father had about that many books."

"Your father had a library like this? But I thought . . ." The remote expression on his face silenced me.

"Oh, he made enough money," said Fisk. "And every fract of it went into books. He had the best history collection on the coast—even better than a university's."

"What became of it?" I asked.

"He willed it to the university. Sort of a 'see, I really was a scholar after all' gesture. It gave him a lot of satisfaction, in the end." Fisk's gaze roved over the shelves with a kind of hungry hatred. Then his eyes narrowed. One set of books had the tall, lean look of ledgers. They filled most of two shelves.

"I suppose we have to check," said Fisk slowly. "Though I'll bet the ledgers we want are tucked in a secret compartment somewhere. Rich people love secret compartments."

"Mayhap he disguised it to look like an older ledger—then he could hide it in plain sight."

By now we both stood before the bookshelves. "He might have done that, but it'd be risky. Why don't you check them out. Forget the dates, he could put down any date. Check the ending balance of each book and make sure it matches the beginning of the next." Fisk took the last ledger to the desk and spread it in the lamplight.

"What are you doing?" I asked, obediently opening the first ledger. The date on its first page was over twenty years ago.

"Um? Oh, I'm curious about the state of our charitable friend's finances about eight months ago." Fisk was already half lost in the columns of figures, so I started going through the older ledgers, though my mind wasn't on them. What kind of father leaves his one valuable asset to others, for vanity's sake, and his family impoverished? But at the same time, he'd given them so much love that they still grieved. And couldn't forgive. I wished I could give Fisk's father back to him, but childhood scars go deepest. And judging by my own relations with my father, I was in no position to give anyone advice on that score.

I wouldn't have recognized evidence of tampering if it had bitten me, but the sums matched and each was larger than the last. I traced the rise of Worthington's fortune, slow at first, then swifter. It didn't take long and I learned nothing but what I already knew—Worthington was a very wealthy man.

"Nothing." I crossed to the desk, where Fisk had appropriated the master's chair. "What have you found?"

"It's not what I found, it's what I haven't. He was telling the truth, that he didn't have much to invest eight months ago—two ships out on long voyages. One's due back soon, the other in three months. Several large loans, mostly to the new mining towns that have the smiths and metalworkers so upset. Those notes aren't due for over a year, though the towns are making small payments now."

"That's just what he told us."

"Ah, but what I don't see is any record of him investing in the cargo that burned—not even a fract. According to this, he hardly had a fract to spare."

"But he said he'd invested. Just not much."

"It was probably known that he invested something, so he couldn't deny it entirely. I'll show you something else that's not here." He turned a few pages and opened the ledger wide. I had to peer closely to see the edge of the neatly cut page.

"Clerks do cut pages out of ledgers sometimes," I said. "When they've spilled ink on them, or some such thing."

"So do merchants," said Fisk. "When that page

records a large loan from an out-of-town bank that they have no legitimate means to repay. This"—he ran a finger down the cleft where the page had been—"is where his hidden ledger starts. All we have to do is find it."

'Twas easier said than done. First Fisk took a ball of string from his pocket and we measured the width of the interior walls by running the string first from door frame to door frame, and then from the door frames to the interior wall on either side. This showed us the wall's thickness—about five inches. The wall that held the bookshelves was the same width.

"At least 'twas a clever idea," I commented.

"I wish I could take credit for it," Fisk replied. "But I once bribed a carpenter who built secret compartments. He taught me a lot."

"So where do we look next? Floors and ceilings?"

"Fireplace and furniture. Old Scroggin said you could hide a chest full of stuff in a fireplace, if you knew what you were about."

Given the amount of heat the glowing coals generated, I was glad to leave it to him. As Fisk rapped and prodded amid the carved wood and marble, I searched the desk. I found the usual quills, inkwells, penknives, paper of assorted weights, string, glue, ribbons, wax, seals—the list went on and included seashells, a cache of nuts and a silver nutcracker, a broken jumping jack, used pen wipers, tacks, keys . . .

What I didn't find were ledgers, or any compartment in which they might have been concealed. The hardest part was replacing everything so my search wouldn't be apparent.

"This is taking too long," I told Fisk, feeling the padding of the chair for concealed objects. I found nothing but padding.

"Relax. We were inside before he even reached the marish. Even if he came straight back, we'd have another hour, and Nettie's Ma promised to keep him talking."

"If he doesn't kill her." I had been searching the bottom of the chair; now I leaned against one side of the desk and gazed at the floor, fighting the worry that had lurked beneath my thoughts ever since this silly plan was first proposed.

"That'd delay him too," said Fisk calmly.

I'd have been furious if I hadn't known he didn't mean it. "Could you hide a compartment in the floor?"

"You can, but Scroggin said most people don't because of the possibility that someone will step on the trip lever. The bookshelves are a better bet."

I ignored him and started crawling about the floor, pressing the squares and rectangles of the pattern.

After a few minutes I decided to be methodical, starting at one side of the room and working from left to right and back again.

Fisk gave up on the fireplace and went to the bookshelves.

I had covered over two-thirds of the room before I found it, beside one wall and set a little lower than the rest of the floor, so that even if someone stood on it, it wouldn't trip the lever. But the small square yielded to my tired fingers with a click, and a section of flooring beside it lifted half an inch.

Fisk had a cat's hearing, too. He was at my side instantly, though he waited for me to raise the clever lid. My heart was pounding. I almost feared to look—but inside the shallow box in the floor lay a tall thin ledger.

"Prettier than gold, isn't it?" said Fisk.

I lifted it out with a care close to reverence. "It is pretty—'tis bound just like the others."

"Of course. That way if someone catches him working at it, they won't think anything of it. He could leave it on his desk in plain sight and no one would look at it twice."

"But he doesn't. He conceals it."

"And we're going to find out why. Bring it over to the lamp."

Fisk pressed the compartment lid closed, and we went to the desk together. His face glowed with triumph—this was the evidence that could return his sisters to safety and wealth, and 'twas he who would give it to them. Even I could see that it would be nice to have Maxwell in his debt after what had passed between them.

Fisk took the big chair again, spreading the ledger before him, pushing the false one aside. I pulled a smaller chair around to sit beside him. He opened the book. "Let's—"

The faint click of the opening door silenced him, and my blood ran cold as I looked up and beheld what stood there. Had it been some curious manservant, I could have leapt around the desk and tackled him— indeed, I'd already half risen to do so. Had it been some dreadful monster out of the tackier ballads, I might have fought somehow. But faced with a small girl, mayhap eight years old, with sleep-tangled hair and a rumpled nightgown, I was paralyzed. I couldn't fight her. I couldn't even threaten her.

Her eyes widened. She took a deep breath and opened her mouth to scream.

"Go ahead," said Fisk cheerfully. "But they're going to be mad when you wake them up."

The girl's mouth closed. She scowled. "I thought

you were burglars. This is Master Worthington's study, and no one's allowed in without permission."

"But we have his permission," said Fisk. "We're accountants from the Ropers' Guild, working with Master Worthington on the charity fund. I'm Master Neals, and this is Master Abercom. And you, Mistress, would be . . . ?"

She liked being called Mistress, but she wasn't so easily seduced. "I'm Bessie Tate, the housekeeper's girl. How do I *know* you're not burglars?"

"Hmm." Fisk thought this over. I sat down again and wiped damp palms on my thighs. "You don't, I suppose. But if we're burglars, why are we sitting here going over the ledgers instead of stuffing loot into sacks?"

Bessie looked around—no loot sacks. Her face fell. "Oh. But Master Worthington went out. How come you're in here without him?" She moved one foot to cover the toes of the other, in the manner of children who've forgotten their slippers. For the first time, I noticed the small white pitcher in her hand.

"Because he got a note that called him away for a while, and we decided to go on working while we waited for him. And what are *you* doing out of bed at this hour, Bessie Tate?"

"I got thirsty." She held out the small jug. "Are you

sure you have permission to be in here without Master Worthington? He gets mad if people mess with his desk."

"Positive. Wasn't there enough water in there to give you a drink?"

"I forgot to fill it. And I'm scar . . . I don't like pumping water by myself. The pump's too tall for me." She gazed hopefully at my squire.

"I'll wager you manage just fine in the daytime," said Fisk.

The look she gave him was wonderfully haughty for a lass that age. "I'm not a baby."

"Of course not." Fisk stood, the very picture of grown-up resignation. "And if I don't go pump, I suppose you're going to stand there talking all night—or report us as burglars. I think it's very bold to ask a burglar to pump for you. . . ."

She led him off to the kitchen, chatting softly, and I remembered that my squire was not only a skilled burglar but a man with three sisters. It also occurred to me that there might be someone else in the kitchen, even at this late hour, but if there was, Fisk would deal with it. I turned my attention to the ledger, but 'twas some time before I could concentrate.

By the time Fisk returned, I was almost ready to wish for more alarms. I'd gotten into my current predicament trying to *avoid* spending my life bent over cramped columns of numbers.

"Find anything yet?"

"Did you get Mistress Bessie back to bed?"

The questions clashed, and Fisk replied impatiently, "She's all tucked in with her drink. What have you found?"

"Not much." I pushed the book toward his chair as he sat down. "It begins with the loan—these initials are probably the bank in Fallon he borrowed from. But all his business dealings are in here, so it's cursed complicated. And for some strange reason he failed to label any of the entries 'embezzled funds.'"

"Hmm. I wonder when his loan came due. Here, you check this ledger. Look for the initials of the Fallon bank—he may have used honest money for some of the payments."

I opened the other ledger and scanned down the proper column, starting just after the time of the fire. I'd almost reached the time Maxwell was framed when Fisk made a sound of satisfaction. "Here it is! No notation, the clever bastard. He just added a one in the thousands column—nice to embezzle round numbers. And hard to catch with a simple scan. It could even be passed off as a mistake if someone noticed it. But he has to have taken more than a thousand. How much was the loan for?"

"Fifteen thousand gold roundels."

But it wasn't I who'd replied. Worthington stood in the doorway, mud and snow dripping from his boots. His expression was a combination of anger, amusement, and . . . respect? Or mayhap 'twas regret. The four men who stood behind him, swords drawn, had the town crest and crossed swords of deputies embroidered on their cloaks. My heart raced, but I rose to my feet slowly. So as not to provoke him to any hasty action. Like our execution.

A ledger slid into my hands—the fake. Fisk held the other, and by the sudden narrowing of Worthington's eyes, he'd no idea which was which. What was Fisk up to?

Fisk stepped back. The window was behind him, and only someone standing where I was could have seen his free hand slide between the closed curtains.

"Very clever," said Fisk, "to buy yourself some deputies. No wonder Potter never found anything on you. But tell me, how did you get away from Nettie's Ma so fast?" He was stalling.

"The old woman? What does it matter? It's only in ballads, Master Fisk, that the villain stands around confessing to the captured hero." Worthington turned to the deputies. "Kill them."

"Wait!" Fisk and I yelped together.

"If we're killed in your house, in the middle of an investigation, Potter will ask a lot of questions," Fisk went on urgently. His hand still fumbled between the curtains. He couldn't stall forever. I had to draw their attention, but how? I'd only a dagger against four swords—if I threatened them, they'd laugh. A coal snapped in the fireplace. Fire. Fire and magic. Mayhap I could create a distraction, after all.

Worthington was answering, ". . . but these four men will swear they found you piling my valuables into traveling packs, and between your known past and your friend's character—"

I leapt back, thrust the ledger into the coals, summoned the magic within me, and willed it to burst into flame. A great explosion of fire that would draw all eyes.

Nothing happened.

Worthington and his henchmen gazed at me, puzzled. I tried again, reaching out to the fire, my magic charged with my need. Nothing. The ledger's cover began to smolder. Worthington snorted.

"Get that out," he told one of the deputies. The man took up a fire poker and pulled the charred ledger from the hearth. I should have known better than to trust my freakish Gift. But at least they were looking at me.

Worthington smiled. "I don't know what you think you're—"

Fisk leaned back. For a moment I saw nothing amiss, but as he continued to tip, the windows flew open and he toppled out.

'Twas a good twenty feet to the ground, and for a moment fear for him displaced my fear for myself. Then I remembered the thick bushes around the house. I wouldn't have known whether there was a bush beneath that window, but Fisk must have or he wouldn't have done it. My squire takes great care of his own skin.

"After him," Worthington yelled. The deputies ran for the window. "No, not that way, fools. Down the stairs, you and you—quick! He knows about you!"

Two of the deputies hurried out and thundered down the stairs, loud enough to wake . . . well, not the dead, mayhap, but at least the staff. The others turned toward me.

I had backed away when they rushed the window, which left me cornered against the bookshelves. With just a dagger, even two swords were too many. One of them started behind the desk after me and the other came around the front.

"Wait!" Without Fisk's to echo it, my voice sounded thin. "If you kill me and Fisk escapes, you'll add murder to the charges against you. *He's* already killed, but you haven't."

Murder is a debt that can't be redeemed in gold, and sometimes the judicars demand a life in payment. The deputies stopped, casting uneasy looks at their employer.

"He's right," said one. "If the other one gets to Potter . . ."

Worthington smiled. "This one is unredeemed. No one can touch you for killing him, and if *he* talks to Potter . . ."

They turned back to me. "Hold on! Don't you want to know what happened to the last man he bribed?"

Evidently they didn't, for they kept coming. I grabbed a small chair, threw it at the one behind the desk, and hurled myself at the other, dagger drawn.

He whipped up the fake ledger and my dagger struck . . . and stuck quite firmly. I might have worked it free, but my opponent wrenched the ledger away. I took advantage of this brief distraction to launch a kick at his groin. It connected so solidly I winced, but that didn't slow me as I ran past him.

Worthington stood in the doorway, reaching for his dagger, but he was too late—I crouched and charged like a bull, ramming him into the wall opposite the door.

He fell, and I ran to the stair that would take me down to follow Fisk. I'd gone down only three steps when two rumpled brown heads appeared, coming up. Servants, sufficiently low ranked to sleep near the kitchen. One carried a poker, the other a broom. They looked more appalled to see me than I was to see them, and that was saying a lot. I didn't pause to curse my luck but turned and ran back past Worthington, who was climbing to his feet. There were more stairs at the other end of the hall.

"He's going up!" Worthington yelled. "We'll have him trapped!"

I prayed 'twas not so. Taking Fisk's route out a third-story window would break bones, even if there were bushes beneath me.

Fortunately it took my pursuers some time to get organized; Worthington was still yelling for them to follow when I reached the top of the stairs and started down another hall.

In most manors this size these rooms would be

guest rooms, and mayhap house the most respected servants as well. I hoped they were unoccupied. In the middle of the corridor a semicircular niche opened amid several windows. But the couches and chairs placed there afforded no promise of cover or escape, and I ran on, trusting that the end of the corridor would hold a stair going down.

I never learned if it did or not. Just past the hallway's midpoint I heard voices, and boots upon the stair, and I opened the door of the nearest room, springing inside.

'Twas dark within, but the Green Moon had risen and I could make out the windows, the pale shape of the empty bed, the chairs by the fireplace . . . and the pitcher and basin on the washstand.

My sore wrist protested the pitcher's weight but I ignored it, hurrying quietly back to the door to listen. I was just in time to hear two men run by, and prayed they'd all go thudding past and up—or down—the stairs.

In the cold, quiet room my breath whistled like a forge's bellows, and sweat stuck my shirt to my body.

"Hey!" My pursuer's voice was muffled but the words were clear. He sounded like he was right outside my door, pox rot him. "What if he went into one of these rooms? We ought to wake the others and search 'em."

The reply was too distant to understand, mayhap because my pulse was pounding in my ears.

"Maybe somebody ought to watch the stair," the first voice said. "And make sure he doesn't come back this way."

I crouched and pressed my face to the floor. I could see his feet in the corridor outside. Bare feet, with hairy toes. There wouldn't be a better chance.

I rose to my feet, tightening my grip on the pitcher as I reached for the doorknob.

"Well, I dunno," he was saying. "I think we ought to wake—"

He yelped as I flung open the door, and the pitcher swung up and struck his head with a sickening thump. I hoped I'd not damaged him badly. If I killed someone, unredeemed as I was, there'd be no mercy for me.

'Twas the servant with the broom, and he dropped it as he staggered. I dropped the pitcher and snatched up the broom, though it made an unwieldy weapon. Speed was my best defense, and fear lent my feet wings as I dashed back down the corridor, pursued by shouts and running footsteps.

The windowed niche loomed on my left, and I

swerved in to snatch up a chair and cast it under the feet of the deputy who led the chase.

He went down with a shout of pain, and the servant behind tumbled over him. With both of them rolling on the floor, I'd have gained a good lead, were it not for the portly dame who emerged into the corridor in her nightgown, awakened by the noise.

Her heart was as stout as she was. She stepped into my path and grappled with me. We danced a few dizzying turns before I broke away and ran down the stairs, leaving the broom in her furious clutch.

The servants' cries drew Worthington out of the study. As I clattered down the stairs, he had plenty of time to draw his dagger and brace to meet me. "Stop, you rogue, or I'll—"

But I didn't stop and he lifted the dagger to strike. 'Tis the kind of amateur mistake that Fisk so scorns. I caught his wrist in my left hand as he started to bring it down, punched him in the stomach, and ran on, barely breaking stride.

The staircase that led to the front door was long and wide, but the hall below it was clear, and hope flooded my heart as I hurtled down. Then the front door opened and red-cloaked deputies streamed through, at least a dozen, more than I could ever fight, and I stumbled to a stop and looked up.

One of Worthington's deputies stood at the top of the stairs. His posture was hunched, like a man recently kicked in the groin, his expression as unfriendly as the drawn sword in his hands. His partner limped up to join him, and Worthington tottered forward, clutching his stomach, and shouted to the men below, "Kill him! He's dangerous! He's unredeemed! He robbed my house and assaulted me! *Kill* him!"

This was the moment to burst into eloquent accusations against Worthington. Fisk would have done so. But I could think of nothing to say that would convince them to take the word of an unredeemed man over Worthington's. I was also out of breath.

The mob below parted around a smallish man, who pulled off a fur-lined cap to reveal his shining pate.

Worthington cried, "Potter, he's dangerous! Kill him! Now!" He shoved the deputy beside him toward the stair, and I realized he was giving his men an excuse to act. They realized it, too, and started toward me.

I looked wildly about for somewhere I might go, or something I might do, and found nothing.

Potter looked up at me. "Why should I kill him? He's not going anywhere. And I advise you two"—his glare pinned Worthington's deputies in their tracks—"not to do anything rash."

"Before anyone does anything, you should listen to

me," I put in. It wasn't eloquent, but it seemed to be enough. Potter nodded reassuringly and started giving orders to his men.

But I stopped caring about Potter, for another man had pushed through the crowd, bareheaded, with scarlet scratches on his face and hands. Fisk. And beside him, small and neat, was Nettie's Ma. She carried Worthington's ledger.

I sank down on the step, though I've no idea why the joyous singing of my heart made my knees give way.

Fisk and Nettie's Ma climbed up and sat beside me. Up close, Fisk's scratches were even more impressive—which you'd expect from a twenty-foot fall into a juniper bush. But I already knew most of his story.

"What happened in the marish?" I asked Nettie's Ma. "I feared for you when Worthington came back so soon."

She snorted. "He never got a chance to lay hands on me. But he was clever enough to realize he couldn't, and as for keeping him in talk . . ." A wry smile twisted her mouth. "He agreed instantly to any term I set. Why not, since he didn't mean to keep his word? After about ten minutes it became pretty obvious I was stalling. He's not a fool. I don't know what he thought was going on, but he turned around in the middle of one of my speeches and took off for home. I followed him till he picked up his henchmen. He passed by two other deputies before he found one he wanted, which made me realize we'd better get some law on our side as well."

I gazed at Nettie's Ma in amazement. "I thought you never left the marish."

"I mostly don't," she said. "But there's no reason I can't. And this seemed like a good time for it."

"She went for Potter," said Fisk. "And I ran right into the pack of them, with Worthington's men on my heels and gaining. They'd probably have caught me in the grounds, if they hadn't had to wrestle with that ridiculous mutt."

"So we've won." I could hardly believe it, even now.

We all turned to look at Worthington. He sat in a chair in the upper hall, ignoring the servants and deputies milling around him. His face was pale but composed, and you could see thoughts racing behind it. His eyes flicked to the ledger Nettie's Ma held, and his face turned a shade grayer.

"Aye, we've got you, you sleek bastard. Here's for that poor lad whose pack I've got."

"And Ginny Weaver," I said softly, remembering her courage and goodwill.

"And Max," said Fisk. "Rats."

"What? What's wrong now?" I demanded.

"Well, nothing's wrong exactly. But this means Judith really didn't do it."

I couldn't help but laugh.

CHAPTER 14

Fisk

It was dawn before Michael and I finished telling Sheriff Potter all we'd done and learned. We left Worthington and the ledgers in his hands, and he'd already sent one of the honest deputies to roust a couple of judicary auditors out of bed to start considering the official charges, so essentially it was all over except for the shouting. Though I expected lots of shouting. I was looking forward to it.

We escorted Nettie's Ma back to the marish, since she declined to stay the night at Max's. Daybreak streaked the frozen sky when Michael and I finally made it home to bed, but I made up for that by sleeping past noon.

I rapped on Michael's door on my way downstairs, but his room was empty. He'd probably been up at the crack of midmorning.

My sisters were still in the dining room when I came down, though the table was covered with lists and dress patterns instead of mid-meal. They jumped up and kissed me—or at least Anna and Lissy did, and Judith's rare smile was the equivalent.

Then they hustled into the kitchen and brought back food, sweeping aside the plans for Lissy's wedding. The first thing she'd done, after Potter told them Worthington had confessed, was to ask if she could marry Tristram Fowler. Max, either stunned by his good fortune or more aware of the situation than I'd thought, consented immediately. I must say they weren't making much progress with the wedding plans; the lists of people to invite, menus for the feast, even the all-important wedding dress, were pushed aside while I ate and my sisters exclaimed over Worthington's villainy.

Anna and Lissy were completely shocked, and even Judith admitted she'd never suspected him. I'd have rubbed that in, but I hadn't suspected him either. Ordinarily that wouldn't have stopped me from bragging, but today I simply felt too good.

Michael had gone off on some errand. He was safe now, for the story had spread through town like wildfire. Max was holding court in his study, receiving the congratulations and apologies of all his acquaintances, and Anna said he wanted to speak to me when it was convenient.

Now was good. I waited until the current caller left and went in, noting that the front door was manned by a strange servant, probably on loan from one of the neighbors.

"What happened to Trimmer?" I asked as I came into the study and took a seat by Max's desk. The furnishings were still a bit sparse, but the joyous relief on Max's face would have made Nettie's Ma's hut look like a palace.

Even the shadow that slipped over his face at my question couldn't banish his happiness. "Rob Potter arrested him. I've been talking to some of my friends in the judicary, and while I won't, of course, be allowed to hear the case against Ben or any of his accomplices, they said they'd listen to my recommendation when Trimmer is sentenced. They let the victims speak, sometimes, though they don't often take their advice. Oh, I'm to have my job back as soon as it can be arranged. I'm a judicar again." He puffed up like pigeon with the pride of it.

"What will you advise in Trimmer's case?" I already knew—Merciful Max was too happy to want to punish anyone.

"I'll recommend that he be required to pay back the

bribe, and the usual ten percent plus court fees. No payment in blood, for he shed no blood. He claims that all he wanted was enough money to escape his wife, and that I can well believe. But giving up the bribe will leave him bankrupt. Since no one here will hire them, the Trimmers will be forced to leave together, and I have no doubt she'll see to any additional punishment he might deserve. Speaking of deserving"—embarrassed color flooded his face—"I have to thank you, most profound—"

"Never mind that," I said. I was in a merciful mood myself this morning. "What about Worthington? I'd have sworn he was thinking up some scheme. Why did he confess?"

Max snorted. "That was his scheme. And it worked, too. He offered to give a full confession, naming all his accomplices, if the judicary would agree not to demand life as his repayment."

"What? They agreed to that? He murdered two people! *Four* if you count the old men who died in the fire."

"That wasn't forgotten. But it's easier to do your judging if you have a full confession—then you can be certain of guilt." Max's mouth twisted. Anna had told me he cried this morning, when Potter assured him that the men he'd hanged really were guilty. That

Worthington himself had composed Ginny Weaver's "suicide note" for the forger. He wasn't crying now, but he looked uncomfortable again. "I really do thank—"

"You already did. Are you telling me they're going to let him *off*?"

"Oh no. The judicary promised him life, but they refused to abjure any other form of payment in blood—and murder can be repaid no other way. His fortune is forfeit. And whatever state he leaves this town in, he'll bear the mark of an unredeemed man on his wrists. I'm not at all certain asking to keep his life was the wisest thing to do."

A cold chill passed over my flesh. At least Michael could work, even if some people cheated him when they learned he was unredeemed. But Worthington would be a maimed beggar, driven from town to town, for even the Beggars' Guild won't permit an unredeemed man to work their pitch. "He'll survive," I said. "He's too smart to die. But you're right—it may not have been the wisest choice."

Max's mouth curved down, and I remembered that he'd once considered Worthington a friend. "He showed a ruthless streak in some of his business dealings, but I didn't think . . . The worst of it, to my mind, is that he seems to feel so little remorse. He said Ginny

Weaver was dying anyway, and in so much pain that her death was a mercy. Clogger was a gambler, drowning in debt, of no use to anyone. The old men were accidents, not his fault, and he harmed me as little as possible. And your friend was unredeemed. Indeed, he can't be charged for trying to frame Sevenson, though the arsons are on his account. The city council will use the court's share of Worthington's fortune to lay more fire pipe."

I like irony too. "What happens to the rest of his money?"

"Most will go to his victims' heirs, though that's at the judicars' discretion. In fact, some say that since Den Skinner felt Worthington's original 'bribe' to Ginny Weaver was sufficient payment, the court will leave it at that. Clogger's heirs, and the old rope makers, will get a great deal."

I really do like irony, and we smiled at each other, for once in perfect accord.

"I'll get some too," Max went on briskly. "Nine months' back pay will almost recoup my loss on those cargo ships."

"Plus ten percent," I said.

"And the owner of the brothel that burned will be able to rebuild. Oh, did you know Worthington chose Thrope's home as his second target just to make him more angry with Master Sevenson?"

"I guessed it. And because he had access to the key. I suppose Thrope gets reimbursed too, plus ten percent?"

"As is proper," said Max primly. But he didn't look happy about it.

"The Ropers' Guild will get the most," Max continued. "It'll take time, but once Worthington's ships return and those loans are repaid, their charity fund is going to be full. The accountants say his fortune will be almost gone once the financial debts are paid. The blood debts . . . let's just say I'm glad I won't be ruling on this case. And it's because of you, Fisk, that I'll be ruling on other cases in the future. Speaking of which, have you thought about your future?"

"Not lately." I blinked at the sudden turn of subject. "I've been busy."

"Just so." Max straightened a pile of paper on his desk. It had looked quite tidy before. "Well, I have thought about it, for you and Sevenson both. I know you share your father's turn for scholarship, and I have several friends on the faculty of Fallon's university. I might be able—"

"No."

"But why not? You could be well settled in a respectable career. As for Sevenson, a nobleman's son must have some experience in estate management. His being unredeemed is . . . unfortunate, but I think I could arrange a post. You could—"

"No," I repeated. I wasn't sure if the emotion tightening my gut was amusement or fury, but it was a struggle to sound civil. "We can take care of ourselves."

"But I too owe a debt." Max realized he was fidgeting and let go of the papers. "Don't stop me. I see now that I was wrong to ask you to leave before. That I misjudged you. That's a hard thing"—he smiled fleetingly—"for a judicar to say. Now I owe you my return to my profession, my reputation, my . . . my peace of mind."

So why did he sound like someone trying to cozen a tax collector? "Max, you don't have to—"

"Yes, I do. You need to hear this, and to know that I know it. Because . . ." He took a deep breath. "Because that's what makes it so difficult for me to ask you to leave."

Long seconds of disbelief beat past before I got my voice working. "What?"

"I'm sorrier than you'll ever know." Max's face was scarlet, but his expression was unyielding. "But I realized this morning, talking to the townsmen, that it will take time for this incident to fade from people's minds. It may be years before I'm wholly trusted again, and I can't afford a . . . I can't afford any kind of scandal or disrepute. Councilman Sawyer made it clear that even without your friend he—"

"We rescued you." I was standing, staring down at him. "We risked our lives to restore your poxy, precious reputation, Michael no less than me, and you're *kicking us out*?"

Max's eyes dropped. "My offer is still open. The university. And you might be able to return someday. Or for special occasions. You could come back for Lissy's wedding."

"When pigs fly," I snarled. I don't remember whether or not I slammed the door, but I took the steps two at a time and burst through Michael's door without knocking.

"Pack. We're leaving."

He had his purse out on the bed and was counting his money, something he almost never did. Now he dropped the pitiful handful of coins and stared at me in astonishment.

"Why? Has Potter—"

"It's nothing to do with Potter. Or the girls." Max hadn't told them his little plan. I hoped they gave him a world of grief. For years. Judith, at least, was capable of it.

I told Michael what Max had said and watched his

expression change from astonishment to sympathy. Unfortunately, the sympathy wasn't for me.

"'Twould be terrible to care so much what others think that you'd wrong a kinsman for it. His conscience will punish him for years to come."

"I'd rather see him punished with a horsewhip!"

I yanked Michael's pack from under the bed and discovered that we'd been here such a short time that he hadn't unpacked much. Just a few days. Just long enough to see my sisters grown, to meet Becca and Thomas, to walk the streets and remember . . .

"Come on. You can help me pack."

I'd hardly unpacked more than Michael and was stuffing in the last of the shirts when a soft tap sounded on the door.

I didn't want to talk to my sisters.

My hand closed on Michael's arm to silence him just as he called, "Come in." But it was Sheriff Potter's shrewd face that appeared in the doorway.

"The servant said you two were up here. Though it looks"—he eyed our bags—"as if my errand was unnecessary."

I stared at him in amazed fury. "Don't tell me you were going to throw us out too? That fits. That's just perfect. Come on, Michael."

But Michael caught my arm, stopping my angry exit.

"A moment, Sheriff. It seems to me we've done naught but good for this town and its folk. Why cast us out?"

Michael's voice was a lot milder than mine would have been. Milder than his would have been when he first came to Ruesport. I think Potter noticed the change too, for he studied Michael's face as he replied.

"You're right, Sir Michael. You and Fisk have done nothing but good in this town, and as its sheriff, I thank you. But I pride myself that I'm a pretty good judge of character."

I opened my mouth, trying to think of a properly cutting reply, and Michael gripped my arm harder.

"You think us villains?" he asked curiously. "Despite all that's passed?"

"On the contrary," said Potter. "I think you're good men. Most of the time, at least." His gaze had drifted to me, curse him. "But I also think that you and your squire are trouble on two legs, and I'd rather have you out of my town before the next batch starts. Am I wrong?"

Given the amount of trouble Michael had dragged me into over the last few months, it was a hard point to argue, but I'd be hanged if I'd agree.

"Jack Bannister once told me that a good deed will get you a stiffer sentence than most crimes, and I see he was right." I picked up my pack and left, my exit somewhat marred by the fact that Michael chose to walk down the stairs with the sheriff.

I caught bits of their conversation—it sounded like Potter was making Michael a gift of something he'd intended to buy, and it was in the stable. Whatever it was. Michael was pleased, but my faint curiosity evaporated as we reached the bottom of the staircase and heard the angry voices in the study.

Angry female voices. Max had told the girls. I still didn't want to talk to them. I grabbed Michael's arm and pulled him toward the door, which the wooden-faced manservant opened for us.

I swept us rapidly through the yard. The sun had come out, and though the untouched snow was still pristine, the places where folk walked were ankle deep in slushy muck. It would be ice by nightfall, and I hoped we'd find someplace to sleep by then. A barn loft, by the look of Michael's purse.

I flung open the stable door and stamped in, then turned to flee as a brindled shadow leapt for my throat. Muddy paws printed my doublet, and a wide pink tongue swiped my face before the mutt hurled itself on Michael with a husky, voiceless rasp that identified it all too clearly. Even when I'm angry I'm not stupid.

"You bought this mutt? Why? Even if we were staying, the last thing we need is a dog. A mute dog. A mute *watchdog*. You're out of your mind."

Michael had somehow convinced the beast to sit before it tracked mud over him, and now he rubbed its head and chest. By daylight its color was a mottled gray and tan, fading to dark gray around the ears and feet, and lighter tan on its chest and belly. It cocked its head when I spoke, and its long tongue slithered out. I had a strong impression that it was laughing.

"Why not?" Michael replied. "He belongs to no one now. As for his muteness, he treed you neatly enough. Besides, I didn't have to buy him. Potter gave him to me."

I closed my eyes. "The usual reward for capturing a murderer is gold roundels, not a mangy mutt. And we could have used the money. Can we even afford to feed it? What does it eat, besides burglars?"

"Soup bones would be good," said Judith calmly. "I packed several for him."

Her silhouette was a dark exclamation point in the sunlit doorway, and she carried two lumpy sacks in her hands. "There wasn't much in the kitchen that was suitable for travel, but I brought what there was."

She handed the sacks to Michael and stepped back, eyeing me coolly. I'll take food over hysterics any day.

I heard the jingle of coin as the sacks changed hands and considered an angry refusal, but the thought of cold barn lofts dissuaded me.

My months on the road last fall had made me a fair hand with horse tack, but today I fumbled so badly that Michael took over. Leaving me with nothing to do but talk to Judith. "Will you marry that Darrow what's-his-name, now that Max is respectable again?"

"I'll think about it." Anticipation glinted in her eyes. "He's not a bad man, just a bit spineless. I believe I could make something of him."

At least one spineless bastard would get what he deserved, but I didn't say it aloud. If nothing else, Judith was quite capable of taking the sacks back. And speaking of spineless . . . "I heard Max and Anna fighting. They sounded pretty bitter."

Michael looked up from loading bread and hard cheese into the saddlebags. "I hope 'twill not cause trouble between them."

"*I* hope he'll sleep in a cold bed for years," I said, and watched with irritation as Michael and Judith looked at each other and smiled.

"You'll both get your wishes," she predicted. "Fisk for a time, and Michael in the long run. She really does love him."

I couldn't be sorry for it. She'd be happy, in the long

run. And Judith would live life on her own terms. And Lissy . . . Lissy would go right on growing into a woman I barely knew, and now I never would.

Judith was watching my face. "You should write. We'd send a letter anywhere it could reach you."

"Would Max allow it?" I asked nastily. Michael led the horses from their stalls, and Tipple gave me a friendly sniff.

"He'd have allowed it last time," she said. "But you stormed out before he could say so."

Just like this time. No, not quite. This time, not being thirteen, I was keeping the money. I swung into the saddle. "I'll think about it."

"Good fortune, brother. Not that you won't make it if you have to—by hook or by crook." Her eyes gleamed, and not with tears.

"Good fortune, sister. Not that you won't bully it out of the hapless world."

I kicked Tipple into motion before she could reply, for a battle of wits with Judith was always risky.

Riding through the familiar streets for the last time might have been a painful ordeal. As it turned out, trying to keep Michael's mutt from chasing cats, spooking carriage horses, and treeing the butcher's apprentice was a full-time job for half a dozen men. It kept us both occupied until we were far enough out of town that Michael could release it from the improvised leash. Michael had been speculating on a name for the beast. Disaster was what came to my mind, with Nuisance a close second.

The horses were fresh, too—their prancing splattered the icy mud to an unbelievable height. But as the traffic thinned, and the dog was freed to range at will, I finally had time to think.

I didn't want to think, and I noticed that Michael had fallen silent too. "You were awfully meek when Potter threw us out," I commented. I suddenly remembered that Potter had called him Sir Michael and referred to me as his squire, without even noticing he'd done it. Was the lunacy that contagious?

"'Tis part of my new persona," said Michael. "It ill becomes an unredeemed man to argue with sheriffs."

I'd hoped he was over that—and the thought didn't seem to depress him as it had. "Well, I hope you've learned to conceal those tattoos from now on."

"Oh, I've learned that. I've been thinking about the way folk perceive others. They hardly ever see who you truly are, especially at first, for their expectations twist their perceptions all out of true."

"Of course. That's how con men get strangers to trust them instantly. And keep their trust, even in the teeth of the evidence."

That silenced him, but only for a moment. "So it can be both used and abused," he said slowly. "But the thought in my mind is that in concealing those marks, in lying, I actually help them see the truth of me more clearly. Strange, isn't it?"

It seemed to me those broken circles were very much part of the truth of him, though not in the way most people would perceive it. In any case it wasn't a decision I was going to discourage, no matter how backwardly he'd come to it.

"Absolutely," I said. "I'm all for using lies to arrive at the truth."

Michael snorted. "Or any other point you wish to reach? No, don't answer that. I'm sorry I said it. But mayhap using folks' tendency to misperceive will let me conceal this other strange Gift."

He was talking about magic, and I was relieved that he saw the need for concealment, but . . . "You're sure you wouldn't consider using that as well?"

"No," said Michael firmly. " 'Tis too unreliable a Gift—or curse. Besides, 'twould be an unfair advantage. Even in the pursuit of adventure, honor must be upheld. To use such a thing—"

"Adventure? You haven't had enough adventure yet?"

The cold wind ruffled Michael's hair, and his grin

was so infectious I found myself smiling as he replied, "Of course not. Adventure and good deeds are the trade of a knight errant and squire. There's no such thing as enough."

I stopped smiling. I'd heard him say this sort of thing before, but now he said it with confidence. With more than confidence—as if he was now so certain, he could laugh about it himself and still mean every word.

I'd wanted to restore him to himself—why hadn't I remembered that his normal self was a lunatic? This was all my fault, and every uncomfortable, ridiculous, suicidal *adventure* he led me into in the future would be my fault too. Good deeds carry stiffer sentences than crimes. You'd think I'd learn, wouldn't you?

The sound of my swearing followed us down the road for a long, long time.

HILARI BELL retired from a career as a librarian to pursue writing full-time. Most would call her a fantasist, but her novels offer memorable characters and a potent mix of adventure, mystery, and fantasy that defies classification. Her growing list of titles includes THE LAST KNIGHT, a Knight and Rogue novel, THE PROPHECY, THE WIZARD TEST, GOBLIN WOOD, and A MATTER OF PROFIT.

Hilari often visits schools and attends conferences to talk about her work. When asked what question she hears most often, she says: "When I do author gigs, one of the questions kids almost always ask me is, 'Which of the books you've written is your favorite? Which one do you like the best?' I tell them that each of my books has something I like about it—that one has a strong character conflict, or a great humor, or my favorite chase scene, or an incredibly twisty plot, but that I don't actually have a personal favorite. And when I say this, kids think that it's an adult copout, that of course I must have a personal favorite, but it really was true . . . until now.

"The Knight and Rogue books may not have the twistiest plot, or the coolest chase, or whatever, but of all the books I've written, they are the ones I like the very best. I love both main characters. Michael and Fisk are an absolute blast to write . . . and I have some wonderfully nasty plans to make a mess of their lives in future books, too."

Hilari lives in her hometown of Denver, Colorado. You can visit her online at www.sfwa.org/members/bell.

READ THESE OTHER NOVELS BY
HILARI BELL

THE LAST KNIGHT　　　THE PROPHECY　　　THE WIZARD TEST

A MATTER OF PROFIT　　THE GOBLIN WOOD